SUBTERFUGE

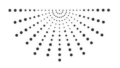

ERVIN KLEIN

ISBN-13: 978-1-937979-54-6
ISBN-10: 1-937979-54-7

Enigma House Press
Goshen, Kentucky 40026
Enigmahousepress.com

DEDICATION

To my wife, Linda, the first person who encouraged me to write and who has gently, but unfailingly, guided me when she felt I could do better.

CHAPTER ONE

December, 1945
  Berlin

The train gained speed as Ernst grabbed the snow-covered ladder. His feet slipped, leaving him dangling by his hands. He kicked the air, seeking support, his freezing fingers beginning to slip. Just before he lost his grip, his foot connected with the rung again. Pulling his body up, he climbed to the top of the coal car.

He was at the back of the car, and could see Axel standing at its front, his left foot on the edge as he prepared to jump the four-foot distance to the next car.

Suddenly the train whistle blew a blast that could only mean someone was on the track ahead. The cars smacked together as the train slammed on its brakes. Ernst saw the chain reaction of controlled collisions, one after the other as the braking moved from the front of the train to the rear. Axel, however, seemed hypnotized, staring only at the car in front of him.

"Axel, get back!" Ernst yelled, but Axel was in a trance. If his timing had been right, it would have been a jump of beauty; but the collision threw him head first between cars. He managed to grab the edge of the front one, but it had a full load. Ernst saw that his friend's grip was not secure; he couldn't pull himself up.

"*Ernst! Ernst!*" Axel cried.

"I'm coming," yelled Ernst, but he couldn't run across the mounded coal. He had no idea what he was going to do even if he got to Axel.

Ernst couldn't see what happened to Axel when he fell, but saw the end result. Axel's body, minus his legs from mid-thigh down, was on the side of the tracks.

Ernst watched, mesmerized, as his friend lay writhing on the ground, blood spurting everywhere.

Ernst clambered down the ladder, jumped clear of the train, and ran back. When he got to Axel, his friend was shouting "*Gott im Himmel! Gott im Himmel.*" God in Heaven; but God had taken the day off.

Ernst told him, "Lie still," but Axel kept pushing himself up with his arms, trying to stand on legs that no longer existed.

"I've got to get home," he said, over and over, until he couldn't struggle anymore and fell back. By then, the rest of the gang was there.

"He wants to go home," Ernst told them, as if everything would be all right if they could just get Axel back to the hole in the ground he called home.

"He can't go anywhere," said one of the other boys. "He doesn't have any legs."

"It's all right," Axel said. "I'll stay here tonight."

In five minutes he was dead.

"We need to tell the Americans," someone said.

"Yeah, and explain that we were stealing coal off the train?" asked Carl. "I don't think so."

"Then what are we going to do?" asked another.

"We're going to get the hell out of here," said Carl. "This won't be the first dead body the Americans find. Remember, nobody knows anything. Now, scatter."

The boys ran off in different directions; none even glanced back.

"Where have you been?" Aunt Marta asked when Ernst got home.

"Getting coal." Ernst put a lump by the fireplace and brushed himself. His clothes, face and hands were filthy from the wet coal, but he had managed to get the piece home without having it stolen by a bigger boy, so it had been a good day.

"Where do you get such large lumps of coal?" his aunt asked, examining it.

"Lying on the ground near the train tracks. I guess they fall off the train when it hits a bump."

She looked at him sternly and put her hands on her hips. "There are no bumps on train tracks."

His eyes widened and he shrugged. "Then I don't know why they fall off, but there they are, lying on the ground. I bet you want me to wash up," he said, scooting into the bathroom.

Even though he was only eight, Ernst was familiar with death. Most of the other deaths, like his parents', he had only heard about; this time it had happened right in front of him. He had no intention of ever telling Aunt Marta about Axel. If he did, he'd have to tell her about climbing on the trains and stealing coal. Either one of those admissions would give her

3

all she needed to forbid his hanging out with the gang, and he wasn't going to let that happen.

The next day, Axel was replaced by Wolfie, a boy a year older and a head taller than Ernst. He was chosen by their leader, Carl, who had put the gang together to scavenge anything of value they could find. Whatever they scavenged, they sold for cigarettes, which they could exchange for some bread or, on a really good day, a little meat.

The military authorities didn't call it scavenging, they called it stealing; but the Americans had all the food they desired, and could kick people out of any of the homes still standing in Berlin if they wanted it for their own housing. Meanwhile, Germans of all ages, even orphaned children, lived in the rubble of destroyed buildings, hiding like Axel had in holes they had dug in the debris.

"You have to prove yourself," said Carl to Wolfie, as the gang gathered the next day.

"All right," said Wolfie through gritted teeth. He balled his hands into fists. "What do I have to do?" he asked, but Ernst could tell from the fists he made that he already knew.

"You have to fight one of us," Carl replied.

"Do I have to win?" Ernst watched him roll his shoulders to loosen his muscles.

"No, you just have to show that you're willing to take a beating for the gang," said Carl, smiling.

"Or give one," said Wolfie, with a smirk. "Who do I have to fight? You?"

Carl shook his head. "You choose. It can be me," he swept his hand toward the motley bunch of boys, "or anyone in the gang."

Of the nine youths in the gang, Ernst was by far the smallest. Sometimes people mistook him for five years of age. The last four boys to join had chosen to fight him, but there was nothing he could do about it. Carl started the gang,

Carl made the rules. As long as he was so much smaller than the others, he expected to be picked. He kept hoping they'd get someone smaller than him so that he wouldn't automatically be chosen.

The rest of the gang, as if to emphasize his small stature, began to move away from him as Wolfie looked them over. Spying Ernst, his eyes lit up. Wolfie pointed straight at him and said, "I choose him."

Ernst reached into his pocket and cupped his hand around a rock. It was smooth, fit perfectly inside his fingers, and made his fist hard as a hammer. He immediately walked toward Wolfie, squinting at something behind the new boy. "What in the world is that?" he asked, as he approached to within five feet of his opponent.

"What?" asked Wolfie.

"*That*," said Ernst, pointing over the boy's head with his empty hand.

The new boy turned and looked behind him. As soon as he did, Ernst pulled the rock out and swung his fist as hard as he could, burying it in the boy's stomach. Gasping, Wolfie doubled over, grabbed his stomach, and struggled to pull air into his lungs. Ernst brought his knee up into the bigger boy's face, standing him up straight. Blood spurted from his nose, and Wolfie raised his hands to cover it. Ernst brought his rock-hardened fist into the now exposed stomach, again, and Wolfie dropped to the ground like a lump of coal the boys dropped off the train. His hands gripped his stomach. Ernst drew his foot back and prepared to kick him in the face, but sensed that his adversary was already whipped.

He squatted down next to Wolfie and said, "This is where I would normally kick your teeth out. If you agree you're beat, I won't."

Wolfie nodded his head quickly.

Ernst stood up, and stepped back, the whole time continuing to watch Wolfie. "We're done, Carl," he said over his shoulder.

"You didn't fight fair," gasped Wolfie between hard-to-draw breaths.

Carl laughed and walked over next to Ernst. Putting his hand on Ernst's shoulder, he said, "I didn't say it had to be a *fair* fight. I just said it had to be a fight. Welcome to the gang, and let this be your first lesson. Somebody's always out to trick you, so be prepared." Looking at Ernst, he said, "That makes five wins in a row."

"I'm tired of it, Carl," said Ernst, walking behind his recent adversary and putting his hands under Wolfie's armpits. Lifting him up, Ernst said, "One of these days my 'look-over-there' routine's not going to work and I'm going to get my ass kicked. Why don't *you* fight the next one?" Ernst looked at Wolfie. He was bent over, hands on his knees. "And Wolfie," Ernst said, "when you're in a fight, *never* look away. My papa taught me that when I was three. *Verdammt.*"

It was two days before Wolfie felt like climbing onto trains. Before he did, Ernst warned him about falling. "You've got to stay away from between the cars," Ernst said. "Axel fell between the cars, so he landed on the tracks."

"Was there a lot of blood?" asked Wolfie, as they walked toward where the train would be slowing down on its approach to the station.

"Yeah. It was everywhere. I even had some on my shirt. I had to rub some of the coal on top of it to keep Aunt Marta from seeing it."

"You got family? You're the only boy I know with family."

Ernst shrugged. "Most of the people I know are dead. My

father, my mother, grandparents, Axel. I could be next. I've learned to expect it."

"Me, too. But you don't seem to mind. I hate my parents for dying. Why did they have me if they were going to die? It's not fair." He kicked at a clump of coal, then hopped on one foot for a few steps when it hurt his foot.

"I guess I mind about Papa," admitted Ernst, on the lookout for American soldiers, "because I don't know for sure he *is* dead."

"What do you mean?" asked Wolfie.

They were about twenty feet from the train, the locomotive having already passed. It was on a curve away from the boys so the engineer wouldn't be able to see them. "I'll tell you when we finish," Ernst said as he broke into a trot. "Time to get some coal, now." He jumped up, grabbed the ladder, making sure he got his feet in the rungs, and climbed up, followed immediately by Wolfie.

It was too noisy on the car to talk. Ernst had learned to get four or five lumps over the side, then get off. Getting greedy and staying too long was the surest way to get caught. Besides, the railroad men didn't seem to care if they limited themselves to just a few lumps each.

When they were finished and were walking back toward the rest of the gang, Ernst said, "Papa was a U-boat *kapitän*. He came home for Christmas one year, then we never heard from him again. Nobody told us anything.

"It wasn't like Carl's father. He was on the *Scharnhorst.* Somebody came to his house and told them it sank and Carl's papa was dead. If my papa *is* dead, I want them to do that for me, but they never have." Ernst kicked a bottle, as if he were kicking some unknown, uncooperative messenger. "Aunt Marta says they don't have time to do that for the U-boats. I don't care about the boat, I want to know what happened to Papa."

The two boys were almost back to where the rest of the gang was dividing the coal they had scavenged. Wolfie said, "Maybe he's still alive."

"Maybe," said Ernst. "I knew a girl who thought her father was dead. Then he showed up one day. Two months later he left again and never came back. He was in the army. Why'd he even bother to come home if he wasn't going to stay?"

"What happened to him?"

"I don't know, but the girl was killed by the Russians. I heard they fucked her to death, but I don't know how that kills you. Do you?"

Wolfie shrugged and shook his head.

"Anyway, everybody dies; that's what Aunt Marta says."

"Why can't we find out what happened to Papa?" Ernst asked his aunt that night.

"Because we don't even have tram service right now," she replied. "How do you expect them to know what happened to a U-boat halfway across the world four years ago when we can't catch a tram down at the corner in the morning?"

He didn't understand the logic of that statement, but Aunt Marta was going to have a baby and that made her more grumpy, less logical. She didn't seem happy about having a baby, which didn't make sense, either, because she used to tell him she wanted lots and lots of babies. But Ernst decided he shouldn't ask about that, either.

Later that evening, Ernst wrote a list of things he shouldn't ask his aunt about.

1. Papa
2. The babie
3. The soljiers. Spechally the soljiers. It makes her hed hurt.

Despite his age, Ernst understood that his father probably was dead, for the reason he had given Wolfie. Everybody in his family except Aunt Marta and him were dead. Nevertheless, he *hoped* Papa was still alive. And sometimes, on those nights that Aunt Marta stopped crying and drifted off to sleep before him, Ernst would sneak out of bed, open the box he kept hidden under it, and pull out a bosun's pipe with "U-112" inscribed on the side of it. Clutching it, he would pretend he and his father were sailing on the open sea. In his imagination, Ernst stood next to him, waiting for a command. When papa gave him one, he would pretend to blow it on the pipe, just like his father had told him sailors did. Then, before he put the pipe away, he would speak into the void that was his life.

"I'm going to find you one day, Papa. I promise."

CHAPTER TWO

1 December, 1939
   Office of the *Sicherheitsdienst des Reichsführers-SS* Berlin
   Office of the Security Service of the Reichführer-SS
Berlin

Günter Hahn looked around the wood-paneled office in which he sat, waiting. At the end of it was a large wood desk, behind which hung a large portrait of Adolf Hitler, the Nazi armband prominently displayed on the *fuhrer's* upper arm. Hanging on the other walls around the room were pictures commemorating high points in the Nazi leader's life; the Nuremberg rallies, speaking to the Reichstag, and entering the city of Vienna in 1938, after the Anschluss. In the last picture, huge Nazi flags hung from every Viennese building and the ten-deep crowds on the sidewalks waved small versions of it. Hahn's spirit soared with pride.

   He was tall, six-feet-two, very thin, with blond hair and blue eyes-the perfect specimen of what Hitler referred to as the 'Master Race.' He was proud of his accomplishments, that he had risen to this level in the party. He was proud of the party, that it had brought new life to the Fatherland. He was proud of *der Führer*, that he had molded the country into what it had become.

"*Sieg Heil!*" The guards at the door yelled, while snapping to attention. Hahn leapt to his feet as Colonel Heinz Jost, the Chief of *Ausland-SD*, the Foreign Intelligence Service, strode into the room. Hahn's right arm shot out in the salute that terrorized Europe. He held it until Jost stopped in front of him and returned the salute.

Jost said, "Congratulations, Ensign Hahn."

Jost was a small man in his late thirties. His eyes were deep-set and seemed to drill a hole into Hahn when he looked up into the Ensign's face. He had a prominent nose and close-cropped hair that was mostly gone from the top of his head. Smiling, he held out a paper to the younger, taller man and said, "Here is your new identity."

Taking the paper, Hahn looked at it and saw his new name, followed by biographical information on who he was becoming.

"Learn this well. This is who you are, now. You will go through all additional training with your new identity. You will be listed as a senior petty officer with your new name, but you will carry the rank of *Korvettenkapitän*. Günter Hahn no longer exists. You have no family, no past."

Hahn blinked quickly, but otherwise showed no emotion, so Jost continued.

"Your psychological testing said you were 'especially suited for unsupervised responsibilities.' As an agent of the SD you will put that ability to use. Do you have any questions?"

"Yes, sir. What were my family told?"

"That Hahn was killed in a training exercise. Your family, his family, was given an unrecognizable body recovered from the Polish campaign, along with his Gold Wound Badge. They buried him last week."

Hahn pursed his lips.

"You knew we would tell them this when it came time to give you a new identity," the Colonel said coldly.

"I know, Sir. But I would not be human if I did not worry about my mother."

"And you would not be standing here if you had not agreed to make this sacrifice."

"Yes, Sir," said Hahn, regaining his composure. "It will not happen again."

"That's a fine man and a good Nazi," said Jost, smiling broadly. "Do you have more questions?"

"Where will I be assigned when I complete my training?"

"Your first assignment will be to U-112, to observe and report. We want you to watch the officers, particularly the *kapitän* and first officer. They both came up through the *Kriegsmarine*, not the party mechanism. *Unser Führer* does not believe the navy is as loyal as he needs them to be, so we like to keep an eye on them. As a *korvettenkapitän* you will be senior officer on the boat, but no one can know this except in an emergency."

"Will I be the only agent on the ship?"

Jost cocked his head and said, "You must call it a boat. Surface vessels are ships. *Unterseeboots* are called boats." Hahn nodded. "There will be no other agents. You will have full authority to take any action necessary to protect the party."

"Any action?"

"Yes," said Jost. He reached out and put his hand on Hahn's shoulder. "Including the liquidation of traitors. You will be rewarded for anything you do on behalf of the party."

Jost removed his hand from Hahn's shoulder and the two men stared at each other for a moment.

"Do you have any other questions?" Jost asked.

"No, Sir," said Hahn. He raised his right arm and shouted, "*Heil*, Hitler!"

Jost returned the salute. "Heil, Hitler! Dismissed."

Hahn turned and marched out, his new identity in his hand.

CHAPTER THREE

17 April, 1941
Near the Shetland Islands

We're fucked, Captain Seligman thought as the fog parted and three enemy destroyers came rolling out of the mist. The lead ship was virtually on top of them.

"Alarmm! Alarmmm," he yelled. *"Clear the bridge. All crew to the bow."*

Watch Officer Watts and Seamen Frick and Bauer immediately unhooked their safety harnesses and descended into the hatch. Ensign Hoerter struggled, however. As the boat tilted downward, he remained strapped to the bridge. Panic overtook him and, no longer trying to release the latch, he tugged hopelessly at the harness.

Seligman was about to drop through the hatch when he realized Hoerter's plight. He jumped to the ensign's side.

"Stop struggling," he shouted over the sound of the sea, "or you'll never get it loose."

He reached in front of Hoerter and snapped it open just

as a wave washed over the bridge. Instinctively, Seligman held his breath and grabbed the rail, but the inexperienced ensign was enveloped in the wave. It knocked him to the deck and bounced him like a pinball, pushing him along on his back until his head hit against the conning tower. Hoerter gagged and coughed against the water in his mouth.

The destroyers were so close Seligman could see the recoil of the guns as they lobbed shells toward his boat. A spray of machine gun fire clanged off the conning tower. Keeping his head low, he grabbed the ensign's collar just as Hoerter slid across the hatch. Lifting him by his slicker, he dropped the youngster ten feet straight down into the upper command deck. Scrambling through the hatch, he reached up to pull the watertight door closed. Before he could, though, another wave washed over the bridge, pouring water into the opening. It splashed over his shivering back. Grabbing the hatch, he pulled it closed just before the next freezing wave hit.

"Hatch secured. *Dive*, take us to eighty meters," he yelled. Putting his feet on the outside of the ladder, he let his hands slide along the side rails, giving him a controlled fall to the upper command deck.

"Rig for silent running," Seligman ordered, then waited for the destroyer to plow into his boat. He hadn't been rammed before and didn't know what to expect. Would it shove the boat into a downward spiral until it hit its crush depth and the silence of the sea absorbed them? Or would it slice a hole in the side, allowing the frigid sea to pour in while his crew struggled to shut it out?

Seligman heard the closest destroyer's propellers churning the water overhead. It passed so close, its wake forced the boat to one side, then bounced it back in the opposite direction like a pendulum. But death would not come courtesy of being rammed. Scant minutes later the propellers of the other two destroyers passed overhead, then all three faded in the distance. The encounter must have caught them as much by surprise as it had Seligman, because they didn't drop any depth charges as they passed overhead.

In his haste to avoid the destroyer, Chief Siegfried, the lead engineer, had the boat in a steep dive. Too steep, Seligman's trained feet now told him; Instead of the fifteen to thirty degrees it should have been, he estimated their angle of descent at fifty degrees.

Hoerter lay collapsed in a heap at the bottom of the ladder, his foot at an odd angle. Seligman did another controlled slide down the ladder, landing on top of the ensign, who cried out in pain. "Get him out of here," Seligman ordered two seamen. As they grabbed Hoerter's arms, he vomited all the seawater he had swallowed. They pulled him along backwards, dragging him through his vomit. The steep pitch of the boat made it impossible to carry him, so they slid him along the deck toward the crew's bunks.

The boat was sinking like an anchor. "*Slow us down,*" Seligman yelled at the chief. "What's the matter?"

"It's not responding," said Siegfried. This was the Chief's first patrol as lead engineer. More importantly, it was his first crash dive while under attack. The boat hadn't practiced crash dives as much as the Captain had wanted.

"Did you put the aft plane down?" Seligman asked.

"Aye, I wanted to get us down fast."

I should have trained him more, thought Seligman. Only with experience does a chief learn how much to put the aft plane down in an emergency. Their out-of-control dive was Seligman's fault, not Siegfried's.

As if to remind Seligman that the threat from the destroyers still existed, Radioman Kretchmer called out, "Propeller closing fast." Moments later a series of depth charges exploded near the bow, racking the boat. Light bulbs exploded. Leaks sprayed the crew.

"Both planes up, Chief," Seligman yelled.

"Aye, *Kapitän*," he replied. "But I can't get them to respond. The sea is holding them in down position."

Depth charges continued to explode, but they were not the crisis now. The chief had to gain control of the descent. Seligman rushed to his side and helped him turn the wheels to raise the diving planes, but they wouldn't budge.

"One hundred-fifty meters," called First Officer Neumann as he monitored the plunge. "One hundred-sixty." Then, "two hundred meters." The boat was sinking too fast for him to call out every ten meters.

"Two hundred forty." As he spoke, the bow crashed into the ocean floor at a speed of fifteen knots. Seligman was sent flying. He collided with various crew members before bouncing off the overhead, then dropped like a rock to the floor.

He jumped to his feet just in time to steady Radioman Kretchmer, who was scrambling back to his chair. Quickly, Kretchmer picked up his headset which had flown off, pulled himself into a kneeling position next to the hydrophone, and again reported, "Propeller closing fast." Thirty seconds later the concussion from depth charges peppered the crew's eardrums.

"Can we reverse and pull the boat free?" Seligman asked the chief as soon as the onslaught of explosions passed.

"Possibly, sir, but we'd have to go full reverse and the destroyers will hear us."

The *Kapitän* calculated in his mind. They had been on the surface only long enough to get a half charge in their batteries, but they did ventilate completely. That gave them enough air to stay down maybe thirty-six hours, if no one exerted themselves. The destroyers were shielding the convoy

Seligman had been stalking, so they would have to move on at some point to catch up to it. He calculated that he could allow the boat to remain stuck until they left, and get loose from the grip of the ocean floor then.

Seligman knew that at times, over beer when they were on leave, the crew would morbidly discuss the advantages of dying by depth charge as opposed to being trapped undersea and slowly suffocating. They all agreed they preferred the swiftness of a depth charge. It was no longer a philosophical discussion, but a real possibility, that one or the other *would* kill them, either immediately or in a day or two.

"Propeller closing fast." Kretchmer's words brought the captain back from his calculations.

Two, four, six explosions, each louder, each closer. More lights blew out and new leaks erupted every time a depth charge exploded. Men rushed to stop the leaks in their progressively dark environs.

"How deep are we?" Seligman asked.

"250 meters," Navigation Officer Winter replied.

No one spoke for a moment. The crush depth of each submarine depended upon its overall condition but the recommendation from command was to not exceed 230 meters. As if on cue, the hull started creaking.

———

In the crew quarters, Hoerter had managed to get back into his bunk. His ankle throbbed and he moaned. Seaman Frick, confined to a bunk during silent running, had landed on top of Hoerter when the boat hit the ocean floor. Now Frick lay in the bunk across the aisle. As Hoerter's moaning got louder, Frick quietly got out of the bunk and stood next to him.

Taking Hoerter's hand in his, Frick whispered, "Don't

moan. Squeeze my hand, instead." He smiled into Hoerter's pained eyes.

"Are we going to die?" Hoerter asked.

Frick shook his head. With his free hand he raised his index finger to his lips and mouthed the word, "Quiet."

Just as he did, two depth charges exploded within a second of each other. Hoerter had not been through underwater bombardment before. He couldn't tell that the explosions were too far away to do serious harm. Frick clamped his hand over the ensign's mouth, still wet with vomit, to keep him from yelling in panic. It felt strange to be comforted by a man he outranked, as if Frick was the ensign, and he the seaman.

On the lower Command deck, Seligman thought about how he was going to get the boat loose from the sea floor, so he could avoid the slow suffocation of his crew. Already the boat had grown so quiet it seemed destined to be their tomb.

He listened to the radioman repeat, "Propeller approaching rapidly" for the next two hours, but Seligman knew from the randomness of the attacks that the destroyers were just trying to cover the area with depth charges. The explosions were moving away from them. Just a little longer, and the destroyers would probably return to the convoy.

Finally the attacks stopped. Seligman waited another thirty minutes to be sure the destroyers were gone, then assessed their damages.

One seaman, Karl Schmidt, had died, crushed by a torpedo that had shifted when the boat collided with the sea floor. Schmidt had been with Seligman on two previous patrols. He was a quiet boy of eighteen, a hard worker that everyone liked. Kretchmer, Schmidt's best friend on the boat, took his death personally.

"I want to kill one of them myself," he said to the *Kapitän*. Seligman nodded. Although only twenty-five, Seligman realized he was a father figure to the enlisted men, many of whom were no older than the dead seaman.

The rest of the crew had bumps and scrapes, but no one else was seriously injured. Hoerter's ankle was broken.

"Blow all tanks?" the Chief asked.

"No," said Seligman. "If we blow the stern tanks and don't get the bow free, the stern will rise up. Then we'll be at too severe an angle to move about. Blow bow tanks, only," he ordered. "All reverse full."

The crew listened to the water being pushed from the tanks and waited in vain for the boat to begin rising.

"Cut engines," Seligman ordered after a minute of useless churning. Then, since most lights were out, Seligman ordered, "By auxiliary light, all men to the stern torpedo room." He would use the men as ballast to bring the stern down and pry the bow loose.

The pitch of the boat dictated that the men had to crawl. They pulled themselves along the aisle by grabbing anything that would give them purchase. They were wet from sweat and from seawater seeping in from various depth charge-induced leaks. Their faces were covered with grease. Some had pissed themselves. They crawled along silently, as if robots. No one was exempt, so Hoerter, his foot dragging behind, took his place with the crawling party. Thirty minutes later, all men were to the stern. It lowered only slightly and the bow did not budge. Seligman, Neumann, and the chief huddled again.

"I think we'll pull loose if we blow the stern tanks," Siegfried said.

"No," said the *Kapitän* shaking his head. "It's too risky. If we don't pull loose, we won't be able to maneuver."

Neumann nodded in agreement.

Instead, Seligman ordered half the crew to form a bucket brigade to move the water gathered in the bow to the stern bilges, where it would help pull the stern down. The other half began stopping all leaks.

Seligman knew their choices were limited. They could conserve oxygen by remaining still, but they would make no progress in freeing themselves. They were too deep to escape and make it safely to the surface. Unless they could free the boat, they were doomed. Better to try something and die in sixteen hours than sit and wait for death in thirty-six.

The water being passed hand-to-hand in buckets was salty and oily, and every time the filthy mix splashed onto the crews' abrasions it added to their misery. The angle of the floor and the oil in the water that inevitably spilled created a treacherous path for the men to navigate. Frequently, one of them slipped and went caroming down the deck. More often than not he took someone with him, and tempers flared.

As the hours stretched and the water gradually began to fill the stern, the men cursed their predicament, the boat, and the water that splashed them. The air became increasingly foul from lack of oxygen and the smell of diesel fuel. Occasionally one of the men vomited. The stench from that made more men sick.

Finally, after six hours of fighting fatigue and the urge to resign themselves to their fate, they switched off, the other half of the crew replacing the bucket brigade. Most leaks had been stopped and they could see progress, albeit slow. After twelve hours, when the first brigade returned to duty, those not light-headed from the lack of oxygen were sick from the stench. Some unfortunate souls were both. Seligman ordered a stop to the water brigade and all men to return to the stern.

Straining for air, the men fought their way toward the stern. It took forty-five minutes for all to get there. Then, imperceptibly at first, what the men judged to be a miracle occurred. The bow began to groan against the floor holding it.

"All reverse," shouted Seligman, showing the chief a smile only a man delivered from death can display.

The electric motors kicked into action. Inexorably, the boat pulled free of the ocean floor. Then, as the bow began to rise faster than the stern, Seligman ordered the stern tanks blown. The boat leveled and began its trip to the surface, a journey most crew members had thought would never occur.

The chief called out every ten meters as the boat rose out of the depths. Not stopping at periscope depth to check for danger, they chased the surface and the precious fresh air they needed and craved.

"Open all hatches," the captain ordered as they broke the surface. When they opened, the fresh air revived the men. The fog, the destroyers, and the convoy were all gone.

"Damage reports," Seligman ordered.

"Forward torpedo room reporting, sir. Moderate water leakage. Pumps are maintaining. We'll have leaks stopped in under one hour."

"Aft torpedo room reporting, sir. No damage."

"Engine room reporting, sir. Damage to number two diesel."

Seligman pointed at an unfamiliar ensign standing to the side, trembling. "Come with me," he said. "Second watch to the bridge."

The second watch, led by Second Officer Watts, with Ensign Braun taking Hoerter's place, climbed through the conning tower and opened the hatch to the outside world.

"What is your name, ensign?" Seligman asked the young man when they reached the bridge. The ensign stood there, shaking. Watts and the other three members of the second watch fanned out to search for enemy ships and planes in all directions.

"Wagner, sir."

"Are you married?" As he talked, he never lowered the binoculars with which he scanned first the horizon, then the sky.

"No, sir."

"Do you know how to use this?" he asked Wagner, holding up a safety harness.

"I've seen it, but I don't get to the bridge often."

"I don't want to lose a man because he can't get it unhooked." Seligman showed him how to use the safety harness and had him practice fastening and disconnecting it until he could do it as fast as the captain. All the while, despite the four sailors standing watch, he kept an eye on the sky. Then, directing his voice into the communication tube, he called to the engine room for an updated damage report.

"Number two diesel still laboring. It might be the camshaft."

"Estimated time for repairs?"

"One hour, sir, and the boat's vented."

"Clear the bridge, dive to 100 meters," Seligman ordered. "Engine room, let me know when the number two is repaired, so we can surface and charge the batteries. Navigator, set a course for Kiel. We need to take care of our injuries and inspect the boat for damage. Radio man, notify command we're coming in for repairs and injuries. As soon as number two diesel is repaired we will return to the surface and bury Seaman Schmidt."

When submerged, Seligman turned the boat over to second officer Watts, and went to his quarters to catch up on the boat's log.

First Officer Neumann stopped by to check on him.

"That was a close call," he said. "We've got to get better radar detection or we'll not last the war."

Seligman tried to smile, but couldn't. He recognized Neumann's words as truth. Reaching into his pocket, he pulled out a picture of himself, a pretty woman and a toddler. His mind returned to Dresden, his wife and son. He remembered the three year-old's last words to him as he left for this patrol, his fourth as *Kapitän* of U-112.

"Papa, come home soon."

He could almost feel the touch of his wife's fingers on his face as she added, "Yes, papa. Come home soon." She had smiled and cried at the same time. It had been so long ago, at a home so far away.

Finally, mustering a smile, he said to Neumann, "I remember as a boy helping my father harvest crops. Another attack like that and I fear the sea will harvest us."

"*Ja*," said Neumann. "*Das ist wahr.*" This is true.

CHAPTER FOUR

20 April, 1941
  The Baltic Sea, just off the port of Kiel

"Surface," Seligman ordered. In the periscope he watched a *Kriegsmarine* minesweeper approaching. It would escort them through the minefield guarding the entrance to the Kiel harbor. "Second watch to the bridge."

He opened the hatch and crawled through the conning tower, followed closely by Watch Officer Watts, Seamen Frick and Bauer, and Ensign Wagner. The first spray from the ocean caught the Captain full in the face. That first one always invigorated him, especially if it was from the cold Baltic Sea.

"Wagner!" Seligman shouted, when he saw the young ensign. "Welcome to the bathtub!" Another wave sent spray into their faces. "Glad you can fill in for Hoerter. His ankle's going to have him laid up for a while, I'm afraid."

"It would appear so, sir," Wagner said.

Seligman and the four watchmen raised their powerful

binoculars to their eyes simultaneously. Each man scanned a quadrant, first the sky for planes, then the ocean for ships. Seligman focused on Wagner's quadrant because of his inexperience.

Seligman scratched his new beard and said, "A fine morning, *ja?*" to no one in particular.

Sensing someone crowding past him, Wagner glanced quickly to his side and saw Seaman Braun, who had just emerged from the hatch carrying the four banners denoting the ships that they had sunk on their patrol. He would hang them from the periscope to let everyone in port know of their success.

Returning his eyes to scanning his quadrant, Wagner said, "If you say so, Sir. But I had hoped we would be flying a few more banners when we returned."

"There will be other patrols, and, besides, we are *alive.*" Seligman raised his arms as he shouted 'alive' but his actions belied his agreement with Wagner. This was the first time he had fewer than six banners to show on their return.

"*We* are alive," Wagner said, "but not Schmidt. And, anyway, our lives are not my greatest concern."

"You have my attention," said Seligman. "What concerns you most?"

Watts shot a quick glance at Wagner, then went back to his search as he, too, waited to hear Wagner's reply.

"That the Fatherland prevail, and *Der Führer* have the opportunity to reshape the world," replied Wagner.

"Of course, we all want the Fatherland to prevail," Seligman said. "But we have a long war ahead of us, Ensign. We do the Fatherland no good rotting at the bottom of the sea. I shudder to think what happens if the United States comes into the war."

"I am not afraid of the United States. *Unser Führer* says we will prevail. Do you not believe him?"

26

There was danger in the young ensign's question. Nazis never seemed to worry what they said to their superiors, and it gave the captain pause. Glancing over the ensign's shoulder, Seligman saw Watts shaking his head. Seligman raised his binoculars to his eyes, then placed his mouth over the speaking tube and ordered an adjustment in the boat's course.

"We will never prevail if we don't get this boat to dock," Seligman finally replied. "Keep a sharp lookout, Ensign."

The captain kept his own counsel as they sailed past the Kiel Lighthouse, and an hour later passed the *Kriegsmarine* War Memorial. Seligman bowed his head as he passed it, a silent tribute to those who had died at sea for the Fatherland.

The Bay of Kiel widened and naval traffic picked up, putting everyone on high alert lest they collide with an outbound ship. Two and one-half hours later, they were docked at Tirpitz Pier.

The Captain had experienced better homecomings and more successful patrols, but they were nevertheless greeted by a band and by women. Always, there were women. Seligman wondered how many were paid to be there. Probably most of them. He searched briefly for his wife. He knew she was in Dresden, but hoped for a miracle.

The women threw flowers on the boat and the band played *Gruss an Kiel Marsch*. Then Hans-Rudolf Rösing, third flotilla commandant, saluted them. When Commandant Rösing shook his hand, Seligman leaned in and said, "A moment of your time?"

Checking his watch, the commandant said, "My office in one hour."

Seligman gave First Officer Neumann instructions on

arranging the men's accommodations in this port to which they only came for repairs, took a quick shower, and made his way to the commandant's office. It was up a hill from the dock and very similar to all the other buildings in the port, a small concession to security in case of an air attack.

"I hear your patrols are usually more successful," Rösing said to him when they convened in the commandant's office a little later.

"Yes, they are, but I'll cover that with Dönitz when we do my patrol critique. I asked to see you about another matter."

"What can I do for you?"

Though Seligman had been to Kiel on at least three other occasions, *Korvettenkapitän* Hans Rösing was new to his position and they had never met. His immediate superior was *Korvettenkapitän* Heinz Fischer in Lorient, but at Rösing's headquarters and while Rösing's men were repairing his boat, Seligman needed Rösing's permission for leave.

"Repairs to the boat will take two weeks. My first officer can oversee them. I'd like permission to travel home for ten days to see my wife and son. Then I can go to Lorient to see Admiral Dönitz for the patrol review."

"I wish I could let you do that, but I'm under strict orders to turn these boats around as fast as I can. If we have *eins eins zwei* ready before you get back and I can't send it out, there will be hell to pay. I will let you have four days to see your family. We'll turn your boat around in that time and you can go back out. We will consider it the same patrol and you can do your review with Dönitz when you return. I'll clear it with him."

Seligman weighed his options. Dönitz held a review board at the end of each patrol and would not be happy about *eins eins zwei* going back out without one, even if it was Rösing's idea. Further, if he went to Dresden instead of Lorient, he would have to ask Rösing to take care of his other request, and he did not know him well enough to do that. Was he a member of the Nazi party? Was he a sympathizer? Or was he, like Seligman, a Naval Officer sworn to protect the Fatherland regardless of who sat in Berlin? Asking the wrong man for the wrong thing could end his career, or even his life.

"In that case, sir, I'd like four days to travel to Lorient."

"Duty, first, eh, *Kapitän*? Since your wife doesn't even know you're in port she'll never know what you're up to. Is she a beauty?"

"She is lovely, yes. I will show you her picture."

Pulling out the picture of him, his wife, and son that he always kept in his pocket, he showed it to the Admiral.

"This is us with our son, Ernst. He was two in this picture. Now he is three."

"Not your wife, man!" Rösing tilted his head back and laughed. "The mademoiselle you are going to see in Lorient. Is she pretty?"

Seligman flushed, but couldn't upbraid this man who insulted his faithfulness but also outranked him.

"There is no mademoiselle in Lorient. I need to see Admiral Dönitz and *Korvettenkapitän* Fischer."

Rösing slapped him on the shoulder and winked. "That's right," he said. "Stick to the party line. That won't get you shot."

CHAPTER FIVE

08:00 CET (Central European Time) 24 April, 1941
   German Naval Base, Lorient, Brittany

Despite his anger at the Commandant's comment about his 'mademoiselle,' Seligman grudgingly understood it. The streets around the Lorient naval base in western France were swarming with women from the *'etablissements'* nearby, their open arms better than the tentacles of an octopus at ensnaring a sailor. He knew most of his crew would make use of their services while they were in port.

The compound itself was clean and closely guarded. Camouflage netting had been draped over several docks where submarines were being prepped for sea duty. Construction had recently begun on the reinforced concrete bays that would, when finished in January, 1942, withstand many attacks by the enemy. At 8 A.M. Seligman reported to *Korvettenkapitän* Heinz Fischer.

Fischer returned his military salute, walked around his

desk, and sat down. He looked up at Seligman and said, "Please be seated. Nice beard."

Seligman sat down and said, "Thank you, Sir. I haven't had a chance to shave since we returned four days ago. I'll take it off this afternoon, then start a new one as soon as we leave."

"When will that be?"

"Rösing says he'll have *eins eins zwei* ready on the 26th, so that's when we provision. Leave on the 28th."

"I understand you wanted to see me about something. Why did you not ask Rösing?"

"I didn't know if I could trust him and you are my flotilla commander."

"All right, what is it you want that is so important you skipped seeing your family?" Fischer pulled a French cigarette out of a pack and lit it.

"I'd like to have one of my ensigns reassigned," he told his commander.

"That is not something you need to travel here to ask. You could have sent me a telegram."

"I didn't want a record of my request. If you turn me down I'd like it to stop here. I certainly don't want Admiral Dönitz to know about it."

"Understood. Who do you want reassigned?"

"Ensign Klaus Wagner," said the captain.

Fischer thought for a moment, then a look of recognition washed over his face, followed immediately by a regretful frown.

"Now I understand why you didn't want a record, but I'm afraid that is impossible," he said. "Ensign Wagner has been placed on your boat by someone in Berlin."

"Do you know who put him on my boat?"

"If I did, I would not be allowed to divulge it. It could be

Dönitz. The Lion is an admirer of the Nazis. It could be someone in the party. For an ensign, he has some impressive connections. There is speculation that he is with the *Sicherheitsdienst*."

"So I am being spied upon," said Seligman. "But why?"

Fischer held up his hand. "Don't jump to conclusions, Captain. Yes, the *SD* wants to know who is loyal and who is not, but that doesn't mean you are the target, or that Wagner is the agent."

"I don't care who he is watching. I don't like it. And if he is a *bordgeistlicher* he's not much of one. The first time I noticed him he was about to wet himself."

"Then maybe you don't have much to worry about. On the other hand, that may be part of his undercover work."

"I still don't like it."

"And I don't like any of my *kapitäns* being under suspicion. But the fact remains that we have some very intricate codes. We cannot afford to have them broken."

"The Tommies are listening to us every time we transmit by radio."

"True. Let them listen to us all they want, as long as they don't break the code. *Der Führer* has ordered the *SD* to investigate every risk. They might think someone on your boat is not loyal. Regardless, if he *is SD*, neither you nor I, nor Heaven nor Hell, will get him off your boat."

Seligman nodded.

"Don't forget the patrol critique with Admiral Dönitz this afternoon at two. Dismissed."

Seligman took his leave. As he walked back to his room he ran over in his mind the points he wanted to make with Admiral Dönitz in the critique, but his mind kept wandering to the possibility of a Nazi plant on his boat. Was he under suspicion? If not him, then who? And why?

14:00 CET

Office of *Vizeadmiral* Karl Dönitz, *BdU* Commander, Lorient Naval Base, France

"The Admiral will see you now."

The secretary smiled at Captain Seligman and led him into a rectangular, wood-paneled office with a long table in the middle of it. Paintings of U-boats hung on the wall. Off to the side was a desk from which Admiral Dönitz now stood up. Four other officers stood behind seats at the long table, two of whom Seligman knew. *Fregattenkapitän* Eberhard Godt was Dönitz chief of staff, and *Kapitän zur See* Meckel was a signals specialist who tediously analyzed every signal sent by every *Kriegsmarine* boat at sea.

"*Kapitänleutnant* Seligman, allow me to present to you *Kapitäns zur See* Schmidt and Engel. They will be meeting with us today. Schmidt is in charge of U-boat escorts and Engel is an operations officer. I believe you know everyone else."

As the lowest ranked officer, Seligman saluted the others. They returned his military salute in kind, except for Engel, who threw his arm in the air and shouted "*Heil* Hitler".

He handed his official patrol report to Dönitz, then turned to Schmidt, whom he had not met before.

"We lost a good young seaman named Schmidt on this patrol. Was he kin?"

"I'm not aware of any relationship," said Schmidt. "I am sorry for your loss."

"Thank you," said Seligman. "And thank you for your fine escorts into and out of all the mine fields. We'd lose a lot more men but for their help." Schmidt nodded in acknowledgement.

Dönitz had received Seligman's preliminary report a few days earlier so that he could review it prior to the meeting. "Not as successful as your previous patrols," he said, as he took his place at the head of the table and waved for the others to sit. The other end, facing Dönitz, was reserved for Seligman.

"We survived," replied the captain, sitting down. "Sometimes that is a success by itself."

"Perhaps for you," said Engel, "but Berlin is not happy with survival. Death before defeat, *Kapitän*."

For the next four hours the group read U-112's logs, reviewed its signals, and critiqued the tactics used on its patrol. Seligman had to justify every decision while they suggested alternatives and asked if their ways would have been better.

When they were discussing the entrapment on the ocean floor, Godt asked, "Did your chief let you down, *Kapitän*? I notice that this was his first patrol as chief of the boat."

"No," Seligman said, shaking his head. "I should have practiced emergency dives more. I did the same number of tests we always do, but as you note, I had a new chief. I should have put him through the ringer before the enemy did." Seligman paused, then continued. "He did not let me down. I let him down. I should have trained him better, faster."

"You don't want a new chief, then?" asked Dönitz.

"No. Siegfried was promoted to Chief after serving on *eins eins zwei* as *Electro Obermaschinist*." Electric motor officer. "He knows our electrical system inside out. He knows the boat, the crew. Rest assured the next patrol will see us making emergency dives until we're doing it under thirty-five seconds every time."

Engel leaned forward and said, "Your honesty is refreshing, *Kapitän*. However, I want to remind you that fifty or more men place their lives in your hands. You just admitted that you almost lost a crew plus a U-boat because of your misjudgment. Does that mean *eins eins zwei* should have a new *kapitän*?" A foreboding smile bared Engel's teeth as he watched the captain's face for any emotion.

Seligman weighed his words carefully. Engel had shown his feelings from the start with the Nazi salute, and Dönitz certainly admired Hitler. Nevertheless, Seligman didn't like being challenged by an inexperienced Nazi who got his commission because he clicked his heels in front of the right people.

"I am very much aware that when my boat is being chased by destroyers and subjected to depth charges exploding around it, I am solely responsible for every man inside that iron coffin. This was my fourth patrol as *Kapitän*, with numerous others as Chief of the Boat or First Officer. Would you have me replaced with a novice? Someone who might blame the chief and thus fail to give the needed training?

"I serve at the pleasure of the Fatherland." He nodded at Dönitz, then continued. "If the Admiral wants to replace me I will not like it but I will accept it, and I will seek other ways of serving." This was Seligman's fourth debriefing, and they were always grueling. He wondered if any U-boat captain emerged from one unscathed.

"I don't think *Kapitän* Engel was advocating your replacement," said Dönitz.

"No," said Engel, still smiling like a dog about to bite. "But I trust it will not happen again. After all, we *are* at war."

"Really? I thought those depth charges the Tommies were dropping on us were just to let us know they were in the neighborhood. Do you even know what it's like to experience a depth charge attack, *Kapitän* Engel?" Seligman asked, his voice rising and his eyes boring into Engel.

"I think we've all made our points," said Godt. "Let's move on."

Seligman nodded toward Godt, but not before noticing Engel frown at the Chief of Staff.

"I'd like to ask a question about tactics," Schmidt said. "This is not the first time I've heard of a *kapitän* sending the crew back and forth to influence movement of the boat. Do they teach this in your training?"

"They do," replied Seligman. "It's fairly common. When we want to dive quickly we send everyone to the bow to help the diving planes bring the boat down faster."

"But this time you were stationary on the ocean floor, and the second time you did it the bow came free. What would you have done if it had not worked?" asked Godt.

"Died," said Seligman. "I would have tried all-full reverse again, and blown the stern tanks, but the lack of oxygen was severe by then. In all likelihood we would have suffocated. We were too deep to use our Drager breathing apparatus to escape."

That statement was followed by silence, the ticking of a clock the only sound as the officers silently acknowledged the risk of their profession.

Dönitz broke the silence by asking, "Have the Tommies come up with any new anti-submarine tactics?"

"I think they've come up with better radar. They were finding us too often. We had to dive six times in one twelve hour period."

"We've gotten reports from other boats, also," said Dönitz, "but I can't believe their radar is improving that much. Ours hasn't."

"Admiral Dönitz thinks we have spies," said Meckel. "He thinks they are on board and are somehow getting signals to the enemy to help them locate our boats." As a signals specialist, Meckel participated in most patrol critiques and was thus exposed to many of the *Vizeadmiral's* thoughts.

Dönitz nodded. "Berlin promises us they've got new technology on the way that will allow us to detect when radar is in the area. Then let's see if they continue to find us. In the meantime, we must find any spies and kill them."

Seligman thought of Wagner. Did *BdU,* the U-boat command, suspect a spy onboard *eins eins zwei*? If they did, they'd probably assign someone from *Ausland SD* to his crew to ferret them out.

Seligman asked, "We're hearing rumors of a device that will allow us to stay underwater longer. Any truth to that?"

"Absolutely, *Kapitän*," said Engel. "It should be available very soon. Our Nazi scientists are unrivaled. Any day now you'll be able to cruise underwater indefinitely. The device is called a snorkel and testing shows that ..."

"I don't know about the 'any day now' part," said Dönitz. "My reports indicate it is a little farther off, but yes, it is being worked on."

Engel's gaze shot daggers at Dönitz for cutting him off in mid-boast, but he didn't push back against the *Vizeadmiral*.

Dönitz's comment was disappointing to Seligman, but at the same time gratifying. *Der Lowe*, the Lion, as the men of the U-boat fleet called the Admiral, was an admirer of Hitler and all things Nazi, and yet he was apparently unwilling to give his men false hope.

Seligman silently compared Engel and Dönitz. Both admired Hitler, but Seligman could see a difference. Engel was a true believer; he was sure that everything Hitler said was true. Dönitz had seen promises of miracle weapons delayed. The Admiral's generation had kept the *Kriegsmarine* alive despite the restrictions of the Treaty of Versailles, only to be sneered at by the Nazis for their alleged inadequacies during the Weimer Republic, which ended when the Nazis came to power. Dönitz was not a true believer, yet he respected Hitler as Germany's best chance for prosperity.

Turning to Dönitz, Seligman said, "I can assure you, these devices can't come too soon for the men on the boats."

Deliberately avoiding eye contact with Engel, Dönitz said, "If no one has anything else to add to this, we are finished." Standing, he extended his hand to Seligman and said, "*Kapitän*, it was good to see you again. Happy hunting. Bring me back a battleship, why don't you?"

"It would be my pleasure," Seligman said, saluting Dönitz, then shaking his hand. Turning to the other officers, he saluted, and received another "Heil, Hitler" from Engel.

As Seligman walked toward the barracks where he was billeted he heard someone calling his name. Turning, he was disappointed to see it was Captain Engel, hurrying to catch up with him.

When Engel got within fifteen feet, he called out, "*Kapitän* Seligman, I wanted to ask you how soon you think Ensign Hoerter will be able to resume his duties."

"I hope he will be sufficiently healed for our next patrol." As Seligman spoke, Engel walked to within a half-foot and gazed closely into his eyes. Pushing his chest toward Seligman, he waited for the slightly taller Captain to step back, perhaps as other *Kriegsmarine* officers did when he crowded them, but Seligman held his ground.

"How do you know Hoerter?" Seligman asked.

"He was in the Marine Hitler Youth group. I spoke to them occasionally. He expressed an interest in the Navy as his career and I took him under my wing. Fine young man. I hope you will see that he receives some extra attention. He has a bright future."

Have I been wrong about Wagner? Seligman thought. *Is Hoerter the SD spy? Both? Why would there be two?*

He thought of his son. At age ten Ernst would be required to join the German Youth. Then, four years after that, the Hitler Youth. What would happen when he was exposed to someone like Engel?

"Can you do that?" Engel's question broke into Seligman's thoughts.

"I treat all my ensigns equally," Seligman said. "Good day, *Kapitän* Engel."

Seligman turned to leave but Engel stopped him with a firm hand on his arm. His smile bared his teeth, like a wolf threatening its prey.

"Truly, *Kapitän*, I am sure you can spare a few minutes to mentor the young man. For the good of the Reich."

"I treat all my ensigns *equally*. For the good of the *Fatherland*."

For a moment their eyes remained locked, neither blinking. Then Seligman said, "At first it sounds like thunder off in the distance. As it gets closer, the noise changes, and you think you are enclosed in a large barrel that someone keeps hitting with a sledgehammer. Each hit is closer, louder, and there is *nothing* you can do to stop it. Soon your ears ring; sometimes they bleed. The whole boat shakes and you can't control it. Water sprays in from leaks you hope stay small. Light bulbs and glass gauge covers explode, and sometimes you get glass in your eyes. The stench of fifty men who haven't bathed in weeks mixes with the smell of diesel fuel and causes some men to vomit. Or maybe it's the fear that makes them puke. The smell of the vomit makes more men sick. At first, you pray to live. Soon, though, you pray for a quick death. You think the boat is being shaken by a giant octopus. Grown men shit on themselves and piss their pants."

Engel's Adam's Apple bobbed up and down. "What *are* you talking about?"

"A depth charge attack," Seligman said through clenched teeth. He pulled his arm loose. "I have a plane to catch."

As he turned his back and walked away he heard heels click. Engel shouted, "*Heil*, Hitler."

Seligman didn't look back.

CHAPTER SIX

25 April, 1941 Afternoon
Kiel Naval Base

The next day, upon his return by plane to Kiel, Seligman went immediately to the pier to check on preparations for their next patrol, scheduled to start in two days. Second Officer Watts waved to him from the deck, where he was overseeing the stacking of food stuffs, lubricating oil, and ropes. Once all materials were accounted for, they were lowered through the one narrow hatch as Watts checked each off his list. Meanwhile, First Officer Neumann oversaw the loading of torpedoes.

"Make sure you spread the food around," Watts called out continuously. "We don't want to upset the trim as we eat it."

As the crew reported, Watts inspected any personal items they had. Crewmen might bring a toothbrush, a few family pictures, writing supplies, but nothing more; space would not allow it.

A few books would be traded throughout the crew.

Limited space for water storage meant that once the boat left port no one would shave or shower until they returned. Beards would take a few days to start appearing, longer for the younger men; the stench of the unwashed would start almost immediately. Once below deck, the majority of the crew, if they didn't have watch duty, would not see sky or breathe fresh air until they returned to port, unless the Captain let them come topside for some special sighting.

Watts confiscated a few bottles of liquor, mostly from new crew members who didn't believe they really couldn't bring it on board, and turned away a few who had too many clothes. The men grumbled over the liquor more than the clothes.

"Your locker is in the engine room," he told Seaman Krause, reporting for his first patrol. "Number 17."

When Krause came back on deck he told Watts, "I barely have room in that locker for my toothbrush and soap. You've even got the second latrine filled with supplies. Are you telling me we've got fifty men on board and only one latrine?"

"No," said Watts. "We have fifty-*two* men on board with only one latrine. And woe be unto the man that tries to flush it when we're deeper than 25 meters."

"Why?"

"The pump's only so strong. At 25 meters, the sea is stronger. When you enter the latrine you sign the log so we know who to blame if we get a load of *scheisse* all over everything."

CHAPTER SEVEN

27 April, 1941
Lorient Naval Base

A final task remained for Seligman. He hated it, and he always put it off to the last. He gathered paper and pen and began a letter to his wife. It wasn't an ordinary letter, though, where he asked about Ernst, family, the home front, and told her anything he was allowed to tell her, knowing that the censors would nevertheless delete most of it. This was a letter he would leave with his personal belongings in Lorient, all packed and addressed to his home in Dresden, to be sent when his U-boat sank.

Seligman always made sure his will was there, signed and up to date. He found it to be easy, almost perfunctory. How many different ways can one say, "My wife gets everything?"

The letter was different. If delivered, it would be days, weeks, even months after she knew he was dead. He wrote a new one every time, to be sure Marie would know she had been in his thoughts, even as he prepared to leave. She would never see more than one of his "last" letters, but he couldn't escape the thought that each had to be new and different.

He read his most recent "last" letter so that he would not repeat it. He thought that if he had to write enough of them with fresh thoughts every time, he would eventually have to fill the page with "I love you"; line after line of "I love you." How many times, he wondered, could he contemplate his death, Marie and Ernst having to go on without him, and come up with fresh observations, heartfelt sentiments?

Fortunately, he was not yet out of words. Picking up the pen, he wrote,

My Dearest Marie,

I have struggled with this letter for some time. I hate that I must write it, but I hate more that you must receive it.

I did not want to leave you, nor for you to raise Ernst alone. It was not my desire that he grow up without a father, and you be without a husband. But even worse would have been if you had to live with me knowing that I had not done my part. Worse, too, that Ernst grow up knowing that his father shirked his duty to family and Fatherland. Please know that I died comforted by the knowledge that I did all I could, that I answered the call. No man can do more than that for his family. In the end I died as I have lived, for you, Ernst, and Fatherland.

In death, I was comforted also by the knowledge that I had the best love a man could have, that of a best friend, confidant, lover, and wife. You were all those to me and more. I struggle for the words to express how I feel, but they will not come. "I love you" is too simple, so I leave you the world. Not the cursed and depraved world we see now. I leave you the glorious, sensuous, world we knew when we first met, before duty called me away.

Do you remember it? I do. It was Dresden, on the Elbe. We were both eighteen in the summer of 1934. I had been sailing on the Elbe, and had just returned to shore when you came over to admire my boat. I told you to get in and although you were hesitant, your

mother told you it was all right. I think she knew what lay in store for us, even before we did.

So we sailed that day, and every day for the next three weeks, until my duty with the National Labor Service took me away for a year. As we sailed I told you of my love for the water, how my father had wanted to be a sailor but family obligations had kept him on the farm. How I had developed his love for the sea.

When I returned from the mountains in 1935, you were waiting for me, and we sailed every Saturday until I had to leave for the Naval Academy. When we married later that year, you hoped I would give up my love for the sea, but I didn't. So you watched bravely as I left for duty, but then, with Ernst in your arms. I loved you for the support, and for the child you gave me. That is the world I want you to remember.

And every time you hear the wind catch in a sail, or someone singing Eine Seefahrt Die Ist Lustig, as I sang it to you that first day we met, when you see the sunset as we watched it on the Elbe that day, or smell your beloved daffodils that I gathered for you, you will know I have truly loved you.

Yours,
Wilhelm

CHAPTER EIGHT

10:00 28 April, 1941
Kiel Naval Base

After days of mundane duty on land, Seligman was satisfied that the men had properly repaired and restocked the boat; it was time to fete the crew before their departure.

They gathered in Barracks C for a farewell feast and all the flotilla staff turned out to wish them Godspeed. Hoerter, his ankle in a cast, moved among them on crutches. Seligman avoided both him and Wagner, who bounced from *fräulein* to *fräulein*, throwing out a ridiculous *Heil Hitler* salute each time he left one to move to another, a bee pollinating flowers.

Seamen Krause and Schulz had arrived together for their first patrol the week before. When Seligman met his new crew members, they expressed astonishment at everything that was there for the crew.

"Do you believe this?" asked Schulz. "Civilians can only dream of this. We've got roast pig, sauerbraten, potatoes, turnips, fruit pies, bread, and champagne."

"And look at this French wine," said Krause, showing Schulz a bottle marked, "Reserved for the Wehrmacht." "Not only have we taken over France, we've taken over their wine." The two laughed smugly; Seligman smiled, but didn't tell them the French were marking their lesser wines in that way to keep the better products for themselves.

Commandant Rösing approached Seligman, who was standing with Neumann, and told them to enjoy being together while they could. "You should have your own boat soon," Rösing said to Neumann. "I'm pushing for you." Then, to Seligman, he said, "I am sorry you were unable to get to Dresden to see your family. The next time you are in port you must be sure to get there. Leave the mademoiselles alone."

He winked at Neumann, and nudged Seligman in the ribs with his elbow. Seligman stared at him silently, lips pursed, until Rösing became uncomfortable in his glare. Lifting his glass in the direction of another boat captain, he walked away from Seligman calling, "*Kapitän*, a moment of your time."

"What a *dummkopf*," Seligman muttered.

"Don't be criticizing my patron," the First Officer joked. "He's going to get me a boat. He must think I want one."

Seligman scowled, and ignored Neumann's disdain for a command. "Your *patron* thinks because I went to Lorient to attempt to get rid of Wagner instead of going to Dresden to see my family I must have *gefickt* some French whore."

"If you need me to *fick* a whore for you, I'll be happy to. After all, I'm your second in command."

Seligman frowned. He was in no mood for jokes. For all the good the trip to Lorient had done for him he might as well have gone to Dresden. At least he would have been able to see Marie and Ernst.

He watched Neumann ease away from him. Seligman

couldn't help being on edge; he was always in a better mood when he finally got his boat to sea. He listened, silent and alone, as his first officer struck up a conversation with Navigator Winter, who wasn't quite as carefree as Neumann, but was more so than Seligman. Neither his first officer nor his navigator had the pressures of being a captain to stir their emotions like a butter churn.

"How was your leave?" Neumann asked Winter.

"Fine. Fine. I spent most of it laid up at Madame Rose's. Different girl every night. What a way to live. How about you?"

"I did get by Madame Rose's once or twice myself," replied Neumann. "What a way, indeed." He and Winter toasted each other and laughed.

Rösing, too, must have sensed Seligman's dark mood for he cut the revelry short by offering a final champagne toast for Captain and crew, this one with wishes for a successful mission. Seligman curtly acknowledged it, then approached Neumann, still talking to Winter about the comparative assets of the women of Madame Rose's.

"Have the men assembled on the deck at 13:30," he interrupted.

"Aye, *Kapitän*."

At 13:30, Seligman stood on the bridge and scanned the deck that was now clear of all the materials that had swamped it only two days before. Hoerter limped around amongst his crewmates, talking to them until Neumann sent him ashore.

Calling the men to attention, the First Officer shouted to Seligman, "Permission to report." Seligman nodded. "All hands present and accounted for. Engine room ready; all decks cleared for departure."

At the *Kapitän's command,* the crew cast off the lines that had held the boat unwillingly to land while a band played *Torpedo Los* and *Ritter der Nordsee,* adding pep and patriotism to the activities. Well-wishers tossed a few last flowers onto the deck, then U-112 backed slowly from Tirpitz pier and began its fifth patrol, all under the command of Captain Seligman.

The *Maschinisten,* whose duty was to maintain and operate the diesel engines, had been below for an hour preparing them for departure. As the boat slowly maneuvered through the harbor Seligman allowed them topside and gave them and the remaining crew one last opportunity to see land and breathe fresh air, then ordered them below. He allowed himself one last look at the coastline rapidly falling away, took the picture of his family from his pocket and looked at it for a moment, then put family and home out of his mind. His attention was seaward.

18:00 April 28, 1941
  Baltic Sea, east of Denmark

"Alarmmm," called Seligman down the speaker tube from the bridge. "Dive, Dive! All hands to the bow!"

Seligman knew from experience what was happening iIn the bowels of the boat; Neumann repeated the command. Crew members spun valves and threw levers. Through the passageway down the center of the boat every free hand ran in a hunched-over position toward the bow. When they got to the fore section each one crowded into any space he could find. The diesel machinists who had just shut down their engines and turned over the propulsion of the boat to the electric motors brought up the rear, and *eins eins zwei*'s bow shot downward.

Seligman and the watch crew dropped through the hatch, the captain locking it in place. He took his position in the control room and yelled, "Rig for depth charges, rig for silent running. Chief, take us to fifty meters, then flatten your angle and steer down to seventy meters."

"Fifty, then seventy. Aye, Sir," said Siegfried.

As they approached fifty meters the Chief had his planesmen adjust the bow and stern planes to slow the descent.

"All hands to silent stations," Neumann called.

The boat became a quiet tomb as everyone waited for the eruption of the depth charges. Tolle, the radioman on duty, listening intently to his hydrophone, said, "No propellers."

The *Kapitän saw it in their faces.* A plane, then, they thought, swooping in to drop bombs on them.

But in a moment, Seligman asked Neumann, "What was our time?" Everyone within hearing sighed in relief and smiled. No emergency; their first test of the patrol.

"Thirty-eight seconds," answered Neumann.

"Three seconds slow," said Seligman. "Chief, you've got to get ten meters of water over our hull three seconds faster than that, or we'll all be dead." Seligman's voice was flat, but the rebuke was clear.

"Aye, Sir," said Siegfried.

"Secure from depth charges. Crew return to their stations." Neumann repeated the order.

28 April, 1941
    War log of U-112
    15:00 Cleared port. Set course for quadrant AL
    18:00 Test dive; thirty-eight seconds

18:10 Surface
21:00 Test dive; thirty-five seconds; Adjust trim
22:30 Surface

29 April, 1941
War log of U-112
2:00 Test dive. Torpedo exercises
5:30 Practice alarm. Emergency drill and deep dive. Difficulty diving due to surface tension holding boat. Had to make extreme adjustment of hydroplanes.
7:34 Practice alarm
10:05 Practice alarm with deep dive; adjust trim
12:15 Surfaced and continued toward quadrant AL

CHAPTER NINE

6 May, 1941
   Quadrant AL 9115

A few hours before sundown, Seligman was in his bunk area just off the Command Deck reviewing navigational charts while U-112 cruised on the surface at grid quadrant AL9115 They were south of Iceland and west of Ireland, in the northern route for convoys from the United States to Great Britain when he suddenly heard, *"Kapitän* to the bridge."

In ten seconds, Seligman's head came through the hatch, followed by shoulders which the men had told him always looked a little broader when he prepared to take them into battle.

"I spotted a smudge on the horizon," second watch officer Watts told him, pointing west. The captain focused where Watts directed him, then called to the chief through the speaking tube, "Come left to due west."

"Left to due west. Aye *Kapitän."*

"That's a lot of smoke," Seligman observed. "Probably a convoy. Let's maintain course and see if it's coming our way."

Seligman and Watts both watched the horizon from where the smoke emanated, while the rest of the watch crew focused on their quadrant.

After ten minutes Watts said, "It's heading straight toward us."

"Yes, it is," said the Captain, licking his lips in anticipation. "We'll wait for it underwater. Sound the alarm."

Seligman, Watts, and the rest of the second watch cleared the bridge as the dive alarm rang out. The horn blared off and on and red lights flashed in the interior to warn the crew. As soon as they were submerged Seligman ordered periscope depth. The seas were rough, though, and he had to continuously work the periscope up and down in order to see without being seen.

"Convoy range 8000 meters," he said as he began to see the outlines of the freighters. "Still heading straight for us."

"Aye, right way around," said Watts. "It will be loaded with supplies for the Tommies."

"I estimate it's coming at seven knots," the captain said as he continued to observe the convoy.

After twenty minutes, he noted, "Range 4000 meters. Three destroyers spread across the front of the convoy. Usually have four. I wonder if there's another. And why are they all in front? Neumann, get the register."

Neumann quickly went to the Captain's berth and returned with the *Groner*, a book that had pictures of all known ships. Seligman described the destroyers as Neumann flipped pages furiously, looking for a match.

"All are similar. One stack. One four-inch gun on the foredeck, four anti-aircraft guns. Looks like four heavy machine guns. Multiple torpedo tubes, but I can't tell the exact number because of the rough seas."

Neumann narrowed his choices to several pages. "It looks like they are probably K class, maybe J class. A ship number would help."

"Of course a ship number would help, and as soon as I can make one out you will have it," Seligman barked. "Until then, use what I've given you."

"There it is," the captain said, when the ship presented its bow. "F53. That's the only one I can make out. The other two ships look the same, though."

"F53 is a J-class," said Neumann, and returned the *Groner* to the captain's berth.

"The boilers are vulnerable, but the ship itself is highly maneuverable," said Seligman, reciting from memory the attributes of the J-class destroyer. "I was hoping for some of those lend-lease jokes the British got from Roosevelt."

Seligman had come up against the lend-lease destroyers twice, and had no problem with them either time. He suspected their commanders were afraid to engage a U-boat because they handled so poorly, and the *Kriegsmarine* told captains to be aggressive when confronting them. The British had had to modify them just so they could prove seaworthy. As fighting ships, they made great anchors. The J-class, however, was a formidable challenge, provided its crew was experienced.

A new sound joined the rhythm of the convoys screws. Quiet at first, its volume soon increased. It sounded like a hammer hitting the hull. New crewmen looked around nervously and Seamen Schulz asked, *"Was ist das?"* his eyes widening. No one answered, but the experienced members went about their jobs as the pings of the destroyers' sonar grew louder.

"Multiple destroyers approaching," said the Radioman Tolle. "Convoy turning southerly."

Seligman rotated the periscope to locate the destroyers. "Three destroyers, distance three thousand meters. Steady on course." The sonar pings from three destroyers grew louder, but Seligman ignored them.

All the crew were quiet for a moment, then Seligman shouted, "Prepare all tubes for firing. Neumann, come see this!"

The First Officer replaced Seligman at the periscope and smiled. "There are at least forty in the convoy. The destroyers are headed this way."

Seligman resumed his position at the periscope. Sweeping the horizon, he saw the destroyers closing fast. He had already decided to take evasive action rather than attack them, saving all his torpedoes for the supply-laden convoy, but their rapid approach meant the evasion had to start immediately.

"Down periscope! Dive fast, chief. All crew to the bow. Prepare for depth charges. How deep is the water here?"

"One hundred fifty-five meters," the Chief replied.

"Take us to one hundred thirty. After their first pass we'll drop to the floor. Tolle, let me know as soon as they have moved past."

"Aye, *Kapitän*."

Men looked for handholds as the bow of the boat tipped downward. After a few minutes the boat leveled and Siegfried called out, "Depth 130." Now to wait.

Fifteen minutes later everyone on the boat heard the frightening sound of a ship closing in. "One destroyer only," said Tolle, listening intently on the boat's radio, and indeed, the pinging from two of the destroyers had stopped.

"Good," said Seligman. "That improves our odds."

"Depth charges dropped," said Tolle.

There was a pause while the bombs drifted downward

through the water, then Seligman heard the first muffled explosions, sounding like thunder in the distance, but causing no harm.

But then four more exploded, two at a time. Being under attack always made Seligman think of crossing a train trestle on foot and suddenly realizing a train is approaching. As the danger approaches, all the pedestrian can do is persevere. Will he clear the trestle before the train gets to him?

The third and fourth sets of four were overhead, and though they caused the boat to shake, the explosions were too shallow to cause serious damage.

"Destroyer moving away," Tolle said.

"Get us to the floor, Chief," said Seligman.

"Dive to the bottom," Siegfried ordered and the hydroplane operators set the bow plane to hard down, the stern plane to down.

The destroyer made two more passes and even though the depth charges were closer than the first pass, the boat's position on the ocean floor confused its sonar. The pedestrian had cleared the trestle.

As the high-pitched whine of the lone destroyer's fast screws faded in the distance and was replaced by the methodical thumping of the slower props of the merchant ships, Seligman ordered a gradual rise to periscope depth. When he raised the periscope he could see that the convoy was now to their east. He would not be able to attack until he caught up, which required surfacing.

"How long to nightfall?" he asked.

"Full dark in forty minutes, Sir."

"We wait until then. Bring us around to five degrees north of east."

After thirty-five minutes, all spent with Seligman peering through the periscope and Tolle on the hydrophone listening for the destroyers, the watch assembled and prepared to climb to the bridge. The convoy had put some distance between it and the unseen threat, but the size of the fleet of freighters still allowed the crew to hear dozens of propellers pounding the ocean.

"They sound like a waterfall," said Schultz.

When the time was right, Seligman ordered, "Blow all tanks," and shortly thereafter U-112 broke the surface. Seligman cautiously opened the hatch, to avoid the difference in pressure inside the sub blowing it open too fast. He caught the wind-driven spray in his face, ducked it momentarily, then climbed out. He was followed to the bridge by the four-man watch, headed by Neumann.

Thin clouds covered a half moon, not a perfect night for a hunt, but better than no clouds at all. Once on the surface they quickly began to close the distance between them and the freighters.

"Anyone see the destroyers?" Seligman asked.

"*Nein, Kapitän*," four voices rang out.

"Then we lost them," Seligman exulted.

"*Kapitän*, a question?" Ensign Schwarz glanced at Seligman expectantly, then looked back at his watch quadrant.

"Yes," said Seligman.

Schwarz continued his watch while asking, "Why did the destroyers split up? Aren't they supposed to attack in threes?"

"Yes, they are. Their sonar may have detected other U-boats and they decided to pursue them. They don't have to sink us to be successful. They just have to stop us from sinking any of their freighters."

"But it was right on top of us. I could hear them without hydrophones."

"Don't worry, you'll have other opportunities to get sunk by a depth charge," said Seligman. The other men made eye contact and nodded. "Just give thanks that they are too inexperienced to pick one target and go after it."

Eins eins zwie steadily closed on its prey. As it did, Seligman and Neumann studied the convoy and plotted their strategy.

"There are just five rows," Seligman told Neumann. "Usually there are twice as many."

"*Ja*," replied Neumann. "The rough seas must have them worried they will be scattered. Good for us they are close together. It will improve our hunting."

"I estimate 1500 meters between each row. I think we can maneuver right in between two columns without being seen. The destroyers' radar will be confused by all the freighters around us so they won't know a U-boat has joined their convoy. We'll attack on the surface. We move forward until we have two ships behind us to starboard. We'll shoot four forward to port, farthest target first, then two aft to starboard, farthest target first. What do you think?"

"I like it," said Neumann, smiling. "Have you ever hit six targets in one attack?"

"Not until tonight," said Seligman, anticipating success.

He began a ritual he went through every time *eins eins zwei* launched an attack. *Our Father in Heaven*, he thought to himself, *I must kill the enemy of my Fatherland, and even though they are our enemy, they are also men. I ask that you protect them from the cold of the water, from the fire of the oil, from the explosions of the torpedoes. If you can, guide them safely home.* Just without a boat, he thought wryly, after pausing a moment. He didn't want that part to go to the Heavenly Father.

The men he killed would bother him until the next time his boat came under attack. Then the Captain would be able to put the dead out of his mind with the realization that they would just as willingly have sent him and his crew to the bottom.

"Maintain full ahead, steady course," he told the Chief through the speaker tube.

"Aye, *Kapitän*."

"It will take us about one hour to get far enough inside the convoy to pull this off," Seligman told the men of the watch. "Until then, keep a sharp eye out for destroyers and any change in the position of the freighters."

"Aye, *Kapitän*," said four voices.

They closed the distance steadily until they were between two rows, then continued forward to position two of the targets behind them. Seligman fretted constantly that the clouds might suddenly uncover the moon. If it did, there might be enough light to identify them as the enemy. He would have to submerge and would lose the advantage of surprise.

He went to the speaker tube and called for the Navigator. When Winter responded, Seligman said, "Take this down for the war log. 'Preparing for surface attack on convoy from rear. Half-moon covered by clouds.' Note time."

"Aye, Sir."

Three times the moon toyed with them, threatening to pop out of the clouds. Seligman knew if he was forced to submerge, however, the boat would lose too much distance, and all their advantage. The only way they could pull off the surprise was to stay where they were. And each time, just as Seligman was about to order a dive, the clouds gathered to cover it.

The third time it happened, Neumann said, "*Heute abend, Gott ist Deutsch.*" Tonight, God is German. This caused everyone but Seligman to laugh quietly.

"Enough of that," he said. "Do you want to jinx us?" His reproach caused an awkward quiet to descend over the men.

With no one talking, Seligman listened to the slapping of the waves against their hull as the sea tossed the boat about. He appreciated the way *eins eins zwei* was moving, rolling on top of the sea as if it were a part of it. Although the sea was rough, there was a rhythm to the waves that coincided with the motion of the boat, and it slid down the back of every wave just as the next one began raising the bow. The captain likened it to a horse and rider negotiating an evenly spaced series of jumps.

He wondered about his first officer. If anything happened to him, Neumann would take command. Too often, however, he seemed to want to be one of the guys. Would he be ready if leadership was thrust upon him? Seligman decided he needed to spend more time preparing him for command, especially if, as Rösing had insinuated, he would soon be getting his own boat.

He looked at Neumann now, busy plotting the path of the torpedoes with the *standzielsehrohr*, the bridge periscope used when attacking on the surface. He knew his first officer didn't like the Nazis any more than he did, but they both had a job to do and it was Seligman's responsibility to see that it got done. Would Neumann's anti-Nazi stand override his duty to the Fatherland?

"Let me know when you have your targets plotted," he said to Neumann, breaking a long silence and startling several members of the watch. To them, he said, "Remember, you are responsible for your sector. Be alert at all times and do not allow yourself to be distracted by our attack. I'll cover Neumann's quadrant while he directs the attack."

"Aye, *Kapitän*," said each of the three watchmen.

A moment later, Neumann confirmed his ranges and bearings, and reported he was ready.

"Commence the attack," Seligman said, with all the

excitement he would show if ordering breakfast. The time was 01:40.

"Tube one," said Neumann, "ready, fire! Tube two, ready, fire! Tube three, ready, fire! Tube four, ready, fire!" Simple commands that propelled hissing torpedoes, death, and mayhem toward unsuspecting ships in harm's way.

"*Torpedos los,*" reported the torpedo man. Torpedo away.

"Left full rudder," Seligman commanded, and the boat quickly swung to port. "What is the estimated run time on the first torpedo?"

"Fifty-eight seconds, sir," said Neumann.

As soon as they were in position, Neumann called out the command to fire the stern tubes while Seligman checked his watch and waited for the first explosion.

"*Torpedos los,*" repeated the torpedo man.

"Right full rudder until we return to original course, then hold steady," Seligman instructed the chief through the tube. "As soon as there is an explosion, full reverse." The crew members waited in anxious anticipation.

When the first torpedo hit almost a minute later, a secondary explosion followed immediately. The freighter blew apart with a ferocity that indicated it was carrying munitions. Seligman felt the boat slow as the chief executed the full reverse order. Then, the second and third torpedoes ripped into two more ships, and dozens of flares emerged from the freighters, lighting the cloudy night sky as if it were a cloudless day.

The convoy changed course, causing the fourth torpedo fired forward to miss the mark. But not the fifth and sixth, fired aft. Those two torpedoes hit their targets in the bow area. The freighters immediately started listing as the forward motion of the ships forced thousands of gallons of water into the gaping holes in their hulls. Seligman knew that as the water quickly flooded underwater compartments, men who had survived the explosions would drown.

U-112 ducked in behind the burning hulk of a doomed 7,000 ton freighter, hiding behind the flames. None of the undamaged ships slowed to pick up crew members who were now flailing wildly in the water. In the icy North Atlantic they would be dead before a ship could stop, either from the cold of the water or the burning oil on the surface. It seemed incongruous and cruel that their bodies below their shoulders could be freezing while their heads were burning. The lucky ones were pulled underwater by the undertow of the sinking ships and drowned.

They had hit the first ship on its starboard side. The secondary explosion took out its underside from midship to bow. In two minutes it was listing heavily to the right. It sank bow first in less than three minutes, her angry props spinning in the air as they vainly grasped for traction.

Two others broke in half, dumping their crews mercilessly into the water. The four halves of the two boats bobbed for a few minutes, then disappeared.

With engines on *eins eins zwei* in full reverse, the convoy was pulling away, but the last two stricken freighters had been behind the boat when the attack started. Now they were next to it. As multiple explosions ripped them apart, they sent huge chunks of steel splashing into the water all around. The watch crew maintained their discipline and continued watching their quadrants until Seligman yelled, "Hit the deck!"

He saw a large cloud of shrapnel descending on the boat, as if it had been flung at them out of the sky by an almighty hand. "*Gott ist Deutsch?*" he thought to himself as he dived for the deck, and silently cursed Neumann for having said it.

At first it appeared the molten hot shards of steel would never get there. When they did, it seemed the terror pelting down on the men would never end. For almost ten seconds burning metal rained down, severely cutting Schwarz on the back of his head. The others managed to avoid direct hits, but they all received minor cuts and burns.

As soon as the storm of metal stopped, Seligman called for crewmen to come topside and remove Schwarz. When he was out of the way, Schulz hurried up the ladder to replace him and he and the others resumed the watch.

"I've located the three destroyers," said Ensign Braun, pointing forward. "Five thousand meters ahead." Seligman trained his binoculars in that direction and could see the destroyers moving away from *eins eins zwei*, which was riding so low the waves washed over its deck.

"We don't even need to dive," said Seligman. "They can't see us and their radar can't find us so close to the convoy. The luck of the hunt!"

"*Ja*, hitting forward and backward both seems to have them confused as to where we are," said Neumann.

The captain set a course to continue stalking the convoy from the rear and ordered the tubes be reloaded for a second attack.

"Radioman, notify Headquarters of our success. Plot on the grid our exact location."

"Aye, *Kapitän*," Radioman Frick replied. He turned to the *Kriegsmarine* grid system, calculated that they were in quadrant AL, sector 91, and relayed this information to headquarters.

7 May 1941
   Quadrant AL 9222

.   .   .

At 03:45 Neumann reported to Seligman that all torpedo tubes had been reloaded.

"But we must move quickly," he said. "Sunrise is at 04:42."

U-112 was already positioned to launch another attack, but as Seligman prepared to order it, Radioman Tolle stuck his head through the hatch.

"Sir," he yelled, to be heard over the ocean's roar, "We've received a message from headquarters."

"Read it," Seligman said.

"*DO NOT MAKE FURTHER ATTACKS. TRANSMIT BEACON SIGNALS. AWAIT FURTHER ORDERS.*"

"*Damn*," said Seligman. "They want to bring other boats in to help with the attack," he said to Neumann. "We've got them right where we want them, their escorts can't find us, and we can't attack."

"The luck of the hunt," said Neumann laconically. Seligman was not amused.

6 May, 1941

War log of U-112

21:30 Convoy sighted moving east toward our position while patrolling Quadrant AL

21:35 Dove to await convoy

22:05 Identified three destroyer escorts as J-class

22:06 Dive to ocean floor 155 meters to evade destroyer attack

22:15 Destroyers evaded; no depth charges

22:45 Rose to periscope depth; convoy out of range for underwater attack

23:25 Surfaced and began approach from rear of convoy

6 May, 1941

War log of U-112

01:40 Commence attack on convoy

01:48 Six torpedoes fired. Five freighters sunk-Two 7000 ton; one 5000 ton; two 3500 ton

01:50 to 03:45 re-loaded torpedo tubes to prepare for second attack on convoy

03:50 Received order from Command to transmit location beacons and await other boats

03:51Attack cut off.

CHAPTER TEN

26 May 1941 16:20 CET (Central European Time)
  Quadrant AL

"*Kapitän* to the bridge," came the terse message from Second Watch Officer Watts. He had spotted smoke on the southern horizon. Seconds later, Seligman stood next to him, hoping he betrayed no visible hint that he'd just awakened.

"There," Watts said, pointing.

"*Ja*," said Seligman. "*Gut gemacht.*" Well done.

The Captain quickly gave commands adjusting the direction of the boat, then estimated, "We should be in a position to attack from the North just after sunset. We'll need to move around them. Let's track them long enough to get their direction, then parallel them at full speed to get ahead. When we're in front of them we'll submerge and do a periscope attack."

Going to the speaking tube, Seligman called below, "Chief, how are our fuel reserves?"

"Good for two days at top speed, if it takes that long,"

Siegfried replied. The chief knew that if conditions were right they would stalk and attack, stalk and attack, until they were out of torpedoes. Or sunk. They were the hunters, closing in on their prey; but it would be hours before they would be in a position to launch an attack and at any time a simple twist of fate could make them the hunted.

Speaking into the tube, Seligman said, "It will be a while before we attack. Until then the crew should carry on as normal."

The initial spotting of the convoy sent a ripple of anticipation through the boat, but soon the tension of impending attack slackened and routine returned. In the front crew area, Krause had organized a game of euchre, using a torpedo to hold the kitty. Tolle, Schulz, and Frick were the other participants. No one seemed at all put off by the thought that their makeshift table could possibly send a ship and crew to the bottom of the ocean in a matter of hours. The game was occasionally interrupted by the cards sliding off the torpedo when the boat rolled in a particularly rough patch of water.

"What do you think of Wagner, always giving the Nazi salute?" asked Krause. "Doesn't he know we don't salute when we're out, not even a regular one?"

"Maybe it's his training," said Frick. "And remember, he's an officer, you're not. Be careful what you say."

"Oh, so you're one of those 'there's a spy onboard' nuts," said Krause. "I don't buy it. We're sailors for the Fatherland first. If there are any Nazis on board they better care about the Fatherland first, the party second. That's what I think. What do you say, Tolle?"

"I say that's a dangerous 'think'. Our government is run by

the Nazis and they have a right to demand respect. Maybe Wagner's trying to show respect to the Reich."

"So when did you become a Nazi?" asked Krause.

"Hitler has brought respect to Germany. I admire Wagner for honoring that," Tolle said and knocked on the torpedo to pass on trump.

"Not so hard," said Schulz, also knocking. "You'll blow us up. I don't think the *Kapitän* agrees with that."

"Picking it up," said Frick, reaching for the top card.

"Why do you say that about Seligman?" Tolle asked Schulz.

"Watch him when Wagner salutes. He always makes a face, and he never tells him we don't do that when we're out. It's like he wants to show Wagner as a fool to the crew," said Shulz.

Tolle nodded, but didn't reply.

Wagner, Kretchmer, and Seaman Schuster were holding their food trays on the foldaway table that doubled as the navigator's charting board. As First Officer Neumann approached carrying a plate of food, Kretchmer finished his meal and cleared a space.

"Here you are, Sir. I'm finished. You can fit in here."

"*Danke,*" said Neumann. He set a plate filled with beets and sausage on the table and stood next to Wagner.

"Watch my tray while I get a knife," said Wagner.

"My pleasure," said Neumann, but as Wagner turned his back the boat was tossed suddenly and his plate of food slid off the table, scattering beets and sausage all over the floor.

"I asked you to watch my plate," said Wagner in a much quieter voice than he would have used with anyone who didn't outrank him.

"Yeah," said Neumann, keeping his hand on his plate, lest it suffer the same fate as Wagner's. "I was watching it. If you wanted me to hold it down you should have asked me."

The color in Wagner's face matched the beets now strewn across the deck as he struggled to hold his anger in. Schuster tried to contain his laugh, but Wagner could see his shoulders shake as he looked down at his plate. Wagner wanted to give the lowly seaman a dressing down but thought better of it in front of Neumann, *his* superior, so he turned on his heel and walked quickly away.

"Are you finished with this?" Neumann called after him, pointing to the mess on the floor. "Because if you are, I'm eating it." Wagner didn't look back.

Turning to Schuster, Neumann said, "It's just wrong to waste food like that, don't you think?"

Schuster nodded his head sagely, and grinned.

At 21:25 CET, just as U-112 was prepared to make contact with the convoy again, Radioman Handelman came hurriedly through the hatch.

"*Kapitän*," he said anxiously, "an emergency message from *BdU*. I just got it decoded."

Handelman gave it to the Captain, who read it and swore quietly. Going to the speaking tube, he called down to the Navigator, "Plot a course for BE 29. All engines ahead full on that course."

Watts looked at him with raised eyebrows, and asked, "We're calling off the attack?"

Without replying, Seligman handed him the decoded message.

Watts read, *'EMERGENCY ALL U-BOATS WITH TORPE-*

DOES TO PROCEED AT ONCE AND AT FULL SPEED TOWARD BISMARCK GRID SQUARE BE 29.'

"What do you make of it?" asked Watts.

"The *Bismarck* is in trouble."

CHAPTER ELEVEN

27 May, 1941 6:55 CET
Quadrant BE 21

"A transmission from U-556, sir."

Seligman awoke from a restless sleep to find Radioman Kretchmer shaking his shoulder. He swung his legs off his cot and sat on its edge, his feet bracing him against the rolling of the boat. Rubbing his face with his hands, he asked, "What does it say?"

Kretchmer grabbed at Seligman's desk as the boat was tossed by a wave. "It says the *Bismarck* was struck by a torpedo dropped from a Swordfish. It cannot maneuver to defend itself."

Seligman was stunned. He thought back to late July of 1938. He, Marie, and not quite one-year-old Ernst had been in Hamburg visiting her family. He took an afternoon to look up his friend from the Academy, *Kapitänleutnant* Gruner, who was to be assigned to the *Bismarck*. Gruner took him on a tour of the monstrous battleship then under construction.

"It is a beautiful ship, both in engineering and capabilities," he said to Gruner.

"*Ja*," Gruner replied. "I'd like to see the ship that can take it down." He spoke like a proud father.

But it wasn't a ship that was her undoing; it was a plane, one left over from the Great War. The most powerful battleship in the world taken down by a twenty-five year-old British bi-plane.

Bismarck, Gruner, and more than 2000 others were on their way to a common grave. He wondered what Gruner was experiencing right at that moment. Maybe he was already dead. One more friend from the academy gone. Would any survive the war?

"Thank you, Kretchmer. That is all."

Seligman pushed back the curtain on his space and watched Kretchmer lurching away. He saw Neumann on the Command Deck, monitoring the boat's activity and Navigator Winter reviewing charts.

"Winter, are you busy?" he asked.

"Nothing that has to be done now, Sir."

"Relieve the First Officer at the command, if you would." Turning to Neumann, he called, "Let me update you."

Neumann quickly reported to Winter on the status of their location, bearings, and speed while both of the men steadied themselves in rough seas. In turn, Seligman told Neumann all he knew about the *Bismarck*, and that it sounded like it would not survive the battle.

"The hardest thing for me to deal with," said Neumann quietly, "is that here we are in rough seas but we're not under attack. We can pretend there's no war; yet somewhere, right now, fellow Germans are losing their lives."

"I know," Seligman replied.

"And for what?" Neumann's voice was no longer quiet.

"So that Hitler can win a trumped- up war he started because he's not over 1918 yet."

"Careful," said Seligman. "What you're saying can get you shot."

"We've had this discussion before. I know you agree with me."

"Whether I agree or not, we have a duty to the Fatherland."

"And the Fatherland is the only reason I launch those torpedoes. I understand that the Tommies think they own the seas: 'The sun never sets on the British Empire!' Well, fuck them. They want to keep us bottled up and landlocked. I understand. We have a right to be angry about that. But the Nazis are out of control, and it's all because of that one arrogant man."

Seligman stood up and looked outside his curtain. When assured that no one was listening, he said, "As your commander, I have to warn you to stop making these treasonous statements. I won't have you shot, but I believe there is someone on board who will, if he hears you."

"The difference between you and me is that you're a politician, I'm not. You agree with me, but you won't say it."

"I have a family, and I believe in the Fatherland."

"And that requires you to fall in line? I don't have a family, but I believe in the Fatherland, too. But are you willing to die for a cause that is wrong? Don't you owe it to your family, don't *we* owe it to the Fatherland, to say, this war is wrong?"

Seligman said, "You *must* keep your voice down. I will discuss this with you, but not for everyone to hear. What am I willing to die for? I'm willing to die for my family. I'm willing to die for the Fatherland."

"But can you separate Fatherland from Nazis?" Neumann leaned close to the Captain so he could speak quietly and still be heard.

Seligman nodded. "That, of course, is the difficulty. Who *are* we fighting for? I'm fighting for the Fatherland, which is at war with an enemy that will kill us just as surely as we try to kill them. I'm fighting for my family, so that my son can live in a country of which he is proud. So that my wife and I might have other children who will have a future, and not be a slave to Great Britain."

"What about Russia? Are they our enemy?"

Seligman shook his head. "We're not at war with Russia."

"Yet."

"That's right. And maybe we should be. They're sending communist organizers into Germany, and we all know it." Neumann nodded, and Seligman continued. "Is it right for them to do that?"

"Of course it's not right. But what country have we invaded that was seriously a threat to Germany?" Neumann's face was about six inches from Seligman's as he hissed through clenched teeth, "Not a one." He leaned back.

"If you feel this way, how can you carry out your duties?"

Neumann shrugged and shook his head. "I try not to think about it. I remind myself it's kill or be killed. But I'm telling you, Willie, I don't like it."

Seligman was surprised at the use of his first name diminutive. He and Neumann had served together since he had been in charge of *eins eins zwei* and they had worked well together, but theirs was a professional relationship. Seligman did not consider them to be friends. Neither had met the other's family. Neumann had just said he didn't have one, and Seligman realized he didn't know much about his first officer. Was Neumann reaching out to him for friendship? If he was, it didn't matter at the present. Right now, Seligman had to determine whether he could count on Neumann to carry out his orders.

"All right," he said, "we agree the war is immoral; we don't agree on the politics of it. But we are officers of the *Kriegsmarine*. We have both taken an oath. I must know that I can count on you to carry out orders. The Fatherland must know that it can count on you if you must take over my duties."

Neumann appeared to be deep in thought. "Well?" asked Seligman.

"I will do my job. I will defend the Fatherland. But our oath was not to the Fatherland. That little man with the little mustache made us swear allegiance to him. I feel no obligation to live up to an oath of allegiance to a crazy man."

"That's not a good enough answer. Our country is at war, and it is our duty to fight that war. I need a First Officer that will carry out that duty. If you cannot you need to transfer out."

Neumann looked as if he was going to be sick. "Willie..."

"Dismissed," said Seligman.

Neumann looked at Seligman for a minute like a puppy looking for an alpha dog, then he stood and walked out.

While the Captain and his First Officer struggled with their differences below deck, the sea pitched the boat like a cork in a tub. A storm was gathering, but still U-112 pushed on toward the *Bismarck's* location. Rain began pelting the second watch, which was again on the bridge. High winds and seas slowed their progress, then enemy destroyers forced them into a detour, delaying them by two hours.

At 11:55 CET Handelman approached Seligman, who was still in his quarters.

"Sir," he said, "another message from *BdU*."

Handing it to Seligman, he waited as the Captain read, *'BISMARCK VICTIM OF CONCENTRATED ENEMY FIRE. ALL U-BOATS IN VICINITY TO SEARCH FOR SURVIVORS.'*

CHAPTER TWELVE

2 August, 1934
Reich Chancellory announcement

By order of *Der Führer*, effective immediately, all members of the armed forces will take the following oath.

"I swear by God this sacred oath, that I shall render unconditional obedience to Adolf Hitler, the *Führer* of the German Reich and people, Supreme Commander of the armed forces, and that I shall at all times be prepared, as a brave soldier, to give my life for this oath."

CHAPTER THIRTEEN

War log of U-112
   28 May, 1941 15:45 CET

Arrived at BE 65, location of last transmission from Battleship *Bismarck*. Waters are calm with a heavy layer of oil and detritus.
   28 May, 1941 15:45-May 29 20:30
   Joined U-557 in search for survivors. None found. No bodies recovered.

CHAPTER FOURTEEN

Dresden
20 June, 1941

"I'm looking forward to seeing my parents tomorrow," Marie whispered in Seligman's ear, then kissed his cheek. They had waited for Ernst to fall asleep, then made love as quietly as they could, considering they hadn't been together for four months. Every time they bounced, the squeaking bed threatened to wake him. He had stirred once, causing both of them to freeze at a moment when freezing was not that easy, but he didn't wake up. If he had, he would have left his bed in the corner and crawled in with them.

"We'll get there at 17:45," she continued in a whisper. "Mama said you haven't been there since the war started; just Ernst and me, and he and I haven't been there since last Christmas. She's afraid Ernst will grow up and not know them."

"Ernst is three and a half. He has plenty of time to get to

know them," Seligman said. "Aren't you worried about the bombing in Hamburg?"

"Aren't you worried about the depth charges in the sea?"

He sighed, shook his head, and said, "All right, I'll be on the train. I don't know why I had to marry such a quick-witted woman."

"You had no choice once I decided I wanted you," she said, massaging him back to life. "I had you following me around like a hungry fish chasing bait." She tugged on him, as if landing a fish.

He chuckled, then pulled her over on top of him. The bed let out a groan and they both looked toward the corner. "We need a quieter bed," he said.

She nodded imperceptibly, then kissed him. She made a face, then said, "Tomorrow, you shave."

Seligman knew she didn't like him with a beard, but he he'd been in a hurry to get home, and hadn't bothered to shave before leaving the base in Lorient.

He had arrived earlier in the day for a ten-day visit, and he didn't look forward to spending more than half of it either at her parents' house in Hamburg, or in transit. He wanted Marie and Ernst to himself, but when she'd found out he would be home, she had written that she had purchased train tickets for all of them.

He liked her parents, but he had so little time at home. And Marta would be there. Marta! She was so...exuberant was the only word he could think of to describe his wife's sister. She sang along with the radio and would spontaneously dance around the room with an imaginary partner. She talked about the most inane topics, like movie stars and boys on whom she had a crush. She would ask him what he thought of something, then before he could answer she'd tell him what *she* thought. She laughed about everything, and even though she was seven years younger, flirted with him incessantly.

The next morning as they set out for the train station Ernst hopped happily from one foot to the other. "Yay," he shouted, "We're going to see grandfather and grandmother!"

"And Aunt Marta," said his mother.

"Yay, Aunt Marta!"

"I hope she doesn't sit on my lap again," said Seligman, lifting their bags onto the tram. "That was embarrassing."

"Only for you," said Marie, smiling at the memory of their last visit together. "Everyone else thought it was sweet."

"I can't believe you were OK with it."

Marie deposited their fare and, with Ernst holding her hand, followed Seligman down the aisle to a seat. "Who said I was OK with it?" she asked as they sat down. She pulled Ernst into her lap.

"You seemed to be."

"She was only fourteen, trying to be a woman. She'll be eighteen on her next birthday. If she tries it now, I'll put a stop to it."

If he wasn't married, and to her sister, no less, Seligman would have reciprocated her flirting. She may have been a child, but she was oh, so pretty. He had to be careful not to imply he liked the attention, or Marie would be angry. Their father would not take kindly to it, either, and he had a connection in Berlin. Dieter would never discuss who his connection was, but Seligman suspected Marie's father could seriously hurt his career if he wanted to.

The train ride was long, crowded, and hot. It took most of the day and Seligman was actually relieved that they had to change trains at Anhalter Station in Berlin. The transfer broke up the almost five hundred kilometer ride and gave him a chance to stretch his legs during the forty-five minute layover. He got Marie and Ernst settled in the waiting room, then said, "I'm going to step outside for a minute. I've heard a lot about the bombing of Berlin and I'm curious to see if there is much damage."

Marie smiled and nodded.

"Can I come, too?" asked Ernst.

"Of course." He lifted Ernst off his mother's lap, set him on his feet, and took his hand for the walk outside.

"I'll stay here with the bag," Marie said.

Despite all the talk in Lorient about how bad Berlin had been hit, Seligman couldn't see much damage during the short walk. If the Tommies had been aiming for the train station, they had missed, so far. Several blocks away, too far to walk in the time he had, it appeared that a few buildings had lost roofs, maybe to a fire; but from what he had seen on the ride into town and his observations now, residential areas were fine.

As they walked back to the train station, Ernst asked, "Papa, what's it like on a submarine?"

"It's not a place where I would want you to be anytime soon," he replied.

"Why?" Ernst let go of Seligman's hand and picked up a rock. He threw it at the side of a building and was pleased when it ricocheted into a vacant field.

"Because it is damp, and cramped, and dangerous."

"Mommy says she gets cramped sometimes."

Seligman laughed. *I'll have to remember to tell Marie about that*, he thought.

He took Ernst by the hand again. "This is different. Cramped means crowded. There are a lot of men in very little space."

"I want to go with you."

"But you can't, *mein kleiner mann*. Why do you want to go with me?"

"Because Mommy says you're brave. I want to be brave, too."

"You are brave, my son."

"Am I?"

"Of course you are. You stay here with Mommy and you help her. It takes a brave boy to do that."

"Mommy says I will be like you when I grow up."

They turned a corner and Seligman saw the station come into view. "You can be like whomever you want to be."

"Then I want to be like Aunt Marta," he said, clapping his hands. "She's fun. She laughs a lot."

"Well, you could do worse." He paused, then added, "I guess."

"Yeah, I could do worse," said Ernst. "What's that mean?"

"It means you should be serious, like your mother."

"Oh."

They walked into the station just as their train was boarding. Marie was pacing, looking for them, so Seligman never broke stride. He picked up their bag and directed Ernst to Marie, who lifted him into her ams, and they climbed aboard.

The ride out of Berlin revealed more residential areas with minimal damage. Civilians were everywhere, and the trams seemed crowded.

When they arrived in Hamburg at 17:45, Seligman picked up the sleeping Ernst and cradled him in one arm as he lifted their bag with the other.

"Marie! Marie!"

They heard Marta before they could see her, as they stepped off the train. Marie's face lit up, and she looked around eagerly, trying to find the source of the voice. Seligman followed her off the train carrying the now-waking Ernst.

The crowd parted and a lithe young woman with short

blonde hair exploded into view. She was wearing a thin, low cut dress that did little to hide her breasts, which bounced enthusiastically with every stride. "Marie," she cried again, practically jumping into her older sister's arms. "It's so good to see you!" Releasing her, Marta lunged at Seligman, pushing against him the breasts she didn't have the last time he visited, and kissed him exuberantly on the mouth, first positioning her chewing gum so that it wouldn't fly out.

Marie was right about her growing up, at least physically. Besides the breasts, she was now as tall as his wife. On his last visit she had been all bony knees and elbows, but now, when she hugged him, her softness was easy to feel through the flimsy dress. Her scent and the way she moved, like a cat looking for quarry, caught him off guard. He didn't know how to react.

She said, "Let me have Ernst, I want to hold him." When he handed Ernst to her, she winked at him.

"*Tante* Marta," said Ernst, patting his small hands on her cheeks as she took him from his father, "where Grandfather and Grandmother?"

"Right over there," said Marta, pointing to a couple squeezing through the crowd. "Let me see you! Let me kiss you," she giggled, smothering Ernst in kisses and sending him into gales of laughter. As their parents approached, Marta held Ernst toward them and said, "Look who I found!" Then, before they got too close, she leaned over to Marie and said, as quietly as was possible for her excited state, "Big news to tell later tonight when we can talk."

Then Marta ran off toward their parents, squealing with delight and swinging Ernst this way and that. All the while Ernst was laughing loudly. Other passengers hurrying to their trains stopped abruptly to avoid colliding with them. Most looked back, smiling, after they passed safely. The toddler's feet flew around haphazardly, the result of the whirling and twirling Marta was doing.

Seligman leaned close to Marie and said, "Hurricane Marta has reached landfall."

"Yes," said Marie, "and I'll be talking to her later about that greeting."

Seligman smiled as he watched his sister-in-law's dress flying up as she spun.

"Don't stare," Marie said. "I've got legs, too."

"I just wanted to make sure she didn't fall with Ernst." He glanced in Marie's direction and saw a smirk on her face, but she didn't say any more.

Elsa and Dieter surrounded their whirling dervish daughter and wrested Ernst from her. Only then did they both hug Marie, Ernst caught between them. Elsa hugged Seligman and kissed him warmly, albeit on the cheek, and Dieter shook his hand.

Dieter's Nazi Party Pin gleamed on his coat lapel. It had a black swastika on a white background in the center, with a red band around it that was inscribed, 'National-Sozialistische DAP'. There was a gold wreath around the outer edge. He had shown it to Seligman once, proudly calling attention to the number on the back and the gold wreath.

"Three thousand five hundred forty-six, meaning only 3,545 people were enrolled in the party before me. Hitler, of course, has Badge number one and now there are more than 100,000. The wreath is only on those awarded before *unser Führer* came to power in 1933. After that, they are just *Angstbrosche*." Badges of Fearfulness. Dieter dismissively waved his arm and laughed with the disdain shown to newer party members by the *Alte Kampfer*, the Golden Pheasants, as those that had joined prior to the Nazi party successes in the Reichstag elections of 1930 were known.

On the ride to their home, they passed some homes that had been damaged in the air attacks.

"Did bombs do that?" asked Ernst, pointing to the houses without roofs.

"*Ja*," said Dieter. "How do you know about that?"

Ernst shrugged.

Dieter said, "They have hit us numerous times since the start of the war. It comes with having a port. But the last time was over a month ago. I think we're out of the woods."

"I hope you are right," said Seligman, though he doubted that Hamburg would be spared future bombings.

"If they do come back, the sirens give us about fifteen minutes' warning. And I have some civil defense maps not meant for the public. I got them from a friend in Berlin." As he said this, he smiled at Seligman. "They have the city marked off in a grid. I can tune the radio to the *Flaksender* broadcasts which tell the anti-aircraft guns which grids are under attack. When they get close to our house we go to the shelter in our cellar. We'll be fine." As he said this, they drove past the blackened shell of a church. One wall and the steeple were all that remained.

After dinner, Marta and Marie washed the dishes while Seligman sat with his in-laws and talked, Ernst asleep in his lap.

Elsa and Dieter Möller were both in their late forties. Elsa's blonde hair was well on its way to gray, but she was still as thin as when they got married. She moved with such grace she seemed to float as she walked. Her prominent cheekbones made it obvious their mother was the source of Marta and Marie's beauty. She liked to sit quietly next to Dieter, sometimes with her hand resting on his.

Dieter's hair was still fairly dark, although there was a lot of gray in his mustache, which was cut similarly to Hitler's and bobbed up and down as he told Seligman, again, how he had been a medic in the hospital where Adolf Hitler was treated for partial blindness after a mustard gas attack near the end of World War I.

"He was under my care when he found out about the armistice," Dieter told Seligman, although his son-in-law could have repeated the story verbatim. "He went crazy!" He swept his arm frantically to the side for emphasis, then continued.

"He has us on the right track now. I notice around town there are fewer Jews. He's sending them off for re-education. Make them decent citizens when all is said and done."

Elsa nodded and smiled at Dieter. *Heaven forbid*, thought Seligman, *that she have an original opinion*. He realized how much he liked Marie's way of challenging him when she disagreed.

They called Hitler "*unser Führer,*" our leader, and despite their rigid belief in his policies, the Möllers tolerated Seligman's more liberal attitude toward Jews and other minorities. The Möllers were good parents, Dieter's medical practice had provided well for their daughters, and they spoiled Ernst every time they were around him. But Seligman worried about the effect their Nazi attitude would have on Ernst.

"We need to invade Russia, kick the Bolsheviks out," Dieter was saying, "then defeat England. Put Edward VIII back on the throne. The Duke of Windsor will work with *unser Führer*. He will. It was crazy that the Tommies made him abdicate, and over what? A woman!" Dieter shook his head. As if on cue, Elsa did, likewise. "Then we can deal with the United States. Teach them to mind their own business."

"Don't give us more than we can handle," replied Seligman. "I worry that the United States will come into the war."

"Bah, let them. They have no business involving themselves in European affairs. Besides, we're working on the *Amerika* bomber. When it is completed, it will be able to fly round trip to the United States without refueling. Give us a couple of islands in the middle of the Atlantic for emergencies, and we'll take the fight to them."

Seligman disagreed with his father-in-law, but knew they would never see eye-to-eye on the Nazis, so he did not reply.

After a pause in the conversation, something unusual when Dieter was involved, Elsa nodded toward Ernst, saying, "He's such an angel." Seligman smiled at her, glad to change the topic of discussion. But almost immediately, the focus returned to the war.

"Where is your uniform?" Dieter asked. "I'd like to take you out tomorrow, show you off to our townsfolk. Let them know we've got a real fighting man in our family."

"I prefer not to wear my uniform when I'm on leave. In fact, since I don't wear it on the boat, either, I would need to clean any uniform before wearing it."

"I can do that for you," said Elsa. "Dieter has been looking forward to seeing you in your *Kriegsmarine* uniform. We've never seen you in it."

"You're not ashamed of it, are you, son?" asked her husband.

"Of course I'm not ashamed of it, but I don't wear it, except on base. I didn't even bring one." He stood up, a limp Ernst in his arms. "I need to put him to bed," he said. As he left the room, he heard Dieter emit a low grumble, and saw Elsa quietly pat her husband's hand.

Marie carried the glass she was drying to the closed swinging door leading into the living room. She pushed on it with her shoulder until she could peer through a small opening and see her husband deep in conversation with her parents. The door swung shut as she walked back to where Marta was washing dishes in the sink.

"How's Friedrich?" she asked casually. Usually he was the first person Marta mentioned when she and her sister talked, but she hadn't, yet.

Marta's eyes glowed and her smile erupted. "That's the big news! Friedrich and I are engaged! He had to leave for the army last week, so we won't get married until he comes home on leave. Then we'll call you to come, and we'll have the *best* wedding *ever*! If Willie's at home he can come, too." Marta, holding a dish dripping water, did an impromptu dance around the kitchen with her arms positioned as if she held a partner.

"That's a big step at your age," said Marie with concern. "Do Mama and Papa know about it?"

"No, and don't you tell them. They think I'm too young to be serious about someone. Papa says only kids chew gum, so until I stop I'm a kid. But I'm not. I'm eighteen." She and her imaginary partner waltzed around the kitchen a second time, dish still in hand.

"Not yet."

"Almost," she said, even though her birthday was seven months away. "I will be by the time he comes home. And you were nineteen when you were married, so it will almost be the same." She stopped her dance, put the dish back into the sink, and took the dish towel out of Marie's hand. She tossed it on the counter and put her right hand over her sister's mouth to quiet the objection that was coming, then took both her hands in her still-wet hands. Laughing, the young girl caught her gum between her lips just as it started to come out of her mouth and pulled it back in with her tongue. "Don't say, 'that's different'. It's not. Isn't it exciting? We'll both be married. Maybe I'll have a little boy and Ernst can be like a big brother."

Marie smiled at her happiness, but said, "It can be stressful being married to a person in the military. I worry all the time when Willie is away. If he's at sea I worry that he'll be killed. If he's in port I worry that he's not alone."

"Willie wouldn't do that. He's a gentleman. Besides, he's in love with you." She let go of Marie's hands and turned back to the dishes.

"Willie's a *man*." She picked up the towel as Marta handed her a pot. "You didn't see the way he was looking at you today when your tits almost popped out of that dress."

"Yes, I did," Marta replied, laughing. "I wore it for him. I wanted him to see that I'm a woman now. I knew you wouldn't mind. "

"You're wrong; I *do* mind, and not just for me. You have to stop teasing men like that before it gets you in trouble. Do you do this with others besides my Willie?"

Marta frowned and looked down at the sink. "No."

Marie spotted, but didn't challenge, the lie. "I don't like you flirting with Willie, and neither will Friedrich. You can't be jumping on his lap anymore; you're not fourteen. When you kiss him it should always be on the cheek, never on the lips. There's a big difference between having a woman's body and being a woman. "

"I kept my mouth closed when we kissed."

"Jesus, Marta, I should hope so! You've got no business kissing my husband on the mouth, open or not. From now on, cheek only."

"You're no fun."

"And you're too much fun. If you're going to get married you've got to settle down."

Marta threw her head back and laughed. "I'll settle down when I'm dead; not before." She handed her sister the last pot. Marie didn't realize how much she was glaring at Marta until her sister reached out and put her hands on the corners of Marie's mouth. She pushed them up. "I like you better when you smile," she said, but when she let go Marie let the frown return. "What's the matter?"

Marie methodically dried the pot. Without taking her eyes off her hands, she said, "I have something serious to ask of you. But first I have to know that you understand what I'm saying. No more flirting. I don't care if it's Willie or whoever."

"I understand. No more flirting or I'll get myself in trouble. What is this serious thing you have to ask me?"

"We'll see how grown up you really are." Marie finished drying the pot, set it on the counter, and hung up the towel.

"That sounds ominous."

"Not really, but it is good that you will be married. I will feel better if there is a man around."

"Why?"

"I will worry less about Ernst."

"When?"

"If something happens to Willie and me."

"What's going to happen to you?"

Marie's eyes locked onto her sister, chilling Marta with their intensity. "I could be killed," her older sister said.

Marta folded her arms across her chest, and looked her older sister in the eyes. "How—"

"Look around you. I saw the damaged buildings coming into town. We're conquering the world, but still British bombers are getting through. Who knows what's going to happen when we invade England? I could be killed by a bomb."

"So what can I do to help you?"

"I want you to raise Ernst if Willie and I both die." She said it very fast, as if she was afraid she would change her mind if she didn't get it out there in the open.

Marta blanched and her eyes widened. "But, but...I'm too young."

Now it was Marie's turn to laugh. She hugged her sister. "I agree." She held her close as her laughter evaporated. "But you telling me that you're too young also tells me that you might actually be as mature as you were trying to convince me a few minutes ago. And you're getting married. You may even have your own family."

Marta broke the embrace, then slid her hands down Marie's arms until she again held her sister's in hers. "Does Willie know you're asking me this? He doesn't like me."

"You don't know Willie like I do. He doesn't dislike you; he's *afraid* of you."

"No!"

"Yes! He's afraid of the effect you have on him. Every time you hop on his lap or shake those tits at him he just about has a heart attack. He's afraid of what I'm going to do to him."

"But it's not his fault."

"I know. It's yours," she said sternly. She tugged her sister's hand in the direction of the table and the two of them moved toward it and sat down.

"I didn't know it bothered you so much." Marta sounded contrite, and she put her hand on top of Marie's.

"It bothers me a lot. And it scares me. If you do that with other men, Friedrich will not be happy, and I wouldn't blame him."

"I guess I've got a lot to learn about being married."

"You'll be OK, but what's done is done." Suddenly Marie laughed. "Lord, the look on Willie's face when you came flying up to him in that flimsy dress! His expression said, 'I can't get an erection. I *must not* get an erection.' I bet he did, though."

Marta hesitated, then put her hands over her mouth and squealed, "He did!"

Marie's eyes widened and both of them laughed, but then she looked very serious and said, "That's why you have to stop. He's going to strain something." They looked serious for a second, and Marta looked at her hands, trying to avoid laughing, but then their eyes met and both broke out in gales of laughter.

When they finally stopped, Marie said, "I haven't told Willie I was going to ask you to raise Ernst. I just decided to ask when you told me you were getting married. I've been denying that anything could happen to us, but it can."

Marie sighed, then continued: "Mama and Papa are too old. And besides, I don't agree with how Nazi they are. You would be the better choice, and Ernst adores you. Willie will get used to it once you quit giving him erections. And you *will* quit giving him erections."

"*Ja, Frau* Seligman." Marta's lower lip stuck out in a pout and she put her chin down on her chest.

"*Danke, Fräulein* Möller." The older sister put her hand under the younger woman's chin and raised her head so that they were facing each other. "So, will you do it? Will you raise Ernst if I die?"

"Yes, but don't die."

"I'll do my best, but when they start dropping bombs they don't look down and say, 'Let me see; where's Marie Seligman?' And with Willie on a U-boat, if they get depth charged there's no place for him to go. So I need to have something arranged."

Seeing Marie's concerned look, Marta hugged her. She realized it was the first time she had offered solace to her older sister, who usually buffered her carefree personality from the harsh world.

They stood up and started toward the door to join the others. Just before they reached the door, Marie turned to her younger sister and said, "One more thing." She rested her hands on her younger sister's hips. "I agree with Papa that you should stop chewing gum; it looks nasty. But I love how carefree you are. It's like every morning you get up and say, 'Let the fun begin.' I hope you do that every day for the rest of your life."

Marta chortled loudly and put her hands on the sides of her sister's face. Squeezing hard, she made her sister's mouth pucker and kissed her full on the lips.

———

When Seligman slipped into bed with his wife that night, his hand immediately went to her breast.

"Honey, we can't," she whispered. "Ernst is restless." She raised up and looked at their son, asleep on a cot at the foot of the bed. "He might wake up."

Seligman pulled her back down and slipped his hand inside her nightgown. He caressed her breasts, and rolled his fingers around her nipples. "He won't hear us," he said. "I've got to have you or I'm going to explode. My balls are aching." He moved his hand to the hem of her night dress, pushing it up past her waist.

"It better be me they're aching for," she said, raising her hips to help.

"Who else?" he asked, pushing the gown over her head, his hands roaming her uncovered body.

CHAPTER FIFTEEN

Hamburg
    21 June, 1941

Seligman awoke the next morning to a dog barking in the distance. He reached for Marie, but she was not in bed. He sat up and looked for Ernst, but he was gone, too.

Seligman swung his legs over the side of the bed and gazed around the room. It was cramped with all three of them sharing it, but had probably seemed large to Marie when she had lived here as a child.

Her presence was everywhere. There were the awards she had won at school. A shelf was filled with books by Luther, Spengler, and Rilke, as well as a Bible. She loved the short stories of Franz Kafka, as well as Thomas Mann's *The Magic Mountain*, but had to read those on the sly; her father would not allow them in the house. Kafka was a Jew, and Mann a member of the *Exilliteratur*, authors who fled the Nazi regime.

He looked at the pictures on her desk, and noticed one

that appeared to be new. He stood up and pulled back the drapes from the window, letting in the morning light. Picking up the new picture, he saw that it was the one she had insisted they have taken by a professional the last time he was home on leave. In it, he stood behind her in his uniform, his hands resting on her shoulders. She held Ernst on her lap, with a smile that could light up all of Hamburg on her face. He ran his fingers over her face in the picture. He smiled and remembered how good it felt to do that in reality. God, he loved her.

He thought of the previous night. He had been consumed with his need for her and his hands moved over her body, stoking her fire until she, at first merely acquiescent, soon burned with a desire equal to his. Ernst, even though restless, slept through it all.

Returning the picture to its spot on the desk, he crossed to the bed, and sat down. He tried to recall another night when they were so in rhythm with each other, but couldn't. Why had he been so aroused the previous day? It was only his second day home on leave, and he was always eager to make up for lost time. On the train to Hamburg, he kept glancing at her, wanting her.

But in his heart he knew that this time it was more than his long absence. This time he had noticed how she held their son so tenderly on her lap, occasionally leaning forward to kiss Ernst on the head as he dozed. He saw her face light up when their son pointed out cows in the fields they passed. Time and again, she had smoothed their little one's hair, even though it didn't need it. He didn't know why he hadn't seen these gestures before. Once she caught him looking at her, and she smiled at him, a flirty smile that set him aflame. He wanted to be by her side forever.

Until now he always equated love with the senses–the way her scent romanced his nose; her voice singing in his ears; her appearance sensually massaging his eyes; the taste of her kiss driving his desire higher; her touch enflaming his loins.

This was different. He needed this woman not just because she satisfied his physical needs so completely. He needed her because of who she was and what she did, and not just for him. Every time he returned on leave, he saw that she had become a more complete person. She cared for Ernst, but she watched the neighbors' children when they needed to run an errand; when it snowed she brought groceries to the old couple downstairs who couldn't get out; she made repairs around their flat, things that she had asked him to do, but he hadn't gotten to them. She never mentioned them again, she just did them. She was no longer an extension of him, but her own person.

He knew that she no longer loved him because she needed him, but because she *wanted* him. Knowing that made him want her, and all the previous day he had ached with that need. They had been together for seven years, but for the first time he truly understood love.

Then, when they arrived in Hamburg, he had not expected Marta to hug him so tightly or kiss him on the lips, and he hoped she hadn't detected his erection. If she had, she might have thought her kiss had caused it; she would have been wrong.

He pulled his clothes on and made his way to the kitchen, where Marta was sitting at the table wearing a thin night-dress, her hands around a coffee cup. The aroma told him it was real coffee like they had on the boat, not the ersatz version Marie made, and he remembered Dieter bragging about being able to get real coffee on the black market. She didn't notice him come in, and jumped when he said, "Good morning." Sitting down opposite her, he asked, "Where is everybody?"

"Mama and Papa took Ernst for a walk."

"But Marie. Where is she?"

"She went to the market." After a pause she added, "We're here alone. Are you scared?" Her smile mocked him.

He returned her smile and leaned back in his chair, folding his arms across his chest. A fly landed on his cheek and began rummaging through the stubble of his one-day beard. Her eyes focused on it, but he never flinched.

Why should I be scared? He wondered.

Gazing straight into her eyes, he said, "I need to tell you something." The movement of his mouth sent the fly scurrying away.

"Sounds serious."

"It is, and I'm glad we are alone so we can talk frankly with each other."

The hardness of his voice made Marta's smile dissolve, and she swallowed.

"You are so very beautiful," he said, with no hesitation. "It would be very easy for a man to love you." He paused to let that register. When Marta smiled slyly, he continued. "But you are not so beautiful when you flirt with me." He paused again, then said, "Do you want to know why?"

"Tell me," she said very quietly, diverting her eyes to the coffee in her cup.

"Because I am your sister's husband, and it shows disrespect to a lot of people. To me, for thinking that I would welcome it. To your sister, for thinking that she can't hold my love. To your parents, who raised you and your sister to support and take care of each other." Marta had blinked at each enumeration. He waited a moment for emphasis, then added, "But there is one person to whom it shows more disrespect than all four of those, and that is *you.*"

She looked up from her cup. For the first time since he had known her, she appeared to be at a loss for words. "It shows disrespect to you because it says you don't think you can find your own true love, that you have to poach your sister's. And by the way, I *do* love you."

She started to speak, but he held up his hand, commanding silence, and to his surprise it worked.

"I love you as a sister. I will *always* be there for you—as a brother. You should cut out these foolish shenanigans before they get you in trouble."

"I've never hurt anyone," Marta said, shaking her head.

"How do you know? If you flirt with other men like you do me, someone has probably thought you were leading him on. Some men have been known to think they are entitled to your…affection because you paraded it in front of them, or dressed provocatively."

She crossed her arms and leaned back in the chair. "I think you are overreacting."

Her gown was stretched tightly across her breasts and revealed her nipples standing erect behind it. "And I think you are a young girl still in school who is going to get a rude awakening when you venture out in the world."

She shook her head from side to side, and started to say something but before she could, Seligman continued. "You can do whatever you want, but I know men. They read things into what you do. They will react totally differently from what you expect. I'm telling you this because you are important to Marie. If you are important to Marie, you are important to me. Your father is a nice man, but he probably doesn't know how to tell you what I am saying. Please listen to me, as you would a big brother."

She leaned forward and laid her hands on the table, her head slowly turning from side to side, as if she were looking for the right words. Her mouth moved, but she said nothing, so he reached out and patted her hands, as if comforting a child. Their eyes met, and he nodded. "Please consider what

I'm telling you," he said. "I say it with love for you and your sister." He placed his hands on top of hers, which were small. His encompassed them.

"You are a good man, Willie Seligman," she whispered, raising her fingers and entwining them with his.

"And you're a good sister. Marie and I love you, as does Ernst. Remember, the flirting will attract some men, but only those who are interested in you for the wrong reason."

"And what would that be?" she asked playfully.

He pulled his hands back. "Ah, I can see you haven't been listening."

She frowned and said, "I've been flirting with boys for so long it's going to take me a while to stop, Okay?" When he frowned she leaned toward him and said, "*Bitte*?" Please?

She looked so earnest that he couldn't help but smile.

Nodding, he said, "Okay."

She relaxed, and asked, "So you're my big brother?"

He nodded.

"Can I ask you for some advice?"

"Fire away."

"Do you think I'm too young to get married? Be honest."

"Yes."

She leaned back in her chair. "My, that was quick."

He frowned. "Do you *have* to get married?"

"Why would anyone *have* to get married?"

"You would know if you had to."

"But what do you mean?"

He hesitated, then asked, "Are you pregnant?"

"*No*! Why would you think that?"

"I don't, but it would certainly change things."

She frowned again, and said, "I want to have a baby very much, but I wouldn't get pregnant without being married." She waved at the fly, which was now surveying her.

"You may be too young to get married, but you are definitely old enough to get pregnant."

She looked down at her cup, again. "Well, I'm not. I just meant, do you think if a certain Friedrich asked me to marry him, should I say yes?"

"Not without talking to your sister and your parents."

"I want to know what *you* think."

"And I gave you my answer." His gaze on her was unwavering.

"I don't like your answer." She smiled.

"You don't have to, but you told me to be honest."

"Lie a little." Her smile grew.

"You're going to marry a certain Friedrich regardless of what I say, aren't you?" he smiled back.

She leaned forward quickly. "Yes! Isn't it exciting?"

"That depends. What do your parents think of him?"

"Papa likes him because he's in the army. Mama likes him because he treats me so good."

"Does his father treat his mother that way, too?"

"Why does that matter?"

"If his father is disrespectful to his mother, he will have learned that it is all right to be that way. Sooner or later he'll be disrespectful to you."

"His father respects his mother. What do you think? Am I old enough?"

"No, but then Marie and I probably weren't, either."

Marta jumped up and started twirling around the room. "He makes me want to dance," she said, making two loops around Seligman and the table. Her arms were outstretched around her imaginary partner, and her thin summer nightgown did nothing to hide her body.

"And Marie said it would be good to have a man around in case I have to raise Ernst," she said. Stopping behind him, she threw her arms around his neck and said, "Oh, Willie, you're the best big brother ever! I'm going to do it. I'm going to marry Friedrich." She kissed him firmly on the cheek. He could feel her breasts against his back, the same as if they were both naked.

As Seligman put his hands on her arms he heard someone clear her throat and looked up. Marie was standing in the doorway, Ernst in front of her, and her parents looking over her shoulder.

"Ernst, maybe you could go play with your trucks in our room," Marie said. "Your father and I need to talk."

"As do we," said Dieter to his younger daughter. "Marta, put on a robe, then meet your mother and me in the parlor."

When Seligman and Marie were alone, she asked, "What was that about?"

"Marta and I were having a heart-to-heart. She wanted to know what I thought about her marrying Friedrich."

"Then why was she kissing you while she was still in her nightgown?" Marie crossed her arms in front of her and leaned back against the doorjamb.

"That's the way she was dressed when I came into the kitchen. If you had heard the whole conversation, you'd know you have nothing to be concerned about."

She uncrossed her arms and sat down at the table opposite Seligman. "Tell me about the whole conversation."

When Seligman finished telling her what he and Marta had talked about, Marie just said, "Hmm."

"She kissed me on the cheek. That's all."

"So she told you she and Friedrich are getting married, huh?"

"Yeah. And she said something about you wanting her to raise Ernst. What is that about?"

Marie swallowed and looked away. "I, uh, I may have asked her to take care of Ernst if anything happens to you and me."

"Really? Don't you think we should have talked about this first?" Her gaze still wandered the room, so he waved his hand in the air to bring it back toward him.

She looked at him and said, "Honestly, yes. I was going to, today, but last night the moment to ask her was right, and I thought you would agree."

"Did you consider my parents at all?"

"No. After I decided my parents were too old—"

"And too Nazi," he said quietly, so they wouldn't hear him in the parlor.

She paused. "Probably they are, but I can't tell them *that.* Anyway, if they're too old, your parents are, too." She studied his face for a reaction, but it was impassive.

"What did Marta say?" he asked.

"She worried that you don't like her and that she's too young."

Seligman nodded. "She is only thirteen years older than him, but I like her just fine."

Marie smirked and he added, "Not in that way."

Marie asked, "So what do you think of her taking care of Ernst? Only if something happens to both of us, of course."

"What choice do I have? You've presented me with a *fait accompli.*" He frowned at her and said, "I'm not upset about the decision, only the process."

"So it's a good *fait accompli,* isn't it? Please don't be mad."

"I'll not be mad at you if you'll not be mad at me because your sister, in a moment of happiness because she's getting married to her boyfriend, kissed me on the cheek."

"That nightgown covered nothing, and she had her arms around you."

"She's enthusiastic about getting married, and I didn't look."

Marie stared at him.

"Ok, maybe a little. Just to confirm what I suspected."

She cocked her head. "What did you suspect?"

"Yours are prettier."

She smiled, then said, "Here's my offer. You agree to Marta raising Ernst and I won't tell Papa to have his friend in Berlin have you shot because you compared Marta's and my breasts."

"Now there's a deal," he said, smiling.

"What do you say?" she leaned back and crossed her arms again.

"Agreed. Please don't have me shot."

"I love you," she said.

He reached out for her, and she extended her hands across the table. When their hands were entwined, he said, "And I love you."

In the parlor, voices rose in anger.

<hr/>

That night Seligman, Dieter, and Elsa sat in the parlor listening to the news on the radio. The broadcaster was denouncing the Soviet Union, saying she was massing troops on her western border and an attack on the Fatherland might be imminent, despite the Molotov-Ribbentrop non aggression pact signed by the two countries in August, 1939.

"*Unser Führer* will show them," said Dieter. "He won't sit idly by and let them attack us."

Seligman recognized the pattern that had occurred right before every recent German invasion, but did not say that he believed it was the other way around; that Hitler was preparing to invade Russia.

<hr/>

In the bedroom, Marie was putting Ernst to bed when Marta

appeared in the doorway. She held a balled-up tissue to her nose and said, "Can we talk?"

Marie leaned forward and kissed Ernst on the forehead. "*Gute nacht, mein kleiner mann*," she said, then stood up and tilted her head toward the door. Marta followed her down the hall to the kitchen.

As soon as the swinging door closed behind them, Marie turned to her and said, "I told you not to flirt with my husband." She glared at her sister.

"You don't understand. I wasn't. Let me tell you what happened." She gestured toward the table.

They both sat down, and Marie said, "This better match up with what Willie told me."

Marta took a deep breath, then told her sister what she and Seligman had discussed.

When she was finished, Marie thought for a minute, nodded her head, and slowly said, "All right, I believe you."

"But what can I do about Papa?" cried Marta. "He doesn't want me to be married. He wants me to take a job as a secretary at the Siemens plant in Berlin. He wants to send me there to live so I'll forget about Friedrich." She spread her arms wide, and said, "*Why?*"

Marie studied her younger sister. *That was just like their father to overreact*, she thought. In his opinion, Marta was too young to marry, but not to move three hundred kilometers away and go to work. Marie agreed Marta was too young to marry, but knew how headstrong Marta was. *No wonder they're butting heads,* thought Marie. *They are just alike.*

"There is only one thing you can do. Take the job, make the move."

"I won't," said Marta, pounding the table like a child. "He can't make me take the job."

"You're right, he can't. But you don't have to commit a crime to be sent to the reformatory. He can report you to the authorities as out of control and a danger to the community, and they'll ship you off so fast you won't know where you are. They could keep you there for years."

Marta began to cry, so Marie reached across the table and took her hands. "Friedrich is in the army, so he will be away from you whether you are in Hamburg or Berlin. Papa won't be able to keep you from writing him if you are in Berlin; if you're in a reformatory they can restrict your writing privileges. It's pretty simple. If you take the job, you can keep in touch with him; if you're in a reformatory you can't."

"I won't go to Berlin."

"Yes," said Marie. "You must. You will be three hundred kilometers closer to Dresden. You can come see Ernst and me on the weekends. Do it for him. He misses his *Tante* Marta. You come see us once a month, and we come see you once a month. Soon this war will be over and you and Friedrich can be together."

"I can see Ernst twice a month?" Her face began to brighten.

"Ah, *meine lieblich Schwester*," said Marie. My lovely sister. She stood up, walked around the table and put her arms around her sister's shoulders. She leaned over and kissed her sister on the cheek.

Marta put her hands on Marie's arms and said, "This is how it happened with Willie this morning."

Marie smiled and patted her arm. "I know."

CHAPTER SIXTEEN

11 July, 1941
Baltic Sea, east of Denmark

Wagner had been manning the helm since *eins eins zwei* had departed Lorient four hours earlier. and was due to be relieved by Seaman Schuster. When Schuster arrived, Wagner looked him up and down for a moment, trying to figure out what looked out of place.

"*Was ist das?* Are you wearing a British uniform?" he asked.

"*Ja*," said Schuster, quite proud of his wardrobe. "It is much lighter than ours, and they have a lot of them in Lorient. I guess we captured them," said Schuster.

"But you are a German. This is not allowed. If you are captured you will be shot as a spy."

"If I am captured, I will already be dead. A lot of the men are wearing them."

"I will speak to the *Kapitän* about this," said Wagner,

turning on his heel and heading to the control room. But when he got there, he found Watts, not Seligman, on duty.

"I must speak to the *Kapitän*," Wagner told him. "Do you know where he is?"

"Somewhere within 77 meters of here."

"You do not know?"

"We are on a U-boat. How many places are there to hide? I'm busy. Leave the control room." Watts called out a course change which Bosun Schwarz repeated and Schuster acknowledged. As he did, the boat slid down the side of a wave, causing both Watts and Wagner to grab the periscope tube to steady themselves.

Watts called up through the speaker tube to the bridge to enquire about the weather and Wagner heard the watch call down that winds were picking up and storm clouds gathering.

"Looks like some rough weather ahead," said Schwarz from the bridge.

Wagner went to the captain's quarters, where he saw Seligman with Neumann. The boat had just passed the longitudinal line where they were to open their sealed orders, and they were now studying them.

Wagner cleared his throat and Seligman looked up from the charts he and his first officer were examining.

"A moment of your time, *Kapitän*?"

"What is it, Wagner? Can't you see I'm busy?"

"This is a very important matter, Sir."

The captain glanced at Neumann, who said, "I understand our orders, *Kapitän*. I'll relieve Watts and you can deal with this *crisis*."

Neumann walked past Wagner, smirking at him.

"Speak," said Seligman.

"Sir, are you aware that Seaman Schuster is wearing a British uniform?"

"As are about half the crew. So what?"

"Sir, this is against regulations."

"*Ensign*," Seligman replied, "It is *not* against regulations when we are underway and I approve it."

"But why do you allow it?"

Seligman had turned away but at Wagner's question he returned his gaze to the ensign's face, and moved toward Wagner until their faces were about a foot apart, causing Wagner to swallow hard. "Not that I have to justify it to you, Ensign Wagner, but these men are living in horrible conditions. If we can make them a little more comfortable we're going to do so. Dismissed."

"Sir, I—"

Seligman pulled the curtain separating his quarters from the rest of the boat, leaving Wagner staring at the green veil three inches from his face. Hearing a muffled laugh coming from behind him, he saw Kretchmer covering his mouth.

"You had best not be missing any important messages," Wagner said to the radioman, and walked away. As he did, he heard Kretchmer laugh out loud.

Kretchmer had just come off duty in the radio room. Balancing a plate of food in one hand and holding on with the other, because the sea was smacking the boat like a cat playing with a ball of yarn, he was looking for a place to sit in the bow compartment. Richter and Krause were already eating there, propped on a torpedo. Krause scooted over a little to make room for him.

"You won't believe this," said Kretchmer. Sausages hung from an overhead pipe, and Kretchmer pushed them out of the way to take a seat next to Krause. "That little prick Wagner was complaining to the *Kapitän* about Schuster wearing a British uniform. Doesn't he pay attention? Just about everyone's wearing one."

"Why do you think he's a prick?" asked Richter.

"Because he *is* a prick," replied Kretchmer. "Don't you ever listen to all his 'Heil Hitlers?' We're on a U-boat. Nobody salutes once we leave port, and I can't think of anyone besides him that uses the Nazi salute. I think I'd rather hear depth charges going off nearby than to hear him click those heels one more time."

Krause nodded agreement.

Richter shook his head. "I don't see any problem. He believes in the *Führer* and the Reich. Don't you?"

"I was drafted," said Krause. "I don't believe in anything."

"Neither do I," said Kretchmer, shaking his head. "This war has already cost me my friend, Schmidt."

"We went to war because Germany was treated as a conquered enemy in the Treaty of Versailles," Richter said. "We weren't defeated, we were stabbed in the back by the politicians. Hitler will make them pay. I like Wagner. And I like that the *Kapitän* has a picture of Hitler hanging in the Command room."

Krause said, "The *Kapitän* doesn't have that picture there because he wants it there. Every U-boat has Hitler's picture there. They have to, or someone gets shot. That's the Nazi way." Krause stood up and said, "I'll be right back. I've got to use the head." He set his plate of food on the torpedo and walked away.

As soon as Krause was out of sight, Richter reached over and shoved his food tray to the floor. It bounced around with a loud clattering. Richter looked at Kretchmer, who raised his eyebrows but didn't say anything.

When Krause came back Kretchmer and Richter were quietly eating.

"Hey," Krause said, "What happened to my food?"

"Didn't you feel the boat roll?" asked Richter. "I wasn't fast enough to save it."

Kretchmer laughed, then grabbed his plate with both hands as the boat slid down another wave. It pitched Krause on top of Richter, who came up swinging.

Kretchmer threw his plate to the side and grabbed Krause, trying to pull him off the other seaman. He was getting the leverage he needed when another wave threw both of them back on top of Richter.

The commotion brought several other crewmen running, including Bosun Schwarz, just off watch duty. Every time the others separated Krause and Richter, a wave would pitch the boat sideways, creating another tangle of sailors on the deck. Many rolled around in the food scattered on the deck.

Finally, Schwarz was able to restore order just as Seligman arrived."What's going on here?"

"The sea pitched me onto Richter, and he was trying to help me up," said Krause. "Then the sea pitched him on top of me, and I was trying to help him up."

"*Ja*," said Richter. "That is exactly what happened."

Seligman looked at Schwarz and said, "Well? You're in charge of discipline. What are you going to do?"

"They were fighting when I got here, Sir. I have no way of knowing what happened."

Krause and Richter stood there, two schoolboys caught brawling.

"I think Bosun Schwarz misunderstood," said Richter, putting his arm around Krause's shoulder. "It wasn't a fight. It was the sea."

"*Ja*," said Krause. "It was the sea's fault. *Verdammt* sea."

Just as Schwarz opened his mouth to render judgment, another wave raised the U-boat, then dropped it down ten feet to an abrupt rest, sending all the men sprawling on the floor, some of them on top of each other.

"See," said Richter. "That is exactly what happened to us."

"*Ja*," agreed Krause.

Schwarz stood up and put his hands on his hips. "Did anybody see what happened?" he asked.

"*Nein.*" "*Nein.*" *Nein.*"

He tried to keep from smiling, but couldn't. "I'm going to warn you both right now, if the sea throws either of you on top of the other one again, you will both report to the cook during your off-duty time for the next three days," he said. "Understood?"

"Oh, yes, Bosun. I am sure that the sea will behave now," said Krause. As he said it, another wave threw everyone onto the deck again.

Pulling himself up, Seligman said to Schwarz, "It's your mess. I didn't see a thing," and headed back to the command room.

When he got there, Seligman smiled at Neumann, who raised his eyebrows questioningly.

"A fight," Seligman said. "Schwarz was there so I stayed out of it."

"Did the bosun crack the whip?" asked Neumann.

"No, the fighters joined forces against the common enemy–him. Blamed everything on the sea. Glad to see it, actually. Now let's hope they do it when we run up against the Tommies."

Eins eins zwei took another roll over a wave and Seligman said, "Clear the bridge. Prepare to dive. That storm's going to wash someone overboard."

Neumann repeated the command up to the bridge through the speaker tube, then looked at the captain expectantly.

Seligman said, "We'll stay down briefly and hope the storm clears. Then we're going to practice dives until the men are too sick from going up and down to fight each other."

Behind him, as the watch crew opened the hatch to come down, another wave washed over the deck, throwing freezing water down the opening.

CHAPTER SEVENTEEN

1 December, 1941
Dresden, Germany

Seligman looked out the window as his train pulled into the Dresden station, grateful to be home. Marie would be surprised to see him, since he hadn't told her of his visit. And Ernst. Oh, how he missed Ernst.

He pulled their picture from his pocket and stared at it until the train bumped to a stop, jerking him forward. Then, putting it back in his inside coat pocket, he stood up and headed for the exit.

An elderly woman struggled with the step off the train and he took her arm. *"Danke,"* she said, and he touched his right hand to his cap.

He walked to the tram, where he sat on the edge of the seat with his duffel in his lap for the fifteen-minute ride. The buildings he passed were familiar, but he didn't recognize the people.

The tram stop was two blocks from their flat. Walking

quickly through the street, he looked around and saw only gaunt women, strangers, all carrying gas masks. When he got to their building he ran up the three flights of stairs. He did not want to startle Marie by walking in, so he knocked on the door, barely able to contain his excitement.

When she opened the door, he first saw the worry lines on her face; but as soon as she recognized him, the tension released.

"Willie," she shrieked, and threw herself into his arms. Behind her, Ernst was sitting on the floor, pushing a wooden truck. Alerted by her cry, he turned and immediately yelled, "Papa, Papa!" Bounding to his feet, he ran to his father, who swept him into his arms.

"*Hallo, mein Liebling*," Seligman said, his arm still around Marie. Her backbone seemed more prominent than the last time he had held her.

"Oh, Willie," Marie said over and over again. "Will you be here for Christmas?"

"If all goes well," he said. "I'm due back on the 27th."

Marie smiled. "Maybe nothing will happen."

"Oh, Papa, I've missed you so much," said Ernst, hugging his father.

He hadn't been home since June, and he noticed Ernst seemed lighter.

"And I, you, *mein kleiner Mann*," he told the boy.

Marie first smiled at her son, then her husband, as tears of joy streaked down her face. "I wish it was night," she whispered to Seligman, "so that we could be in bed together."

CHAPTER EIGHTEEN

2 December, 1941
Dresden, Germany

Seligman sat on the floor as Ernst tugged at his neck.

"Oh, no, you're too strong for me," he declared, as he let Ernst push him over. In reality, though, Ernst's pushes were like a fly trying to lift a car. He had neither grown nor gotten stronger in the time Seligman had been gone.

Marie was fixing dinner. Seligman stood up, walked behind her, and put his arms around her, caressing her breasts. She inhaled deeply, and whispered, "Don't let Ernst see you," but put her hand on his and pressed it against her harder, tilting her head back against his chest.

"Ernst seems thin, and he has no strength," he whispered into her ear, looking over his shoulder to make sure the boy could neither see the way he held her nor hear his comments. As his hands moved over her breasts, he noticed her ribs were more defined, too.

"What do you expect? We have no meat, the bread is

mostly sawdust. Can't you tell my breasts are smaller?" She pushed his hands away as Ernst began to move around the room.

"We have better food than this on our boat, and we have little room to store anything." He stepped back, but kept his hand on her shoulder.

"You aren't paying attention to what is happening. Dresden is lucky. We haven't been bombed, but a lot of cities have."

"We get reports from the Command that the war is going well. Sure, they tell us about occasional bombings, but according to their reports, little is damaged, and British planes are shot down. Goering said they wouldn't get through."

She had moved away from him and removed the lid from a pan to check their dinner. Replacing it, she turned to look at him, one hand on the edge of the stove, one hand on her hip. "Munster was bombed six months ago. You saw the damage in Hamburg when we were there last June. I want my parents to get out, but they won't move. And the British have been bombing Berlin, *Berlin,* for over a year. "

"The U-boats are doing well."

"The civilians are not. I cannot buy food. It does not matter for me, but what will happen to Ernst? He weighs less now than he did last summer. If the propaganda put out by the Nazis was food, Ernst would be fat."

"I will go to the market and get some meat. They will sell it to me," he said, beginning to pace.

"They can't sell what they don't have." She went to the cupboard and picked up three plates. "You must bring us some every time you come home. That is the only way we will get meat."

"You just asked me to commit a crime for which I could be shot."

"I just asked you to feed your child." She handed the plates to him. "Anyway, let's not argue. Set the table. Dinner is ready."

"What are we having?" he asked, as he put the plates on the table.

She hesitated. "Turnips."

He arched his eyebrows, and she said, "It is all we have."

"I understand," he said, as he sat down at the head of the table.

"Mama usually sits there," said Ernst, climbing into his chair.

"When Papa is home, he sits there," said Marie. She slid into the chair on Seligman's right.

"Someday I will sit there."

"Then you better eat," said Seligman. "It takes a big butt to fill this chair."

Ernst laughed but Marie slapped her husband's wrist lightly and said, "Willie! Watch your language in front of the boy," causing Ernst to laugh again.

"I miss you when you're not here, Papa."

"And I miss you, *mein kleiner Mann*," he said, wondering if Ernst's butt would ever grow big on a diet of turnips and beets.

CHAPTER NINETEEN

8 December, 1941
Dresden, Germany

Seligman and Marie rose early. It was cold, but Marie scolded him as he put coal on the fire.

"That's too much," she said.

"But it is only fifteen degrees," he complained. "And the sun won't be up for another hour."

"I'll fix you some coffee. You've spent too many hours baking on that boat. You'll be snug and warm and we'll be out of coal. Ernst and I will be shivering."

"I wouldn't call sweating in 120 degrees while a ship drops depth charges on us being snug and warm," he said, but he reluctantly grabbed the last piece of coal he had placed on the fire and pulled it out. After brushing it off he returned it to the bin. Marie smiled at him as he turned on the radio.

"What could you possibly want to hear this early in the morning?" she asked.

He sat down at the table in the kitchen. "The news. I want to know how things are going on the Russian front."

Marie poured him a cup of coffee. "We are bogged down. Mrs. Schultz two doors down has two sons there." Marie paused, crossed herself, then said, "She had three. The dead one might be the luckiest. They wrote her that they are wearing summer uniforms and it is colder there than it ever gets here. They were told they would be home by November. Now they may never be home. Her husband is too old to fight, but he wants to join. He tells her, '*Mein Führer* needs me.' Poor woman."

Seligman took a sip of coffee and said, "This is horrible. What is it, ground up dog turds?"

"Listen to Baron von Seligman," she said, swatting him lightly on the head as she moved about the kitchen preparing breakfast. "It is chicory. You sailors get all the real coffee. We have to get by on this. Maybe you should bring some with you the next time, along with the meat."

"You seem determined to get me shot." He took another sip and grimaced.

She stood behind him and put her arms around his shoulders. Her embrace tightened as the radio announcer's voice rose in volume. "What is he so excited about?" she asked.

Standing , Seligman walked to the radio and turned it up.

"Not so loud, Willie! You'll wake the boy."

He turned it back down, but put his ear close to it.

He listened for a full minute, then said, "*Gott im Himmel.* The Japanese have attacked Great Britain and the United States."

Marie sat down suddenly. "How does that affect you?" she asked, her hand over her mouth.

"Perhaps we can attack American escorts now."

He walked to the phone mounted on the wall and started dialing.

"Who are you calling?" Marie asked, knowing even as she asked.

It took a few minutes, but as soon as he was connected to Naval Headquarters, he said, "Seligman here. I heard the news. What am I to do?"

He listened intently and Marie clutched her robe to her throat and wept quietly.

Ernst, still in his nightshirt, walked up next to her. "Mama, why do you cry?" She put her arm around him.

Seligman hung up the phone. "I must go." He couldn't look at Marie.

"But Papa, it isn't Christmas yet." Ernst began to cry, too.

"I will give you your present now, my son," said Seligman. He went to his duffel and pulled out a small package wrapped in newsprint. Handing it to Ernst, he said, "Merry Christmas, *mein kleiner Mann.* You should open it now, while I am here."

Ernst looked at his mother, who nodded her head, even as she cried. He quickly tore open the package and looked at the object inside.

"Do you know what that is?" asked Seligman. When Ernst shook his head, he said, "It is a bosun's pipe. We use it to give commands on the boat." Seligman pulled a small book out of his duffel and handed it to Ernst. "This book tells you how to blow it for different events. When I come home next time you should be prepared to blow it like this." Seligman took the pipe from Ernst and sounded the call for the captain to come aboard.

"I want to do it," said Ernst, hopping up and down. He tooted on it a few times, then looked at it again. "What's this say?" he asked, pointing to the side of it.

"It says, U-112," said Seligman. "That is my boat."

Marie was quiet as he gathered his things. In no time at

all he was ready. Ernst marched around the room, tooting with every step.

"Ernst, be a good man and stop blowing the pipe whenever Mama tells you to," Seligman told his son.

"All right, Papa."

Marie stood and he put his arms around her.

"I'm glad we at least had last night," said Marie, looking up into his face.

"And the night before, and the night before that, and the first night home, and that afternoon when the neighbor watched Ernst, and—"

"All right, I get your point," she said, turning her head and putting her ear to his chest. "It was more than once. But I thought we would have until the 27th. I thought we would have *Weihnachten.*" Looking up at his face, she asked, "Why did they have to attack while you were home?"

"I don't think my being home had anything to do with it." He smiled kindly at her and pulled her close. She put her head on his chest again and he kissed the top of her head.

"All I know is you were supposed to be here until the 27th and you're leaving today. Why did I have to fall in love with a sailor?"

"I don't know, but I thank God every day that you did." He kissed her one last time, then picked up his duffel and walked out the door. As he walked down the steps he heard Ernst blowing the pipe, and Marie crying.

CHAPTER TWENTY

12 December, 1941
Reich Chancellery, Berlin

Adolf Hitler paced in front of Grand Admiral Erich Raeder, who stood at attention. On the *Führer's* third pass, he stopped directly in front of the sixty-five year old admiral, turned, and looked into his inscrutable eyes.

"I have pledged to our allies that we will not conclude a separate peace with *any* of our enemies," he told Raeder. "But the United States poses a challenge. How can the *Kriegsmarine* hit them before they have a chance to mobilize their industry?"

"*Mein Führer*, our situation in the Atlantic will be eased by Japan's successful intervention. Already we are hearing reports of the transfer of American battleships from the Atlantic to the Pacific to replace those lost in the attack at Pearl Harbor."

Hitler continued to stare at the Admiral from two feet away, a stare that usually wilted the recipient. But the *Führer* mused that since Raeder had been in the service for forty-seven years, he was not easily intimidated. He was one of Hitler's most intelligent commanders, and his intelligence made him appear arrogant. Or more likely, Hitler suspected, since he did not have great respect for the Navy, his arrogance made him appear intelligent. Hitler took one step toward Raeder, crowding him.

Raeder didn't flinch.

"But, Admiral, the United States has lost prestige with their losses at Pearl Harbor. Won't they attempt to recover it, perhaps in the Azores, Cape Verdes, or Dakar? If they do, it will make our job in the Atlantic more difficult."

"No, *Mein Führer*. They will have to concentrate all their strength in the Pacific. Just two days ago, Britain lost the *Prince of Wales* and the *Repulse* to a Japanese air attack, so they will be reluctant to do anything in those areas. The Americans do not have the ships to support occupation tasks in the areas you mentioned, or even to supply them. All these situations make the east coast of the United States vulnerable right now."

For a moment the two men stared at each other, Raeder's eyes reflecting only discipline. Hitler, unable to read this man and not able to unnerve him, began pacing again, speaking to the Admiral over his shoulder. "But isn't it possible Great Britain and the United States will abandon East Asia long enough to launch an attack against us and Italy?"

"Highly unlikely. This would leave the British vulnerable to attack in India, and if the United States leaves the Pacific while the Japanese have the upper hand their west coast becomes vulnerable. Let me repeat, the east coast of the United States is vulnerable to us. That is where we need to attack. Just this morning I ordered six large U-boats to proceed as quickly as possible to the shipping lanes along the coast. Dönitz wanted twelve but we cannot spare that many. Nevertheless, with six, in a very short time we shall begin to wreak havoc. Others will quickly follow."

Hitler stared into the Admiral's eyes for a full fifteen seconds, trying to get him to blink, flinch, anything, but Raeder didn't budge, so the *Führer* said, "I have a meeting to attend in my private chambers. The Jews started this war. I must let my Party members know that I intend to stand by my promise to exterminate them for this." He turned and started to walk out, but stopped and looked back at the Admiral. "This had better work," he said. "Show yourself out."

Raeder bowed his head to acknowledge Hitler's order, turned and walked to the door.

CHAPTER TWENTY-ONE

19 December, 1941
Lorient Naval Base, Western Coast of France

Seligman stood at the entrance to Second U-Boat Flotilla Headquarters with three other men. They all wore blue over-coats, gray gloves, and blue caps which showed the captain's emblem. When a Horch sedan pulled up, they climbed in and the *Kriegsmarine* driver took off toward the chateau that housed the offices of Admiral Karl Dönitz.

Reinhard Hardegen, befitting his reputation as an aggressive captain, claimed the one seat in front. Seligman, at twenty-five the youngest of the four, volunteered to sit in the middle of the back seat, between Richard Zapp and Ernst Kals.

Seligman did not know the other three, but had heard much about each of them. They were some of the best captains that the *unterseeboot* command had. He decided to listen and learn, a smart plan since the others had plenty of opinions.

"How is your health since the plane crash?" Zapp asked Hardegan. Didn't it cause you stomach problems?"

"Ja, and my leg, but there's nothing to it," said Hardegan. "My last review said I was fit for sea duty, but not U-boat duty. But when I reported to Admiral Friedeburg for assignment, he asked me if I was fit to return to the sea. Naturally, I told him yes. It's not my fault he interpreted that to mean I was fit for U-boats."

The other three laughed heartily. Hans-Georg von Friedeburg was in charge of the Organization Department of the *BdU*, which assigned men to the U-boat crews.

"That's the way to survive in the *Kriegsmarine*," said Hardigan. "Answer only the question asked and don't volunteer anything."

"Did the Lion ever ask about your condition?" Asked Kals.

"He asked if I had been responsible for the slow transfers of my medical records."

"What did you tell him?" asked Zapp.

Hardegan looked over his shoulder, and with a sly smile, said, "I told him, 'I'm not that smart.'"

They laughed, again, although Seligman's had the sound of a person who wanted to be in on the joke but knew he wasn't.

"Then," continued Hardegan, "the admiral said, 'You're lucky I like you, or your skinny ass would be on a mine sweeper in the Mediterranean.'"

Seligman noticed that Hardegan was thin as a flagpole, but Seligman knew his reputation—if anyone mistook his appearance for timidity, they had not served with him and rumor was that his aggressiveness was why Dönitz liked and admired him.

As the sedan crossed the Ter River bridge and continued

toward the chateau, Zapp asked, "Any idea why we're here this morning?"

"I'm hoping we're going to New York," said Hardegan. "I hate to tell you how many times I've had a ship lined up in my sights, only to see the American flag. I'm not happy with the way they've been helping the British, nor that the *BdU* wouldn't let us do anything about it."

"That should all be changed now," said Kals.

When the sedan pulled up in front of the chateau, a Lieutenant walked quickly down the steps and opened both passenger-side doors on the staff car. *"Wilkommen,"* said Hans Fuhrmann, an aide on the Admiral's staff, as the four men emerged. As if on cue, they simultaneously placed their hats on their heads, and the sedan pulled away.

Seligman and the other three captains followed Fuhrmann inside, and hung their coats and hats in the foyer. The lieutenant led them into the situation room and told them, "The Admiral will see you shortly. Help yourself to coffee." He gestured toward a pot on a small table in the corner. Then, waving toward the operations chart laid out on a large table, he said, "Please feel free to look around."

The captains nodded and said, *"Danke."*

After Fuhrmann left Zapp asked, "What do you make of this?" He pointed toward a chart covered with red and blue pins.

They were all quiet until Hardegan said, "I say the blue pins are U-boats and the red pins are convoys."

Zapp concurred. "But if you're right, we don't have many U-boats in the convoy paths in the Atlantic." Gesturing toward a cluster of blue pins in the Mediterranean, he said, "They're all down there."

"Which is why I think we're going here," said Hardegen, pointing to the East coast of the United States and drawing his hand south from Boston all the way to Key West. "I'd lay money on it. What do you say, Seligman?"

Seligman was taken by surprise at the sudden acknowledgement of his presence, but he nodded. Logic said that Hardegen was right.

"You seem pretty sure of all this," said Kals, ignoring Seligman, who turned to look at Kals when he spoke. Kals looked to be in his mid thirties, and was thin to the point of appearing emaciated. That, along with his red hair, and freckled complexion, gave Kals the impression of frailness, but Seligman knew he was highly successful in combat.

"It just makes sense," said Hardegen. "We've been at war with the United States for less than two weeks and all of a sudden the Lion wants to see the four of us. And what do we all command? Type IX U-boats." He paused, looking at Seligman. "That *is* what you command, isn't it, *Kapitän?*"

"Yes, it is," acknowledged Seligman, appreciative that Hardegen again drew him into the conversation.

"See what I mean?" Hardegan asked. "We can go 3000 nautical miles further than the type VIIs. What's that tell you? He wants U-boats that have greater range, because he's sending them to America. Catch the bastards before they're ready, like the Japanese did. I look forward to sinking a few of the arrogant assholes." He leaned his head back and howled like a wolf on the hunt, causing the others to laugh.

Zapp walked to a window overlooking the base and gazed out at the hundreds of workers rushing about to finish two huge, windowless, concrete behemoths. Keroman I, with five U-boat pens, Keroman II, with seven. They sat on the bank of the Ter River and were designed to be impregnable to bombing.

Seligman had heard that Zapp was thirty-seven, which would make him the oldest of the four. He was square-jawed, with a long nose and prominent ears. Whenever he let a smile play around his lips, which was not often, it would display a deep cleft under each cheek. Unlike Kals and Hardegan, he was short and thick. Like them, Seligman knew he had numerous medals and awards attesting to his prowess as a U-boat commander.

"Come look at these," Zapp said to the others. They walked up behind him, and he said, "Look at those roofs. The enemy will never touch them from the air." Indeed, the tops of the bunkers were three and one-half meters of reinforced concrete.

"My boat is being re-fitted over there right now," said Hardegen, proud as a father.

"Which one?" asked Zapp.

"B6," he said, pointing. "It should be ready by the time we finish here. Now all I need to know is where we're going."

"Perhaps the Admiral can help you with that," said a voice behind them. The four captains turned and snapped to attention as Eberhart Godt, Dönitz's chief of staff, entered the room.

"Good afternoon, gentlemen." He returned their naval salute, then said, "Please follow me."

He led them to a door on the side of the room, where he knocked three times, then opened it into the private office of Admiral Dönitz, who was seated at his desk.

Dönitz stood and came around the desk, where all four captains drew up to salute. Returning their naval salute, he went down the line and shook hands with each man, welcoming them, commenting on their medals.

"How's that little boy?" he asked Seligman. "What is his name? Ernst?"

"Yes," replied Seligman, gesturing toward Captain Kals and saying, "Just like my new friend, here." Kals beamed as if the boy had been named for him. "He is fine, at home with his mother in Dresden."

"Another Seligman in the *Kriegsmarine* in twenty years, perhaps," said Dönitz, smiling.

The Admiral returned to his chair. Sitting down, he waved his hand for them to take chairs lined up on the other side of his massive, dark, wood desk. The office was large, and there was plenty of room for them to be joined by Godt.

"Gentlemen," said Dönitz, "you may be wondering why you are getting this briefing as a group and why your Flotilla Commander is not doing it. It is because you are going on the same mission, and I want to talk to you about it myself.

"There will be two other boats involved in this mission whose *Kapitäns* could not be here today. They are U-125, commanded by Ulrich Folkers, and U-109, commanded by Heinrich Bleichrodt. Do any of you know them?"

The other three all acknowledged being familiar with the two captains. Seligman said, "I haven't served with either, but I have spent a few evenings talking with Ajax when we were both in port. Very knowledgeable. He has given me several pointers that I appreciate."

Dönitz nodded. "*Kapitänleutnant* Bleichrodt, Ajax, as you called him, has had the Knights Cross since October of last year, and you know you don't get that until you've sunk 100,000 tons. He and Folkers have already received the orders I will give you today." Dönitz leaned back, then continued.

"I asked *Grossadmiral* Raeder for twelve boats, but he only gave me six. Then, U-128, which was supposed to participate, developed problems that required dry docking. It won't be available for two months. Fortunately, *eins eins zwei* is available to replace it." He smiled at Seligman and nodded in his direction. "But that puts greater pressure on you to perform. You must whip your crew into crack shape."

When Seligman nodded, the Admiral continued. "You are going to be out for a while. Your boats must be provisioned with everything you can possibly fit on them. Test dive as soon as possible, and practice frequently. The Tommies will scour the Bay of Biscay for you. They have become much more aggressive with their search planes. Your survival will depend on you being able to survive their attacks. You must practice until you can dive in under thirty-five seconds. If you cannot do that you will be dead. Maintain strictest discipline. You must not let anyone shirk his duty. Trim your boats frequently, as you will be burning off fuel and need to keep them balanced.

"You are to return to your boats and depart with all due haste. You will receive your standard sealed Operation Order from your Flotilla commander, *Korvettenkapitän* Schutze, just prior to your departure. I'm sure you've met him since he took over for Heinz Fischer in August." The captains nodded assent.

"You will not open those orders until you cross twenty degrees longitude, at which time you will let your officers know your mission.

"You will each work independently, however I want offensive operations to all begin the same day. The exact time of this action will be sent to you as you travel to your assigned areas. You, however, will maintain radio silence. Command will notify you when we want you to transmit. U-653 will be operating in grid AK southeast of Greenland transmitting dummy signals to give the impression of a large number of boats there. This should confuse the British and make them less aware of boats going to America.

"You had an opportunity to observe the maps in the situation room. You no doubt saw how sparse our presence in the North Atlantic has become. This will not last, gentlemen. I want us to *own* the Atlantic. I want you to beat the waters like a drum on this mission." Dönitz brought both his fists down on the desk with a thump. "It shall be known as Operation Drumbeat. Do you understand these orders?"

"Yes, *Herr* Admiral," said the four commanders.

"One last thing," said Dönitz. "We are expecting success on these patrols. The Propaganda Office has had a photographer on some of your boats in the past. They have not always been welcomed. You will all have one on your boat for this mission and will afford him every courtesy. Let him be on the bridge with you as often as he wants and safety allows. Understood?"

The captains again acknowledged the instructions.

Dönitz nodded to Godt, who stood. As the captains rose to follow him, Dönitz said, "*Kapitän* Seligman, a word with you in private, please."

Godt ushered the others toward the door. "He will only be a moment," the chief of staff said to them. "You may wait in the situation room. When the Admiral is finished, a car will return all four of you to your quarters."

Seligman didn't like this. If he was in trouble, why would the Admiral wait until after going over the mission to dress him down? What did the others think of this? He felt his heart flutter.

The Admiral indicated that he should sit down, then shuffled through some papers on his desk, as if he was looking for something. As Seligman sat there waiting, he saw Godt return to his chair. Whatever was coming, Dönitz wanted a witness.

Looking up from his papers, he said, "I have heard some conversation that your First Officer, Oskar Neumann may have some liberal tendencies. This cannot be tolerated."

"I'm sorry, Admiral. I've never been very politically astute. Can you explain to me what you mean by 'liberal tendencies'?"

"Your career would be much enhanced if you became politically astute," said Godt.

"Thank you, Admiral, that is correct," said Dönitz, nodding to Godt. Turning back to Seligman, he said, "I encourage you to cultivate your contacts with officers who are party members. I have heard from sources that you were quite abrupt with *Kapitän* Engel after a debriefing last April. I would encourage you to make amends there. He could be quite helpful to you in your career."

"I have always felt that if I took care of my boat and crew my career would take care of itself."

Dönitz frowned and leaned back. His hawk-like eyes peered out of his thin face and bored in on Seligman, who did not flinch. Dönitz rubbed the side of his head with his right hand and said, "It never hurts to have friends in the party. You will do what you choose *Kapitän*, but I am under pressure to make sure that the correct officers are promoted. I encourage you to think about what I have told you today. I am told that Neumann has expressed opinions sympathetic to the enemy, especially the United States. That indicates he has liberal tendencies. I don't have concrete proof but if he is your friend I suggest you bring him around to thinking more about the Fatherland and less about the enemy."

"May I ask the source of these reports?"

"I don't know who reported it. If I find out and it is a credible source I will have Neumann replaced." He glanced down at the paper on his desk, then waved his arm toward the door and said, "Dismissed."

Godt stood and Seligman followed him back to the situation room.

When they were back in the car, the others ignored Seligman. It was as if they didn't want to be sullied by whatever Dönitz wanted to talk to him about. Their focus was on the mission.

Zapp said, "He didn't mention America. Is that where we are going?"

"Where else?" asked Hardegen. "He just doesn't want it out there in the ether, yet. Wait until you get to twenty degrees longitude. You'll see then."

But none of their conversation registered with Seligman, who was lost in his own thoughts. Who else knew of Neumann's antipathy for the Nazis? And did they know he agreed with his first officer?

CHAPTER TWENTY-TWO

23 December, 1941 07:30 CET
Quadrant BE 7673

"Welcome back." Navigator Winter slapped Hoerter on the back as he and the Ensign passed at the base of the conning tower ladder. "How's the ankle?"

"Good." Hoerter did a quick jig to show how well he was moving.

"All the walking wounded are here," said Winter, as he spied Ensign Schwarz behind Hoerter. "How's the head?"

"Good as new," Schwarz replied. "My hair's even grown back to cover any scarring."

"It's good to have you both back," said Winter. "I had heard you would both be returning. I hope you've both got new job duties. Hoerter, when you broke your ankle Schwarz replaced you. Then he got hit by flying shrapnel. That job assignment is a jinx!"

"Sounds like it," agreed Hoerter. "I'm joining Braun in the forward torpedo room. Schwarz is staying in the jinxed job."

Winter smiled at Schwarz, shook his head and said, "Good luck with that."

"Hey, we're sailing around the ocean with people dropping bombs on us. If I go, chances are, you go too," Schwarz said with a grin.

"You forget, I'm the navigator." Winter stepped aside to let the two ensigns get to the food Maier, the cook, brought up to them. "I get to say where we go. If I wake up dead, it's my own damn fault.

"And speaking of where we're going, we just passed twenty degrees west. I saw the *Kapitän* a few minutes ago, and he was getting ready to open our orders." Winter gestured over his shoulder toward the closed curtain about eight feet away that pretended to give the captain privacy. In such close quarters he probably could hear every word they were saying. "Guess I'll know in a few minutes where I should chart us to."

"Not just that," said Schwarz, "We're in a combat zone. Combat bonuses for everyone!"

Hoerter laughed. "I won't need it if we're going to America. I've got enough bets on that as our destination that when I collect I'll live like a god when we get back to Lorient."

The two ensigns carried their breakfasts to the Petty Officer quarters and sat on a bunk to eat fresh eggs and sausage, a luxury available only because they had just left port. Winter stood at the chart table just outside the captain's quarters sorting charts of the North Atlantic. Seligman, in his quarters with the curtain closed, presumably was reading the now unsealed orders from Flotilla Commander Schutze.

Seligman opened the curtain and called for all officers not on duty. "Close the forward and control room hatches," he ordered when they had all crammed around him. He saw that this caused some chagrin amongst the crew, who subscribed to the well-known *Ubootwaffe* saying that the most interesting things to know on a boat were the things you were not supposed to know.

"Men, we are going to America," Seligman announced when the hatches were closed.

Some of the men repeated,"America," but he was most interested in the reaction of his First Officer. Neumann's face clouded over and he slowly shook his head from side to side.

"Can we see the charts?" asked Winter. "I need to make sure we take the shortest route to conserve fuel."

"That's going to be difficult," said Seligman. Winter looked puzzled, and Seligman smiled mischievously at his officers.

"When the flotilla commander gave me the folder, he told me this had all happened so fast that *BdU* did not have proper supporting documents. For months, Hitler had been telling him not to provoke the United States, then all of a sudden Hitler declared war on them."

Seligman paused for effect, then shook his head. "We have no nautical charts," he said, then waited for someone to take the bait.

Watts was the first to bite. "What do we have?"

The officers of *eins eins zwei* looked at each other. Seligman heard some of them muttering, *"Ja,* what do we have?"

"Here is what we will use to attack America." He pulled out several tourist guidebooks, the kind any tourist could get in a gasoline station. The first was for New York, then Atlantic City. They ranged down the east coast of the United States, until, finally, he had one for Key West.

"Right here is everything you could want to know about

Key West," he laughed, as he held up a brochure that described the recovery of the Keys since the disastrous hurricane of 1935, and a road that replaced a train.

"This is a joke, right?" asked Neumann.

"No, it's not," said Seligman. Up to now, he had been teasing, almost jovial. He knew they should have had better charts, but he wanted to give the impression all was fine. He was no longer smiling when he told them, "It may make our job more difficult, but we are up to it."

"We've got enough fuel to go 12,000 miles," said Siegfried. "We can get there."

"And back," said Seligman.

"Ja," murmured the others.

"For *der Führer*!" shouted Wagner.

"Yeah," said Hoerter, but the rest remained quiet, with awkward glances all around. Neumann was off to the side. Seligman saw the malevolent look he sent Wagner's way, but his expression remained impassive.

"Where do we attack?" asked Watts.

"Our orders call for us to go all up and down the east coast. But we will start at a time specified by *BdU*, unless we encounter a ship that our *Groner* index says is greater than 10,000 GRT.

"There are five other boats on their way. We are to work independently, unless ordered otherwise. Since we have a dearth of navigational information, we are to locate and report beacons, lights, buoys, and anything we see in the way of defenses. When you are on watch, you are to keep a sharp eye out for these, and see that your watch-mates do, too."

"Chief," he said, looking directly at Siegfried, "your records will be extremely important for us. Do not lose track of remaining fuel, keep the boat in trim at all times, log how much ballast you must transfer to do so. Since we have no navigational charts, we'll be relying on your readings of our on-board equipment to tell depths." He paused, then said, "We're going to find out what you're made of this cruise, Chief."

All except Neumann laughed, and those close to him shoved the Chief gently. Siegfried smiled sheepishly.

"Aye, *Kapitän*," said Siegfried, and touched his hand to his forehead in a casual, but respectful, acknowledgement. Seligman appreciated his calm demeanor; the crew had to have confidence in their chief. The captain knew however, that his stomach had to be churning.

"We don't know what the Americans have done in the way of preparation," added Seligman. "Admiral Dönitz thinks we're going to catch them unawares. We'll see, but we need to be diligent against attack from the air. If we are late seeing a plane, it will be better to stay on the surface and shoot it out. If we dive and it has depth charges, we have no way to defend; but if we're on the surface we can use our gun. All orders are to be carried out immediately, without question. And speaking of questions, now is the time to ask them, if you have any."

Schwarz looked around at the others, then held up his hand.

"Speak," said Seligman.

"Who's the new seaman with all the camera equipment? I tried to give him some duties but he said he already had his and didn't have time for more."

"Oh, yes. We have a guest on board. Schwarz has obviously met him. Seaman Fritz Zimmerman is a photographer for the Propaganda Ministry. Please introduce yourselves to him and answer any questions he has about the boat. He will be taking photos of the crew. You are to cooperate with him, and have your men do the same. When we do a surface attack, he will be on the bridge to get pictures. Watch Officers, make sure he gets below when we have to do an emergency dive. I don't want any harm to come to him. Neumann, please take him under your wing and show him around."

Neumann appeared ready to object, but Seligman's jaw shoved challengingly forward, and he remained silent.

"Anything else?" Seligman looked around but the men shook their heads.

"Neumann," he said. Neumann was staring down at the deck. Now his head shot up.

"Aye, *Kapitän*."

"Take the boat down to forty meters. I'll speak to the crew on the loudspeaker. I'd like to see you in my quarters in thirty minutes. Watts, you'll relieve him then."

"Aye, *Kapitän*," both officers replied.

Seligman stepped across to the radio room, picked up the loudspeaker microphone, and gave the crew a scaled-down version of the orders he had just relayed to the officers. There was no celebration from most of the crew, just a business-like acceptance of the job ahead. The winners of the betting pool whooped, but the captain paused in mid-announcement at the sound of celebration and they immediately became quiet.

When he finished the announcement, Seligman walked the ten feet to his quarters and waited until Neumann reported. "Sounds like an exciting patrol," Neumann said before Seligman could start in on him.

"That's what I wanted to talk to you about. The look on your face told me you didn't like it."

"My face said that? Nah. I'll have to make sure I look pleasant for the photographer when I show him around." He looked and sounded sour.

Seligman lowered his voice. "Dönitz told me before we left port that he's heard rumors about you."

Neumann looked surprised.

"Do you want to know why?" Seligman asked.

"I didn't think you put any stock in rumors, especially from *BdU*."

"Don't be insubordinate." Seligman's voice was barely a whisper. He hated that he had nowhere on the boat to have a totally private discussion. "We are at war. I told you last May I needed to be able to count on you, and if I couldn't that I would get a new first officer. You assured me then that I could.

"Dönitz told me he's heard that you have expressed sympathy for the enemy. He called it having 'liberal tendencies.' Do you know what he's talking about?"

"You know how I feel."

"But I want to know what caused Dönitz's interest in you. What have you been saying and who have you been saying it to?"

"All right, let me think." Neumann paused and Seligman stared at him. "It might have been two weeks ago, right after Hitler declared war on the United States. I was at a bar in Lorient. Petty Officers Tolle and Schwarz were there. Those of us without families to go home to. I probably had too much to drink."

Seligman shook his head.

"Now, wait," said Neumann. "Before you start jumping to conclusions, let me tell you what happened."

"What did you say?"

He looked away. "I may have said there was no need for Germany to declare war on the United States."

"Jesus, man, do you realize that could be taken as criticism of Hitler? In front of two officers who have taken an oath of loyalty to him?" He sat on his bunk and roughly shoved a small stool over in front of his subordinate. "Sit down," he said, gesturing at it.

Neumann sat, then looked directly at Seligman and said, "Hitler is *not* the Fatherland."

"But the oath they've taken is to him, not to the Father-land. They are young and naive. It is possible they take that oath just a little more seriously than you. I order you not to say anything critical of Hitler or the Nazis in front of the other men. Do you understand that?"

"Yes, sir." Neumann clenched and unclenched his fists.

"Were Wagner or Hoerter around?"

"No, neither."

"Good. If you want to get something off your chest, tell it to me, but those two better not be around."

"Permission to speak frankly, sir."

Seligman looked around to see who was nearby. Siegfried was on the lower command deck, checking trim. Tolle was in the radio room, but had his headphones on. They were still submerged, so crew members were not moving around. No one appeared to be close enough to overhear anything.

Nevertheless, when he turned back to Neumann, he said, "For now keep your thoughts to yourself. We've had this discussion before and I don't think you can say anything right now that will further enlighten me. I'm better off not knowing your 'frank' opinions." Neumann nodded, and Seligman continued, "What I do need to know is, *are you going to follow my orders?*"

There was the question, a dangerous one for both of them. If the answer was 'yes,' could Seligman trust it to be true? If the answer was no, friendship or not, Seligman had to relieve Neumann of his responsibilities.

When Neumann spoke, Seligman could read no emotion on his face. "I will not let you down, *Kapitän.*"

Seligman glanced toward the command deck again. Siegfried was conferring with Navigator Winter, neither paying any attention to them. In the radio room, Tolle appeared to be taking down a message. Turning back to Neumann, he quietly said, "I have to do a review of your work at the end of each patrol. My recommendation determines whether you get your own boat. How can I recommend you for command when you talk so carelessly?"

"You would do me a favor if you did not. I don't want a command now that the United States is in the war."

"*BdU* won't keep you as first officer here if you aren't recommended to move up."

"Good. I will never have to take a boat into battle in a war I believe is immoral."

"They will assign you to a surface ship where they can hide you with ten others of your rank. Where you will probably be sunk by an *unterseeboot*."

"You'd like that, wouldn't you, Willie?"

"'Sir' or '*Kapitän*' is the proper way to address me."

Neumann flinched and his eyes widened at the rebuke. "We've been together a long time. I thought in private—"

"You thought wrong. To answer your question, no, I wouldn't want you killed." He paused, thinking, then leaned in toward Neumann. "You asked me once what I would die for. I told you. Now it's your turn; what are you willing to die for?"

"The Fatherland."

"What about this boat? Her crew?"

"We've become an arm of the Nazi party. We've even got a propaganda photographer on board. I look hard, but fail to see the Fatherland here."

"So you would not die for this boat and her crew?"

"There are ideals for which I will die, and if the boat can somehow be incorporated into those ideals, Fatherland, fraternity, a noble country, I will die for her. Gladly, if it would bring us peace."

Seligman stood and tried to pace, but only had room for two steps in any direction, so he stopped in front of Neumann. "My boat is *not* an arm of the Nazi party, but it *will* defend the Fatherland, and that includes attacking American shipping. You will help me carry out those attacks and that is an order. Do you understand?"

Neumann stood and drew himself up to his full height, which was slightly taller than Seligman. He looked down at his captain and waited a full ten seconds before giving his reply. "You are my *kapitän*. I will carry out your orders, including showing around the Nazi propagandist with the camera. Really, sir, to order me to babysit him was unfair."

"Almost every *kapitän* would assign that to the First Officer. I'm not going to exempt you from normal duty because you find it repugnant. If I start that, I'll have apprentice seamen telling me what their conscience will and won't let them do. This is a German vessel of war and it will be operated as such. Dismissed."

As he left, Neumann walked past the radio room, where Radioman Tolle sat with one earphone on his ear and the other on the side of his head. He was doing what he had been trained to do. Listening.

CHAPTER TWENTY-THREE

25 December, 1941 08:00 CET
   Quadrant BD 8772

Seligman ordered Siegfried to take the boat to twenty meters, then picked up the microphone.

"Crewmen," he said, "We have some surprises that I will tell you about after I read you a message we just received from *BdU*.

"It says, 'On this German Christmas, I am with you in heart and thought—you, my proud, tough, fighting U-boat crews.'

"This message is signed '*BdU*', so it is from Admiral Dönitz."

Seligman then invited the men to come by the Command deck and see the live *Tannenbaum* they had on board.

"The smell of a tree always puts me in the Christmas spirit. We can thank our support services for making this possible. It is only four feet tall, but we don't have much room so it must be small. I also want to thank Seamen

Schroder, Richter, and Krüger for their work on wiring the tree with electric candles, since for obvious reasons we can't have real ones. When you come by, though, remember we are submerged, so do not make any movements of large groups, and this is only for the next two hours. After that, we will return to our restriction on movement while the boat is submerged and the tree will go away. Chief, while the men are moving around, please watch our trim closely."

Siegfried nodded to the captain from his post ten feet away.

"Next," he continued, "I have agreed to allow each man to receive a few sips of wine on this holy day. At 13:00 the Chief will pass through the boat and dispense it. We will spend most of the day underwater so that you can have a quiet and holy day.

"Finally, the best gift we could receive. Before we left, we asked the families to send us holiday letters, so we have Christmas greetings from our families. Our watch officers will pass them out after our Christmas meal.

"I personally want to wish each of you a pleasant Christmas. That is all."

Almost immediately, the crew began passing by the tree. Most stuck their noses close to it to gather in the scent of the forest, so incongruous twenty meters below the surface of the Atlantic Ocean. The orderly exchange of men from forward and aft compartments made the Chief's job of keeping the boat in trim relatively simple.

After the mail and wine were passed out, Richter pulled out a small accordion that Watts had allowed him to slip on board and began to play *Stille Nacht*. War-hardened men wiped tears from their cheeks, put their arms around their crew-mates' shoulders, and joined in singing. They knew they would have to return to the war eventually, but while they could, they enjoyed the tree, the wine, and especially the letters from home.

Late in the day, Seligman looked in on Neumann.

"You have no mail?" he asked.

"I have no family," said Neumann.

"Nothing? No siblings, cousins? No one?"

Neumann shook his head. "I was the only child of two only children. My father was killed in the Great War–he never even knew I was born. My mother died when I was at the Academy. I've been on my own since." He paused long enough for Seligman to see a look of regret cross his face. "Have you ever felt like you really didn't belong in this world and that you are here by mistake?"

Seligman shook his head.

"I have," said Neumann. "I can be in the middle of a crowd and be so lonely I wonder what I'm doing there. People can extend a courtesy to me, it can be as simple as holding a door when my hands are full, and I wonder why they did that. After all, it's only me." When Neumann saw the shocked look on Seligman's face he smiled, apparently to soften the words.

Seligman had no idea how to respond to such a self-deprecating statement. Instead, he ignored it and said, "I have a letter from Marie and Ernst. Would you like to read it?" Seligman held out the letter to his morose first officer.

"Are you sure this is allowed?" Neumann asked, but his smile as he held out his hand to take it said he appreciated the gesture.

"If it's not, it should be," said Seligman. "Besides, I'm the *Kapitän*. I get *some* leeway."

They had only been out three days, but already the stubble on their faces made them look grimy. Seligman stood while Neumann sat on his bunk.

"I've never met your family," said Neumann as he read the letter.

"Then we need to change that. Next time we are in port, I want you to come to Dresden with me."

"Is that an order?" Neumann looked up from the letter and half-smiled.

"No," said Seligman. "It is a request."

"Then I accept. Provided we get home."

"I will get us home," said Seligman. "With your help, and *Gott erlaubt.*" God permitting. Reaching into his pocket, he pulled out his ever-present picture of Marie and Ernst, with him standing behind them. Showing it to Neumann, he said, "I need to get a new one. This one is getting old."

Neumann took the picture and looked at it. "Your wife is very pretty. Does she have a sister?"

"*Ja*, and she is very pretty also, but a little too enthusiastic. Very nice shape, but also a fiancé".

"My luck," Neumann sighed. "How old is your son?"

"Four in October. He was two when the picture was taken."

Neumann handed the picture back to Seligman, then held his hand out to his captain and said, "*Frohliche Weihnachten,* Willie." Merry Christmas.

Seligman took his proffered hand and said, "*Frohliche Weihnachten,* Oskar." Neumann smiled, but his eyes looked troubled.

CHAPTER TWENTY-FOUR

28 December, 1941 12:30 CET (06:30 A.M. EWT)
  Grid BD5255

Ensign Tolle, carrying a plate of sausage, potatoes, and turnips in one hand and a cup of coffee in the other, sidled up to First Officer Neumann, who sat on his bunk eating the same meal. Tolle looked around and verified they were alone.

He had been waiting for a moment like this for five days. Finally, everything had come together. Neumann's watch had ended, he had come off radio duty, and the boat was submerged.

He wanted to talk to Neumann in as much privacy as one could expect in a 252-foot-long, 10-foot-wide space crammed with mechanical equipment, tubes, pipes, and fifty other men. With the boat submerged, movement was restricted to keep it in trim, so he stood in the galley until Meier, the cook, handed him lunch. Then, with a full plate, he slid the ten feet aft to the officer's bunks and found Neumann alone.

"*Kapitänleutnant*," he said quietly, "A moment of your time?"

"Sure," said Neumann, scooting to one side to make room.

Tolle dropped his lanky frame onto the bunk next to Neumann and carefully positioned his coffee between his legs so it would not spill.

"What brings you to my corner of this underwater world?" Neumann asked affably. Tolle had only known Neumann since the radioman was assigned to the boat and thought the first officer's mood swings made him hard to like. Sometimes when Tolle approached him he was aloof and reserved. Other times, like now, he was congenial and happy. Thank goodness. Tolle needed him now.

"A matter which requires great discretion," said Tolle, between bites. He spoke slowly and quietly.

"Is that so? All right. Let's hear it."

"Do you remember several weeks ago, when we were in Lorient at that sidewalk café? Schwarz was with us."

Neumann's eyes narrowed and he slowly said, "Vaguely. We had a lot to drink that night."

"Hitler had just declared war on the United States." Tolle paused, a cat in the early stages of pursuing a very cautious mouse.

"What about it?"

"You expressed a concern that Germany was…taking on more than it should."

Neumann shook his head. "You are overstating my comments. I want what is best for the Fatherland. I don't want us to lose our momentum in the war." The affability in his voice was gone and his hand shook a little as he used his fork to push his food around.

"I want to help. I think you are planning something, and I want to be in on it." Tolle's words came in a torrent as he looked around again to make sure no one was close enough to overhear.

"I don't know what you're talking about. What would I be planning?" The first officer's voice was low. Tolle interpreted this to mean he was wary but wanted the conversation to continue.

"I know we must be careful," he said. "What we are talking about could get us both in trouble, but it is important to both of us, and to the Fatherland."

Ensign Braun's voice in the speaker tube interrupted before Neumann could reply. The first officer jumped up and listened at the speaker tube. Tolle could hear enough to know that Braun was reporting that the torpedo men would be doing maintenance on the torpedoes. Since none had been fired and they would have to do service on all twenty-two, it would be an all-day process, both forward and aft.

"Very well," said Neumann to Braun. "Carry on."

The interruption seemed to have given Neumann a moment to think. When he turned back to the radioman, he no longer appeared flustered, and said, "You misunderstood my words. *Der Führer* knows what he is doing."

Tolle watched Neumann. A cornered dog is always dangerous, his father used to tell him. The first officer looked around furtively, so Tolle smiled a mild, calming smile, and said, "Perhaps I was mistaken. But your words to the *Kapitän* shortly after he announced our journey to America indicate otherwise."

"What words?"

"Didn't you tell the *Kapitän* that in your opinion, Hitler is not the Fatherland? I heard you say that."

Neumann blinked his eyes rapidly.

"Do not fear," said Tolle. "I'm with you. I heard you tell *Kapitän* Seligman that you knew he agreed with you, but you couldn't persuade him to help you. Not only do I agree with you, but *I* will help. Give me a chance."

"I don't know," said Neumann. His half-eaten meal remained on his plate.

"Yes, you do," said Tolle confidently. He ate his last bite of food and drained his coffee cup. Standing, he said, "Say the word, and I'm with you."

As Tolle carried his plate to the galley in the next compartment, he wondered how Neumann had risen to the position of second in command.

CHAPTER TWENTY-FIVE

8 December, 1942 CET 04:00 (January 7, EWT 10:00 P.M.)
Grid CB7778

U-112 had reached the eastern coast of the United States, near Boston, then turned south. As they waited for orders from *BdU* as to when to attack, they were constantly alert for any ship of more than 7,500 tons. Dönitz wanted a coordinated attack, but had conceded that a vessel of that size justified sinking it ahead of schedule. So far, however, they had not seen any.

Seligman took the boat to the "storm cellar," as he called it, during the day, where they would settle on the bottom, conserving their batteries. Sometimes, however, they would cruise quietly just below the surface, looking for prey through the periscope that barely broke the surface, like the eyes of an alligator gliding through the water. At night, they would surface, activate the diesels and settle in at nine knots, the watch crew looking for targets and studying the activity on shore.

"I can't believe the American cities aren't doing a blackout," Watts said to Seligman, as his watch came off duty after passing New York. "The city was so lit up, it was like daytime. The street lights were blazing and cars were driving about with headlamps full on. We could hear the roller coaster at an amusement park, and the screams of the riders."

"Those poor bastards must think the Atlantic will keep the war away from them," Seligman replied.

At 04:00 CET, January 8, the second watch, with Watts in command, relieved Neumann and his first watch. When Watts' crew arrived on the bridge, Neumann told them, "Get hooked up right away. Moderate seas, occasional swells breaking over the bridge. Storm probably coming in."

Neumann and the rest of his watch dropped through the conning tower hatch, and he spun it shut. On the bridge, Watts and his men quickly scanned the surface of the ocean, but visibility was less than 300 meters.

They had been topside about fifteen minutes when a larger wave than usual swept over the boat from stern to bow, followed by a loud bang.

"What was that?" asked Watts.

The others shrugged their shoulders, but Krause pointed to the port side and said, "It sounded like it came from over there."

Leaning over the rail as far as his safety belt would allow, Watts looked around. "I see it," he said, looking at a compartment door being pushed back and forth by the waves. "That last wave knocked open the port ammunition hatch. If we don't get it closed we're going to lose some of our rounds for the deck gun."

Watts was a muscular young man with blond, almost

white, hair, who bragged to the crew that the sea was his wife. He liked to joke that she gave him less trouble and treated him better than any of their real wives. As a cadet at the naval academy in the late 1930s, he had set his sights on the 1940 German Olympic weightlifting squad. When war broke out, however, the games were cancelled and he found himself assigned to the U-boats. He worked diligently to prove he was up to any task, so that he might someday command a boat of his own.

Perhaps it was the desire to do whatever was needed that caused him to unhook his belt and drop over the rail to close the small door. He checked the placement of the rounds in the container and was securing the lid when the stern began to rise, and the watch crew heard the sound of a freight train bearing down on them. Watts turned and looked up as a wall of water engulfed the bridge. But for their safety harnesses the entire watch would have been swept overboard. As the water receded, the deck was so barren it was hard to imagine that five seconds before a man had been there.

Below deck, Neumann had removed his foul weather gear and walked into the galley when he felt the stern rise up, then drop as the bow thrust violently skyward. Holding onto the table, he sat down with Seligman and several other off-duty officers.

"Who's got the helm?" the first officer asked.

"Wagner," Seligman replied.

Neumann made a face, as if the sudden twisting of the boat was the Nazi sympathizer's fault; but before Seligman could respond to any implied criticism, the call of "Man overboard!" rang through the boat.

Seligman sprinted for the command room, yelling, "Reverse course!" Grabbing a safety belt, shirt, and life jacket, he raced toward the ladder.

"Reverse course, reverse course," Wagner shouted to the helmsman, who immediately hit both port and starboard control buttons with the palm of his hands, turning them to the 30 degree stop limit. Seligman threw on the life jacket and flew up the ladder. As he reached the bridge, Seligman's heart sank. It was an overcast night with visibility down to 200 meters, and seas at five feet. The likelihood of spotting a head bobbing in the water was very small, but he had to try, if only to let the rest of the crew know he'd do the same for them.

"Get the searchlight up here," he shouted into the speaker tube. Turning to the other men on the watch, he asked, "Who is it?"

"Watts, sir," said Krause, the ranking seaman.

"Why wasn't his safety belt on?" the Captain asked, as he clicked his in place.

Krause explained what Watts had been doing and why he disconnected his belt. "It was a huge wave, Sir. Much bigger than all the others. We didn't see it in time to warn him."

I would have rather lost the rounds, Seligman thought. The shirt he had grabbed at the same time as the life jacket he now threw into the water to see which way it would drift. They would follow it, but Seligman knew that with the tricky current for which he had no charts, Watts could be anywhere.

When Seaman Kruger brought the light up less than a minute later, Seligman immediately ordered him below because he did not have a safety belt, then he and the watch crew scanned the surface.

Krause suddenly pointed to starboard and yelled, "There!" When Seligman looked, he saw what appeared to be a shock of blond hair bobbing in the water about fifty meters away, and he directed the boat toward it. As they closed on it, however, a wave enveloped it and the light hair, the white foam on the top of the wave, and the light from the spotlight blended together, then dissolved into the oil-black sea. Twice, after losing sight of Watts, they heard a cry of "Here!" but when the light was shone "here," nothing was there.

Below deck, tension spread. No one talked except when they had to, and then it was in hushed tones, as if they were already conducting a memorial service. Those that had been eating set their food aside. Bunks were empty; those that had been asleep got up as the news spread. They knew it wouldn't help but seemed disrespectful to sleep. Everyone hoped for the cry of "We got him!" but the call didn't come.

After an hour of searching, Seligman weighed the situation. The ocean was high enough to swamp a man even if he was in a life jacket. In the dark, their visibility was limited to a very small area just around the boat. They needed to continue toward the southern coast of the United States to be in place when the coordinated attack began.

"I'm ending the search," he shouted. *I hope if Watts is still alive that he's not close enough to hear me*, thought Seligman. *But with waves this size, he's probably been dead for at least thirty minutes.*

The men passed the searchlight down through the hatch.

Seligman stayed topside, and the boat returned to its south-
ward course.

CHAPTER TWENTY-SIX

9 December, 1942
 Map grid DC 3187

"How deep is the bottom here, Chief?" Neumann asked. He was manning the command room as Seligman got some much-needed sleep. The captain had been topside through the entire search for Watts, then had taken Watts' place on the watch.

"Ocean floor at seventy-five meters," came the reply from Siegfried.

"Let me know if it gets any more shallow," Neumann instructed.

Prior to losing Watts the previous day, the patrol to America had been uneventful. On the 9th, the storm predicted by the rough seas that claimed Watts hit with full anger.

Before he had retired to his quarters, Seligman told his first officer that if the seas didn't abate within an hour, Neumann was to dive to periscope depth, fourteen meters.

"Remember what happened to Watts," the captain had warned. "We don't want to lose any more men."

Topside, the watch crew was finding it impossible to keep their binoculars dry. Between waves they would open the hatch to hand them down into the bowels of the boat. There, one of several seamen would wipe them dry with a soft leather rag and hand them back up to the patrol.

Neumann decided to see how things were on the bridge. He struggled to climb the ladder up to it, though, and twice almost lost his grip on it. When he arrived topside, he immediately hooked his safety belt to the rail and watched the bow.

It would hang on the precipice of each deep wave, then drop down the other side, thrusting the twin screws at the stern high into the air. The waves tossed the boat in every direction while gale-force winds whipped the seas into an angry cauldron.

He had only been there a minute when he saw a monstrous wave, looking like a snow-capped mountain range, bearing down on the bow. The men on the bridge braced themselves. It swept over them and momentarily swamped everything, including the tower. The watch crew gasped for air after the mountain of water passed over.

"Clear the bridge," Neumann ordered. Into the voice pipe he called to the Chief, who was on the lower command deck twenty-five feet below him, "Prepare to dive to periscope depth. On my command." At fourteen meters, they would still receive radio communications but would be protected from the ocean's wrath.

When the watch crew descended into the Command Room and all were accounted for, Neumann called to the Chief, "Dive," and the red lights that signaled a dive began to flash, joined immediately by the dive bell.

They slid under the surface into a calmness where Neumann had time to think. Watts' death came immediately to mind. Watts was one of the older members of the crew, but still only twenty-two. Neumann liked the second officer, but even if he hadn't, twenty-two was too young to die for no reason.

But the men they were trying to kill would die in vain, also, Neumann thought.

Neumann remembered the surface attacks U-112 had launched, where it was his responsibility to calculate the correct bearing for the torpedo and the time to launch it, using the *U-bootzielobtik*. U-boat target optics. Similar to a periscope, the UZO, as it was called, had multiple crosshairs both vertical and horizontal, that enabled him to calculate the angle, speed, and distance of the target, which he then relayed to the torpedo room so the torpedo's trajectory could be set.

But it also afforded him a close up view of the doomed vessel. After the torpedo hit, Neumann could often see the men running frantically around the deck trying to get the lifeboats lowered. If the ship was listing heavily to one side, it was impossible to launch them. Then the men had no choice but to drop into the ocean where death was likely.

Sometimes *eins eins zwei* was close enough that Neumann could see the fear etching the faces of the men, and he knew that they realized they would soon be dead, they just hadn't died, yet. These men had families waiting for them at home, families that would forever wonder what happened to their husband, father, brother, son. How did he die? Who gave the order? Was there anything that could have been done to save him?

This was why Neumann didn't like attacking unarmed merchant vessels, especially of a country with which he did not think Germany should be at war. He knew he had to do something to get out of this untenable situation, to stop seeing the fear on those faces.

Radioman Tolle brought him back to reality when he called out, "A lot of distress calls from merchant vessels tonight." He sat at the radio with one earphone on an ear, the other on the side of his head, so he could listen for commands from within the boat.

"Anything from the United States Weather Services?" asked Neumann.

"They say we have force nine seas and force 10 winds." Tolle paused, rooting through his messages until he found the one he wanted. "You'll like this. One ship heard that and replied, 'the numbers don't go any higher.'" Tolle watched Neumann for a reaction.

Neumann smiled, then said, "Yes, they do. It could be Force 10 seas. I think we'll stay submerged for a while. Any ship's captain with any sense will be staying in port today, so there won't be any targets." *Thankfully*, he thought.

"Is there anything I can do to help you, First Officer?" Tolle's question took Neumann by surprise.

He looked at the radio man, but saw only a blank expression. *Was he referring to their conversation of a few days ago?*

"*Nein,*" said Neumann. "Everything is fine."

"Remember, I can help," said Tolle, but the radioman was no longer looking at him. He had returned to reviewing his messages. Before Neumann could get lost in his thoughts, though, Tolle asked, without looking up, "May I put a record on the loudspeaker?"

"Yes," said Neumann. "Something peaceful, to help the men forget the storm and Watts."

Tolle rooted through some records, pulled one out, and put it on the turntable. He grinned at Neumann mischievously, as *Michel horch der Seewind pfeit*, a military march, started. It was an ode to the sound of the wind at sea.

"Not exactly the soothing melody I had in mind during a storm," Neumann said. He had not seen this side of Tolle before, and wondered what he was up to. It seemed cruel considering they had just lost Watts. When the march ended, Tolle switched to *Tristan und Isolde*, a favorite of the crew.

Tolle went back to his monitoring duties, again leaving Neumann to his thoughts, which turned quickly to his relationship with the captain. Two days earlier, Neumann had asked Seligman if he had any idea about what their target might be.

"Your guess is as good as mine," Seligman said enigmatically.

Neumann was frustrated with him. They had been assigned to *eins eins zwei* at the same time. It was normal that the first officer and captain would become close friends, but every time he thought they were getting close Seligman withdrew.

Then, on Christmas Day, Seligman had shared the letter from his wife and showed him the picture of his family. The letter had some intimate details of his recent visit home, and Neumann felt he was suspended on the ceiling of their flat, peering into the middle of their relationship. The captain had even invited him to go home with him the next time they were in port. He liked Seligman and wanted to get to know Ernst, "*der kleine mann,*" as Seligman called him. The little man.

But that was fourteen days ago. Since then, Seligman had not avoided him, but all conversation was strictly business; where they were, whether to surface, when to ventilate.

He and the captain used to enjoy talking politics, both German and world-wide. Previously, Seligman, too, had questioned the need for war with the United States, but since Germany's declaration of war against America, the captain had refused to engage him in any political discussions.

At 2300 CET he saw Tolle walk to the captain's quarters and pull back the curtain far enough to stick his head in.

"I have a transmission marked '*Offizier*'," Neumann heard Tolle say. "It's from *BdU*."

Seligman's bunk creaked as the captain rose, then he and the radioman crossed the aisle to the radio room table where Tolle had the Enigma machine. As the radioman deciphered the message, he watched Seligman's face change from anxiety as to what the message might be, to curiosity, then finally, relief.

"We attack on the 13th!" Seligman shouted, to all who could hear. He rushed back to his quarters and through the open curtain Neumann saw him pulling out the target orders from the confidential papers safe. Soon everyone would know what they would be attacking. Fates of the defenders would be sealed.

I'm running out of time, Neumann thought to himself. *Do I trust Tolle to help?*

CHAPTER TWENTY-SEVEN

27 August, 1948
Charlottenburg District of Berlin

"Come on, Ernst!" Carl said. "You've got to go with us! Uncle Wiggly Wings is due tonight!" Ernst had been friends with Carl since right after the war, when Ernst had joined his gang to scavenge coal and...survive.

"Who's Uncle Wiggly Wings?" asked Ernst. It was late afternoon. Aunt Marta would be home in an hour, and she didn't like him roaming the streets, especially with Carl.

"He's an American pilot we met at the air field," said Carl. "We asked him for chocolate, but he didn't have any. He said if we watched for him he'd wiggle his wings and drop us candy. He's done it twice and it's time for him to be back again. Come on!"

Carl's parents were both dead and Aunt Marta considered him a bad influence. He was the same age as Ernst, almost eleven, but half a head taller. He stayed in bombed-out buildings, burrowing a hole in the debris to have a place to sleep. Sometimes he was lucky and would be invited to stay a while with a real family, such as Ernst and Aunt Marta. Once, when Carl was at their flat, she asked him how he survived.

"I do what I have to do," he said, giving her a big smile and offering her a cigarette for a sandwich. She frowned, but fixed him the sandwich and took the cigarette, holding her hand out until he gave her a second. With two she could get enough meat on the black market for Carl to have supper with them.

Ernst watched Carl and the others racing down the street. There were eight of them, all of them from the gang. Most weren't as lucky as Ernst; they didn't have an adult like Aunt Marta to give them direction. Instead, they lived like Carl and had one goal–to survive. But today they were all laughing as they ran. Ernst decided to go along; Aunt Marta would just have to deal with it.

"Wait for me," he shouted, as he took off after them.

"Come on," yelled Carl. He waved his arm at Ernst and slowed down until the smaller boy caught up.

"What kind of candy does he drop?" asked Ernst.

"Chocolate bars, chewing gum, different kinds, some-times enough for three cigarettes," said Carl, a master of the black market. "Right now I don't need smokes, so today I can eat any candy I get."

"How far is it to the airfield?" Ernst asked as they slowed to a brisk walk. He had not been there before.

The planes had been coming in low over their neighbor-hood at all hours of the day and night since late June. For the first few weeks Aunt Marta and Ernst both jumped every time one came in extra low. It took them a while to accept that they weren't going to drop bombs.

"About four kilometers," said Carl. "We'll be there in a half-hour if we hurry."

But Carl was overly optimistic. It took almost an hour for them to get to the Templehof Air Field, where the Americans were flying in their food and supplies. Ernst and his friends did not understand why the Russians had blocked all the roads across East Germany leading to West Berlin; all they knew was that Uncle Wiggly Wings dropped candy for them.

Once they got to the air field, Ernst and Carl separated from the others. In about twenty minutes, just as Carl had promised, one of the American planes came over wiggling its wings and soon the children saw packages floating out of the sky on small parachutes. There were about forty children now, all running after the goodies that were falling from the plane. Ernst wasn't fast enough to catch one, but Carl was. Ernst watched as Carl ate a Hershey bar.

"You've got to be faster," Carl told him, laughing.

Ernst heard someone scream, *"It's mine, you can't have it."* Turning in the direction of the voice he saw a bigger boy standing over a fallen girl and rooting through a candy package. Ernst didn't know either of them, but the girl was crying and the boy was laughing at her and eating the candy he held in his hand.

Ernst put his hand in his pocket, and gripped the rock he always carried. He walked quietly toward the two of them, waiting for the thief to look away. When he did, Ernst punched him in the stomach. The boy doubled over from the punch and Ernst laced his fingers together, the rock in the middle, and brought them down on the back of his head. The boy crumpled to the ground, rolled onto his side and put his hand on the back of his head, opening his stomach to a kick, which Ernst immediately provided.

"That should take care of Rudolf," Carl said, but Ernst's eyes stayed focused on the other boy. He picked up the candy bar that the boy had dropped and started to eat it.

"That's why I like having you around," said Carl, watching

Ernst. A smile played around his lips. "You know how to deal with things."

"He shouldn't take other people's candy," Ernst said.

"It's not yours, either," the girl yelled, looking back and forth from Ernst to Carl.

Ernst looked at her. "I got it back from him, so I deserve a reward."

"You're no better than him, if you're going to take it away from him for yourself," she said, starting to cry. "It was *my* candy."

Ernst walked toward the girl, the beaten boy behind him. "Here," he said, holding out the last bite of the candy, "you can have what's left. Enjoy it."

"I think you're a bully, too," said the girl.

Ernst and Carl watched her walk away. Ernst shook his head. "Women," he said. "I'll never understand them."

He had just gotten the words out of his mouth when he was tackled from behind. *Who is this?* Ernst thought, as he found himself face down on the ground, with someone on top of him. A hand grabbed his hair, pulled back, then slammed his face down. He felt blood running out of his nose. It pulled back and slammed his face again, this time splitting his lip.

"*Carl,*" Ernst cried, tasting blood.

Before the assailant could hit his face into the ground again, Carl grabbed the boy off his back and yelled, "Let him go, Rudolf." They rolled to the side. Ernst tried to get up but Rudolf punched Carl, then kicked Ernst, knocking him down, again. Rudolf was on top of Carl, pummeling him when Ernst got to his feet.

"Help me, Ernst," said Carl, who was no match for this punk, Rudolf. Neither were the two of them. Ernst couldn't disengage him from Carl. Ernst had always relied on the element of surprise and when forced into a fight, he'd give it his best, but didn't stand a chance.

The fight ended when Rudolf, tired of beating on them, stood to the side and bent over to catch his breath. Carl and Ernst took off. They weren't sure if they got away, or if Rudolf let them go.

Aunt Marta was already angry at how late Ernst was, but when she saw his split lip and bloody nose, as well as his torn clothes, she let him have it.

"Where have you been?" she shouted. "And you've been fighting, too." She spied Carl limping along behind Ernst and lit into him. "You got Ernst into this, didn't you?" Her question was more of a statement.

"Can I wash up?" Carl asked.

"No, I want you out of here."

"Please, Aunt Marta," said Ernst. "I'd be a lot worse if Carl hadn't come to my defense. Can you clean us up first, then give us hell?"

"Give you he...!" Aunt Marta stood, hands on hips, her mouth gaping open, as she looked from one boy to the other. "Where did you learn language like that?"

"I try," said Carl, shaking his head. "I tell him not to talk like that. I don't know what to do with him, Aunt Marta. I don't."

It didn't seem possible for Aunt Marta's mouth to drop open further, but it did. She stared at Carl, who stood with his arms spread wide. "I can't do anything with him," he said, shaking his head. Carl's right eye was already turning a purplish-blue.

Ernst waited for the explosion. He had seen Carl deal with

his aunt this way before, acting like he was the voice of reason to Ernst's wild child, when in fact, it was just the opposite. He didn't know why Carl did it, because it never worked with her.

"Carl, I will clean you up, and I know I'll never find out the truth, but then I want you out of here. Do you hear me? I want you gone."

She turned and went into the other room. When she returned she had some cotton, a bottle of yellowish medicine that would burn like the blazes when she put it on their cuts, and some tape. She seemed to get perverse pleasure from hearing the boys try not to cry as she dabbed their wounds none too gently.

"What was this about?" she asked, but when Ernst began to answer she said, "I want Carl to tell me."

"A bully named Rudolf stole a girl's candy. Ernst took up for her, and at first, he had Rudolf on the ground. Then he forgot rule number two."

Aunt Marta grabbed Ernst's head so he couldn't jerk away as she swabbed his nose and lip. "Do I even want to know what rule number two is?"

"When you're in a fight, never look away. We both took our eyes off Rudolf to talk to the girl. He snuck up on Ernst, then when I joined in, he beat me, too. I'm telling you, Aunt Marta, if it wasn't for my being there to help, there's no telling what would have happened to Ernst."

"I am Fräulein Möller to you, sir. If that is rule number two, what is rule number one?" Aunt Marta had finished with Ernst and directed her attention to Carl. She shook her head as she looked at his eye, and a cut on his ear.

"Somebody's always going to try to trick you," said Ernst. "Carl made up rule number one. I made up Number two."

"If it is your rule, you'd think you would remember it better," said Marta.

By the time she had finished dressing their wounds,

Marta had softened a little, and Ernst was agreeing with Carl that they would have licked Rudolf but they had run out of time. She almost smiled when Carl told her, "That's right, we had him, but we couldn't finish him off because Ernst said he had to leave because you would be upset if he was late."

She gathered her supplies and looked at the boys. "Let's go fix supper."

"It's so kind of you to offer," said Carl, "you being such a fine cook."

"I didn't offer you," she said, turning her back on Carl and taking her medical supplies into the other room.

When Marta returned, Carl had his hand on the door-knob. "Stay," she said. "I'll have supper ready in a few minutes."

As she worked on supper, Marta asked, "So you gave the candy back to the girl?"

"Some of it," said Ernst, smiling. "I'm the one that got it back, so I ate most of it."

"Ernst!" Marta said. "I'll not fuss you for stealing to survive. Even Archbishop Frings said it's OK to steal necessities. But candy is not a necessity. I don't care if the bully took it from a girl, taking it from him was stealing, unless you gave it back to her."

"No, it's not. You've got to stand up to a bully." He reached for one of the beans his aunt was washing, but she smacked his hand.

"And you see what happens when you do."

"Papa told me, a black eye only lasts for a few days. If you lose your self-respect, that lasts forever."

"Your father told you that? Do you know what it means?"

Ernst nodded. "It means you have to stand up to bullies."

"And look where it got him. He's at the bottom of the ocean leaving me here to raise you."

When they were all seated at the table, Ernst said, "They never told us he was dead. Do you think he's alive?"

Marta sat down opposite Ernst. She put her elbow on the table and her chin on her hand. "No," Marta said. "It's been too long. He would have come home to you and your mother if he could. He loved you both so much." Marta shook her head. "And you're so much like your father," she sighed, standing up. "Always trying to help someone."

"It's good that I'm like Papa, right?" Ernst asked, smiling at Carl.

"Yes." She turned and started toward the counter, but stopped suddenly. Turning toward the boys, she pointed a finger at Ernst. "But he would have given the girl ALL of her candy." Ernst heard a sadness that always crept into her voice when she talked about his parents.

"Someday, I'm going to find out what happened to him." Ernst nodded at Carl.

"Let sleeping dogs lie," she said, peeling a potato. "Trying to find that out already killed your mother." She put her hands on the counter, leaned over and began to cry. "I wish so much that she was here to help me with you," she said.

She walked to her bedroom. Ernst followed, abandoning supper for the moment. Carl started to follow, too, but Ernst told him, "You stay here."

She sat down on the bed and put her face in her hands, sobbing.

"I'm sorry I made you cry, *Mutter*," he said, but calling her "Mother" made her cry even harder. He sat on the bed next to her and tried to put his arm around her shoulder. He wanted to rock her with his arm around her, and say, "It's all right, it's all right," but his arms were too short.

She turned and hugged him. "My dear, sweet, Ernst. You didn't make me cry. Where would I be without you?" She kissed the top of his head, then held him for a minute, saying, "It's all right."

"Come on," she said, standing up. She wiped the tears from her eye and said, "Help me finish supper. Carl must think I'm crazy."

After they ate and Carl had left, Ernst asked, "Aunt Marta, are you better now?"

She smiled at him and nodded her head.

"What did you mean when you said, trying to find out about my father killed my mother?"

Marta stared at him for a long time before saying, "That's a discussion for another time."

Then I guess I shouldn't ask about the soldiers either, he thought.

CHAPTER TWENTY-EIGHT

13 August, 1961
Berlin

It was a bright Sunday morning. Ernst caught the subway in Charlottenburg and rode to the canal where he liked to find a sunny place to read. The other side of the canal was the border between West and East Berlin. Since 1949, when the blockade stopped and the airlift ended, citizens of both East and West Berlin had been able to move back and forth freely. East Berliners one hundred meters away from Ernst on the other side of the canal had the same freedom of movement he had and it was not unusual for Ernst's reading to take place on the other side with no harassment from the Stasi, the feared East German police.

He carried his book looking for a place to sit, occasionally nodding at an attractive woman, when he came upon a spot where a crowd had gathered and was watching some activity on the other side of the waterway.

Across the canal, in plain sight of Ernst and the other

West Berliners, soldiers of the National People's Army of East Germany armed with rifles were forcing people back from the water. Other soldiers, this group unarmed, were unrolling barbed wire along the top of the bank.

Ernst heard people near him muttering. He heard, "barricade," and "why," and although they were too distant to understand what the people across the canal were saying, Ernst could tell they, too, were upset.

What was the purpose of blocking their passage? Ernst wondered. As far as his eye could see, the East German soldiers were stringing barbed wire along what everyone knew was the border between east and west. He saw a few people try to force their way past, but the soldiers pushed them back. If the civilians persisted, the soldiers swung at them with the butts of their rifles, then herded them to the side and forced them to sit with their backs to each other while one soldier stood guard over them.

All of a sudden, one man directly across the canal broke through the soldiers' breastwork. He ran toward the canal as his female companion cried, "*Gustav, nein!*" Diving into the canal, he began to swim toward the west as the soldiers ran to the top of the bank yelling, "Halt! Halt!" and pointing their rifles at him. When he didn't stop swimming they fired their rifles. Ernst heard the explosions and counted six shots, then, ten seconds later, a seventh and final one.

The swimmer went limp and slid under the water, a widening pool of red around him. The woman cried in anguish, "Gustav!" and slumped to the ground. She put one hand to her mouth and stretched the other toward the man in the water.

The soldiers started yelling at the rest of the people, and it appeared that they were trying to disperse those they were not detaining. One soldier walked up behind the woman on the ground and raised his rifle.

"Don't hit her," yelled Ernst, but the soldier brought the butt end of his rifle down hard on the back of her head, and she fell flat on the ground, as still as death. The soldier then looked across the canal and raised his middle finger in reply.

Ernst was standing next to a middle-aged woman who gasped and put her hand to her mouth. Others swore at the soldiers, shaking their fists.

The soldier raised his rifle to his shoulder and pointed it at Ernst and those around him. Everyone else fell to the ground but Ernst remained standing and stared defiantly at the soldier.

"Get down," people screamed at him. "He'll shoot you, too."

Instead of shooting, however, the soldier slowly lowered the rifle, waved his arm dismissively, and walked away.

"You should be more careful," said a woman as Ernst helped her stand. "They could have shot you."

"They aren't stupid," Ernst said. "That poor soul they shot was on the wrong side of the dividing line, but they aren't going to shoot across the border."

A moment later, Ernst heard sirens, but they weren't ambulances. The woman who had been knocked unconscious, as well as the others who had been detained for fighting with the soldiers, were pushed or carried into one of two police wagons that pulled up. One of the soldiers waded into the canal, then swam to the dead man's body. He pulled it to the shore where another soldier helped him drag it out of the canal. They dumped it into the second vehicle as if they were clearing a dead animal from the side of the road. As soon as each was fully loaded it drove off with its siren blaring. The whole process took about ten minutes.

When Ernst was a child his Aunt Marta would tell him, "You better behave. Someone will always know you and if you misbehave, I will hear about it." There were times when he returned home from scavenging that she had spanked him because of something she had heard he did. Now he was an adult, but when he got home he found that she still had her informants.

"What were you thinking?" she called to him from the kitchen as soon as he opened the door to their flat. He hadn't had a chance to reply when she walked out of the kitchen, drying her hands on a towel.

"About what?" He asked, setting his book on a table in the living room.

"My friend from work, Helga, lives near the canal. She called me on the phone and said the East Germans were putting up some kind of a barrier so she went out to see what was going on. She saw the soldiers shoot a man trying to swim across the canal. The next thing she knew, she heard someone shouting at the soldiers, telling them not to hit a woman. She told me it was you shouting, and when one of them pointed his gun at you, everyone got out of the way except you."

Ernst smiled at his aunt.

"Don't be smiling about this. Are you trying to get killed?"

"No. They weren't going to shoot me. It would cause too much trouble."

"Maybe you tempt the one soldier who doesn't care. Maybe he'd like to see trouble started."

She crossed the room and put her arms around him. "I didn't raise you to see you shot like some mad dog."

"No? Then why did you raise me?" He pulled away from her embrace.

She turned her back to him. "You can be so infuriating," she said.

"Look at it this way. As small as I am, from the distance I probably looked like a boy. They would be crazy to shoot a little boy."

"They are bullies. They don't care who they shoot."

"You have to stand up to bullies."

"But why does it always have to be you? I don't want to catch you doing that again."

He smiled mischievously and said, "Oh, I promise you won't catch me doing that again."

She folded her arms and looked at him, frowning. "I know what you are doing," she said.

"Then you know that I will be all right."

"I don't know that at all!" She paused, then growled, "Ohhh, you stubborn man." She picked up his book. "What are you reading?"

"*The Stranger,* by Albert Camus."

"What's it about?" she turned it over and started reading the notes on the back cover.

"It's about a man who doesn't cry at his mother's funeral. His lack of emotion is later used to condemn him to death for murder."

Marta grimaced. "You better watch out," she said, reading the back notes. "That could happen to you; you never cry."

"What good does crying do? It never changes anything."

She set the book down. "It shows that you're human, that you have emotions and play the game."

"What game?"

"The game of life."

He dismissed her with a wave. "I don't play games. I take what I want and get what I need."

Marta walked to him and put her hands on his face. "I know," she said. "No matter what I try to teach you, it's always about you. Your father wasn't like that, and I wish you weren't like that, either."

He removed her hands from his cheeks and sat down. "You always want to lecture me about my father. What say we look for him? Maybe he's still alive. Maybe I can meet this saint."

"You don't have to be so sarcastic," she said, sitting in a chair opposite him. "And you know how I feel about searching the records. We should let sleeping do-"

"Sleeping dogs lie," Ernst interrupted. "Yes, I'm aware of your position. What I don't know is what you don't want me to find out about him."

He got up and walked toward the kitchen, but stopped as he noticed a cloud of gloom descending over her. "What's wrong?"

"Nothing. It's just…"

He waited, but she seemed reluctant to continue. "Go on," he said.

She sighed. "Sometimes I still think of you as a child, someone I can mold, but I just realized, you are the same age as your father when he became *Kapitän* of the U-boat. He was very brave, and so are you. But sometimes you are not honorable like him."

Ernst walked into the kitchen, got a glass of water, and carried it back into the living room. "One of these days I'm going to look for my father, whether you like it or not," he said. "Find out if he was as honorable as you always say he was." He paused, then said, "I wonder why my mother didn't try to find out what happened to him."

Marta cocked her head, as if surprised. "She did. It got her killed." She paused for a moment, then said, "That's why I don't want you looking for him."

"You said that once before, when I was young. You never told me how it got her killed." He sat down in a chair. Tell me now. I want to know."

She studied him for a minute, then sat down on the couch. "Go get us both a beer," she said. "I'm going to need it."

He raised his eyebrows, but stood up and walked to the kitchen, returning a moment later with two beers. He handed her one, then sat down next to her.

CHAPTER TWENTY-NINE

27 June, 1942
Berlin

The train arrived at 14:20 at the Anhalter station. Marie stood up, woke Ernst, and held her hand out to him.

"Carry me," he said, as she struggled to pull the trunk into which she had packed all their possessions.

"You must walk on your own. I have to get our trunk off the train." When Ernst began to whimper, Marie looked out the window and saw Marta on the dock. She had one hand over her eyes to shade them, even though it was overcast, and was trying to look in the train windows to find her sister.

"Look," Marie said to Ernst, pointing toward her. "There's Aunt Marta. You run ahead and see her while I get the trunk."

"Papa always carried me."

"Papa isn't here anymore," she snapped. "You're almost five years old. You have to take care of yourself while I get our trunk." It sounded harsh, even to Marie, but she didn't have the patience she used to have when Willie was there for her to fall back on. She propelled him toward the door with a hand on his back, and watched him go down the steps to the dock. It wasn't fair that he would grow up without a father, but it was beginning to look like a lot of German children were going to do that.

Ernst hadn't cried when she told him his father was dead, nor since. At first she thought it was because he was so much like Willie; strong and stoic. But then he had begun to ask her the questions. *How long would Papa be dead? Can he come back when he stops being dead? Where do you go when you die? How did he get to Heaven? Can I go there and see him? Why not? I'll come back. Please, I want to see him for a little while.*

When the questions started she realized he didn't understand what being dead meant. He thought Papa being dead was like Papa being away at sea–an inconvenience, but not the life-altering event that it was for her. She dreaded that time in the future when he came to understand.

She saw Ernst catch Marta's eye as he stepped off the train. Marta smiled at Ernst, squatted, and held her arms wide. Ernst ran to her and was enveloped in a hug, but the smile was subdued and the hug wasn't the raucous kind she used to give him. Instead, she nuzzled her face between his cheek and shoulder, holding him tightly, and gently rocked from side to side, seeming to get as much comfort from the hug as she gave. As Marie struggled alone with the trunk, she reflected that Marta looked much older than her eighteen years; then she remembered that Marta, too, had suffered a loss.

The letter from Marta had come four weeks earlier, in late May. "I got a letter," it began, and instantly Marie knew what she was going to say. "It had a military return address and a black border around the edge. Stupid me! I thought at first that Friedrich had won an award, or maybe he was coming home on leave. I had to read it twice before I understood. He doesn't even have his own grave; there were so many they buried them all together. Tell me, sister, what do I do?"

Marie grieved for her, but at least Marta knew for certain. She had not heard from Willie since he left the previous December after their early Christmas celebration, and not knowing what happened was driving her crazy. She knew in her mind that he was dead when his pay stopped coming, but her heart wanted to see it in writing. In some ways, she considered Marta lucky and resented that Marta knew Friedrich's fate but she didn't know Willie's.

When she hadn't gotten his pay in February she wrote a letter to the pay office, but before she could mail it she got a letter similar to the one Marta had received. It said Willie had been killed at Stalingrad. Stalingrad? He was *Kapitän* on a U-boat! "You are wrong," she wrote them.

"No, we are not," they replied by letter. "There was no *Kapitän* Wilhelm Seligman in the *Kriegsmarine.*"

She wrote them again, and told them Willie had been in the *Kriegsmarine* for seven years. She gave them his date of birth and city in which he was born.

"The only Wilhelm Seligman from Dresden with a birth date of January 16, 1916 for whom we have a record was in the Sixth Army in Russia," they replied. "He was killed in January at Stalingrad."

"That is not my husband," she said.

"If he was not your husband, why did you take his pay all these years? We sent his pay to your address, and when he was killed in January we stopped it," the clerk wrote her.

How could this be? she wondered. *Why did they think he was in the army?* "My husband was not in Russia," she wrote them.

"Provide us with a copy of his *soldbuch*." His pay book. "If

183

he was in the *Kriegsmarine* it will show that. Otherwise, do not write us again."

Like all men in the military, he was required to keep his *soldbuch* with him. "If I had his *soldbuch* I would have him," she wrote them bitterly.

Three weeks later she got their reply, denying the very existence of her husband, and ending with, "Do not write us again."

She wrote to Victor Schütze, the Flotilla commander, to ask of the status of U-112, but he didn't reply. She cursed herself for never wanting to get to know the men with whom Willie served because now she knew of no one to contact who could tell her what had happened.

All through the spring she had tried to keep busy, but at night when she would lie awake staring at the ceiling, listening to the sweet sound of Ernst breathing rhythmically in his bed, she would quietly cry, trying not wake him. Then the letter from Marta had come.

"Dearest Marta, I am so sorry to hear that Friedrich has been killed," she replied. "I understand what you are going through because I have not heard from Willie since December and his pay has been stopped. I fear the worst but am angry that no one can tell me what happened. I am running out of money and must do something. If I moved to Berlin maybe we could live together and I could get a job at Siemens with you."

After expressing her sorrow over Marie's inability to find out what happened to Willie, Marta had encouraged her and Ernst to move to Berlin. "Siemens needs secretaries," she wrote her sister. "You can find work with me, but we will have to share a room as my flat is small. We can fix a pallet for Ernst next to our bed. Come on a Saturday and I will meet your train at the station."

Today was a Saturday.

Marie dragged the trunk off the train, bouncing it on each of the three steps down to the dock. She and Marta embraced quietly, a far cry from homecomings they had shared in years past, when she, Ernst, and sometimes Willie, would go to Hamburg for a visit. Back then, Marta had been unable to contain her enthusiasm, swinging Ernst like a rag doll, hugging everyone, running up and down the dock.

"I was surprised you wanted to come here," said Marta as they hugged. "I thought you would go to Hamburg to be with Mama and Papa."

The two sisters found a hand truck and loaded the trunk on it while strangers rushed by, ignoring their need for help. "I thought about it, but Berlin is being bombed less than Hamburg. Also, I decided I didn't want to hear Papa defending..." Marta nodded in recognition and Marie looked around quickly to see if anyone was listening, but everyone else were afraid they would be sucked into helping the two women struggling with the trunk if they stopped to listen or talk. "Besides," she continued, "things are different. I have to move forward without Willie. Going to stay with them would have been too much like going backwards."

"Damn, this trunk is heavy," Marta said, as they struggled to push the truck along the dock. "You must have everything you've ever bought in here."

"It is our life. Everything we have, everything we have left from..." She noticed Ernst listening to her, so she stopped without saying, 'Willie.'

"Have you heard anything? Will anyone talk to you?"

"No, no one. The pay office clerk told me that families are losing people every day and I should get on with my life. How do they expect me to do that?" Marie started to cry and Marta quit pushing the truck to hug her. Soon both sisters were standing there together, crying, with Ernst tugging on their skirts. He started to cry, too, and Marie dropped down on one knee to comfort him.

"Don't cry, son." As she spoke, a man with a swastika armband and his face buried in a map tripped over them.

"Get out of the middle of the sidewalk, you crazy woman," he yelled as he stood up and dusted himself off. "I could have broken an arm." He grumbled for a moment, then turned and walked off.

"Let my momma alone," yelled Ernst, shaking a fist at the man, and Marta had to grab him to keep him from running after the man.

"Come here, *mein kleiner mann*, before you get us all in trouble," said Marta, picking him up and laughing in spite of their predicament. "Wow, you've grown," she said, although she was surprised at how light he felt. She tried to help Marie push the luggage truck while holding on to Ernst, but finally gave up and set him on the trunk. "I can't carry you," she told him, "but you can ride here."

Ernst smiled, happy to be a passenger, as his mother and aunt pushed the truck. When they got outside, Marta said, "We need to cross the street to catch the tram to my flat. Lucky for us it stops right in front of the building. I hope there is someone there to help us lug this up three flights of stairs."

But there wasn't, so, one step at a time, the sisters pushed and pulled the trunk up the stairs. They stopped at each landing to rest. It took over thirty minutes but finally the trunk was in Marta's living room.

"Leave it here," she told her older sister. "We'll unpack it and carry everything into the bedroom. I cleaned out a side of my *shrank* so you can hang your clothes in it next to mine. We both might have to get rid of some things."

"It's fine," said Marie. "I don't know what..." her voice drifted off and she sat down on the trunk and cried, again.

"It's OK, Mama," said Ernst, patting her back. "It's OK." But she knew he was too young to understand just how bad things were.

———

After supper, the sisters sat together on a sofa and talked in whispers. Blackout curtains covered the windows and they used minimal lighting. People were more subdued in the dark of a blackout, although there was no logic to it; the crews on the planes bombing them could not hear the voices of those on the ground, even when they screamed in the throes of death. Nevertheless, the mood of the dark carried over to the peoples' voices.

"Tell me about your job," said Marie. "And what you think there may be for me."

"It is a mess right now. I work for a group of engineers who design the electric motors for the..." Her voice trailed off.

"You can say it," Marie replied. "They design the electric motors for U-Boats. I can't expect people to never mention the *Kriegsmarine* or U-boats around me, especially if I'm going to work at Siemens."

"It's good you realize that," Marta said. "One of the engineers, Herbert Baum, one of the nice ones, was arrested by the Gestapo in May. Turns out he's been involved in anti-Nazi activity since before the war began. He even tried to sabotage some of the operations at work."

"How did they find out about him?"

"Have you heard of the *Lustgarten?*" When Marie shook her head, Marta told her, "Everybody likes to go there. It's like a park and it's on an island in the River Spree. They have a lot of outdoor events, parades, concerts, exhibits. The Nazis put up a display there that they sarcastically called 'the Soviet Paradise'. It was supposed to show everything that was wrong with the Soviet Union. Apparently, *Herr* Baum and some other communist sympathizers planned to set fire to it, but the authorities found out and arrested them before they could."

"What will happen to him?"

Marta glanced at Ernst, but he was asleep with his head in Marie's lap. "He killed himself while in custody. A lot of people seem to do that." Marta rolled her eyes. "Anyway, I talked to my boss, the lady over the secretaries. She said they can use you in the maintenance office, typing up repair orders. You have to be careful, though. When they found out about *Herr* Baum's activities, they really started watching who they hire. You can't do or say anything that can be interpreted the wrong way."

Marie nodded. "And Ernst? You said your neighbor will watch him while we are at work?"

"Yes. She has a boy who is two and a baby girl who is six months old. Her husband works at Siemens, too. We'll ride the tram to work with him. He must be pretty important there. Never talks about what he does, and he's not worried about being conscripted."

"What does she want for watching Ernst?"

"She wants us to watch her children on the weekend, so she and her husband can get away." Marta stopped for a moment, her lips a thin line and her brow furrowed. "It's not fair," she said. "You've lost Willie and I've lost Friedrich but we have to help her spend time with her husband."

Marie nodded. "I know, darling sister. It is not fair, but it is life."

"What are you going to do to find out what happened to Willie?"

"I'm going to see Papa, ask him to use that Nazi Party Pin he's always bragging about to get someone to talk to me."

"Do you think he'll do it?"

"I don't know. He doesn't like anyone questioning anything the Nazis do, but I've *got* to find out." Marie brought her fist down on the sofa.

Ernst awoke. "Momma, is Papa here?" he asked, rubbing his eyes. Sitting up, he said, "I want to see him."

"Ernst, honey," Marie said, rubbing his back, "don't you remember? Papa's dead."

"Still?"

"Yes, sweetheart. Still."

CHAPTER THIRTY

13 August, 1961
Berlin

"So she went to see Grandfather?" asked Ernst. Marta nodded. "And she was killed while she was there?"

"Yes. She couldn't go right away because of work. They needed her six days a week, and sometimes on Sunday. Your mother was very smart, so they had her doing other work besides secretarial. Siemens wouldn't let her off for over a year. When she finally went, it was July 1943. She wanted to take you, but I wanted you to stay here. The British were bombing Hamburg all the time, and I was afraid for her. But she was an adult and was going to do whatever she wanted. Thank God I convinced her to leave you here."

"If she had taken me I would have been killed, too?"

Marta nodded.

Ernst swallowed, his Adam's apple bobbing, and glanced out the window. It was still light and he wanted to hear more. "I'll be right back," he told Marta. Their beers were

190

empty, so he carried the bottles to the kitchen and got two more. Before he returned, he peeked around the corner at his aunt, who was sitting very still, staring into space. Seeing the East German soldiers kill the man trying to swim the canal had raised some memories. *Would I have a chance to ask about the soldiers?* he wondered.

CHAPTER THIRTY-ONE

Hamburg
25 July, 1943

"I can't believe this heat." Dieter Möller sat up in bed and looked at the clock ticking on the nightstand. Five minutes to one. Feeling the other side of the bed to see if Elsa was there, he located a lump that grunted when he pushed it. "And it's so dry. My garden is ruined. I think I'm going to lose all my beans, maybe the rest of my vegetables." He mopped his brow with a handkerchief.

"Go back to sleep," Elsa said.

"I can't. It's too hot."

"Then be quiet so I can sleep."

He got up and walked into the kitchen to get some water, passing the closed door to the room where Marie was sleeping. She had arrived the day before in the midst of the epic heat wave. Elsa had gone to bed at ten but he and Marie had stayed up until close to midnight discussing what had happened to Willie. She wanted him to use his connections in the party to find out what was going on. He snorted, remembering her naïveté. There was a war, that was what was going on. His death was no more expected or unexpected than the next. So what if the government said he was a soldier, not a sailor? Dead was dead. Still, her tears moved him and he would do what he could.

He stopped halfway across the kitchen and cocked his head, listening. *What is that?* He wondered. *It sounds like planes, but why haven't the sirens gone off?* As if to answer his question, the sirens started wailing. Five seconds later multiple planes roared overhead.

He ran toward the bedrooms, shouting, "Elsa! Marie! Wake up!" He needn't have bothered. The sirens had brought both of them scurrying out of their bedrooms.

Outside, bombs were exploding, each one sounding closer. "*Gott im Himmel!*" Elsa shouted, "How did they get so close without the sirens going off?"

"I don't know," shouted Dieter, "but we've got to get to the cellar." The entrance to the cellar was outside, and as they dashed out the kitchen door a bomb exploded a hundred meters from their house. Dieter saw Marie stop to look, seemingly hypnotized by the debris thrown toward them. Initially looking as if it were moving in slow motion, in just seconds chunks of wood, brick, and other debris began raining down near them. Dieter grabbed Marie's arm and pulled her toward the cellar just in time to avoid having chunks of concrete dropped on her. "This isn't fireworks," he told her. "The next bomb could be on our heads."

They huddled in the cellar almost an hour, listening to the methodical destruction of their neighborhood. They didn't dare venture outside to see what was happening but they could hear their house collapsing above them. Elsa and Marie huddled under the protective spread of Dieter's arms, and he was glad neither said a word when an explosion occurred so close that it caused him to wet himself.

When they emerged from the cellar, the roof and second story of their home were gone. What remained was in shambles. "My furniture, mother's china, our clothes. They're all gone," Elsa said through her tears as she walked through the ruins of their house. Broken dishes were strewn over the floor. The few pieces of furniture that remained were damaged beyond use, and what clothes they could find were beyond wearing.

"The house is gone," said Dieter. "We will have to stay in the cellar."

"Our family pictures!" Elsa cried from what had once been the living room. "Where are our family pictures?" Marie put her arm around her mother. Most of the walls where the pictures had hung were gone, and those that were still standing were bare. There was broken glass everywhere, but they could find no pictures.

———

In the Berlin flat she and Marie shared, Marta arose at 6:00, clicked on the radio, and put a pot of water on the stove to make coffee. The announcer was saying something about bombings; she couldn't tell where, only that there had been massive destruction. A knot formed in her stomach as she thought of Hamburg, her parents and sister, and said a prayer.

Finally, the announcer confirmed he was talking of Hamburg; she felt the knot tighten. She thought for a moment she would be sick. When the sensation passed she went to a shelf and picked up a picture. Sitting down in her chair in the living room, she pulled her bare feet up under her and held the picture in her hands, staring at it. Her mind wandered back to 1934, when it was taken. Marie was eighteen, she was ten. They sat together in a chair, with Dieter and Elsa standing behind them, his arm around his wife's shoulders. Marta and their father were laughing; Marie and their mother, serious–the normal state of affairs.

As she sat there staring at the picture Marta felt tears overflowing her eyes and tracking down her cheeks. She walked to the bedroom door and whispered, "Ernst?" She heard him stir, but then he was quiet again.

Marta continued to listen to the radio but frequently walked to the bedroom door and watched Ernst sleep. Marie had always told Marta that he looked so much like her, his *Tante* Marta, when she was a little girl.

She adjusted the dial to get a better signal but heard Ernst stirring, so she went to the bedroom and picked him up. She carried him into the living room and sat in the chair with him on her lap, rocking her body back and forth. *Please, God,* she prayed to herself, *let them be OK.* She repeated it in her mind over and over, and kissed Ernst on the head, saying, "It's all right," as the radio announcer reported that the planes had somehow slipped into Hamburg with no warning. He went on to say that the radar had not malfunctioned, but that the British had probably done something to make the radar fail. Once past the city's defenses, they made repeated attacks against the innocent civilian population. Time and time again, the announcer said that the *Fuhrër* would see that vengeance would be visited on British cities.

It was a Sunday, so Marta listened to the radio all day. According to the reports the Americans and British alternated so the raids were virtually non-stop. All day Marta tried to telephone her family. When she couldn't, she tried reaching friends, but the phones were down everywhere. Finally, Marta tried Alwin Hoffmann, the gardener their father had hired when she was a child.

She said to herself, *Please answer. Please answer*, as she heard the phone futilely ring. Finally, just as she was about to hang up, she heard a weary "Hello."

"*Herr* Hoffmann," she said, "this is Marta." She paused. He didn't respond, so she added, "Marta Möller. You do yard work for my father."

"Yes, Marta. I can barely hear you. Can you speak louder?"

"I'm trying to reach my parents," she yelled into the phone, even though she didn't want Ernst to hear. She had forgotten how hard of hearing *Herr* Hoffmann was.

"There was much damage in their area of town, Marta. I live in Hammerbrook. We're a residential section and the British left us alone. Thank God they think there is nothing of value here."

"*Herr* Hoffmann, I need you to help me. Can you go to their house and see if they are all right?"

"*Nein, nein.* There is too much bombing, both day and night. I could be killed."

"*Herr* Hoffmann, when I was a child you and Otto had the fever. My father found out, and he came to your house. You and your son were sick in bed and had no one to take care of you. Papa brought you both to our house and got you medicine; my mother took care of you for three days. *Three days.*"

"True, but the Brits weren't bombing the city. I'll be killed."

"How is your son? Is he alive?"

"Otto is manning the flak battery in the park. He is alive, but a sixteen-year-old should not have to do that."

"But you know he is alive. I've got to know if my parents are. My sister is there, too." Marta began to cry. "I'm scared. Please do this for my parents."

There was a long pause. "*Herr* Hoffmann?"

"*Ja*, all right," he said reluctantly, "but only because they took care of us. I will go right now while there are no bombs falling on our heads."

"*Dankeschön, Herr* Hoffmann. *Dankeschön.*"

She hung up and said, "Please, God. Please, God." She looked up and saw Ernst standing in the bedroom door looking at her. As soon as he saw her look at him, he dashed into the bedroom and jumped into bed, throwing the covers over his head.

Dieter, Elsa, and Marie were huddled in their cellar when they heard someone calling their names.

"Who could that be?" Dieter asked.

"Go look," said Elsa, just as someone started pounding on the cellar door.

"Dr. Möller!" the voice called.

"*Herr* Hoffmann?" said Dieter, recognizing the voice. It took great effort, but he pulled open the door that was crooked on its hinges and said, "What are you doing here?"

Hoffmann stood there straddling the rubble in the cellar passage, his shoulders hunched over as if he were expecting a bomb to drop on his head at any moment. "*Ach*," he said. "You're alive. When I saw the condition of your house I was afraid you would be dead." He stood there waiting to be invited in.

"Yes, we're alive," said Dieter. "But surely you didn't come all the way from Hammerbrook just to check on us."

"Yes, actually. Your daughter sent me. She wants me to take you to my flat." When he wasn't immediately invited inside he looked over his shoulder to see if any planes were in the air. He flinched at every sound behind him, then ducked and threw his hands over his head, expecting the heavens to open up and shower him with parts of buildings.

"My daughter is with us," Dieter said, surprised.

"*Nein*, Dr. Möller. Your other daughter. The one in Berlin."

"Marta, Papa," said Marie. She saw how nervous Hoffmann was and pushed past her father. "Please come inside," she said.

When the gardener was inside Dieter said, "But your flat is smaller than our house."

"You no longer have a house," said *Herr* Hoffmann. "Is this where you want to stay?" he asked, sweeping his arm around the unkempt cellar.

Elsa nodded in agreement. The cellar had a coal furnace in it, a tub with a scrub board, and a table with four chairs. There were no windows and the floor was uneven brick, some of them sticking up far enough to trip a person. "And our Audi is inside the garage with the roof crushed," she said. "I don't know how you will be able to see patients."

"I can only hope my office is still standing so I have some medicine," Dieter said. "Otherwise, I won't need a car, but in the meanwhile, I will have to get a bike to ride."

"Did you bring your truck?" asked Marie.

Hoffmann nodded. "But you will have to ride in the back," he said. "It only has one seat, for the driver. Bring any food you have. We may need it."

As they drove through the streets they had a hard time knowing where they were because all the familiar landmarks, even the church steeples and the brightly-colored facades, were missing, destroyed by the bombs. Time after time, first one, then another, would gasp in despair as they saw a favorite shop, or the house of a friend, leveled to the ground. The smell of fire and the heat from the smoldering embers were everywhere. And another, more pungent, odor.

"What is that smell?" asked Elsa.

Being a doctor, Dieter recognized it. "Death," he replied,

and indeed when they looked closely they realized some of the piles of rubble in the streets were actually bodies mangled and burned beyond recognition. The bombers were coming too frequently for anyone to bury them, and in the heat they had begun to rot.

When they reached Hoffmann's house, the Möllers called Marta and told her that they were all right.

"We don't know what is the matter," Dieter told his younger daughter. "We can't trust the sirens, it's like they have gone crazy. Sometimes they give a 'pre-warning', followed by the 'alarm-over' signal. Then they sound 'alarm', then 'alarm over'. We don't know what to believe."

"When can you go home?" she asked, relieved that they were alive.

"We have no home to go to. If we return there we will have to live in the cellar. Otto is on duty with the home guard and Hoffmann says he hasn't been here for days. The Americans attack during the day, and the British at night, so he stays at the guns and sleeps when he can. We're going to stay in his room and Marie will sleep on the sofa. We may be here a while."

They were there three days.

CHAPTER THIRTY-TWO

27 July, 1943
Royal Air Force Headquarters, London

At the Royal Air Force headquarters in London, Prime Minister Churchill arrived in a fog of cigar smoke. As he handed his umbrella to an aide, he asked Air Chief Marshall Arthur "Bomber" Harris, "Where will you be bombing tonight?"

"Hammerbrook, Hamm, and Borgfelde are the primary targets," said Harris. "They are full of war industry workers. We'll be using a combination of explosive bombs, followed by incendiary bombs. If we can kill the workers we will kill the industry."

Churchill nodded. "Carry on," he said.

The bombs started dropping in Hammerbrook shortly

before midnight. *Herr* Hoffmann, Elsa, Dieter, and Marie all made it to the bomb shelter in the cellar, along with twenty-one other people. Before they entered it, they could see nearby neighborhoods already ablaze, and soon the entire town was on fire.

The shelter was well-built, and withstood the bombing, including one near hit, but soon the occupants noticed other problems. Elsa, Dieter, and Marie were huddled together despite the heat. Dieter was the first to complain.

"I'm having trouble breathing," he told them.

Marie was sitting next to her mother, sweat rolling off both. Elsa pulled at the collar of her dress, even though it fit loosely around her neck. Dieter stood up, but immediately sat down next to Marie. People throughout the shelter removed their outer clothing, but they still couldn't get cool. Everyone panted, as if they had just climbed ten flights of stairs.

"Why do I feel my body being pulled toward the outside wall?" asked Marie.

"Because the air is being sucked outside by the fire," said Dieter. He tried to continue, but his throat locked up. He couldn't talk; his throat, already parched from the unusual heat, was completely dried out by the firestorm raging all around them.

Dieter took his wife's hand in one of his and his daughter's in the other and noticed how hot they were. The others were lucky–not being doctors they didn't realize they were suffocating. Dieter tried to tell his family he loved them, but couldn't speak, nor could he breathe. There was no longer air in the room.

3 August, 1943

Hamburg

"Halt," shouted the captain. The motley group of British prisoners of war stopped in front of the burned out carcass of an apartment building. They could feel the heat rising up from the ruins, even though the firestorm had died out six days earlier. There were still plenty of hot embers, however, raising the ground heat even more than the already hot temperatures.

"You, you, and you," said the captain in English, pointing at three prisoners at random. "Over here," he said, indicating where he wanted them to stand. The three Brits shuffled to where he pointed.

"Guard," said the captain to the *Wehrmacht* soldier nearest him, "take these men into the ruins of the buildings in this block and look for bodies. Those you find will be brought out and put on a truck for burial." He looked at his watch. "The truck will be here in fifteen minutes."

The guard waved his rifle in the direction of the closest building and followed as the three prisoners made their way toward it.

Turning his attention to the remaining prisoners, the captain said, "The rest of you will search for unexploded bombs. When you find one you will disarm it."

"How are we supposed to do that?" asked one of the prisoners. "We don't know anything about bombs."

"They are your bombs. You will disarm them," said the captain, walking away.

The three British prisoners, along with the German guard, could see that the only thing left of the building was the bricks, still hot to the touch. When the men pulled on them, they crumbled.

The stairwell was filled with debris. One prisoner crawled over it on his stomach, feeling the heat in the rubble. Sticking his head through a small opening he made, he stared in amazement into what had once been a cellar. "What the…" he said, confused.

"What is it?" asked one of the others.

"I have no idea," he replied. "Come look."

He stood up and a second Brit took his place. After a moment the second prisoner said, "Are they dolls?"

"Let me see," said the third. They changed places and the third stuck his head through the opening. "That's what it is," he said. "This was somebody's doll collection. But why are their clothes so big?"

"They are not dolls," said the guard, who had been listening to them. "We must dig our way in."

When the POWs cleared the debris and gained access to the cellar, they found it contained twenty-five bodies, none of which bore any visible injuries. They looked as if they had gathered for a party, except that they had removed their outer clothing.

"Are they children?" one asked. They were half the normal size of an adult, but some of the males had beards, and the females had breasts, small, but proportional to their bodies.

"You see what you British do?" asked the guard. "This is not the first time I have seen this. They suffocated because the fire took all the air. Then their bodies shrank. I have a friend who is a doctor. He told me the heat evaporates all the moisture in their bodies." His eyes bore into the British prisoners. "These were good German people," he said, his voice rising, "and your government killed them. Are you proud of this?"

One of the prisoners squatted in front of the Möller

family, studying them. Marie lay between Dieter and Elsa, her mouth forming an O, her eyes open, staring at him with a look that would haunt him the rest of his life. Even in death he could tell she had been beautiful. He had no way of knowing that but for her sister's intervention, there would have been a five-year-old boy next to her.

CHAPTER THIRTY-THREE

13 August, 1961
Berlin

"Why did you call the gardener?" Ernst asked.

Marta took a sip of beer. Just thinking about what her family went through shook her, and she needed to gather her thoughts before she continued. "His house was in a working class neighborhood. I thought our family would be safe there because until that time the British had stayed away from residential neighborhoods. But they and the Americans changed their strategy. They started bombing the neighborhoods where the workers lived, including Hammerbrook, *Herr* Hoffmann's neighborhood."

"And my mother never found out what happened to father's boat?"

Marta shook her head. "If she did, she didn't live long enough to tell me."

"It makes no sense that a boat could just disappear and no one know what happened," said Ernst.

"It happened all the time; you were too young to know. U-boats would just stop communicating with headquarters. We would hear about surface ships, they could signal before they sank; U-boats seldom could." She stopped and drained the last sip of beer, a far-away look in her eyes. *Poor Friedrich. What happened to him?* she thought, as she set her bottle down.

She felt Ernst's hand on her shoulder; it brought her back to the present and she smiled wanly. "I prayed for months that they survived, that your mother would come back, but then the Russians came to Berlin and I—we—had our own problems. By then I knew they were all dead." There was an emptiness in her eyes and her voice sounded as if she were in a deep well as she said, "It's like it just happened yesterday."

Ernst had never been able to remember much from that time. Sometimes he had said he remembered something happening, only to have Aunt Marta tell him his mind was playing tricks, that what he remembered had never happened. Eventually, his memories were so muddled he shut down all thoughts of that time. He had done it for so long that now he wasn't sure what he imagined and what was real.

Some things were clear. Marta had been a carefree teenager, so different from now. She was always laughing, and his mother always serious. Others were less clear. He thought he remembered a baby named Greta, but what had happened to her? As he sat there with his aunt, he tried to gather random thoughts into a coherent memory.

He asked, "Did soldiers come to our flat in Berlin?" As soon as he asked he wished he hadn't. Marta's eyes grew wide, her face went white, and she put her hand to her forehead.

She stood up and said, "Come on. Let's have supper."

CHAPTER THIRTY-FOUR

January, 1946
Berlin

Marta wanted to return to work, but Siemens had to rebuild the factory. Marta went to see her supervisor in January, 1946, to ask when that might be. The woman told Marta she could come back to work immediately, but she would have to help repair the factory first. The only other option was to wait for it to re-open.

"I can't do manual labor; I'm pregnant," she told *Frau* Hufnagel, the supervisor of secretaries.

"And I am very sorry for you," she replied, but Marta knew she was lying; they had never gotten along, and *Frau* Hufnagel enjoyed being hard on her. "Maybe you should have had an abortion," she told Marta. "A lot of women did, but not you. Now you have to live with that decision."

Others had also suggested that Marta get rid of the baby, but

Marta had seen enough death. She wouldn't be personally responsible for another one.

"Isn't there anything I can do without standing all day? I will have the baby soon, then I can do whatever you want me to do."

Frau Hufnagel looked at Marta from head to foot, then shook her head. "You can sit here and clean these as the other women gather them up," she told Marta, putting a chair next to a pile of used bricks. "We need to get all the mortar off them. We can't get enough new ones, so we have to re-use them."

Marta sat down and began cleaning bricks with a small, hand-powered machine with two blades in it. The blades were not sharp enough to cut anything, but they were a brick's width apart and when Marta put one in the gadget and pushed down on the handle the blades dropped like a guillotine, scraping the sides clean.

Marta worked there all day, loading, cleaning, and stacking bricks, but at the end of the day when *Frau* Hufnagel returned, she frowned.

"Is this all you managed to do? My grandmother could have done that many in an hour," she sniffed. "Come back after you have the baby, and be prepared to get some blisters on your hands, instead of your cunt."

"*I didn't get pregnant by whoring around,*" Marta yelled at her.

"Whatever you say, Marta. I'm not asking anything of you that I'm not doing myself." True to her word, she had her hair tied back, hands covered with work gloves, and feet swaddled in boots. As she walked away from Marta, she swung a shovel up on her shoulder and shouted, "Get back to work" at a group of women who had stopped to talk. "Start shoveling that rubbish into the truck," she ordered.

A lot of women Marta's age were doing fine, but they weren't pregnant. They could get what they needed from the Americans, as long as the soldiers got what they wanted from the women.

For a while, Marta also did all right. She and Ernst had to eat, and even though she was pregnant, she wasn't showing, yet. Her looks, even compromised by the hard times, still attracted attention. She rationalized that it wasn't prostitution because she never took money, only cigarettes. She ignored that cigarettes were used like money.

Once her pregnancy became obvious, her regulars no longer sought her out, afraid they would be named as the father, and she had to start approaching random soldiers again. She had been told by one of them that certain men found pregnant women "a delicacy," as he put it. She hoped she could find a few of them, but she had no luck.

"You're pregnant. Not interested," said one soldier after she approached him on the street a few weeks earlier, asking for help. She stared at the candy bar he was eating and absentmindedly licked her lips. "Make you a deal," he said, watching her do that. "I'll give you two cigarettes to fuck your mouth."

Two cigarettes would get her eight ounces of bread. She looked up and down the street, then followed him into a nearby alley where she found some cardboard to kneel on to protect her knees from the rocks and debris. She made him give her the cigarettes, which she dropped in her purse, then knelt in front of him.

When she opened her mouth he shoved it in as far as he could, causing her to gag. He soon developed a slow, steady, rhythm with which she could keep up, however, and he let her set the pace.

When he finished, he helped her struggle to her feet. "You're not bad once you get into it," he said, watching her gently touch her lips. "It's a shame you're pregnant."

She watched him strut away, then stepped behind some trash cans. She retched a few times, but nothing came up.

Ernst liked the bread they had that night.

———

The baby was born on February 2nd, and Marta named her Greta. Marta knew immediately that she didn't have enough milk for her, and Greta cried with an accusatory tone as if demanding to know why Marta had let her be born when she couldn't take care of her. Marta cried, too, at her helplessness, but she held Greta close, singing to her and cuddling her. By February 6th , Marta's milk had totally dried up. On the morning of the 7th Greta wasn't crying, and Marta knew her baby would never be hungry again.

Marta had always wanted a child. She wanted to experience giving life to another human. But this child was cursed from the start, and in the five days Greta lived, she never knew anything except cold and hunger.

The Occupation government had requisitioned land for cemeteries and Marta took her daughter's body to the morgue they had established. The next day she, Ernst, and their neighbors, *Herr* and *Frau* Kleist, traveled just outside the city to see Greta buried in an unmarked grave with scores of other starvation victims.

When they returned home Marta began to focus on keeping Ernst alive, but the Americans weren't much help. They didn't distinguish between Nazis and other Germans. If you were either, you were both. They didn't trust the Berliners, and were still forbidden by the American government to fraternize with them. Some soldiers had always ignored the rules, and eventually the Army lifted the no-fraternization order as it concerned the children. That's when Ernst's industriousness really kicked in, and he kept them fed until Marta returned to work.

"Aunt Marta," Ernst called, as he ran into their flat one afternoon a few weeks after Greta died, "look what I have."

He held a small piece of bread and two bratwursts like a mother would hold the hand of a child. Remembering what she had been doing to get food, she immediately scolded him.

"I didn't do anything wrong," Ernst said. "A soldier needed his boots polished, and I did it for him. Then another one saw me polishing the first pair, and he had me polish his. They said if I come by every afternoon they'll have something for me to do and they'll give me food for helping them."

Marta said, "You shouldn't have to do that, you're only eight."

Ernst's smile faded. "I thought you would be proud," he said.

Marta saw the effect her words had on Ernst, and said, "I am proud of you, *Schätzchen,* but you shouldn't have to polish the Americans' boots."

"They have so much," he told her. "I bet I can get everything we need when they're not looking. If we don't need it, I can trade it to some of the other boys, and get something we do need."

She looked at him for a long time, contemplating how to respond to that, but hunger overtook her. Squatting down, she said, "Which do you want? You earned them, you get first choice."

He smiled and showed her one of the bratwursts that was missing an end. "I already took a bite of this one," he said.

"So you did! Then it's decided." Taking the other one from him, she said, "This one's mine."

Walking around the table he sat down opposite her, and

said, "Now that I'm working, if you want to have another baby, you can."

She had just taken a bite of bratwurst, and his words caused her to choke. She held her hand up to her mouth and spit the food out. Getting up, she ran into her bedroom and sat on the side of the bed. She hated the Germans for starting the war, and the Russians for their vengeance. She hated her family for getting killed, and the Americans for treating the Germans like outcasts in their own country. She put her face in her hands and cried, for a moment hating everyone.

She sensed someone next to her and jumped, but it was Ernst. "Are you sad, Aunt Marta?" he asked.

She nodded, not looking up. She felt him climb up on the bed next to her. He put his arms around her as far as he could, and she felt him begin to rhythmically push her away, then pull her back. On the third cycle, he said, "It's all right, *Mutter*. It's all right, *Mutter*."

Marta put her arms around him, and they rocked together, her saying, "It's all right, Ernst" and him saying, "It's all right, *Mutter*." They stayed like that for a quarter-hour, then, when she had composed herself, they went out and finished their bratwursts.

CHAPTER THIRTY-FIVE

17 August, 1961
Berlin

Marta walked into the kitchen as Ernst was packing his *zwischenmahlzeit,* his in-between meal. She and Ernst had long ago adapted to having their largest meal of the day in the evening, with a light snack in place of lunch. "Good morning," she said.

He put a container of yogurt in a bag, moved it to the side, and picked up an apple from a bowl on the counter. "You must be feeling better," he said.

"I am. The headache is finally gone. Good thing, too; I need to get back to work. Give me one of those apples, please," she said as she picked up a yogurt from the refrigerator.

Ernst got another apple from the bowl and set it on the counter next to her. "You've been there since before the war ended, you're entitled to some time off."

"I know. Still, I've been off with a migraine every day this week. There's work to do, and if I can't do it, they'll find someone who can."

"You used to have migraines a lot. This is the first one in a while. What caused it?"

"Maybe it's best I don't think about that, or I might get another one," she said.

"That sounds like you know what causes them. Is there something in particular that starts them?"

"No," she said.

"You don't sound very convincing."

"Off to work," she said, pushing him toward the door, "or you'll be late. I have to leave in a few minutes, too."

He picked up his lunch bag and started toward the door, but as he opened it he turned. "I'm beginning to see a pattern to your headaches," he said.

She smiled wanly. "I'm beginning to see a man miss his bus. Those Mercedes aren't going to build themselves," she said, as she walked toward him. Putting her hand on his back, she guided him out. "If I knew why I get these headaches, I'd talk about it," she lied. "Now go to work."

She watched him walk to the bus stop and studied him while he waited for his bus. She appreciated how protective of her he always was, but it bothered her that he was not like that with his girlfriends. With them, he was selfish, he would break up with them at the drop of a hat. His father had been kind to everyone. Why couldn't Ernst be more like him?

One thing they had in common was toughness. Despite his size, Ernst would stand up to anyone, just like his father. *His size doesn't matter*, she thought. *He proved that in 1945.* She laughed darkly, but instantly willed herself to stop. *That's nothing to laugh about*, she thought.

She watched as Ernst's bus arrived and he stepped aboard.

CHAPTER THIRTY-SIX

Berlin
26 June, 1963

Ernst stood in the crowd of 450,000 outside the *Rathaus Schöneberg* with his girlfriend, Emilia. He was excited to see Willy Brandt, the Mayor of Berlin, and German Chancellor Konrad Adenauer, as well as a number of other dignitaries. He had come, however, to hear the President of the United States, who had just declared to the world, *"Ich bin ein Berliner."*

"Did you notice his pronunciation was not very good when he spoke German?" Emilia asked, as the crowd began to filter away. "But despite that, he's an awesome speaker, and so handsome."

"I wish there was some way I could shake his hand," said Ernst.

Emilia put her hand above her eyes to shield them from the sun and scanned the podium. "I don't see him anywhere."

Ernst continued to look around, trying to find a way to

meet the President. When Emilia's and his eyes met she smiled and said, "Sorry."

They began to walk through the crowd, weaving this way and that, trying to navigate.

"I've got an idea," she said. "Let's go back to your place and see your aunt. I haven't seen her in a while."

"I've got a better idea," he said. "Let's go back to your place so I can have some of this." He grabbed her butt and squeezed.

"Stop it," she said, twisting away from him. An elderly woman, who had seen what Ernst did, frowned at him and shook her head.

"I don't like it when you do that," Emilia said.

"What, this?" he asked, stepping behind her and firmly grabbing her left butt cheek.

"Damn it, Ernst," she said, as she pirouetted to get away from him. "I asked you to stop. Now I'm telling you." She leaned close to him and whispered, "If you stop now, when we get home you can squeeze it all you want."

"Oh, you're too good to me," he said.

Suddenly, there was a commotion to his side. He turned just in time to see a man grab a woman's purse and push his way through the crowd. As the thief tried to get past him, Ernst grabbed his forearm and did a quick judo sweep with his foot, putting the purse snatcher on his back. Ernst placed his foot on the man's chest and jerked the purse out of his hand.

It all happened so fast that people had to scatter to keep from getting bowled over. Emilia screamed and jumped back, so Ernst looked at her and said, "Don't worry. It's under control." Looking around, he shouted, "Is there a police officer nearby?" but by now the crowd was moving away from them and people were once again focused on getting home. A broad area around the two cleared out and Ernst was on his own.

Ernst continued to pull the man's arm while keeping his foot firmly planted on his chest so that the thief couldn't knock him down. In a calm voice he said, "I'm going to let you up and you're going to walk away. If I have to take you down again, I will break your arm. Do you understand me?"

The man was not yet ready to give up. He made one more attempt to push Ernst's foot off his chest, but Ernst applied enough pressure to the back of his elbow to convince the thief that he could break his arm if he chose to.

"*Ja*," he said, wincing. "Let me up."

Ernst backed away, but as the man stood up he lunged at Ernst, who quickly side-stepped, then shoved him from behind, causing him to fall again. When the attacker tried to get up Ernst walked behind him and brought his foot up between the man's legs. He immediately collapsed on the ground and grabbed his crotch.

"You crushed my balls, you bastard," he yelled.

"You asked me to crush your balls," Ernst replied, then turned to the woman whose purse he was holding and said, "I believe this belongs to you, and I think a reward of ten marks is in order."

"*Ernst*," shouted Emilia, hitting him on the arm. "That's soooo rude."

The woman, her eyes widening, said, "I don't have that much money."

"How much do you have?" asked Ernst amiably, opening the purse.

The woman snatched it out of his hand and looked inside. "I have five marks," she said. "Here take it." She wadded up the bill and threw it at him.

"*Dankeschön*," he said, catching it.

As they hustled away from the thug still writhing on the

ground, Emilia said, "I can't believe you made her give you money. Where'd you learn to act like that?"

"I learned to take care of myself here in Berlin, after the war, if that's what you're asking," he said. "There was a group of boys I worked with, stealing things. We'd climb on trains and steal coal." He paused, then said, "One of them fell one day. His legs were cut off by the train wheels and he bled to death."

Emilia stared at him in disbelief.

"Like I said," Ernst told her, taking her hand, "nothing in life is free, but life itself is cheap."

"It's still not right to demand money. Where did you learn that move you made?"

"It's judo. I used to get into a lot of fights. When you're small, you have to land the first punch. I'd wait until the other person wasn't watching, then I'd lay into his stomach."

Emilia stopped walking and stared at him, her mouth open. While they were stopped Ernst checked to make sure the thief was still on the ground. When they started walking again, Ernst took her hand and continued.

"Once I got the other guy on the ground I'd kick the crap out of him. If I didn't get the first punch in, I was in trouble. As my reputation as a sucker puncher grew, more often than not, I didn't get the first punch in. Aunt Marta got tired of me coming home with black eyes and bloody lips, so she made me take judo. She said if I insisted on being short, she insisted I learn to defend myself. She didn't know I was already a pretty good street brawler. The judo made me better."

"I was afraid you were really going to break his arm."

"I thought about it, but the kick in the balls was enough. He was clumsy. That made it easy."

They walked until the crowd had thinned out and Ernst thought they could get a taxi. He released her hand, held up

ERVIN KLEIN

his, and yelled, "Taxi." When a black cab pulled up in front of them, he opened the back door. As Emilia climbed in Ernst reached under her skirt and put his hand between her legs. She quickly sat down and slapped at his hand.

"That's enough," she said. "I told you to wait until we got home. Since you can't, you won't be staying at my place tonight."

He pulled his upper body out of the cab and took out his wallet. Leaning into the cab again, he handed the driver three Deutsche Marks and told him, "She'll give you the address. Keep the change." Backing out of the cab, he pointed a finger at Emilia and said, "I won't let you treat me like that. Good bye, Emilia." He closed the door and tapped twice on the front window.

Ernst saw the back window rolling down and heard Emilia call out, "Ernst, wait," but the cab kept moving. Ernst walked away, whistling.

"Is that you, Ernst?" Aunt Marta was in her bedroom, but she came out and met him in the hall. "Where's Emilia? I thought she'd be with you."

"Emilia is no more," smiled Ernst.

"What? Why?" asked Marta, folding her arms across her chest.

Ernst looked at her and furrowed his brow. "It appears she doesn't like playing grab ass in public. Can you believe that?"

Marta put her hand to her mouth and said, "Please tell me you didn't grab her in public."

"Ok, I didn't. But anyway, she's gone. Good riddance."

"What is the matter with you? Women don't like to be treated like a piece of meat, especially in public."

"I don't think what I did was that bad, and anyway, I was tired of her."

He walked into his room, Marta following him.

"Your father would never treat a woman like that. Not only did he respect them, he wanted a woman to respect herself."

"Is that so? I wouldn't know, would I, since I never knew my father and a certain aunt, who shall remain nameless, has always discouraged me from finding out anything about him. You'll tell me about my mother, but who can I talk to about my father? No one."

Marta sat down on his bed and watched him as he began to pace. "Searching the German military records won't teach you about your father," she said. "You should listen to what I tell you about him."

He pulled a chair away from his desk, turned it to face his aunt, and sat down.

"But you've told me everything you know about him, and I want to know more. I want to know when he died, where he died, what successes his U-boat had. You can't tell me that. Aunt Marta, I love you, but you're not being fair. I think there's something you don't want me to know."

"No," she said, standing up. "There is nothing to hide about your father."

"Then why shouldn't I find out what the records say about him?" As Marta started toward the door, Ernst said, "I think it's time."

She turned to look at him. "I don't. And by the way, I'm going to miss Emilia. In the three months you dated her, she was good for you."

"It was my decision."

Marta smiled. "I know. She was too sweet to break up with you."

As Marta turned to leave, Ernst asked, "Sometimes I

remember soldiers at our house. Am I imagining that?" He knew he said it almost as a taunt.

Marta seemed to stumble, then caught herself. "*Yes,*" she almost shouted, but wouldn't turn around to make eye contact.

CHAPTER THIRTY-SEVEN

22 March, 1972
Berlin

"Is Katrin coming for dinner?" Marta had just come home from work and breezed through the living room as Ernst sat looking at the paper. He always got home about fifteen minutes before her.

"I'm not seeing Katrin anymore," he said, without looking up.

Marta, on her way to the kitchen, turned on a dime and re-entered the living room. She stood staring at Ernst, who wouldn't look up from the paper, so she walked over to where he sat and pulled it out of his hand.

"Why?"

Ernst stood up, left the newspaper in a wad on the sofa, and walked toward his room, saying, "What difference does it make? I told her to get lost." He tried pushing the door closed behind him, but Marta, following close on his heels, caught it with her hand, and followed him in.

"Ernst, what were you thinking? She is a good woman. Why do you treat women like that? You're never going to get married if you won't meet a woman half way."

"How do you know I didn't?" Ernst finally turned to face his aunt. "Isn't it possible she wasn't the right one for me?" He raised his eyebrows questioningly.

"Ok, you're right. I'll give you the benefit of the doubt."

He smiled and looked away.

"What did she do to make you break it off?" Marta asked quietly.

Looking at her again, Ernst said, "I don't want to talk about it. It's done, that's all."

"I know it's done, but can't you see I'm worried about you? I don't want you to be alone. I won't always be here to keep you company."

"Let's fix dinner," said Ernst, walking toward the door. He stopped when Marta took hold of his arm.

"No," she said. "You're not getting off that easy this time. How many times have you been seeing a nice girl, only to drop her just when she got interested in you? And for what? For some made-up wrong that you think justifies breaking up. No one is perfect; we have to learn to accept a person's flaws with their good points."

Ernst laughed. "This from a person who doesn't even date, let alone get serious with someone."

Marta flinched. "I have my reasons. Besides, we're not talking about me, we're talking about you."

"True. But why are we *always* talking about me?" Ernst pointed a finger toward her and said, "Let's talk about you for once. Why don't you date?"

"I don't think that's any of your business," Marta said, turning her back on him.

"But my sex life is *your* business, is that how it works?"

Marta's back stiffened and she turned to face Ernst. "I

never ask you about your sex life, nor do I want to know, but yes, that's how it is. I have never dated, so there's nothing to talk about there. You go from one woman to another, you treat them like dirt, then you drop them. You always show me respect, but not your girlfriends. Your father wouldn't have done that. He was kind, he listened, he let a person live their life, and he lived his."

Ernst smiled. "It's interesting that you lecture me on how my father was, but all these years, every time I've wanted to find out what happened to him, you have some reason why I shouldn't look for him. Why is that?"

Her face went blank.

"I'll make you a deal," said Ernst. "You tell me why I shouldn't check the military records to find out when my father died, how he died, where he died, and I'll tell you why I broke up with Katrin. Deal?"

Marta stared at him, not moving.

"I broke up with Katrin because she only liked the missionary position. I tried to get her to do it dog–style but she wouldn't. There, happy?" He started laughing and said, "I guess you could say she put her paw down."

Ernst never saw it coming as Marta raised her hand and slapped him. He continued to stare at her and she said, "Apologize for talking to me like that."

As soon as he caught sight of the tears in her eyes, Ernst softened. *Dammit*, he thought, *why can't I stand to see her cry?* It never bothered him when one of his girlfriends cried, but let just a few tears trickle down his aunt's face and his insides turned to mush. With every tear he'd see her standing between him and danger. She was the one constant in his life. So many of his friends grew up on the streets without parents; a lot of them died because they had no one to tell them not to do stupid things. He was alive and he had Aunt Marta to thank for it.

"Of course, you're right," he said. "I'm sorry, *Mutter*. I don't know what gets into me sometimes."

She smiled at him, but there were worry lines on her face, as if the smile cost her every ounce of effort she could put forth. As she pulled his chair away from the desk where she had helped him with his homework so many times, she pointed at his bed. He sat on it, and she sat on the chair, facing him.

"I'm sorry Katrin couldn't...satisfy your needs," she said. "But I won't let you talk to me like that, either. Relationships are a two-way street, ours included." She paused, then continued. "You're right–I cannot expect you to behave like your father but deny you the opportunity to learn about him." She took a deep breath. When she spoke again, she surprised both of them.

"How he died might give you some clues as to how he lived. I admired your father so much and my sister was lucky to have been married to him. You will be a better person if you live more like him. But the more you delve into the war, the more likely it is that unpleasant memories will come back to haunt both of us."

"We're both adults. I think we can handle that."

"Don't say I didn't warn you." She stood up, ruffled her hand through his hair, and walked to the kitchen. It was suppertime.

CHAPTER THIRTY-EIGHT

Morning 11 April, 1972
Bundesarchiv, Wiesentalstrasse 10, Freiburg, Germany

Ernst and Marta stared up at a rectangular, twelve-story glass building as if they were climbers sizing up Mount Everest. Marta took a deep breath and said, "This is the address. If we are going to find anything they should have it here."

Ernst wore a gray suit, white shirt, and dark red tie, all new, all bought for this trip. The shirt was a little large around his neck, but the tie, which she had tied for him, was knotted perfectly.

"Come on," she said, and started toward the building, but he didn't move, so she stopped. "We should go inside," she said.

"I know, *Mutter*, but now that we're here, I'm nervous about what I will learn. Was he a Nazi?" Ernst held a lit cigarette in his shaky hand.

She smiled at him. He raised the cigarette toward his

mouth, but before it got there she took it from him and, putting it to her thin lips, inhaled a long, relaxing puff.

"I love when you call me *Mutter*, but you only do it when you are anxious. Relax. I can assure you he was *not* a Nazi. He was a good man. He loved the Fatherland." She dropped the cigarette and ground it out with her foot.

His brow furrowed and he shook his head. "Then why did you warn me I might find some unpleasant memories?"

When she reached out instinctively to straighten a tie that didn't need straightening he placed his hand on hers. "Well?" he asked, holding her hand against his chest.

She looked uncomfortable, and said, "It was wartime. Desperate times call for desperate measures and people do things they don't want the whole world to know about." She pulled her hand from under his. "It wasn't your father I didn't want you to find out about. I didn't want you to remember the way we lived." She put her right hand on her chest and said, "Looking for your father will raise questions I didn't want to answer."

"Did it ever occur to you I might already remember those things? And, anyway, there is *nothing* I could learn about our lives then that would make me ashamed of you, *Mutter*."

She smiled at him. "Let's go," she said, taking his arm in hers. Her high heels clicked on the concrete as they approached the National Archives Building.

Inside, a woman who appeared to be in her twenties, with short, blonde hair, mischievous blue eyes, and an engaging smile sat at a desk chewing gum. Over the desk hung a sign that said, *'Informationsschalter.'* Information desk. Her name-plate said, 'Greta Sachse.' As they approached she smiled brightly, creating dimples deep enough to plant corn in.

"Guten Morgen," he said. "My name is Ernst Möller. I want to find any records you have about my father. He was the *kapitän* of a U-boat during the war."

"You are fortunate he was in the navy," said the woman, continuing to chew. "A lot of the army records below the divisional level were destroyed during the war." Picking up a pencil, she prepared to write on a notepad on her desk. "So, your father's name was Möller?"

"No," he replied. He placed his hand on his aunt's shoulder, and said, "My aunt adopted me, so I took her name."

"Oh, I thought you were his wife," she said enthusiastically. She leaned forward and giggled. "You don't look old enough to be his mother or his aunt."

"You are kind," Marta replied, annoyed by her air of familiarity. "I was young when I adopted him, but I am plenty old."

Greta nodded as Ernst reached into his coat pocket and pulled out a piece of paper. "Here is the information on my father," he said. "His name was Wilhelm Seligman, and he was born in Dresden on January 16, 1916. His boat was U-112."

"What is it you wish to know about him?" Greta asked, as she looked at the paper Ernst had handed to her.

"How he died," said Ernst, "Where he died, and what happened to the boat."

"Very good," said Greta, standing. Ernst immediately noticed her diminutive size. She was wearing heels, but was still shorter than him by two inches, and he was only 5 foot 3.

"I'll show you what records we have. Follow me." As she led them down a hallway, her spiked heels clicked in time with Marta's. Ernst watched the sway of her hips in her tight skirt until his aunt snapped her fingers in front of his eyes and glared at him. He shrugged, but was pleased when Greta quickly glanced over her shoulder and smiled at him.

Fifteen minutes later they stood at a table studying a book labeled "*Kriegsmarine Geschichte.*" Kriegsmarine History.

"Are you sure it was U-112?" asked Greta, chewing her gum incessantly. "According to this, U-112 was never built."

"Of course it was built," Ernst said. "My father was on it."

"Could you be mistaken?"

"Could *you*?" asked Marta. "You said many records were lost late in the war."

"Yes, but generally the lost ones were of individuals. And mostly the army. These are *Kriegsmarine* records. They are intact, as far as we know. If a ship or a boat was built, it would be in this record," she said, placing her hand on the book.

"Then how did I get this?" Ernst asked, withdrawing a small box from his pocket. It was scuffed and the corners broken, with a rubber band wrapped around it. He removed the band, lifted the lid and extracted a small pipe.

"Oh, yes," said his aunt. "Show it to her."

"What is it?" asked Greta, cocking her head to get a better look.

"Are you familiar with a bosun's pipe?" asked Ernst.

She shook her head and reached to take it from him, but Ernst held it firmly.

"On sailing ships commands were given with a pipe. It was easier to hear than voice commands when the sailors were climbing amongst the sails."

"Do one for me," Greta said. She clapped her hands in front of her and bounced on the balls of her feet.

Marta rolled her eyes. "It will be loud," she said.

"It will be fun. Please!"

Ernst put the pipe to his mouth and blew one low blast, then one high. Heads came out of doors all up and down the hall to find the source of the shrill whistle. Greta's mouth formed an "O", her eyes grew wide and she clamped her hands over her ears as she looked down the hall at the commotion the noise had caused.

"I just gave you a command," he said to her.

Greta smiled wickedly, leaned toward him, lowered her voice, and said, "How dare you command me to do that!"

Marta frowned, but Ernst laughed and said, "Hey, can't blame a guy for trying."

"Both of you behave," said Marta. "We don't have time for frivolity."

Greta looked chastened, but as soon as Marta looked away she winked at Ernst and playfully smacked his hand. "So what *was* that command?" she asked.

"The first note was to prepare to pull on a line and the second was to commence pulling."

"This is interesting," said Greta, ignoring Marta's frown. "But how does it prove your father was on U-112?"

"It was Christmas in 1941 and he was home on leave, but he was called back early because we declared war against the United States. I was four years old and it was my Christmas present from him. He gave it to me right before he left." Ernst paused, swallowed hard, and said, "It was the last time I ever saw him."

"May I see it?" asked Greta, and Ernst handed it to her.

"Be careful. It is all I have from *mein Vater*."

"It is lovely," Greta said, holding the pipe as if it were a national treasure.

"Look at the other side," said Marta.

When Greta turned it over she revealed, engraved on the side of the pipe, 'U-112'.

CHAPTER THIRTY-NINE

9:25 CET 12 April, 1972
Bundesarchiv, Wiesentalstrasse 10, Freiburg, Germany

"Mr. Hunt," said Greta, "I have a question to ask you." Gunther Hunt was very old—at least fifty; probably older than her father. He had been in the army during World War II. And not the Home Guard, that motley group of young boys and old men. No, he had been in the *heer*, the real army, in Italy when the Americans invaded. He had killed men and seen men killed. He was wounded and walked with a limp because of it, although whenever questioned about it he changed the subject.

Greta stood in the doorway to his office waiting for him to look up at her, but on this chilly spring morning he apparently wasn't in the mood for questions. *I know he only sees me as this gum-chewing clerk,* she thought.

"I'm busy," he said, drinking his coffee and scanning the newspaper.

"Perhaps later, then." When he was in a good mood he

would explain things to her and be almost nice. Most of the time, she was best served by keeping her distance.

As she turned to leave he said, "Oh, all right," and closed the paper. "If you're going to badger me until I answer your inane question, let's get it over with."

"Are you sure?" she asked, turning to face him again. Her voice was as bubbly as the fizz in a soda. "I don't want to interrupt you if you're busy."

"You're wasting my time. Get on with it." He stared through her, and she diverted her eyes.

"A man came in yesterday with his aunt," she began, looking at the ceiling. "He wanted information on his father, a sailor in the war, and I tried to help him. He said his father was on a U-boat and gave me the number, but when I looked it up, our records said it was never built."

"Then it was never built," said Hunt. "You have no question. Why do you bother me?" He looked down at the paper again.

"They are coming back today. I told them I would try to find out why our records say it wasn't built."

"Because it *wasn't built*," he said, staring at her for a moment, then turning away to look out the window.

"But he had a pipe," she said.

He pondered that statement for a moment, keeping his back to her, then said, "What *are* you talking about?"

"He had a bosun's pipe he said his father gave to him. It had the boat number on the side of it."

Hunt quickly spun around, fixing his steady gaze on her. He inwardly smiled when she flinched. "So he found a bosun's pipe and put a number on the side of it. That proves nothing."

"Will you speak to them? He and his aunt will be here at ten. He's very nice and I told them I'd see if you could talk to them." Chew, chew, chew.

"Always making promises for me. What time is it now?"

"It's 9:30. You have a half-hour if you need to do anything." This was about the time of day he made a trip to the bathroom, where he would disappear for up to a half-hour.

"All right," he said. "I'll be here a little after ten. They'd better not be late."

Greta watched him carry the paper down the hall, harrumphing with every limping step. She smiled, her jaw and thoughts going a mile a minute.

When Ernst and Marta arrived at five minutes before ten, Greta was at her desk to greet them.

"Did you bring your pipe?" she asked, her big smile pushing those immense dimples into her cheeks. "Mr. Hunt is going to want to see it. If anyone can help you, he can. But let me warn you." She folded her hands, leaned forward on her forearms, looked around to make sure Hunt wasn't lurking nearby, and whispered, "He can be grumpy. I think he's constipated."

Marta laughed. "There's not a thing we can do about that," she said.

Ernst looked at her and said, "Aunt Marta, that's the first good laugh I've heard from you since we got here."

"Good for you, Aunt Marta," said Greta, making a fist and swinging her arm in front of her as if to say, "way to go". Marta stopped laughing. "I'm so happy I made you laugh," Greta continued, but when she saw that Aunt Marta was no longer laughing, she added, "If only for a minute," and looked at her hands.

"I'm not used to being called 'Aunt' by anyone other than my nephew," Marta said with a frown.

"I want us to be friends," said Greta, her smile returning, but not big enough to make her dimples pop nor to stop her gum chewing.

"We are," said Ernst immediately.

Greta rewarded him with a dimpled smile, but Marta wouldn't meet her gaze.

As Hunt approached, Greta noticed his limp was more pronounced in the presence of these strangers. As she tried to introduce them, Hunt brushed her aside and held his hand out to Ernst.

"Gunther Hunt, Archivist. You have a question about a U-boat that was never built?" The older man towered over Ernst and leaned forward, making Ernst seem even smaller, but Ernst held his ground.

"I believe it *was* built," Ernst said, taking Hunt's hand and holding his ground. "My father was its *kapitän*."

"I'll be the judge of that," said Hunt, releasing Ernst's hand and holding his arm out toward his office. "Follow me. Greta, you may return to your desk. And stop that smiling. You have work to do."

Ernst glanced at Greta as she headed to her desk, then he and Marta followed the archivist to his office. When they sat in Hunt's office, he asked Ernst, "Why are you so sure your father was on this U-boat?" Before Ernst could answer he continued, "What did you say the number was?"

"*Eins eins zwei*. My father gave me a bosun's pipe from it."

"Show him," said Marta.

"Yes," said Hunt, nodding and holding his hand out. "Show me."

Ernst handed him the pipe with the engraved 'U-112' facing up, and explained again that his father had given it to him for Christmas.

"This is very nice," said Hunt. "And I'm sure it has sentimental value. But bosun's pipes did not have their ship numbers engraved on them. Anyone could have done this at any time."

"It was like that in 1941 when he gave it to me."

"What was your father's name, birthdate, and city of birth?"

"I gave that information to Greta yesterday."

"Then give it to *me* today. She won't have it anymore. She only knows how to chew gum. It takes her five minutes to find her ass using both hands." Seeing Marta blanch, he quickly added, "Please pardon my language, Frau."

Ernst repeated his father's information, slowing down when Hunt held his hand up, unable to write as fast as he was talking.

When he stopped, Hunt continued to write for a moment, then looked at what he had written. Without looking up, he said, "Can you come back at 15:00?"

"Yes, but why?"

"You've been searching for a U-boat number. I want to see what I can find out about your father. I need some time to look through veteran records."

"All right. We will be back at 15:00. But my holiday is almost over. I need to know what you find today."

"I am an archivist," said Hunt, bristling. "Not a miracle worker."

12 April, 1972 15:00 CET
Bundesarchiv, Wiesentalstrasse 10, Freiburg, Germany

Hunt ushered Ernst and Marta into his office and waved them to the chairs they had occupied that morning. After a staged pause during which he stared at Ernst, he went on the attack.

"Your father was not on a U-boat. In fact, he wasn't even in the *Kriegsmarine*." Hunt stared imperiously at them. His words were directed at Ernst, but Marta responded.

"That can't be. I remember my brother-in-law talking about the U-boat."

Turning to face her, Hunt's eyes bored in. "Did you ever see this U-boat?"

"No, but--"

"Did you ever see him in uniform?"

"No, I lived in Ber—"

"Then how do you know he was in the *Kriegsmarine*?"

"This is absurd. How do you know he wasn't?"

"The records, *Frau* Möller. Here they are." He picked up a piece of paper and read from his notes:

Seligman, Wilhelm.

Date of Birth: 16 January, 1916.

Place of Birth: Dresden, Saxony.

Branch of military: Heer.

Unit: Sixth Army.

Rank: Private.

Date of Death: 30 January, 1942.

Place of death: Stalingrad. Executed for war crimes against the Russian population.

Buried: In a common grave with other criminals.

He flung the paper across the desk, where Ernst picked it up and read it. Marta stood to look over his shoulder.

"This is nonsense," said Ernst. "*My father was not a war criminal.*"

"Is that your father's birthdate and place of birth?"

"Yes, but *he was in the Kriegsmarine.*"

"These are my records. You wanted to see them. You have

seen them. It is obvious that he concocted a story about a U-boat that was never built."

"But why?" Ernst leaned across the desk.

From the other side, Hunt leaned toward him. "Isn't it obvious? Haven't you heard about the war crimes committed by the Sixth Army during Operation Barbarossa? In August of 1941, the children of Bila Tserkva were massacred by the men of the Sixth Army. Your father was executed, probably for something like that."

Ernst clenched his fists and started to rise, but Marta's hand was on his arm. "We won't be bothering you any longer, *Herr* Hunt," she said, standing. "*If* that is your real name. And *if* that is a *real* limp from a *real* wound."

"Oh, it is real; I can assure you of that."

"And I can assure you of this," said Marta. She placed both hands on Hunt's desk, leaning forward, before she continued. "Ernst has no reason to be ashamed of his father. He was a good and honorable man. If you had known him, had served with him *on the U-boat,* you would be a better man than the rude, constipated wretch you are."

"*Tante Marta!*"

Standing straight up, she ignored Ernst's shocked exclamation, held out her hand to Hunt, and said, "Give us the pipe and we will be going."

"You have no right to speak to me like that. I have a job to do."

"Then *do it*! You show us records that we tell you are wrong. We have personal knowledge, you have a piece of paper. If you can't help us, direct us to someone who can. If this were *your* father would you accept what you have told my nephew?"

Hunt rolled the pipe in his hand as if he might not give it up. Then, as he handed it to Marta his voice softened and he said, "You are right. If it were my father I would continue to search. My records are all I have, but there is someone you should talk to in West Berlin; a professor by the name of Horst Bredow. He might be able to help you."

"Why will this man be able to help us when you can't?" Ernst asked.

"He *might* be able to help you. He has an extensive collection of information about *unterseeboots*. He has items we don't have here." Hunt spread his arms as if to encompass things he could not reach. "He seeks people out to talk to them; we take what is given us. If our records are incomplete he might know things that can help you. I have sent people to him before."

"So the records may be wrong?" asked Ernst.

"Incomplete, *Herr* Möller. It is possible."

"Well, *Herr* Hunt," Marta said, "if you knew that, you had no reason to imply my brother-in-law was involved in war crimes without proof."

"You are right, of course," said Hunt apologetically. "But why do you say I'm constipated?"

"Your eyes are brown. Good day, *Herr* Hunt." When she reached the door, she turned to face Hunt again, cocked her head back, and said, with magnificent dignity, "And it is *Fräulein* Möller."

On their way out, they stopped at Greta's desk, where she was on the phone.

"I have to go," she said quickly, and hung up. She looked at them in anticipation, still chewing.

"It looks like our next stop will be back home in West Berlin," Ernst told her.

"What's there?"

"Not what, who. Apparently there is a professor who

collects U-boat memorabilia. Hunt thinks he might be able to help us."

"Oh, I hope so," said Greta. "I want you to find out about your father," she said, smiling at him. Out of the corner of her eye she saw Marta staring at her and she started shuffling papers on her desk.

"And I owe you an apology," said Marta.

Greta's head shot up to look at her, eyes widening.

"We got off on the wrong foot," Marta said. "You reminded me of a baby I once knew named Greta, and it brought back unpleasant memories, but that is not your fault. Please forgive my rudeness." She extended her right hand toward Greta.

"You don't need to apologize," said Greta, standing up and taking her hand in both of hers. "Compared to the way Mr. Hunt treats me, you were wonderful."

"*Jaaa*," said Marta, dragging the word out. "It was seeing him in action that made me realize I had been less than pleasant to you. *Danke fur ihre hilfe.*" Thank you for your help.

"*Bitte.* And please, let me know what you find out in Berlin."

"I will leave that to Ernst."

"Then I expect to hear from *you*," said Greta, closing one eye and pointing a finger at him as if she were aiming a pistol.

"It will be my pleasure," he replied.

"And please, dear," said Marta, "you would be so much more attractive if you didn't chew that gum so loudly."

"Such a forward young lady," said Marta, as they walked down the steps.

"*Ja*, I like that in a woman."

Marta looked at Ernst disapprovingly but his smile melted away her rebuke. She put both her arms around his left arm and drew him close to her.

"Oh, Ernst," she said with exaggerated weariness. "Where *did* I go wrong with you?" She kissed him on the cheek.

"You don't approve of her, do you?" he said, watching the cobblestones pass under their feet.

"She has no filter. In the brain, out the mouth."

"But what a pretty mouth. And those dimples. Wow!"

Marta stopped and pulled his arm to turn him toward her. "Are you *attracted* to her?"

"Would that be a bad thing?"

"She doesn't seem to be your type." Marta waved her arm dismissively. "And that gum chewing!"

"If I'm going to have a family, I need to start soon."

Marta stared at him and said, "If you're going to have a family, you need to be more respectful of women–more like your father."

"You've made that clear to me. I don't want to be single and alone." *Like you*, he thought.

Marta continued to stare. She seemed to know what he was thinking because she said, "There are good reasons why I never married, I just haven't discussed them."

They began to walk again, and Ernst put his arm around her shoulder. "I told you yesterday, there are a lot of things I know that you think I don't," he said.

"Is that so?" she asked.

"Yes. You never married because you believed you were…" He searched for the right word. "Damaged. You thought no man would want you. But you *weren't* damaged." He paused. "A lot of women had to do what you did to get food."

Marta stopped their slow walk and again turned him

toward her. "I've never told you about that. How did you know?"

They were next to a park, and Ernst directed her to a bench. They sat in silence for a moment, then Ernst said, "People talk. I heard what happened." He paused, then continued. "And I remember American soldiers coming to the flat."

Marta looked away.

"Am I right?" he asked. She nodded yes.

"And the baby named Greta that you mentioned back there. She was your child by an American soldier, wasn't she?"

"Yes, she was mine," Marta said, tears starting to flow. "But her father wasn't an American."

Ernst studied her and she began sobbing. He put his arm around her again and let her cry until she could calm herself, then asked, quietly, "Who was the father?"

Marta took a deep breath. "I don't know. She was *Russenkinder.*"

"What? I don't remember Russian soldiers."

"See, you don't know everything you think you know." Marta looked around, as if looking for someone.

Ernst stared at her, his mouth open. "How did that happen and I didn't know about it?" he asked.

"I made up stories so you wouldn't know what was happening, and sent you to the cellar. I didn't want you to see what they did to me."

Memories flashed through Ernst's head. A uniform on the floor, and a naked man, Aunt Marta screaming. He couldn't process it, and Aunt Marta's voice brought him back to the present.

"Greta at the archives made me think of her. My baby Greta, would have been twenty-six last February. About the same age."

Ernst took her hand, and asked, "What happened to your Greta?"

"She starved to death." Marta looked at her hands, wringing them in her lap. "I wasn't eating enough, and I had no milk."

They sat quietly and watched a young father being chased by his two toddlers. He laughed as his children "caught" him. *"Oh, sie haben mich erwischt,"* he yelled. You caught me.

Ernst chuckled. Then, without looking at Marta, he said, "It happened to a lot of women in Berlin, with both the Russians and Americans."

Both continued to watch the father and his children, as if by not looking at each other, their conversation was about someone else, not them.

"I know. They gave me no choice." She put her head down for a moment and sobbed, and finally Ernst turned to her and held her as she cried. "The Russians took what they wanted and left nothing. At least the Americans gave me food. Or cigarettes. We had to eat."

"I appreciate and respect everything you did for me," Ernst said. He realized how strong his aunt was, and he was ashamed for all the times he had let her down.

After a moment, Marta said, "Did you know I was engaged at the start of the war?"

Ernst looked at her. "No! Why didn't you tell me?"

She shrugged. "We were too busy surviving."

"Tell me now."

She sighed, and at first Ernst thought she was going to retreat into silence, but then she went on. "I had gone to school with him but he had to join the army in 1941, when he turned eighteen. We were in love and couldn't believe that some little war would come between us, so when he asked me to marry him I said yes.

"This is where your father comes in, and why I liked him

so much. He was so handsome, and brave. I was infatuated, even though I was engaged to Friedrich and your father was married to my sister, so I flirted with him all the time. I wanted to get his attention. Your father scolded me for that, but gently, and he told me I did it because I didn't respect myself enough."

As Ernst pointedly watched traffic pass, Marta continued. "After he told me to behave and stop flirting with him, as well as other men, he asked me about Friedrich, and really listened to me when I told him about my beau. Your father was the first person to treat me like an adult. He knew I was going to marry Friedrich even though he told me I was too young, and he told me he was happy for me. My own father wouldn't tell me that. Then Friedrich never came home."

"Do you know what happened?"

"Only that he was in the Sixth Army." Ernst turned to look at her. "Yes, the same Sixth Army that *Herr* Hunt claims your father was in. So Friedrich was killed in Russia and buried where he fell. At first I thought I would go there someday to put flowers on his grave, if I could find it. I had studied Russian in school and could speak it some. But after … after Berlin, I didn't think it would be a good idea."

"How do you not hate them all?"

Marta pulled her hand out of his and shrugged. "I have reason to, but I don't." She paused, watching the father and children, then said, "There has been enough hate. *Gott im Himmel*. Fifty million dead, including my Greta, your parents, my parents, and my fiancé." She shook her head.

They sat quietly for a minute, then she said, "And you. I've *never* figured you out." She playfully pushed his shoulder. "Sweet one minute, a terror the next. Not at all even-tempered, like your father. You treat me fine, but you are not respectful of your girlfriends."

"It's not easy losing your parents," Ernst said, as if that

was a reason for being difficult. He looked off into the distance.

She reached out and turned his face to look at her. "I understand that. Don't forget, I lost mine, too."

He looked at her, dumbstruck. *Of course, she had,* he thought. *I've been so focused on myself I didn't realize this. She lost everyone that was important to her, and still protected me from harm.*

Marta sighed again. "Now I just want us to be happy. We should look to the future. You and I are all that is left of our family, which is why I was wrong to insist you not look for your father. You need to put flowers on his grave, if he has one. He was a good man; you can be, and it seems you already knew a lot of my secrets."

"Are there more?"

She pinched her eyes, as if a sharp pain just shot through her body. "A woman is entitled to some secrets." She paused. "But someday you will meet a woman who loves you and, if you will learn how to behave around her, our family will continue. Greta is certainly interested in you." Then lowering her voice, she leaned toward Ernst as if she were confiding some dark secret, and, imitating Hunt's powerful bass, said, "But it takes her five minutes to find her ass using both hands."

Ernst smiled and said, "Maybe I can help. Four hands might find it faster." Marta rolled her eyes and shook her head. "Do you really think she's interested in me?" Ernst asked.

"Yes," said Marta. "But is she right for you? That is the question." She put her hands on her knees, and said, "Now it's time we got back home to West Berlin and look up Horst Bredow."

"There's something that puzzles me," said Ernst as they stood up and began walking to their hotel.

"What's that?"

"Yesterday, when I told Greta my father was in the *Kriegs-marine,* she said I was lucky, because a lot of *heer* records were lost. Yet, in just a few hours, *Herr* Hunt found *heer* records on my father, and he wasn't even in the *heer.*"

Marta raised her eyebrows. "Interesting," she said.

CHAPTER FORTY

8 July, 1972
Berlin

The door opened and a man in his late forties greeted Ernst, Marta, and Greta. He was short with thick arms and a receding hairline. His thinning hair had flecks of gray in it, and there was a cleft in his chin. He was dressed casually in a blue sweater covered with a light blue diamond pattern, and the collar of a shirt showing out the top.

"*Willkommen*," he said, as he waved them inside. "I have been expecting you."

"Mr. Bredow," said Ernst. "It is so nice of you to see us."

"Nonsense," Horst Bredow said. "The pleasure is mine. From our phone conversation, I'd say we have a mystery to discuss." He glanced at the two women, but waited to be introduced.

"Oh," said Ernst, gesturing toward Marta. "This is my aunt, Marta Möller. "

Bredow nodded and Aunt Marta smiled in return.

"And this is my friend, Greta Sachse."

Greta held out her hand, and said with a giggle, "I'm his girlfriend," to which Marta rolled her eyes.

Bredow took her hand and said, "Charmed. I am sorry, my wife Annemarie, is out this afternoon. She loves visitors as much as I do."

They were still in the hall, so Bredow said, "Well, come in, come in." They walked into the foyer of a comfortable flat with a dining room to the left and a living room to the right. Ernst glanced into the dining room long enough to notice a small table with four chairs and a *schrank*, but it was the living room that got his attention. In the middle were a sofa and a chair with a table next to it, but around the walls he saw bookcase after bookcase laden with binders, each with a number on its spine. There was even a bookcase in front of the only window in the room.

"You noticed my collection, eh?" said the teacher. "I have a binder on each U-boat. The number on the side is the number of the boat." He pulled one off the first shelf and proudly showed it to the trio. "This is for U-22," he said, pointing to the number on the binder's side. Turning pages as he spoke, he said, "Here's the list of crewmen who served on it; Here are its patrols; Here are its commanders." He shook his head sadly. "The whole crew lost somewhere in the North Sea on 27 March, 1940. We don't know what happened to them."

He closed the binder and, still shaking his head, put it back on the shelf. "May I offer you something to drink? Some juice, or water?"

"No, thank you," said Ernst, as Marta and Greta shook their heads in agreement. "We're taking up enough of your time already."

"Does it look like I mind?" he asked, spreading his arms wide and smiling at Marta, then said to Ernst, "On the phone you said that your father was *kapitän* of U-112, is that correct?" He directed them to a sofa with a wave of his arm.

"Yes. I was told you might have some knowledge that you could share with me," said Ernst, following Marta and Greta to the sofa.

As they sat, Bredow took up residence in the well-worn brown chair facing them. There was a binder on the table next to the chair, but the spine faced away from him, so Ernst could not see the number. A fat cat jumped into his lap, circled twice, and curled into a ball, Bredow's hand resting proprietarily on its back. "This is Romeo," he said, stroking the cat and eliciting a loud purr from it.

"I'm afraid in regards to U-112 there is little more than rumors," Bredow said. He saw Ernst's body sag and his lips purse, so Bredow quickly added, "Which can be innuendo or even canards, but sometimes they are *true*. That is why we must investigate, right?"

Ernst smiled but thought that if rumors were all he would get from this man, it was a wasted trip. Rather than voice his doubt, however, he asked, "What have you heard?"

"I will share that in a minute. First, tell me why you think your father was *kapitän* of that boat."

"He told me he was its *kapitän*."

"But you told me when you went to the Archives they had a record of your father being in the *heer* in Russia." He shook his head and said, "That seems to shoot down that story." Despite his words, the soft tone of Bredow's voice seemed to be guiding Ernst rather than challenging him.

"Show Mr. Bredow the pipe," said Marta. Bredow's eyebrows, bushy and prominent, raised as Ernst reached into his pocket and pulled out his bosun's pipe. He handed it to the professor.

Turning it in his hand, he said, "I see it is engraved with 'U-112.'"

"Yes, but Gunther Hunt, the archivist, said a pipe from a true U-boat would not be engraved."

"He said a lot of things," Greta remarked. "I think he was constipated."

"Now is not the time," said Marta, not looking at the younger woman. Instead, she sent a dazzling smile in Bredow's direction.

"He's right about the engraving," said Bredow, ignoring the women's comments. "It doesn't mean the boat existed, but it doesn't mean the boat didn't exist, either." Looking at Ernst seriously, he said, "You are, however, the first person to ever tell me you had family on *eins eins zwei*. And by the way, I have met *Herr* Hunt. The man can be prickly, but he knows what information he has, and what he does not have."

Bredow leaned forward in the chair, and said, "It's a beautiful pipe. And you say your father gave it to you?"

"Yes, sir. The last time I saw him. I was four."

"Treasure it, then," said Bredow, returning it to Ernst.

Greta patted Ernst on the knee.

"But the *rumors*, *Herr* Bredow," said Marta, her voice rising impatiently.

"Oh, yes. I almost forgot," he said, giggling like a schoolgirl. "All records say that *eins eins zwei* was never built."

"Yes, we know that, *Herr* Bredow," said Marta. Ice dripped from her voice so Ernst reached over and patted her hands, which were busy twisting a knot in the handkerchief she held tightly.

"But there are those that don't believe the records," said Bredow, ignoring the interruption.

"*I* don't believe them," said Ernst, "and I want to know what's going on. Why are there no records of U-112? And why, if so many *heer* records were lost, was Hunt able to find records in just a few hours that said my father was in the *heer*, in Russia? Can the records be wrong?"

"Of course records can be wrong," said Bredow. "The end of the war was a cataclysm and we lost a lot of *Heer* records, although we saved most of the *Kriegsmarine's*. Do you know why *Herr* Hunt told you to see me?"

"He said he was aware that some of their records were incomplete and you might have something that the archives did not," said Ernst.

"All I have is the rumor. I have nothing in writing that the archives don't have because if I find a new document I share it with them." He paused, then continued. "I wanted to hear what you had to say, though, because I have always been suspicious of the story of U-112. There's nothing in writing to substantiate anything I am about to tell you about your father's boat. If you ever find anything concrete about its existence you will be the first. However, here is the story as I understand it."

He paused, as if in thought, then said, "Just a moment." He gently urged the cat to the floor and stood up. "For this, we need some schnapps."

"None for me, please," said Marta, but when he returned with a tray there were four glasses on it. Ernst and Greta immediately took one; Marta hesitated, then did so, too.

Bredow set the tray on the table next to his chair and sat down, the cat immediately rejoining him. He picked up the remaining glass, lifted it in the air, and said, "To the officers and men of U-112, whoever they were, and wherever they may be." The others took a sip, but Bredow downed his. "A good libation for a good story, I always say."

"And the story, *Herr* Bredow?" said Marta. "Why do you know about it and Gunther Hunt does not?"

"First, let me tell you what I know," said Bredow. "Then I will tell you why I know it and *Herr* Hunt does not. The story is that U-112 *was* built and commissioned. Its crew was screened to find only those with no family." Ernst started to say something, but Bredow held his hand up with his palm toward Ernst, and continued. "How your father would have ended up on it I have no idea. I can only tell you the story, which is that it was sent on a secret mission in early 1942, but it was sabotaged by someone on the crew and lost with all hands."

"Sabotaged?" asked Ernst.

"Yes. As to your curiosity about how I know this and *Herr* Hunt does not, I will tell you this. *Herr* Hunt is a bureaucrat. He is trained to believe only what he can see. If the records say *eins eins zwei* was not built, to a bureaucrat, that means *it was not built.*" Bredow slapped his hand down on the arm of the chair, causing Romeo to jump out of his lap. Greta blinked at the sound of his hand hitting the chair.

"I was a sailor on an iron coffin," Bredow continued. Greta looked confused, and he explained, "That is what we called them. We played cat and mouse; first we were the hunter, then we were the hunted. And sometimes the government played cat and mouse with us. They would not tell us things that could have helped save lives."

"Like what?" asked Marta.

"For example, they knew our radar detectors were antiquated," Bredow replied. "But instead of telling us so we would stop using them, they let us think they were fine. They were too proud to admit that sometimes the Allied machinery was better than ours. Thus, a lot of men were lost that should not have been. My own boat, U-288, was sunk while I was on land recuperating from injuries suffered on a previous patrol. No one knows for sure what happened to it." As he said this, he held his hands outward, palms up. "So what happened to U-112? Records could have been changed to spare the government...let's just say, embarrassment."

Greta and Ernst looked at each other, puzzled.

Bredow continued. "After the war I decided to spend all

my disposable time finding out what happened to each boat and letting the families know. People tell me stories. Some stories come from the families. Some come from other crews who knew men in the *unterseeboot* service. The same stories are ignored by *Herr* Hunt because they are not backed up with documents."

"Who told you about *eins eins zwei's* secret mission?" asked Ernst.

"I've talked to so many people over the last twenty-seven years, I don't remember. But I know I've heard it from more than one source. Unfortunately, it is very hard to track down who told what to whom. Maybe it originated with one person who told two people, who told two, and so on, until I heard the story from different sources, but the original person was the same."

"Do you believe U-112 was built, Mr. Bredow?" asked Marta.

"What I *believe* is irrelevant. The pertinent questions are, first, could it have been built? It could have. Second, could it have been sent on a secret mission? It could have. And third, could it have been sabotaged? It would not have been the only one."

"Where was U-112 supposed to have gone?" asked Ernst.

"America."

Ernst and Marta looked at each other. "Really?" asked Ernst dubiously.

"It is not far-fetched," insisted Bredow. "When do you think your father died?"

"He gave me the pipe when he was at home for the last time. It was in December of 1941, when the Japanese attacked Pearl Harbor."

"That's right," said Marta. "We never heard from him again. He must have been killed on his next patrol."

Bredow nodded. "So it was when we were at war with

America. Did you receive his belongings? They usually sent these to the family when boats were lost. A lot of families got a last letter from their beloved after he died."

Ernst shook his head. "I'm not aware of us receiving any of his things." He picked up his glass and finished his drink, then said to Bredow, "All right, let's look at this logically. You've researched the fate of many U-boats. If you were me, where would you look next?"

"America."

Ernst cocked his head and asked, "Why?"

"In January of 1942 Admiral Dönitz began Operation *Paukenschlag*. Records indicate that he sent five Type IXC boats to the East coast of the United States. What if he actually sent six, but something happened to the sixth that was embarrassing to the Nazis? Sabotage would certainly qualify for that. What would they do?"

Ernst paused momentarily, then said, "Lie about it?"

"Exactly. The Nazis were masters of the Great Lie. You say it often enough and people will believe it. You change the records and people begin to believe the new records."

Bredow paused and furrowed his brow, then continued. "You should search the prisoner of war camps in the southern part of the United States. That's where most of the attacks in Operation *Paukenschlag* occurred. If U-112 was sunk by sabotage, the saboteurs most likely planned their escape from the boat. If they succeeded in getting to shore they may have been interned in a POW camp. You should look for anyone who was listed as part of the crew of *eins eins zwei*. Even though the boat never officially existed in Germany, if you find something in America it will have existed there."

"I don't understand," said Ernst. "The boat either existed or it did not." Greta nodded her agreement.

"You're not devious enough," said Bredow. His voice

sounded like a growling dog. He leaned forward and held onto Romeo so he wouldn't be dumped onto the floor. "You must think like a schemer. Remember what you said— if you were in a position of authority in Germany and the sinking of a U-boat would be difficult for you to explain, you would lie. If the Nazis eliminated all records of the boat then it would no longer exist in Germany. But if you find a record of it in the United States you know it existed."

Ernst shook his head. "It seems so far-fetched."

"We don't know what went on behind the scenes," said Bredow. He picked up the binder on the table next to where he sat and held it so that Ernst could see its spine, on which was written, 'U-112'. "I've told you everything I've heard about U-112. That one rumor is all I have in here. I have no crew, no patrols, but now I am going to write in your father's name." He opened the binder, picked up a pen, and started writing. "I hope when you get back from America you can give me some additional names," he said as he finished and set the pen aside. "Now let me give you a few more things to consider."

Ernst leaned forward. "What about?"

"The U-boat high command, the people that were in charge when your father was at sea."

"You speak as if you believe my father truly was a U-boat *kapitän*."

"And why should I not? I'm not *Herr* Hunt, bound by protocols. I'm Horst Bredow, a seeker of the truth. I know that the Nazis lied to the world, so it's not hard to believe that they lied to the families of U-boat crews, or that they lied to you. I know, for example, that on 3 September, 1939, at 19:40 Central European time, when the war had barely started, the *SS Athenia*, an unarmed passenger ship of the United Kingdom, was sunk by U-30, commanded by Fritz-

Julius Lemp. But from 1939 until 1946, the German government covered up that fact."

"Why?"

"128 passengers and civilian crew were killed, 28 of whom were United States citizens. The German government was afraid the United States would use this as a cause célèbre to join the war. Admiral Raeder did not believe that any U-boats were in a position to sink the *Athenia*, but when U-30 returned to base on 27 September, 1939, Lemp told him that he had mistaken it for a vessel of war and sank it."

"What did they do?" Ernst asked.

Greta nodded, turned her gaze from Ernst to Bredow, and asked, "Yes, what?"

"Dönitz ordered Lemp to Berlin where he had to report his mistake to Raeder, who in turn reported it to Hitler. *Der Fuhrër* decided that the incident would be hidden for political reasons. Instead of ordering Lemp punished, Hitler ordered Raeder to cover up the sinking. Lemp had to change the war log of U-30 to delete all mention of the sinking and was sworn to secrecy about it. Hitler then claimed that it was deliberately sunk on orders from Winston Churchill, who hoped to bring the United States into the war. For seven years the Nazis successfully hid German involvement in its sinking which was, by the way, a violation of the *Kriegsmarine's* own rules concerning the sinking of an unarmed ship."

"But the coverup was unsuccessful in the end," said Marta.

"Only because of the Nuremberg trial of 1946. No one outside of the *Kriegsmarine* high command knew what had happened. It only came out because Nazis were charged with war crimes. What if the war had ended with no war crimes prosecution? It would *never* have been discovered. And, this was the first war where the victor prosecuted the defeated, so the Nazis had every reason to believe their mistake would never be discovered."

Ernst shook his head. "OK, it happened one time. So what?"

Bredow smiled smugly. "All right, you want more. On the 20th of June, 1941, *Kapitän* Reinhard Hardigan of U-123 mistook a neutral Portuguese freighter for a British ship. He sank it, but the Portuguese government didn't know who did it and blamed a British submarine that was in the area, which played right into Dönitz's hands. He ordered Hardigan to change his war log to show no sinking on that day. Hardigan, too, was sworn to secrecy. Only after the war, when Hardigan wrote his memoirs, did the true story come out."

"Wouldn't the crew know what they did?"

"No. You've never been on a U-boat. Most of the crew can't see what's going on, so only two or three people know what was sunk and the location of the boat when they sunk it. You threaten to shoot a few people and you get their cooperation."

"How does this relate to my father's situation?"

"Don't you see?" asked Bredow. "If there was misconduct to cover up the records that they had to change would be *Kriegsmarine*, and if someone created false records that said your father was in the *heer* it would have been done by the *Kriegsmarine*. If they did create false records, Hunt would not have found them in the *heer* archives; he would have found them in the *Kriegsmarine* archives. That would explain why he was able to find them so fast."

"But," said Ernst, "why would a *Kriegsmarine* record say my father was in the *heer*?"

Bredow's eyes widened. "*You're right,*" he exclaimed. "If the record says your father was in the *heer*, it *should* have been a *heer* record." His brow furrowed and he rubbed his chin. "Unless they simply made a mistake and forgot that his *heer* record should be in the *heer* archives." Bredow shrugged, then smiled, and said, "Oh, what a tangled web we weave, when first we practice to deceive." He shook his head, and clucked his tongue, emitting a "Tsk, tsk."

Marta's head had been on a swivel during this exchange, looking first at Bredow, then at Ernst. Now she focused on Bredow, nodded, and said, "All right. But what misconduct were they covering up?"

"Remember," said Bredow, raising his palm toward Marta as if to say slow down, "We are presuming they covered something up. We don't know for sure that they did, and probably never will. If not for the Nuremberg trial, we would not have known about the *Athenia*. If not for *Kapitän* Hardigan's memoirs we would not have known about the change in the U-123 log. But the fact that these logs *were* altered shows that the Nazis were willing to change records to cover up incidents. Who knows if other changes were made that never came to light? But if you go to America and find records of crew members of U-112, you will have evidence that records were changed in Germany. And what a story that would be. You could write a book! Be sure to mention me." Bredow laughed.

His guests looked at each other, laughing. The professor said, "Now, I must start our dinner before my wife gets home. May I offer you a final drink before you leave?"

Ernst, trying to process all he had heard, held up his hand to say no, but Marta picked up her glass, drained it, and held it out to Bredow. "Yes, please," she said. "And don't be skimpy."

"Oh, I like this woman," said Bredow, smiling, as he filled Marta's glass.

CHAPTER FORTY-ONE

10 July, 1972
Berlin

Before they left for work, Marta asked Ernst what time Greta got home. Greta now worked as a secretary at the Mercedes plant, a job he'd lined up for her when she moved to Berlin to be closer to him.

"Why do you want to know that?" Ernst asked.

"Just wondering what her schedule was," she told him, hoping she sounded vague. Her intentions were anything but vague, however.

She took the subway and arrived at Greta's flat about half an hour hour after Ernst said she would be there. "I've never met anyone like her," Ernst had told his aunt that morning. *Nor I*, she thought to herself. "She loves people to drop in on her," Ernst continued. "When they do, she always wants to cook supper for them." Marta was certain she wouldn't be staying for a meal.

When Greta opened the door, she had a big smile, as if

Marta had made her day by knocking, but it quickly vanished when she saw who it was.

"Aunt Marta! This is unexpected." A frown formed on her face.

This is one drop-in visit she didn't want, thought Marta. "I think we should talk," she said. "May I come in?" She stepped forward without waiting for Greta's reply.

"Yes, please do." Greta said. As she stepped back to get out of Marta's way, Greta slipped a wad of gum out of her mouth and wrapped it in a tissue she had in her pocket.

Marta had not been to Greta's flat before, and she was struck by how small it was. The furniture looked hand-me-down but it seemed cozy. A single plate sat on the table and the wonderful smell of dinner cooking wafted into the living room. A small black and white television blared out the day's news from a metal stand in the corner, next to a bookshelf filled with books and family pictures.

Marta walked to the shelves and looked at the pictures. One showed a younger Greta with a man and woman Marta presumed to be her parents. Several others had a boy and another girl in them. From the looks of the other children, Greta was the oldest, and she looked different from them, more attractive.

Greta turned off the television. "My family," she said, when she saw Marta looking at the pictures. Coming over next to her, she pointed at the people. "This is my mother and father, and these are my brother and sister. My brother is away at college now, and my sis—"

"May I sit?"

"Of course." Greta gestured toward a chair, but Marta sat on the day bed opposite it. She looked around and wondered how often Ernst visited here. He wasn't home in the evening as frequently as he used to be, and once or twice in the two months since Greta had moved to Berlin he had called to say he wouldn't be home at all.

"Would you like something to drink?" asked Greta politely.

"I want you to know I like you," said Marta. "But I raised Ernst, and I can't let him make what I see as a big mistake."

Greta tentatively sat down on the edge of the chair and leaned forward, as if afraid to get too comfortable. "What mistake?" Greta swallowed hard.

Marta looked at the blank television, then straight into Greta's eyes. "I don't think you are right for him."

Greta spread her hands questioningly. "Isn't that for Ernst to decide? Aunt Mart—"

"I would prefer you to call me Marta. Or *Fräulein* Möller. That would be even better."

Greta folded her arms across her chest and looked away. "I only called you that because I thought we were becoming family."

"I think that's premature and inappropriate."

Greta's eyes focused again on Marta. "If you're worried about losing Ernst to me, you won't. You raised him to be a good man. You will never lose him." She covered her face with her hands.

Marta wasn't about to acknowledge that the younger woman was right. She said, "You're younger than him. Don't you want a man your own age?"

Tears had begun to roll down Greta's cheeks.

"Don't do that," said Marta, looking away. "That's not fair," but the younger woman made no effort to hide them.

"You don't understand," Greta said, holding her head proudly. "I moved here to be near Ernst. I know what I want, and he is it."

"You are beautiful and can have many men. You will find another."

"I don't want another. He is the type man my mother told me to look for."

Marta tilted her head at an angle and said, "Really? "

"Yes, and it's because of the way you raised him."

Marta blinked as if she had been slapped. "Really?" she repeated, in a slightly higher pitch. "He has never treated his girlfriends with the respect they deserve. I know, I've seen his behavior."

"He has told me about that. It is something he struggles with, but he has a great deal of respect for you. That is why I know he is right for me."

Greta stood up and began to pace nervously. After two trips back and forth across the small room, she stopped in front of the bookshelf and picked up one of the pictures. Turning, she showed to Marta the picture of a stern looking woman about her own age. "This is my mother when she was younger," Greta said proudly. "She reminds me of you in many ways. Woe be unto the person that crosses one of her children. But, *fräulein*, I have not, and will not, cross Ernst. I love him."

Marta leaned back on the day bed, and it scooted a little, causing her to jump. Sitting up straight, she said, "I'm afraid he might cross you."

Greta sat down again in the chair, clutching the picture of her mother to her chest, but in a way so that Marta could still see the image. "When I first went out with Ernst, I was afraid of that, too. But he told me not to worry about it. He said he used to be disrespectful to girlfriends but that you had always commanded his respect. For years you asked him not to search for his father, but when you relented, he realized if you could change, he could, too. Not only that, but you told him he needed to change, that he would never find a woman to love him if he treated them so poorly. You have tremendous influence over him, and always will."

"Hmmm," was all Marta could reply. After a moment of thought, however, she said, "Tell me about your mother encouraging you to look for a man like Ernst."

Greta nodded. "When I was a teenager, I tried to fit in with the popular group. I didn't see it at first, but they took advantage of the other teens." Greta stopped talking and swallowed. She looked like she might be sick. "I don't talk about this very often."

Marta leaned forward, put her arms on her knees, and said, "If you would prefer not to talk about this…"

Interrupting, Greta said, "I want you to accept me, to know that I am good for Ernst and he is good for me, so there are things I need to tell you, even though I'm not proud of them." She paused and took a deep breath. "There was this boy I really liked, and he said he liked me, but he didn't." Greta's eyes wandered the room, as if looking for what to say next. "When he got what he wanted, he wouldn't have anything to do with me. Everybody at school knew about it. My mother found out from her friend who was a teacher."

Greta looked straight into Marta's eyes, then continued. "She didn't yell at me, just asked if I was pregnant. When I told her no, she said I could do one of two things. I could let it define me and turn me against all men or I could learn from it. She said I hadn't been very smart in choosing boys, but I could learn from the mistakes when it came time to choose a man."

Greta hugged her mother's picture tighter and seemed to be searching for the right words.

"You don't have to say any more," said Marta.

"*Ja, mache ich.*" Yes, I do. "I want you to know how smart my mother is. And how tough, much like you."

Marta blinked several times and cocked her head to the side, but said nothing.

"She had many problems, and on some days she was not a

good mother. But that day she was the best mother in the world. What she said has guided my thoughts about men ever since. I share it with you now so that you will know I am sincere when I say Ernst is the man I will love for the rest of my life.

She went on: "My mother asked me what I was looking for in a man. She told me, 'Stop thinking about *boys*. What do you want in a *man*?' I told her I wanted to have fun. 'And was what happened fun for you?' she asked me.

"Of course, it wasn't, and I told her so. She said, 'Then you are looking for the wrong things. Again, I say, stop thinking about *boys*. They only want one thing. Think about a man. Look at your father. Do you like the way he treats me?'"

Marta started to say something, but stopped. Greta paused, but when Marta didn't speak, she continued: "I told her I liked very much how my father treated her. He was not your usual German father. He helped her around the house. He kissed her when he came home and when he left. He listened to her opinions. They did things together.

"'That is what you should look for in a man,' she told me. 'I am the luckiest woman alive, because he knows me, and he knows what I went through, and still he loves me.' You see, *Fräulein*, my mother was not always easy to like, let alone love."

Greta stopped and put her face in her hands, as if ashamed at what she had just said about her mother. She sat there for a moment, then raised her head and continued.

"She was…she…she suffered from depression. Sometimes she wouldn't get out of bed for days. Father never pushed her to get up and do things. Sometimes she yelled at him. He never yelled back. Sometimes the house was a mess. He didn't complain, just helped my siblings and me clean it when he got home from work. More often than not, he fixed our supper and breakfast. She loved us, but oh, the demons that raged inside her head. My father saw *her*, not the demons. He loved her in spite of them. And he loved me, in spite of everything."

"You were his daughter," said Marta. "Why would he not love you?"

Greta sat quietly for a moment. When her answer came, the words were slow and measured.

"He was *always* my Papa, even though I was not his daughter." She placed the picture of her mother on the table next to her and sat on the edge of the chair, leaning forward. Her hands were clasped together in front of her so tightly Marta could see the white in her knuckles. Greta looked at her, eyes pleading for Marta to understand.

"So your mother had been married before and he was your stepfather?"

Greta leaned back and looked at the ceiling. A tear ran down her cheek and onto her neck. "No," she finally said. Her voice became hard, as if she were speaking of some vagrant in the street. "I am *Russenkinder.*"

Marta put her hand to her mouth and said, "*Gott im Himmel!* Was your mother in Berlin?"

"*Ja.*" Greta was still looking at the ceiling, but nodded her head slightly.

Marta exhaled loudly and lowered her hand. She watched as Greta picked up her mother's picture, ran her hand over it, then hugged it to her chest. "I am very sorry for your misfortune," Marta said, "but what does this have to do with my Ernst?"

The room became so quiet Marta could hear a clock ticking in another room. Outside, a car horn sounded. She could tell that whatever Greta was going to say would shape their relationship, one way or the other, for years to come.

Finally, Greta said, "I could tell, from the way Ernst

treated you, that you had taught him to respect you. And if he respected you, he would respect me, too, regardless of my background. *Fräulein*, I knew from that moment at the Archives when you told me about the baby named Greta."

Marta sat up straight. She and Greta stared at each other in silence, until finally, in a voice so quiet Marta almost missed it, Greta said, "*Du hast auch dämonen, nicht wahr?*" You have demons, too, don't you?

Marta sat still as a statue, staring at the younger woman. Then, very slowly, Marta nodded her head. Her own voice sounded like someone else's as she said, "*Ja. Ich habe dämonen, auch.*" Yes. I have demons, also.

Marta picked up her purse, stood, and slowly walked to the door. Opening it, she stepped outside and pulled it shut behind her, never looking back. She looked around and even though she saw traffic on the street, a plane flying overhead, and a dog tied to a chain barking at her, she heard nothing. *Ich habe dämonen, auch,* she thought. Leaning back against the door, she stood perfectly still. It took her a minute to remember where she was, and how to get home.

CHAPTER FORTY-TWO

10 May, 1945
Mecklerstrasse, Berlin

Marta hadn't worked in several weeks. A major portion of Siemens' manufacturing work had been moved to other locations beginning as early as 1943, but her clerical job in the main office continued until April 20, when the electronics company bowed to the pressure of the collapsed economy and closed everything in Berlin. No one seemed to notice the irony of it being Hitler's birthday.

The Russians had occupied most of the city since soon after the plant closed and everywhere the German citizens went, they heard reports of violence against the populace, especially against women. So far the brutalities had not found their way to Mecklerstrasse, but each night the residents of the building, Marta and Ernst included, gathered in the cellar to compare notes about what they had heard during the day, and to listen to the dilapidated radio in the corner.

Since her forced sabbatical from work, Marta and Ernst spent most of their time in their top floor flat, making it as weather-tight as they could, which was not an easy task. The roof leaked everywhere and there were gaping holes in a few places. There was no glass in any of the windows and the exterior wall was missing in their kitchen so that, when they ate, people walking by in the street could see them sitting at the table four stories up. They stayed out of the kitchen after dark for fear they would step out into the void, but most days they could get water from a pump in the street, and they wouldn't need heat for several months. In a world of adjusted expectations, they adjusted.

Marta had found the abandoned flat after theirs was destroyed during heavy bombing in March. As always, they had gone to the cellar when the bombing started, which saved their lives; but when they emerged, the building was virtually leveled and their furniture was destroyed. More hurtful to Marta, though, was the loss of the family pictures she had managed to salvage when Marie and her parents were killed almost two years earlier. Marta had left Ernst with a trusted neighbor and travelled to Hamburg to sift through the rubble of their childhood home, managing to recover a few family portraits but precious little else. The destruction of her flat had cost her even those few memories. Her parents and sister were dead, Wilhelm was lost at sea, and Friedrich lay dead in Russia. Now she had no pictures of any of them.

For several months Marta, Ernst, and the rest of the Berlin population had listened to the sounds of war drawing closer to the city, day and night. They couldn't escape the blaring of the air-raid sirens, the planes flying low overhead, the bombs exploding, or the buildings collapsing. Then, a few weeks earlier, they heard the artillery, and finally machine gun and rifle fire. Today, however, there had been an eerie, almost frightening, silence. It continued as the sun set, except for an occasional drunken Ivan in the street.

The previous day a neighbor shared some horse meat with her, not out of the goodness of her heart, but because the meat was old. Horses killed by the fighting did not last long in the street, but this one had not been found right away and was beginning to rot. She and Ernst had eaten it yesterday and Marta was trying to decide if she could salvage any more when she heard someone coming up the back steps. She braced herself, expecting more scavengers or, worse, Russian soldiers, but it was *Herr* Kleist, the baker who lived on the second floor with his wife.

"They have my wife!" he called to Marta through the busted door, a look of terror on his face. "Please, talk to them in Russian."

"My Russian isn't good."

"It's better than mine. Please help us."

She wiped her hands on her dress front, told Ernst to get in the closet in the bedroom and stay there until she returned, then said, "Let's go."

When they got to the Kleist's second floor flat she started in, but he said, "No, we were in the bomb shelter with neighbors." Marta nodded. Everyone had gotten used to going there during the raids, and now it was a communal gathering place.

In the basement Marta and the baker found twenty people, maybe more, standing in a semi-circle. Some lived in the building, but some were homeless and stopped in looking for a place to stay. They were watching two Russians pulling at *Frau* Kleist's underclothes, the soldiers having already removed her outer garments. She kept swinging at the Ivans, but one grabbed her right arm and the other managed to pull her underpants off.

"Stop it! what are you doing?" Marta asked, immediately

challenging them. She dared not touch the soldiers but hoped that confronting them would shame them into leaving.

"What does it look like?" said the more belligerent one. "Your soldiers took our women. Now it is our turn." He said more, but Marta couldn't understand it; he talked too fast. She understood the meaning, though–German women were fair game.

They turned their attention back to *Frau* Kleist and Marta ran up the stairs and into the street. Seeing a Russian officer, she ran to him and said, in broken Russian, "You must come. Your soldiers cause problems."

He waved her away, but Marta insisted. "You must," she said, placing her hand on his forearm. He glared at her as if she had committed an unforgivable sin by touching him; but when she removed her hand, he followed her back to the basement.

The soldiers had *Frau* Kleist on the floor when Marta and the officer entered. The belligerent one was on top of her, his pants to his knees. Her face was turned toward the wall and the other soldier held her arms over her head against the cold, stone floor. The other tenants stared, mesmerized, as if watching a snake charmer; they knew they could do nothing. Their quietly muttered obscenities seemed intended more to express their outrage to *Herr* Kleist than for the Ivans to hear. Meanwhile, *Herr* Kleist clenched and unclenched his fists, and the neighbors restrained him from intervening, an action that would have surely gotten him shot.

"Is this all you were worried about?" the officer asked Marta. "She will not get a disease. Russian soldiers are healthy."

"Stalin said this would not happen," Marta bluffed.

"And yet it does." He looked at Marta and sighed. "All

right," he finally said. "But be assured, I cannot be bothered with this all the time."

Looking at the soldiers, he said, "Release the *kartoffelesser*." The potato eater. The crowd murmured restlessly at the derogatory term the Russians frequently used, and the soldiers argued with the officer in Russian, the Ivan on top *Frau* Kleist never missing a stroke.

"This woman is going to file a complaint," the officer said to them, gesturing toward Marta. "Stop, or you will be shot."

After a moment, the soldier reluctantly stopped. The other released *Frau* Kleist's arms and the soldiers stood up. As they buttoned their pants and followed the officer toward the door, they glared belligerently at Marta.

Frau Kleist rolled onto her side, her back to the crowd, and pulled her legs toward her chest as her husband gathered up her clothes and covered her with them. He touched her shoulder, but she pushed his hand away. "You let them do this to me!" she shouted, the words coming out of her mouth like bullets out of a machine gun.

He walked around her to where she could see him and stood with his arms outstretched. "I tried to stop them." He gestured toward the others. "They held me back. They knew I would have been *shot*."

"So instead, I was raped!"

"So you would rather I be shot, and *then* you raped?"

Frau Kleist waved her arm dismissively, and arranged her clothes to better cover herself. Her husband looked to the others for support, but they were talking among themselves.

"We should go to the commandant and report this," said a woman Marta didn't know.

"What good will it do?" asked another newcomer. "We are at their mercy."

While they argued, Marta watched the officer walk away, then went to where *Frau* Kleist still lay on the floor. Looking around, she found a torn sheet in the corner and draped it over the naked woman, then helped her to her feet, all the while holding the sheet to cover her. When she was standing, Marta said, "Let your husband help you to your flat."

"He should have helped me before," she said, glaring at him.

"He couldn't," said Marta. "But he can now."

Frau Kleist continued grumbling, but when Marta, her arm around the older woman's shoulders, nodded her head toward *Herr* Kleist, he came over and put his arm around her waist, and she let him lead her toward the door.

Marta turned to the others in the cellar. They were milling around, no one having anywhere to go that was any more secure than where they were. The two women were still arguing over whether to report the attack.

"We must make this space more secure," Marta said to several old men who were there, but they turned away from her as if they hadn't heard. Several others had followed the Kleists out the door, so that there were only about ten people left, mostly older people she knew from the building and the two women she had never seen before who, Marta guessed, had nowhere to go.

She needed to check on Ernst, so she walked to the door and slowly opened it, looking around for more Russians.

Too late, she saw the same two lurking nearby. They exploded through the half-open door, with more charging in behind them.

The two who had attacked *Frau* Kleist held Marta's arms while the others tore at her clothing. She screamed as loud as she could, hoping the officer would hear her and return, but one of the Ivans hit her in the face and told her to shut up. His blow caught her on the side of her cheek and the corner of her mouth, and she tasted salty blood.

In seconds she was naked. She felt hands grabbing at her

body everywhere. The assault was almost like a choreo-graphed dance, down to the last grab. One soldier entwined his hand in her hair and propelled her forward, shoving her in the direction of an old, beat up, easy chair someone had brought down from their apartment. She tried to brace her feet on the floor but another put his hands between her legs from behind and lifted her as a third soldier, a new arrival pushed her upper body down over the arm of the chair. The one holding her hair pushed down hard on her head, planting her nose firmly against the seat cushion. Marta smelled the stench of all the bodies that had sat in it. She struggled to stand but a hand between her shoulder blades kept her bent over the chair arm.

"I can't breathe," she mumbled. The hand in her hair turned her head to the side. Her mouth dropped blood on the chair where it dragged across the seat, and she stared into the mocking face of the belligerent one as she felt hands pull her resisting legs apart. She heard a belt being loosened and felt hands grabbing her hips, pulling her back as the invisible invader shoved forward. It felt like a knife when he entered her, and she cried out in pain. The Ivan holding her hair laughed at her, his foul breath filling her nostrils.

"This will teach you not to complain about us," he said. "Now learn your lesson."

The first soldier finished and was replaced with another, then another, even as still more Russians arrived. Soon, they had all raped her, and when some of them got in line again, she feared it would never end. She actually hoped some of the soldiers would tire of waiting and turn their attention to the other women, but they were there to punish her, and for over an hour they did.

There were ten other Germans in the cellar, only a few she knew from living in the building. She heard them talking quietly. Every now and then one of the soldiers would tell them to shut up or they could take Marta's place, but the Russians had no intention of letting up on her.

She feared they would kill her, and at one point even hoped they would, rather than what they did, but then she remembered Ernst. What would happen to him if she were dead? Even if they left her alive, what was she going to tell him happened to her when he saw her body all bruised and battered?

When she thought it couldn't get any worse first one, then a second, took her like she was a man. She tried to fight them off but others immediately pushed her down again. She had never before experienced that, and the Ivans laughed at the way she squirmed, trying to get away. "Like a butterfly pinned to a display board," said one.

"Anybody else?" the belligerent one yelled when he finished his second turn, but there were no takers. Her ordeal was finally over. The hands released her and she tried to push herself up, but was too weak. Two soldiers grabbed her arms. She thought they were going to help her but instead they lifted her and, turning to face the others, displayed her to them as if she were a trophy. The Ivan who taunted her pointed at Marta and said, "This is what we do to troublemakers," all the while looking around the room at the others. He turned to Marta and said, "We'll be back."

***

Ernst had fallen asleep on the floor of the closet shortly after his aunt had told him to stay there, but he awoke as he heard the door open. He walked into the living room and immediately cried, "Aunt Marta! What happened?"

She looked like she had fallen off her bike. Her mouth was a bloody mess with streaks of dried blood on her chin and her lip puffed out on one side. Her hair, which she usually kept combed, was tangled as if someone had run an eggbeater through it. She held her torn clothes around her body.

"Ernst, honey," she said through her split lip, "I got beat up." She sat down very slowly and grimaced when she did.

"Who beat you up?" he asked. "I'll get a gun and shoot that bad person." Ernst started toward the door, not even realizing he had no gun to shoot anyone with, nor any idea who to shoot.

"Honey," she said, "things are different. We don't have to hide from the planes anymore, but we have to be careful of the Russians. Some of them are mean. Some of them do bad things."

"I won't let them do bad things to you. You need to stay with me."

Marta smiled in spite of everything. "You are my hero," she said, "but you must be careful who you say things to. I don't want you to talk to the Russians. You know what their uniforms look like, don't you?"

Ernst nodded. "But I think we should get a gun and shoot them if they hurt you." Ernst held his hands like he had a rifle and yelled, "Pow!"

"We can't do that," said Marta, smoothing his hair, "even if it would be fun to do. Now, will you get a wash cloth and get some water from the pump so I can clean up?"

While Ernst ran down to the well, Marta looked at the calendar and counted the days from her last period.

CHAPTER FORTY-THREE

15 May, 1945
Mecklerstrasse, Berlin

The two Ivans arrived shortly after dark. They shoved the door open and were standing in her flat before she could react. Marta recognized them from the gang rape of five days previous. They brought along a new one who walked with a noticeable limp. When Marta saw them, she felt like she would throw up.

"Ernst, you go to the cellar and don't come back until I get you," she said, as her hand in the middle of his back propelled him toward the door. Before Ernst got there, though, one of the Ivans grabbed him.

"He should watch," the soldier said. "Let him see how real men handle a woman."

Marta picked up a butcher knife lying on the table and said, "If you let him go downstairs I will do whatever you want. If you keep him here I will kill myself before you can do anything." She was bluffing; she would never leave Ernst to fend for himself, but the Ivans didn't know that. Ernst looked at her quizzically; he had never heard her speak Russian before.

The soldiers argued amongst themselves for a moment, then the belligerent one waved his arm at Ernst and yelled, "*Gehen!*" Go.

Ernst yelled, "*Nein!*" and moved between his aunt and the soldiers. Before the Ivans could respond Marta grabbed him, placed herself between him and the soldiers and spoke soothingly to him. "Ernst, these are my friends. I want to talk to them and I need you to go to the cellar."

He looked at her dubiously.

"I know I told you not to trust Russian soldiers, but these are my friends."

Ernst looked at the knife in her hand. Her eyes followed his to her hand. She laughed and said, "We play the silliest games, don't we?" as she set the knife down. "Please," she said to him.

He walked slowly toward the door, then stopped and turned around, cheerfully saying, "I can play a silly game, too."

"No," she said, smiling at him despite the sick knot in her stomach. "This is a grown up game. Now go; I will come get you when we are finished." She must have sounded sufficiently convincing because he turned and walked out. When he left, she closed the door and put a chair against it since the lock was broken. Without looking at the soldiers, she walked toward the bedroom, unbuttoning her dress. The three soldiers followed, dropping their uniforms along the way.

She was true to her word and did everything they wanted. *At least there are only three*, she told herself over and over. She was still sore from five days earlier, but besides the physical pain, the one that walked with a limp kept saying horrible things in her ear about the beautiful *Russenkinder* he would leave her with. He moved on her so long that finally the other two told him to finish. At least they had quick triggers.

When they were finished with her, she curled into a ball on the bed, pulled a blanket over her nakedness, and cried, trying not to think about what she had just done for Ernst's sake. She heard them rummaging in the kitchen and hoped they found the horse meat she was going to throw out; it was becoming rancid. Let them eat that—maybe it would kill them.

When they left, she stumbled to the bathroom, and washed herself as gently as she could, looked to see if there was blood on the wash cloth, then brushed her teeth. Her lip, busted in the previous assault, was split open again. When she had done all she could, she broke down and cried again. *I must get more water from the well*, she thought, picking up the bucket. On her way there, she stopped in the cellar to get Ernst.

CHAPTER FORTY-FOUR

16 May, 1945
Mecklerstrasse, Berlin

"I can't take this anymore," Marta said. She and *Frau* Kleist were in Marta's flat, Marta recounting what the men did to her the night before. "On top of it all, one of them tore my last underpants. I told him I would take them off. Now what can I wear?"

The women looked at each other, both of them surprised at how offended they were at the shredding of her pants, considering the other brutalities the Ivans had inflicted on her. Some women killed themselves, but others discovered that a dark humor helped them survive. Marta and the *Frau* were survivors.

She had gotten to know the Kleists soon after she and Ernst started living in the building. Their only child had died in the epic tank battle at Kursk–the only family detail they had shared. Marta called them '*Herr*' and '*Frau*'; they called her *Fräulein*. In a world where privacy seldom existed, it was a nod in that direction. Marta found it comforting to have this woman to talk to, even if the Kleists were old enough to be her parents.

Frau Kleist looked around to make sure Ernst didn't hear her. "My last one told me that I was tighter than Ukraine women. I think he was an officer. So polite. Not at all rough."

"The ones that come for me are. They didn't beat me this time, but only because I agreed to cooperate if they let Ernst leave. I have to put a stop to it."

"Kill them." The *Frau's* voice was hard.

Marta shook her head. "And get shot? No."

"Go somewhere else. There's nothing holding you here."

"That won't work," said Marta. "They are still mad at me for what I did when they attacked you, for what little good it did us. They will track me down. And we can't leave the city without permission of the Russian command, which hasn't given it to anyone."

"Stand up," said *Frau* Kleist. "I have an idea."

Marta stood and the baker's wife looked her up and down like she was for sale.

"Well?" Marta finally asked, feeling a blush coming to her cheek.

"You're young. What are you, thirty-five, thirty-six?"

Marta gasped. "I'm twenty-two. Do I look that old?"

Frau Kleist shrugged. "None of us look young after what we've been through. But you're pretty, even for thirty-five."

"What is your idea?" Marta asked.

"Some of the women have a 'lone wolf' to protect them."

"What do you mean?" Marta sat down.

"You find an officer, the higher the rank, the better. You feed him, mend his uniform, give him whatever he wants. He protects you from the enlisted men. You only have to fuck one Ivan."

Marta looked at *Frau* Kleist and wondered what had

happened to them. A week earlier the most personal thing they would have told each other was what they had for dinner. That was before the Russians. What *Frau* Kleist was describing was almost prostitution, and Marta was considering it.

"Wait a minute," said *Frau* Kleist, holding up her hand as if to interrupt Marta's thoughts. "I have a better idea. *Herr* Kleist and I used to live in this flat several years ago. We moved downstairs because I didn't like climbing all the steps, and two older sisters moved in until the shelling started. There was an attic that had access in the ceiling of the closet in the bedroom. *Herr* Kleist and I stored old clothes up there. Come," she said, standing up. "Let's look."

They went into the bedroom and opened the closet door. Looking up, the women saw a trap door in the ceiling.

"I remember the space up there was at least six feet high," said the *Frau*. "If we had a ladder, we could climb up there when we heard the Russians, pull the ladder up behind us, and put the wood panel back in place. In the dark they will never see the opening, or if they do, they won't think we had any way to get up there. And if they do think we're up there, they'll have to find a way to come get us. The Ivans are lazy; they won't want to work that hard. They'll leave and find someone else."

"But how do I get a ladder?" Without one, the attic was useless.

Frau Kleist grinned. "The wall is missing in your kitchen. We can have my husband get some wood out of the rubble. Anyone seeing him will think he is just starting the clean up. He can pull the wood into the bedroom and build a ladder out of sight. If the soldiers come around before it's finished he can hide it under the bed. All you have to do is let us hide with you in the evening when the soldiers get drunk and come around. They never come inside during the day. When they can't find us they'll think we drowned ourselves in one of the lakes. A lot of women they raped did that, you know."

Marta knew, but that was not an option for her. Her desire to live was too strong and, besides, she had Ernst to consider.

Herr Kleist started working on the ladder that same day. With no interruptions, by dusk he had a ladder tall enough to reach the opening in the ceiling. It was rough, but serviceable.

"Come on, Ernst," she told him that evening as she and the Kleists prepared to climb to their hiding place. "An adventure awaits!" she said, hoping he would see this as fun.

The four of them had barely pulled the ladder into the attic when they heard someone rummaging through the flat. They quietly lowered the hatch cover into place so that the opening would not be seen. Marta looked at Ernst and put her finger to her lips. "Quiet," she mouthed to him.

When the soldiers were gone, *Frau* Kleist said, "Tonight we have to lean against these boxes, but tomorrow we will arrange blankets to sleep on."

"It's like camping," said Ernst happily.

"Yes," said Marta. "Didn't I tell you it would be fun?" She hugged Ernst and kissed him on the top of his head. "Look," she said, holding up a bucket. "We even have a toilet," drawing a laugh from everyone.

When the Ivans came back the next night, Ernst and the three adults were already settled in. After a week, the soldiers gave up.

Except for one.

CHAPTER FORTY-FIVE

Berlin
    12 July, 1972

The sun was shining brightly in the late afternoon as Marta got home from work. She had called in sick the day before with a migraine the likes of which she hadn't had since she was young, and the time spent alone gave her the opportunity to sort through her life, something she had refused to do since the war. Greta, however, had confronted her about her demons, as Greta called them, in a way that was gentle, yet indomitable. For years she had tried to block all memories from the time of the Russian occupation but two days ago, when Greta had told her that her mother had been raped by the Russians and she suspected that Marta had, too, they all came flooding back to her.

Maybe I'm getting better, she thought; she got over the headache in a day. In the past, when Ernst would ask her about some awful memory he had that conflicted with what she had told him happened, she would take to the bed for days, sometimes a week, as the reality of what had happened overwhelmed her. She would sleep day and night until she succeeded in shoving the memory to the recesses of her mind.

It was like the time Ernst asked about his mother's death. It was when he saw the Berlin Wall being built. He had returned home and told her about seeing a man shot and a woman beaten. As they talked, Ernst asked about his mother's death. Marta had managed to keep her composure with the help of a few beers as she told him for the first time of the death of her sister and parents. But then, out of the blue, he had asked if he was correct in remembering soldiers coming to their flat. So many times Marta had told him that she had some police friends who would come by in their uniforms, and she thought he had believed her. But then he asked about the soldiers, and she had spent the next three days in bed.

What Greta said about her mother's demons stunned Marta at first, and she thought about it all night. *And I wonder why I had a migraine*, she thought, but she also smiled. The conversation released something inside of her, and when the migraine left, so too did the knot in her stomach.

If Greta's mother had not been raped, Greta would not be here today to fill Ernst's life with love, she thought. She never thought something good could come out of something so horrible, but Ernst was happy, something she had wanted since he had been born. It was time for her to live her life, and she was prepared to accept Greta as part of Ernst's life.

I'm ready to accept Greta as part of my life, too, she thought, and what an uplifting feeling that was. Her family would grow, and maybe there would be babies. She wondered if Ernst knew that Greta's father was an unknown Russian solder. *Who cares?* She thought. *Ernst wouldn't.*

As she set the table for supper, she heard Ernst coming

down the hallway. From his animated conversation she knew Greta was with him. Normally Marta could hear Greta's laugh as soon as they came out of the stairway, but today it was Ernst's she heard. Their flat had never been one for raucous laughter, nor even idle banter. It wasn't like her own home growing up, where she and her father were constantly joking. And the teasing they did! Especially of Marie and their mother, the two serious souls in the family.

Where had that fun gone? She wondered, then realized that Greta had given her the answer. The demons had stolen it. *Well,* she thought, *it's time for an exorcism.*

The door flew open and in they came, arms intertwined. As soon as Greta saw Marta, though, she let go of Ernst.

"Great news," said Ernst to his aunt. "I've got two plane tickets to America. You and I will be leaving in two weeks."

"Me and you?" Marta asked.

"Yes," he said. "You'll go with me, won't you?"

Marta looked at Greta. She didn't appear to be disappointed, more resigned to what she thought was inevitable. *I can fix that,* Marta thought, then said to Ernst, "Not this time."

Ernst looked surprised.

Marta took a deep breath, as if she was breathing in fun. She felt happier than she had since she and Friedrich had gotten engaged because of what she was about to do. "I think you should take someone else," she said, still watching Greta. Marta saw Greta's eyes grow wide as she covered her mouth with her hands. She seemed to read Marta's mind.

"Who?" Ernst asked.

Bless his clueless heart, Marta thought, and smiled. "I think you should take…" She paused, then, imitating Greta's actions the first time they met her at the Archives, closed one eye and pointed at Greta like she was pointing a gun. "Greta."

Greta bounced on the balls of her feet like she had to go

to the bathroom and patted her cheeks with her hands. She said, "Oh, *Fräulein* Möller, that is so nice of you, but I could never take your place."

"Don't worry, child. You are *not* taking my place, you're making your own. And *Fräulein* Möller is way too formal. I think you should call me Marta. Or Aunt Marta. Would that be OK with you?"

Ernst looked back and forth at the verbal tennis match being played between his aunt and his girlfriend, but all their attention was focused on each other.

"Oh, Aunt Marta!" Greta said, and rushed to her, throwing her arms around Marta's waist. "*Dankeschön!*"

"Whoa," said Marta. "I'm not a big hugger." Her arms were suspended in the air, as if she didn't know what to do with them. Marta looked to Ernst for help, but he just shrugged. Greta continued to hug her, and gradually Marta brought her arms around the young woman to return the hug, albeit not quite as enthusiastically. She patted Greta's back and when she realized Greta was crying, her hands settled there and she said, "It's OK, it's OK".

She looked at Ernst, who was standing to the side, his head shaking slightly, his lips forming the word, "What?" over and over, but no sound coming out.

"Ernst," said Marta, "don't stand there looking confused. Set another place at the table."

Ernst's eyes widened, and he hurried into the kitchen to get another plate, but instead of gathering up a place setting, Marta saw him peek around the corner at Greta and her. She pretended she didn't see him looking and kissed the top of Greta's head, just as she had done to Ernst so many times in his childhood; just as she had done with a hungry baby that she couldn't save. Greta sobbed loudly. "My Greta, my Greta," Marta said, and began to rock her back and forth, holding her tighter and tighter.

"We are family now, my Greta," she told the young woman. "We are all family." Soon, she, too, was sobbing, her shoulders heaving and her head shaking. She couldn't remember the last time she had cried so hard but she knew what she was crying for; her lost baby, her lost family, but also for all the lost years. All those years when she had forgotten what her sister Marie had told her the night she asked her to raise Ernst. *It's like every morning you get up and say, 'Let the fun begin,'* She remembered Marie saying to her. *I hope you do that every day for the rest of your life.*

But Marta hadn't. She hadn't done it since the day the Russians pushed her over the arm of a chair and raped her. Then the baby, *her* Greta, the daughter she loved in spite of having been conceived in hate, had died. When Ernst had caught one of the Ivans in the midst of his foul deed, she... well, for years *that* memory consumed her, controlling where they lived, what she said. Marta had to go on living for Ernst's sake, to cleanse his memory of the horror, but she had lived all these years without laughter.

She rocked Greta from side to side as she cried over her baby, her family, Friedrich, all lost. She knew, however, that this was the last time she would cry for them, that when she stopped and her tears dried, her life would begin anew. She could see the rebirth of her happiness with Ernst and Greta. She leaned down and whispered in Greta's ear, "*Lassen sie den spass beginnen, meine Greta.*" Let the fun begin, my Greta.

And she smiled through her tears.

CHAPTER FORTY-SIX

1 August, 1972
   Fort Benning, Ga. U.S.A.

"Have you ever noticed how all military bases look alike?" asked Ernst, as he and Greta drove toward the main gate into Fort Benning. "Not just in the United States, but those in Germany, too." He downshifted and brought their rental car to a stop at the entrance gate.

"I guess I hadn't noticed," said Greta, looking around for similarities.

"For starters, they all have these gates with a little building where the guards can hang out. And all the buildings look alike, especially the barracks."

The guard barely glanced up before waving them through, but Ernst stopped and summoned the guard toward him by waving his hand.

"And none of them want to do anything," he said quietly to Greta. Ernst's window was rolled down, so when the guard asked what he needed, Ernst told him in broken

English the purpose of their visit. The guard nodded and gave them a map of the base with the building containing POW records circled.

"Have a nice visit," he said, touching his hand to his helmet in a modified salute that soldiers reserve for civilians. "I hope your search is successful."

"You're getting really good at English," Greta said as they pulled away.

"I should be. This is, what? The twelfth base we've been to since we got here? I thought sure we'd find something at that camp in Arizona. That's where a lot of *Kriegsmarine* POWs went. I'm glad we were able to fly there. That would have been a long drive for nothing."

"I think we were smart to come back east. That's where Professor Bredow said to look."

"Yes, but if we don't find anything here, I may go home empty-handed. I have to be back to work on Monday." Ernst smacked the steering wheel with the heel of his right hand. *Did I really think I would find something?* He thought. *What were the odds?*

"I don't think you should give up," said Greta, flinching at the hand slap. "Today is only Tuesday. We can get to some of the bases in Florida tomorrow if we don't find anything here, and still have plenty of time. Our flight home isn't until Saturday afternoon. Besides, I think this is where you find something."

"You've said that at every base," he said. They drove past a building marked, "Education Center," then pulled into a parking space at the next building. It had a sign over the door that said, "Base Command."

"I know, but I think this is where it happens. Don't forget to lock your door," she said as she got out of the car. She fanned herself with her hand. "Gee, it's hot."

They walked inside and approached a desk marked

"Information." "How can I help you?" asked the African-American man behind the counter. The stripes on his sleeves indicated he was a sergeant. His pleasant smile gave Ernst hope.

"*Bitte.*" Please. "*Mein* English is not *gut*," said Ernst. Greta stood next to him smiling her best smile, dimples bobbing.

"*Das ist kein problem*," said the sergeant. That is not a problem. He continued in German, "I'm Sergeant Johnson. I just spent a year in your country. We can speak in your language."

"*Danke*," said Ernst. Greta smiled.

"I bet you're here looking for a relative who was our guest during World War II," the sergeant said. He put his forearms on the waist high counter and leaned forward, looking from one to the other.

"*Ja*," said Ernst. "My name is Ernst Möller." Gesturing toward Greta, he said, "This is Greta Sachse. I am looking for information on my father. He may have been a prisoner of war during World War II."

"All right, sir. What was his name and what unit was he with?"

Ernst repeated his story for what seemed the hundredth time since they had arrived in the United States.

"He was rescued off a U-Boat?" said the sergeant when Ernst finished. "That didn't happen very often."

"I don't know if he was rescued, but I've been told that you had prisoners of war here. I am looking for records of *anyone* from U-112 who may have been a prisoner here. I've been to many bases but have not found anything yet, and I must return home soon."

The sergeant led them to the now familiar microfilm machine and showed him the records they had. "Here's the army, its units…"

"No, he was in the *Kriegsmarine*."

"Yes, sir, I understand. I'm just showing you how it is divided up."

"Where is the *Kriegsmarine?*"

"Be patient," said Greta, patting Ernst's forearm. "I bet he can help you."

The sergeant smiled at her, then said, "Wait one. We didn't have too many sailors here, so I don't access those records often." He turned and walked out.

After about five minutes, Ernst rubbed his head and said, "Where did he go? It's taking too long." He started toward the door the sergeant had used to leave, but Greta grabbed his arm and pulled him back.

"He probably slipped out the back door and we won't ever see him again," Greta said, her eyes dancing. "Or maybe," she lowered her voice to a tone she hoped sounded ominous, "he was murdered when he left here."

Ernst frowned, and she said, "What's the matter, *schätzchen?* I've never seen you this nervous before. I'm only teasing."

"I'm beginning to fear I'll never find anything. I can't bear coming all this way to leave empty-handed." As Ernst spoke the sergeant came around the corner with a box of microfilm.

"The *Kriegsmarine,*" he said, as if he had put the records together himself. Pulling one of the slips out of the box, he slid it on the viewer. "This is the index," he said. "You can search by name, hometown, rank, ship, or boat. If you find what you want it will tell you the number of the sheet that the information is on. Then you put that sheet on the viewer to find what you want."

Johnson took a few more minutes to familiarize Ernst with the records, the whole time Ernst saying, "I know how it works. I've used these before."

"*Schätzchen*," said Greta, patting his arm, "let him finish." Finally, Johnson left.

Ernst went quickly through the index until he found 'U'. He was reviewing the numbers when Greta noticed something she hadn't seen before.

"The U-boat numbers," she said. "They're in numerical order, but they don't follow chronologically. Weren't they numbered in the order they were built?"

"Professor Bredow explained that."

"I don't remember him talking about that."

Without looking away from the microfilm, he said, "It must have been when you went to the bathroom. Or maybe you were talking." She poked him in the ribs, and he grinned, then continued. "Germany wanted to make other countries think we had more U-boats than we did, so they weren't sequentially numbered. That way, if U-550, for example, pulled into port somewhere, spies would think we must have at least 550 boats, but we might have skipped a bunch of num—*Gott im Himmel*, Greta! Here it is!"

"Where, where?" she squealed.

"Here. The index says prisoner 114172, from U-112 is on sheet twelve."

Ernst's fingers were shaking and he fought to control them as he looked for sheet twelve. Loading it into the reader, he searched for the prisoner number. Sergeant Johnson may have been right about there not being many sailors, but he only needed one, if it was the right one.

And there he was. Prisoner 114172 from U-112. The euphoria Ernst felt was short-lived, though.

"Is it your father? Who is it?" asked Greta, bouncing on the balls of her feet.

"His name was Erich Tolle." His voice sounded like air escaping from a balloon.

Ernst sat there looking at the microfilm for five minutes

or more, as if his continuing to stare would make 'Erich Tolle' miraculously become 'Wilhelm Seligman'. He hit his fist on the counter, then went back to the index and looked again, first under U-112, then meticulously down each row and column to see if there were any other entries for U-112. He searched for Dresden. He examined any similar number, such as 122, 113, 121. He looked for the name, 'Seligman.' In desperation, he even looked for 'Möller.' Nothing. His elation at finding evidence of the existence of the boat was dashed by his failure to find his father's name.

"Who was Erich Tolle?" Greta asked.

He slowly shook his head as his mind searched for an idea that would unlock the mystery of U-112. "I've never heard of him. The record says he was a Radioman. He survived, but where is he now?"

They walked to the front of the office, where Johnson was talking to another soldier. When he turned and saw them standing to the side, however, Johnson nodded, switched to German, and said, "I'll only be a minute."

When he finished talking to the other soldier, he turned to Ernst and Greta and said, "My German friends. Did you find your father?"

"No, but I found a crew member."

"So you've got a track to follow." Johnson sounded more positive about the process than Ernst, but Greta nodded and bounced a little.

"I told him that," she said.

"Yes, I have a track," said Ernst. "This *is* the first time I've ever found any record of anyone from U-112. The German Archives told me it wasn't built. This proves it was."

"Any other proof?"

"Just this," Ernst said, and pulled out his bosun's pipe. "My father gave this to me in 1941. He was home for Christmas, but he couldn't stay so he gave it to me early. It was the last time I saw him." He turned it so the sergeant could see the engraved 'U-112'.

Johnson looked at it, then put his hand on Ernst's shoulder. "It must be very special to you."

"*Ja.* For the last four months I have been chasing a ghost. People at the German archives said the boat didn't exist; that my father didn't exist, or if he did, that he was executed for war crimes in Russia. I don't believe them." He looked at Greta, who had a contrite expression on her face, as if the Archives not having a record was her fault. "My father was a sailor, a *kapitän.* I want to know what happened to him."

Using his hand on Ernst's shoulder to guide him toward the door, Johnson glanced back to make sure Greta was coming along, and said, "I just got off duty. Let me buy you two a cup of coffee."

Ernst was about to decline the offer when he heard Greta say, "*Dankeschön.*" He turned to look at her, but she conspicuously refused to make eye contact.

After they went through the drink line at the cafeteria and Johnson got coffees for all of them, they sat at a table and Johnson said, "Tell me about yourself, Ernst."

"How far back do you want to go?"

"Start with when your father gave you the bosun's pipe."

Ernst told his story. Occasionally he would use a German word that he'd have to explain to Johnson, but mostly the soldier just listened as Ernst described growing up in Berlin with his aunt. He told the sergeant about his job at Mercedes auto works and his interest in politics. When Ernst started telling about the trip to the Archives, Greta chimed in.

"That's where we met," she said, grinning widely. "I told *Herr* Hunt to talk to them. He isn't easy to get along with." She leaned toward Johnson, lowered her voice, and said, "He's constipated, you know."

Ernst, sitting next to her, did a double take and looked at her sternly.

Johnson's eyes widened. "No, I didn't know that," he said, laughing and looking down at his now empty coffee cup.

"Well, he is," she said. "I think that's why he's so grumpy."

"So why did you decide to check our records?" asked Johnson, still chuckling.

Ernst told the Sergeant about Professor Bredow and his work uncovering the truth behind the fate of lost U-boats.

"It was his suggestion I come here," said Ernst. "He said the Archives could only report what the Nazi records showed, but he said maybe someone changed U-112's records. It looks like that's what happened." Greta nodded.

"Why would they do that?"

Ernst shrugged. "Professor Bredow says we may never know, but he told me about two other times when they did it to cover up something that would have embarrassed the Nazis."

Johnson raised his eyebrows and said, "Man, I wish you could find this guy, Tolle. He could absolutely confirm that your father's boat existed."

"I know," said Ernst, "but *how* can I find him?"

"I've only been here a month. Let me talk to some of the more experienced men. See if they know anything. You go have some supper. How can I reach you?"

"We're staying at the Travel Inn." He gave Johnson his room number, then said, "But please hurry. I must return to Germany soon. I build cars."

"And we have a wedding to plan," said Greta, beaming.

Johnson looked at Ernst, then Greta, and smiled.

"Congratulations, to you both," he said. He looked at Ernst and said, "You old sea dog," as if he had known him all his life.

The phone was ringing as Ernst and Greta returned from dinner. Ernst hurried to pick it up and immediately recognized Sergeant Johnson's German, spoken in a soft, southern drawl. Greta stood next to him, bouncing on the balls of her feet and hoping.

"Can you come over here right now?" Johnson asked. "I have someone I want you to meet."

"Erich Tolle?" asked Ernst excitedly. Greta's eyes widened.

"No, it wasn't that easy. But someone who has information about how to find him. The office is closed now. Let's meet in the cafeteria where we had coffee."

Ernst felt his throat go dry. Despite Greta's optimism, he was afraid that something would go wrong.

"I don't think he'd tell you to hurry back if he wanted to tell you Erich Tolle was dead, or anything like that," said Greta. "I think we're going to get good news."

They drove their rental car back to the base and parked near the cafeteria. Walking in, they looked around. It was much more crowded than when they and Johnson were there earlier, but near the back, at a table on the left, Ernst saw Sergeant Johnson waving at them. He was with another man whose back was to them. Greta bounced up and down, waving her hand and smiling.

As they approached, Johnson stood up and the other man looked over his shoulder. He, too, had a sergeant's patch on his sleeve and when he saw Greta he stood up.

"Ernst, Greta," said Johnson, "I want you to meet Sergeant Thomas. Steve, this is Ernst and Greta."

Steve Thomas held his hand out to Ernst. He had a firm grip and, although not as tall as Johnson, still towered over the German couple. He nodded to Greta, who flashed her dimples and nodded back. She was practically shaking from excitement.

"Sergeant Thomas has worked here for a year and a half," said Johnson. "He has a story I thought you'd be interested in hearing. Want some coffee?"

"Water, please," said Ernst.

"Beer," said Greta.

"My kind of woman," said Johnson, pointing at her. "You sit down here and talk to Steve and I'll get one beer and one water. By the way, he speaks German, too. Not as good as me, but he's looking forward to practicing it again."

"Yeah, yeah," said Sergeant Thomas, waving his hand dismissively at his fellow soldier.

Ernst and Greta sat down, eyes focused on the man across the table from them.

"I understand you are looking for Erich Tolle," said Thomas.

"*Ja.* I think he served with my father. Do you know him? Is he alive?"

"I've met him. Mysterious guy."

Greta graced Johnson with her dimpled smile as he came back and handed her a beer. "*Dankeschön,*" she said.

"*Danke,*" said Ernst, taking a glass of water as Johnson sat down next to Thomas. Ernst took a long drink, wishing he had gotten beer, too. That would have calmed his racing heart. "Why do you say, 'mysterious?'"

"Because he knows something, but he won't discuss it with just anybody. I think he will talk to you, though."

"Why?"

"Let me give you a little background. I had only been here about a month when this fella with a German accent came in to the office one day. Said he knew our staff rotated in and out so he had been coming by about once a year. He wanted to keep everyone posted."

"About what?"

"About him. Wouldn't say anything about himself other than he was known as Erich Tolle. Said if anyone ever came looking for information on U-112 that I should put them in touch with him. Wouldn't tell me why, wouldn't tell me who might be interested."

"Where is he? I must see him."

"He's in Atlanta. From what I understand you're the first to ever come looking for him. I'll give you the address. What's the story?"

"My father was the *kapitän* of U-112, but I can find no record of the boat, or him. German Archives tells me she was never built, but Horst Bredow says maybe she was." Ernst explained to Thomas about Bredow, about his search, and the tangled webs into which it had taken him.

When Ernst finished relating all he had been through the four of them sat in silence for a minute, then Thomas said, "Very interesting. A boat that was never built, a father you can't find, and a man who claims to know what happened. You need to get up to Atlanta."

"*Ja, ja!*" said Ernst. "But first, I must call my aunt in Germany."

"Yes, Aunt Marta," said Greta. Turning to the soldiers, she said, "Aunt Marta raised Ernst."

Thomas slid a piece of paper across the table to Ernst and said, "Tolle gave me this." Ernst looked at it and read, "7177 Mulberry Street, Atlanta Georgia." The sevens all had a line across them, as a European person would write them. There was also a phone number.

"*Ja, das ist gut,*" said Ernst, standing. He smiled broadly, held out his hand to Thomas, and said, "*Dankeschön.*"

They shook hands, and Greta, unable to contain herself, went around the table and hugged first Thomas, then Johnson, who looked very uncomfortable and held his arms out so they would not touch her body.

"Is something wrong?" asked Ernst.

"Yeah. I'm black, and she's white, and this *is* the south," said Johnson awkwardly.

"I don't understand," said Ernst, puzzled.

"Yeah," said Johnson. "Neither do I, but me hugging a white woman could cause big problems."

"Ah, discrimination," said Ernst knowingly.

"Yeah," said Johnson.

Ernst smiled mischievously and asked, "Can a black man get in trouble for hugging a white man?"

Thomas looked from Johnson, to Greta, to Ernst. "I don't think so," he replied.

Ernst walked around the table and hugged first Johnson, then Thomas, repeating, "*Dankeschön, Dankeschön.*"

"Let me know what you find out from the mysterious *Herr* Tolle," said Thomas.

"I'd like to know, too," said Johnson, clapping Ernst on the back.

Greta wasn't happy that she couldn't hug these helpful Americans, stuck out her lower lip like a pouting child, then put her hands together in front of her, as if in prayer, and bowed deeply to Johnson in the manner of the Japanese. Johnson was obviously surprised, but returned the bow. When she straightened, she took Ernst's hand and they walked outside into the late evening sunset, both of them nodding to and smiling at everyone they met, and saying, "*Dankeschön.*"

CHAPTER FORTY-SEVEN

Early afternoon of 3 August, 1972
    Atlanta, Ga. U.S.A. Home of Erich Tolle

"I'm so excited," said Greta, bouncing on the car seat. "I knew this was going to be where you found something. I told you that as soon as we got here." She reached over and punched Ernst on the shoulder.

"You told me that at every camp we visited," he reminded her.

"There you go, again, getting hung up on insignificant details," she said, looking around. "This looks like the neighborhood you and Aunt Marta live in. Oh, Ernst, I'm so excited. We're going to meet Erich Tolle."

"Can I ask you a question?"

"What?" Greta turned to look at him.

Ernst's eyes never left the road, but he smiled and said, "Are you excited?"

"I'm *so* excited." Greta laughed and bounced.

They followed the directions Tolle had given Ernst on the

phone, and only got lost once. A stop at a service station for a map showed where they had missed their turn, only a few blocks back.

When they turned onto Mulberry, Ernst drove slowly, looking for "7177." Twice he slowed almost to a stop to read an address. In the blistering heat, he and Greta were both grateful the car had air conditioning, a luxury they didn't need in Germany.

"There it is," Greta whispered, as if in prayer, and pointed at a one-story stone house. A driveway ran along the left side of the house to a garage in the back yard. As Ernst turned the car into the drive, he saw a man standing in the doorway with the main door open. The man looked through the glass storm door, watching Ernst and Greta get out of the car and approach the front door, his hand on the door latch.

"*Willkommen*," he said, opening the door for them.

"*Herr* Tolle?" Ernst asked.

"*Ja*," I am known as Erich Tolle," he answered in German. Hearing their native language put them at ease.

Tolle was a man in his mid-fifties, a little under six feet tall. He was not thin, but appeared to work out, as he had no belly fat, like Ernst had noticed on so many Americans. His hair was longer than most men his age, with significant amounts of gray. A mustache graced his lip, and lines creased his face. "And you are Ernst Seligman?" Tolle asked.

"Möller. Ernst Möller. My aunt, Marta Möller, adopted me when my parents were killed. I have lived with her in Berlin since 1942."

Tolle nodded and said, "I see."

"But I was born Ernst Seligman, son of U-boat *Kapitän* Wilhelm Seligman." He stopped on the small porch and put his hand on Greta's arm. "And this is my fiancée, Greta."

"Come in, come in," Tolle said, stepping back to give them

room to enter. In the living room, a woman about the same age as Tolle greeted them.

"I'm so glad to meet y'all," she said, in a heavy southern accent. Ernst and Greta nodded, and the woman said, "I'm sorry, but I don't speak any German, 'cept for a few swear words that I've learned from my husband." She and Tolle both laughed, so Greta joined in. Ernst, his limited English baffled by her accent, and anticipation of finally learning his father's fate causing him to clench and unclench his hands, just looked on.

Holding out her hand, she said, "My name is Barbara. Can I offer you somethin' to drink? Water? A beer?"

"*Bier?*" Greta understood that word. "*Ja,*" she said, shaking Barbara's hand.

"*Ja, bier,*" added Ernst, as he shook her hand.

"Thanks, Barbara. I'll have one, too," said Tolle in English. As she walked to the kitchen Tolle switched to German and said, "Let's sit down." He directed the visitors to the sofa, then took up residence in a chair that looked like others sat in only on his invitation. "I'm sure there's a lot of questions you want to ask me."

"*Ja,*" said Ernst, but before he could ask any, Barbara returned with three beers on a tray.

"Y'all have a lot of catchin' up to do," she said. "I'm goin' to let y'all alone so's y'all can talk."

Ernst looked confused, so Tolle translated for him. Ernst and Greta nodded to Barbara, stood up, and said, "*Danke.*" They remained standing until she left the room, then sat down and looked at Tolle expectantly.

"I suppose you want to know about U-112," Tolle said quietly.

"Yes," said Ernst. "In Germany they say it didn't exist."

Tolle's eyes widened. "Huh," he said, "it sounds like the Nazis re-wrote history. I can assure you it existed."

"That's what *Herr* Bredow guessed," Greta said, nodding her head and poking Ernst in the ribs.

Tolle furrowed his brow, but before he could ask who *Herr* Bredow was, Ernst asked him, "Did you know my father?"

"I knew him very well. He was my *kapitän*."

"Tell me what happened to him."

Tolle looked uncomfortably around the room. "Well," he said, "we certainly got to that fast."

Ernst scooted forward to the edge of the sofa and folded his hands together. "I came from Germany to learn about my father. I want to know what happened to him."

Tolle paused, appearing to search for the right words. "I have never told anyone this story before, and even though it was thirty years ago, I still worry that there are those that will do me harm because of what happened. I will share my story with you, but you must not share it with anyone unless I agree. Will you accept that?"

"How can I agree to that when I don't know what your story is?" asked Ernst.

Tolle stared at the younger man. "It is complicated. Hear me out. You are entitled to know, but I must protect myself."

Ernst leaned forward, one hand on his knee. "I thought you invited me into your house to tell me about my father and U-112. Why should I have to agree not to tell anyone?"

"Ernst, please," said Greta. "We should hear him out."

Tolle lowered his voice. "*Bitte.*" Please. "Listen to Greta. I've never even told my wife what I am prepared to tell you. You are entitled to hear what happened; then *you* can judge me. But it is no one else's business."

Ernst wasn't certain, but he remembered the last thing his Aunt Marta had said to him before they boarded the plane in Berlin. She had hugged Greta, then taken him into her embrace. Clutching him to her, Marta had whispered in his ear, "If in doubt, trust Greta's instincts. She is wise beyond her years."

"All right," Ernst said, sitting back. "I will listen to your story. But first, I want to know what happened to my father."

"My story will tell you," said Tolle.

"I want to know how he died *first*." His voice grew louder with every word.

Tolle pursed his lips, sat perfectly still for a minute, then, his voice cracking with emotion and tears in his eyes, he said, "*Erich Tolle tötete ihn.*" Erich Tolle killed him.

Greta gasped. Ernst's eyes went wide, his nostrils flared, and he clutched his hands into fists. He stood up so fast that Tolle didn't have time to react; Greta, however, did. She grabbed the back of Ernst's belt with both hands and, with surprising strength, flung him back onto the sofa. She looked him in the eye, pointed between them at the sofa, and commanded, "*Sitzen!*" like she was disciplining a dog. Then, standing up, she pointed at Tolle and yelled, "*Aber du bist Erich Tolle!*" But you are Erich Tolle!

Both men looked chastened by the blonde tornado in their midst. Ernst silently stared at Tolle, his hands balled into fists. Tolle met Greta's gaze. "*Ja, Ich bin bekannt wie Erich Tolle.*" Yes, I am known as Erich Tolle.

CHAPTER FORTY-EIGHT

11 January, 1942 21:30 CET (3:30 P.M. EWT)
Near the Georgia coastline Grid DB1919

Eins eins zwei lay on the ocean floor waiting for dark, Neumann in command. When he had relieved Seligman three hours earlier, the Captain told him that he would be back at 22:00. At 21:30, though, he climbed the conning ladder up to the command room.

"Still on the bottom?" Seligman enquired.

"Aye, *Kapitän*. If the weather has cleared upstairs it will be a good night for a hunt."

"That it will, number one. That it will. Fill me in on what's going on."

Neumann said, "We're in 55 meters of water; we have 105 minutes to full dark; all torpedo tubes are loaded, and the eels were serviced in the last eight hours. We need to vent in the next eight hours, and will do that when we surface. We're ready to go."

"Fine, number one. Get some rest before your watch begins. Dismissed."

"If it's all right with you, Sir, I'm going to walk the boat and see that everything and everyone are prepared for night. I think we're in for a busy one."

"All right," said Seligman. "But make sure you're ready for your watch at 00:00. It's only two and one-half hours away. I know I'm leaning on you more with Watts gone, but I'm going to appoint Winter to second officer. He's been training Seaman Bauer in navigation, so while he's standing watch Bauer can navigate."

"Thank goodness you didn't choose Wagner. Too pompous. He'd let it go to his head and the men would probably mutiny."

Neumann expected Seligman to reply but after waiting a few seconds realized the captain wasn't going to give one, so he left the command deck and quietly approached the forward torpedo room. There was so much he had to do. He wished Tolle's offer of help had come sooner, so he had had time to think about it. *Is Tolle trustworthy?* Neumann wondered. Finally, he decided, *I don't know him well enough to include him.*

The first officer checked on the location of the scuttling charges in the forward torpedo room. Neumann had helped the Chief distribute all fourteen throughout the boat when they left port. Neumann remembered his days as chief of the boat, when it was his responsibility to put the charges in strategic places in case the boat had to be scuttled to avoid capture. That knowledge of where they were located and how to arm them would come in handy now.

In the forward torpedo room he asked the enlisted men how they were doing, and told them the boat would be rising to the surface to begin the night's hunt in less than two hours. He wondered how many would survive his plan, and suddenly wondered whether he should carry it out. Except for a very few, he liked these men and ran the risk of killing every one of them. If it would stop the war it would be worth it for all of them to die, including himself. *It won't stop it, though, so why do it?* He thought. *I will carry the guilt of all their deaths.*

But that was the yin of the argument. Immediately the yang kicked in. *If I carry out the attacks, I will be guilty of all the deaths of the seamen on the ships we sink. I've got to do something. If not this, what?*

He could deliberately misfire the torpedoes, but after everything he had said to the captain about his beliefs, Seligman would quickly know what he was doing.

He'll just do it himself. Or worse, have that little shit, Wagner, do it. He's an officer, he's been trained on the UZO. But if the attacks we carry out are important to the war effort, it stands to reason that the ones we don't carry out can be harmful to it. Neumann shook his head, as if to clear it.

He would carry out his plan.

At the rear of the torpedo room he passed the head tucked off to his right, a bucket that had been used numerous times overnight sitting next to it. He ducked and stepped through the bulkhead into the engine room. Glancing down at the metal grid work deck, he could see through it to the batteries that powered the underwater motors. The first officer moved quickly over the grid, feeling the heat put off by the batteries rising into the boat. Without this simple, yet effective, venting in the floor, the batteries would overheat. Watching his step, he moved onto the solid surface where the battery compartment ended.

Heading aft, he observed, but did not call attention to, the scuttling charges throughout the boat. As he moved through the command room he heard Seligman order the boat to periscope depth and felt the floor begin to tilt as the electric motors moved it quietly upward.

When he reached the aft torpedo room he repeated the discussion he had had with the crew in the forward room. This time, though, it didn't trigger any internal arguments. As he returned to his bunk to rest until it was time for his watch command, his mind was set.

Everything was in place.

On the command deck, Seligman puzzled over Neumann's comment about Wagner. The captain didn't like Wagner's Nazi ways, either, but he was the commander of a German war vessel, and he had to do his duty. If that meant promoting Wagner to second officer he would do it, and the men would just have to like it. *This is my command*, Seligman thought. *I will command it as I see fit.*

The question that caused Seligman more problems was whether he should relieve Neumann of his duties as first officer. He certainly didn't want to, but he wasn't sure he could totally trust Neumann.

Damn him, thought Seligman. Here we are about to start a surprise attack on Germany's newest enemy and he was distracted from directing the attack while he tried to figure out if he could trust his crew. He liked Neumann, but that couldn't enter into it. Neumann had to be prepared to do his job.

Seligman thought back to their conversation two days before Christmas. Neumann had assured him that he would follow any orders that Seligman gave him. *But what choice did he have?* thought the captain. *If he told me he wouldn't I would have had him handcuffed to his bunk for the duration. My God*, thought Seligman. *I let Neumann con me.*

His decision was made. Before they launched their attack Seligman would relieve Neumann of his duties as First Officer. He would promote the Chief, Siegfried, to the position.

———

Tolle was on duty in the radio room waiting for Frick to arrive and relieve him when he saw Neumann pass by. With their attack to begin on the 13th, just a little over one day away, if Neumann was going to do something to prevent it, he would need to do it in the next twenty-four hours.

Tolle silently cursed Neumann's insistence that he wasn't planning anything. Then Frick arrived and Tolle turned the radio over to him. He reminded Frick to receive messages only, unless Seligman ordered one sent.

"We are to maintain radio silence until we begin attacking," Tolle told the seaman. "Admiral Dönitz doesn't want the Americans to know we are here yet."

"What exactly are we attacking?" asked Frick.

"I'm sure the *Kapitän* will let us know as soon as he thinks we need to know," Tolle said brusquely. *Who does Frick think he is, asking a question like that? Frick isn't an officer. His job is to send and receive messages. Who or what we attack is not his concern.*

Tolle could feel the boat holding steady. The captain liked to come up to periscope depth about this of time of day and hold there until full dark, over an hour off. Tolle made his way to the head. He'd been waiting until they came up from the bottom to use it because when they were deeper than 25 meters the water pressure prevented them from flushing. Below that depth, everyone used a shared bucket that quickly became very unpleasant. He couldn't stand using it.

"I'm going in there," said Richter, the electrician, trying to push past Tolle as the radioman stood outside the head signing the latrine log.

"No, you're not," said Tolle. Putting his arm across the doorway to block Richter's access, he said, "You haven't signed the log. If you make a mess they'll make me clean it up since I just signed it. If you can't wait for me, use that," he said, pointing to the 'honey bucket' next to the head.

Richter looked at it and grimaced. It was already about to run over and Richter gagged at the stench. Tolle pulled the curtain closed, dropped his pants, and sat down.

As Tolle sat on the toilet, he heard Richter complaining to anyone who would listen. Everyone had been on both sides of that argument, though, so he got no sympathy.

Tolle had an idea of what Neumann was planning. If only he knew for sure, he could do something. But Neumann was apparently determined to act alone. *Damn Neumann*, Tolle thought. He heard Richter gag again as he squatted over the bucket just outside the curtain.

Tolle debated whether he should report what he suspected, but if he went to the wrong person he might be prevented from doing what he needed to do. *Who can I trust?* he thought. His instincts and training told him to trust no one.

His decision made and his business completed, Tolle cleaned himself. As soon as he got his pants back up he would find Neumann and threaten to reveal his plan unless he let Tolle in on it.

Seligman saw a shadow seeming to drop out of the clouds. He had been using the observation periscope to scan the sky for planes and the surface for ships. But thick, gray clouds dotted the sky and the sun moved in and out through them as it moved lower on the western horizon. He couldn't definitely identify it as a plane but with full dark less than ninety minutes away, he decided not to take any chances.

"Down periscope," Seligman ordered. "Take us to thirty-five meters real easy, Chief," he called out. "I don't want our screws to create a disturbance on the surface that a plane could see, so cut them back and don't rush it."

Siegfried nodded. "Diving to thirty-five meters," he repeated. "Adjust both bow and aft planes five degrees," he told the helmsmen. "Reduce speed to 1/4 ahead."

Throughout the boat, the order, "Dive to thirty-five meters" was passed from one compartment to the next.

Richter had just finished using the bucket outside the head in the forward torpedo room. Angry at Tolle for not letting him use the toilet, he yelled, "You better empty this bucket when you're finished in there."

In that instant Ensign Braun called from the torpedo room: "Dive to thirty-five meters."

"What did he say?" asked Tolle, preparing to flush the toilet.

From beyond the curtain, he could only make out Richter saying, "You better empty this bucket when you're finished in there," The bucket slid under the curtain toward Tolle.

As Tolle emptied the bucket into the toilet, the boat settled serenely at thirty-five meters.

Tolle realized he shouldn't have emptied all the contents of the bucket, because it filled the toilet almost to overflowing. *Good thing we're at periscope depth*, he thought, grabbing the flushing valve and opening it full. Immediately the contents of the toilet splattered him all over.

"*Gott im Himmel!*" he yelled, spitting to clear his mouth. He pawed his face with his hands, and stumbled back, not realizing what caused his predicament. Meanwhile, sea water came pouring in through the open valve.

Tolle dragged his hands through the excrement on his face and flung it in all directions. Men coming to his aid and moving toward the open valve ended up taking cover to avoid the flying turds. Precious moments were lost as Tolle continued to flail around and fling what should have been in the toilet indiscriminately around the torpedo room.

Braun immediately realized the danger they were facing; sea water was flooding the torpedo room and pouring through the gridwork floor into the battery compartment below. If the sea water hit the batteries, deadly chlorine gas would be formed by a chemical reaction between the batteries and the salt water. The most inexperienced crew member knew this, yet they were too busy hiding from flying feces to address the real crisis.

Braun shoved his way past Tolle and the men aiding him and reached down to close the valve, but the water pressure was too great. He couldn't budge it.

"Notify the *Kapitän*," he yelled, as the first splashes of sea water reached the batteries. "Chlorine gas release! All men use your breathing apparatus!" He continued to struggle with the valve, but soon smelled the chlorine gas in the air. He grabbed a Drager device from a storage locker and quickly put it on, giving him about ten minutes of air. It was imperative that the boat surface to vent the gas.

On the Command Deck, Seligman heard the chlorine gas alarm and ordered an immediate emergency surfacing. "Crew to use breathing apparatus," he yelled. "Prepare to ventilate as soon as we surface. Start bilge pumps! Chief, get your apparatus on, then get us up fast." *I just hope that wasn't a plane*, he thought, remembering the shadow.

The alarm sounded a chlorine gas alert. Men raced to get to their Dragers as gas wafted throughout the boat. Those that were a step slow in donning their breathing device coughed and retched.

"Get your device on now," Seligman shouted at Wagner as he pulled his own on. As Wagner responded Seligman shouted, to no one in particular, "If you see someone fall, get them up. The gas will be more concentrated near the floor. Are the bilge pumps running? I don't hear them!"

Even as he spoke, Seligman heard the pumps start, a necessity to get the water out of the battery compartment.

In the forward torpedo room, Braun gave up on closing the valve. He made sure everyone was out of the room and he and two seamen closed the watertight bulkhead. He checked to make sure everyone was using their breathing device, then ordered everyone to move to the back of the engine room.

"Surfaced," yelled the chief. "Open all hatches for ventilation; start diesels!"

"Watch crew to the bridge," yelled Seligman.

The call to "Open all hatches" rang through the boat.

In the conning tower above the command room, Neumann led the watch crew up the ladder. As soon as he heard the Chief call out that they were surfaced, he opened the hatch, pausing as the pressures equalized, then shoved it back. As he climbed through it and into the dusk of the late afternoon, he heard the diesels and their vent fans start, and felt fresh air rushing down the opening to clear the boat and push the deadly gas out the relief vents. It was 22:30, approximately one hour before full dark.

Each member of the watch crew clicked their safety harness onto the rail and immediately began scanning their quadrant. Neumann, looking aft, noticed the significant wake being generated by the twin screws as the boat moved forward through moderate waves. He knew even after they dove it would remain for a while, a long, white line on a sea of black. It would point toward where they had submerged as if it were giving direction to any plane with a load of depth charges and a desire to kill them. They needed to get underwater fast, but they needed to be surfaced to repair the valve.

After a five-minute eternity, Siegfried's voice through the speaker tube informed them that the boat was ventilated. Now the crew had to wait for the bilge pumps to empty the forward torpedo room of the water and make repairs to the stuck valve that had started all their problems.

But as soon as the Chief declared the boat ventilated and before the bilge pumps could empty the forward torpedo room, Neumann saw Hoerter stiffen, his binoculars to his eyes. His right arm pointed, and he yelled, "Plane, 170 degrees, coming in from starboard aft!"

"Alarmmm! Alarmmm!" shouted Neumann into the

speaker tube and the emergency dive bell immediately started ringing.

The watch crew began dropping through the hatch, Neumann bringing up the rear. Just before leaving the bridge, he glanced one last time at the plane and was stunned to see the pilot so close that he would have known him on the street if they were ever to bump into each other. As he dropped through the opening and secured the hatch, he knew his plan was no longer necessary. Unless the plane was unarmed, there was no way U-112 could escape it.

Seligman realized the crew had no idea of the danger they were in. One moment they were removing their breathing apparatus, preparing to make repairs to the stuck valve, and the next they were seeing the red dive lights flashing and listening to the emergency bell ordering a crash dive.

"All men to the bow," shouted Seligman, forgetting for a moment that the bow was full of sea water behind the water tight bulkhead.

"Cancel that!" he shouted when he remembered. "Careful, Chief. You've got a forward torpedo room full of water!" *At least the water in the room would help pull the boat down faster,* he thought.

"Aye, *Kapitän*" replied Siegfried, then started to call out depths, as he always did in a dive. He had just said "Twenty meters" when three loud explosions near the stern forced the entire boat violently downward. Everyone hit the overhead.

Seligman heard the dreaded sound of sea water thundering in through the pressure hull before he hit the floor. The fall practically knocked him unconscious, but water came pouring forward from the aft torpedo room, rousing him and shoving indistinguishable bodies along ahead of it. All but one were missing arms or legs, and one had no head.

Seligman tried to order the men to close the watertight doors, but he couldn't get his breath to speak.

"Close all water-tight doors," he heard a voice yelling, but he couldn't recognize whose it was. It didn't matter. Water hit him in the face and shoved him along the floor, but it helped to bring him back to his senses. He stood and fought his way back to the foot of the conning tower ladder, where he looped his arm through one of its rungs and held on against the water, which was already approaching his waist. Men struggled to close watertight doors, but the breach was too great; the push of the water made it impossible.

Seligman saw Tolle fighting his way through the water to the radio room, but the radio was already submerged. Tolle moved the short distance from the radio room to the lower command deck, where Seligman clung to the ladder.

"I must send a message to *BdU*," he said to the captain, who nodded, and moved to the side of the ladder.

Tolle climbed into the conning tower, pushed through the men that were there, and found the secondary transmitter. He immediately sent a message to *BdU* telling them what had happened and advising that the boat was sinking. He just had time to send a second message before the pushing and shoving of the men clamoring to get out separated him from the radio.

All compartments below the upper command deck were now almost completely flooded. Heads bobbed in the ever smaller air pockets, where the air was oppressively hot from being compressed by the incoming water.

In the chaos, Seligman finally recovered his breath and yelled, "Abandon ship!" as if there were a ship to abandon. Everything behind the command room in the center of the boat was destroyed by the blasts. With water up to his neck, the captain kept waving for men to climb the ladder to the conning tower, but there weren't many left who could climb.

When he had to tread water to stay afloat, Seligman moved to the ladder and began climbing. He thought he was the last man out of the lower level, but felt something bump him in the back of his legs so he turned to see if he could help someone. It was the body with no head, being pushed this way and that by the water. Checking his Drager mouthpiece to make sure it was positioned where he could get it, he raced the sea up the ladder to the conning tower, where he found Neumann, Tolle, and eight seamen.

"Listen to me!" he said. "We've practiced this before. We were on the ocean floor during the day at fifty meters depth, so that's probably where we will hit bottom. There is no reason everyone still alive cannot get out alive from that depth."

At his last words, the boat hit the bottom hard. Fortunately, it was so full of water the men were not slammed around as they had been when the depth charges ripped it apart. Everyone had their Dragers on, so they waited for the boat to fill.

"Remember, men," Seligman said one last time before putting his mouthpiece in, "you've got plenty of air to get to the surface, as long as you don't panic. Don't go up faster than the air bubbles leaving the boat. Otherwise, you'll get the bends. Neumann, open the hatch as soon as pressure allows. You'll be first out. I'll be last."

Seligman inserted his mouthpiece and thought of his

family. He hoped that Ernst would find someone to be a father to him. He expected to get to the surface. He did not expect to get to shore.

As the water rose over their heads, the pressure inside and outside equalized and Neumann spun the lock on the hatch, pushed it back, and began his ascent to the surface.

Several more left, but the rest were holding back in a small air pocket to the side of the hatch. Seligman took out his mouthpiece and told them, "You have to get out now," but they were incoherent and panicking. One called for his mother; another cursed the boat. Zimmerman, the photographer that had been assigned to the U-boat for this mission, kept repeating, "It's so hot."

As the air pocket diminished, Seligman told them to put their mouthpieces in, but they didn't. Despite their rescue apparatus, they drowned, and only Zimmerman and Seligman were left. The captain looked into Zimmerman's eyes, but the photographer had what was known as the thousand-mile stare; his mind had surrendered to death and when he slipped below the water Seligman reinserted his own mouthpiece and exited the hatch.

As Seligman swam toward the surface, he counted seven men above him. He could tell that several of them were panicking, though. They had plenty of air in their Drager to get topside, but he could tell they were not exhaling properly. He watched several of them become inert, one just as he broke the surface. He hoped that more had escaped from the forward hatch. He knew no one had gotten out the aft hatch.

Neumann was calm when he broke through the surface. Seligman had been right, they hadn't been that deep. He wondered if he would have been able to detonate the scuttling charges if the boat hadn't been sunk by the American plane. He wasn't sure he could have lived with himself if he had been responsible for the deaths of the crew.

He was only on the surface for a moment before other heads began to pop up. Despite the storm of the past few days having moved on, the surface was still choppy, with three to five foot waves. Neumann estimated they were forty kilometers out from shore, too far to swim, and the current would probably pull them farther out. He thought the lack of merchant vessels for the last few days could be because of the storm, and hoped they were in a shipping lane. The weather system had come up from the Caribbean and brought with it unseasonably warm water, so he knew they wouldn't freeze.

"Over here, over here," shouted various sailors. Some sounded relieved, some dazed, some delirious. A few were dead, their drowned bodies pulled up by the buoyancy of their Dragers.

A roar overhead caused Neumann to look up just in time to see a plane with American markings. He assumed it was the one that had sunk them. It was so low he could see the pilot's face looking out the window at them. He waved to acknowledge he saw them. Several of the men cursed the plane, but on a second low pass over them life jackets were thrown out, and on a third, a life raft.

Two men swam to retrieve the life jackets, but the plane dropped the raft farther away, and in the darkness and choppy seas they couldn't find it. The roar of the plane became quieter until, a few minutes later, they realized it had left.

Neumann and the other men kept calling out to each other and finally the first officer heard the captain's voice, ordering the men to swim into a tight circle. When all gathered together in a circle, there were twelve survivors.

"We have to assume there are no others," Seligman said to Neumann. "That means we lost forty."

"Thirty-nine," said Neumann. "We had already lost Watts."

Seligman quickly determined that they had seven life jackets and three Drager devices which still had some flotation qualities, but twelve men. He ordered everyone out of their life jackets.

"I can't take mine off," said Schulz. "I can't swim."

"Someone is going to drown if we don't share them," said Seligman. "The seas are too rough for a man without some flotation aid."

"I won't do it. You're picking me to be the one that drowns."

"We must work together or we will die separately," said Seligman, but Schulz wouldn't listen. He began to flail about with his arms. His feeble efforts succeeded in separating himself from the group. They never saw him again.

The rest did as Seligman had ordered. When the flotation aids were removed, the men tied them together in a circle, so that all could cling to them. Despite this, one man babbled incoherently about the life raft.

"We need it," he finally managed to get out. "I'm going to find it," he said, as he let go of the circle of vests and struck out in a direction that Seligman thought was east. He had only gotten about ten meters when the captain saw his head go under, never to return to the surface.

"Does anyone know who that was?" asked Seligman, but no one replied. They were too busy keeping their own heads above water.

Neumann noticed the man on his left floundering so he reached over and grabbed him by his collar. But the man knocked his hand away, cried, "Mama!" and went under.

It was too dark for the stranded men to really see each other, so Seligman ordered, "Beginning with me, and going to my left, we will sound off our names so we know who is here. Seligman!"

On his left, the next man called, "Schuster."

"Wagner."

"Schwarz."

"Tolle."

"Hoerter."

"Neumann."

"Bauer."

"Meier."

"Gentlemen," said the captain, "we have survived the sinking. Now we await our rescue." He hoped he sounded more convincing to them than he did to himself.

CHAPTER FORTY-NINE

Evening 11 January, 1942 to Morning, 13 January, 1942
    Somewhere off the Georgia U.S.A. coast

The men watched the sun sink in the western sky, growing ever bigger as it approached the horizon. Shortly after sunset two planes passed far overhead, high enough to reflect rays from the sun, despite it having set on the men bobbing in the water fifteen minutes earlier. Even the most optimistic of the group knew that the aircraft were too far up, and the surface of the water too dark, for there to be even the slightest chance of either plane seeing them.

"I think we should swim toward shore," said Bauer.

"We're probably forty kilometers out and the currents are against us," Seligman replied. "Our best chance to be seen is to stay together."

"We had no charts," said Hoerter. "How do you know where the current is going?"

"I know general trends of the currents in this area and

they are against us reaching shore," said the captain. "Our best bet is to stay together to make our group more noticeable and be spotted."

Bauer grumbled, but shut up until two hours later, when the seas had settled. Without a word to anyone else, Bauer started swimming west. He had only gone about ten meters when Hoerter followed.

"Don't do it," ordered Seligman, but the two men ignored him. Seligman understood their frustration but knew theirs was a losing gamble.

Now there were seven.

Meier asked of no one in particular, "What are the odds of our rescue?"

"Luck has been with us," said Seligman. "When we sank the water was about fifty meters deep, I would estimate. We've come through some seas that were hundreds of meters deeper. If we had sunk in those areas we would have never even gotten to the surface. The plane that sank us dropped life jackets, so I believe the pilot will report our location. If they send a ship to look for us, it will know these waters and the currents, so it will know where to look for us. I say we will be found."

"But when?" asked Schuster.

"Not before tomorrow," said Neumann. "They won't even look for us until then."

Overnight the surface remained calm, making it easier to hold on to the ring of life jackets, so the men were able to conserve energy. The air cooled, but the water remained warm so they were comfortable. The next day was a different matter.

Without a cloud in the sky, the sun beat down on their faces. By noon all of them felt their skin drying and beginning to burn. They took off their shirts and covered their heads, but even alternating between covering their heads and their shoulders, by nightfall the skin on their shoulders, arms, and faces was painfully burned.

Shortly before nightfall, when they had been in the water a little more than twenty-four hours, they saw what appeared to be a destroyer heading straight for them, and the men believed their moment of deliverance had arrived. Inexplicably, however, it curved away from them, never coming closer than one kilometer.

The next day, there still wasn't a cloud in the sky and the sun again broiled them, sapping their strength. The ocean picked up again and even in a tight circle the men on the other side were often briefly obscured by the waves. They had been without food or water for thirty-six hours and hunger was an issue, but dehydration was the threat.

Meier was the first to lose his grip on reality. He yelled out that he saw a ship. Everyone's heads came up as they strained to see it. Soon enough, however, they realized there was no ship; Meier was hallucinating. He lost all sense of reality, quit holding onto the ring of life jackets, and soon drowned.

Next was Schwarz. When he started seeing planes, then ships, the others reacted more slowly than when Meier had, and with less hope. The third time he claimed to see a ship, he struck out for it but went under before he swam twenty meters.

When Schuster yelled, "A ship! A ship!" no one even turned his head. Minutes later, in the same way he had let go of reality, he released his grip on the life jackets, floundered, and drowned.

About the time the sun got directly overhead, Seligman

suggested another roll call. There were only four of them left, but he wasn't sure which four. His eyes were assaulted by the burning sun, the glare on the water, and the stinging salt water. He could make out forms but not features, and wondered if he would recognize himself in a mirror.

"I'll go first," he said, "then to my left. Seligman."

It took a moment, but then he heard "Wagner."

Immediately, "Tolle" rang out.

A pause, then, "Neumann."

"We should talk to each other," Seligman told them. "If we talk, we will stay alert. If we stay alert, we-"

"A ship! I hear a ship!" Seligman wasn't sure which man said it, but he knew that whoever it was, he would be the next to go.

But then Neumann said, "Tolle's right! I hear it, too!"

They couldn't see it at first, and when they finally did they understood why. It wasn't a large ship, maybe twenty meters in length, moving slowly south. Seligman said, "It's a fishing boat."

The men were too parched and tired to yell loudly, but even with their dry throats, they made enough noise to attract the attention of someone on the ship, and it began a slow turn toward them.

They heard voices speaking English, and Tolle raised his arm so the crew would see them.

"Good Lord," said one of the men on the boat, "Look how burnt they are. Who do you think they are?"

Tolle heard the engine slip into neutral and felt arms grabbing him, pulling him out of the water.

"Who are you?" a voice asked. Tolle knew enough English to understand what they were asking, and said, "Tolle."

There were three Americans on the boat. Two of them half-walked, half-carried Tolle below deck, where they laid him on the floor. Then they went up the few steps to the open stern and pulled each of the others onto the ship one at a time, placing them on the floor next to Tolle.

"Here's some water," said one, bringing cups to each. When Wagner began to gulp his, one of the Americans said, "Whoa, not so fast. You'll throw it all up." In a moment, their thirsts slaked, they all fell asleep.

"Look," one of the Americans said. "They have no uniforms. They must be merchant marine."

"This one does," said the one that appeared to be in charge, pointing at Neumann. "It's British."

"What the devil are British sailors doing floating around in the waters off South Carolina?" asked the tall one.

"Whatever they are, and whoever they are, they're damned lucky we came by here," replied the captain. "From the looks of them, I'd say in another few hours they would have been dead. Let's get our nets in and head to shore so these poor souls can get some medical attention. Maybe then, they can talk and we can find out what ship they were on and what happened to it."

"Think they might have been swamped when that storm hit last week?" asked the tall one. They walked up the steps to topside.

"But British. What are the British doing here? I bet our Navy's not going to be happy about that."

Tolle had been feigning sleep. As the last of their rescuers pulled the door closed, making the rest of their conversation unintelligible, he raised his head and whispered, "*Kapitän?*" He paused, but got no reply from Seligman.

"Neumann? Wagner?" Neither replied.

He sat up and gave his head a minute to get its equilibrium. They were lying on the floor of the cabin. At first he thought the others might be dead, but then he made out the rise and falls of their chests. *Weaklings*, he thought.

He carefully stood up and looked around the cabin. It was a working boat with no frills. They were on the floor because there were no bunks, just a small cabinet with a large capacity water container sitting on it. He picked up a cup from the floor, shook out the water in it, then filled it. He gulped the water down, then refilled it and sipped it while he reconnoitered the room.

On the other side of the cabin stood several cabinets. A radio sat on top of one. He had to step over the other men to get to them, and almost fell when someone topside opened the throttle and pushed the ship forward. He steadied himself and got to the other side, where he opened several drawers in the cabinets. In the third one he found what he was looking for.

Tolle picked up the pistol and looked it over. It was a .38 caliber five-shot revolver. He opened the cylinder and saw that all the chambers were loaded. Pointing it at Seligman's head, he quietly said, "pow," imagining brains, blood, and bone splattering everywhere.

It would be easy to kill these three as they slept, but then what would he do about the Americans? He would have only two shots left in the gun, and there were three of them. Although he found a box of ammunition, he knew he wouldn't be able to reload quickly enough to kill all the Americans if they came as soon as they heard gunshots.

Tolle dropped some shells into his pocket. He stepped across the sleeping men to get to the cabin door leading topside, grasped the handle and turned his body sideways, holding the gun behind him.

Pushing the door open, he saw two of the Americans standing at the back of the boat, their backs to him. One was smoking a cigarette while the other put his arms over his head and stretched. There was a ladder beside Tolle leading up to a bridge, where he suspected the third American was piloting the boat. Stealthily, he mounted the steps, bracing himself on the top one. Pointing the gun at the back of the man with the cigarette, he fired.

The American staggered forward. His knees hit the back of the boat and he tumbled head first into the ocean. The man on the left turned, his eyes wide, but before he could react, Tolle pulled the trigger and the gun sent a bullet deep into his chest. He fell backward onto the deck and cracked his head on the rail on the top of the stern. He landed on his back, blood pouring from the hole in his chest.

Tolle started up the ladder to the bridge. Halfway up the captain met him, mercifully blocking the sun, which had been causing him to squint. Now Tolle could get a good shot.

The American was looking down at Tolle, his eyes wide. "What are you doing?" he shouted. "We saved you!"

Tolle leveled the gun at the American's chest and rapidly fired twice. His first shot hit a little to the right of center, but the second was straight to the heart, and the American, already knocked back by the first shot, tumbled over backwards. Tolle stepped down the ladder, careful to avoid the blood already on the deck from the earlier shooting, and was reloading when the door from below deck flew open and Seligman mounted the steps, followed closely by Neumann and Wagner.

Seligman stood with his hands on his hips as he, Neumann, and Wagner took in the carnage. Wagner stood on the steps leading down to the cabin and retched at the scene even though there was nothing in his stomach to vomit up, while Neumann walked around shaking his head. Newmann had to grab onto Seligman to keep from falling, however, when his foot hit some blood mixed with water and flew out from under him. Meanwhile, Tolle casually dropped shells into the cylinders of the pistol.

"What *are* you doing?" asked Seligman, looking at the dead American on the stern deck. He had seen plenty of mayhem and death, but usually through a periscope at 1000 meters. To see it this close was unsettling, but Tolle's calm demeanor after killing three people especially unnerved him.

"Let's get him over the side," said Tolle, as coolly as if he were discussing where to go for dinner. He tucked the now-loaded gun in his waist band and grabbed the dead man by his arms. "Grab his feet," he demanded, but, like Neumann, slipped in the blood and almost fell. Regaining his balance he repeated, "Grab his feet." When no one responded he said, "Do you want to show up on shore with dead Americans? They are not combatants. We will be executed."

"No," said Seligman, regaining his composure. "*You* will be executed. We had nothing to do with this and I have no idea why you did it."

"They are the enemy," said Tolle. "We must do our duty to *unser Fuhrër.* I have a plan. Grab his feet." He continued to hold the arms of the dead man.

"I am still your *Kapitän,*" said Seligman. "I will decide what we do. Give me the gun."

Tolle looked at him for a moment, then threw down the dead American's arms. "You disgust me," he said, turning his back on the captain.

Seligman clenched his fists and said, "You will show respect to me as your *Kapitän* and superior officer."

Tolle stood with his back to the captain, as if weighing his options. One-meter waves bounced them slightly from left to right as the pilotless boat made its way west. Neumann moved toward the ladder and said, "I'm going to take the helm. Seems like somebody should be watching where we're going while you two sort this out."

"No," said Tolle, turning around quickly as Neumann put his foot on the bottom step. "I want Wagner to do that."

Neumann stopped but kept one foot on the bottom rung and looked over his shoulder. Tolle pulled the gun out of his waistband. Seligman stared at Tolle, whose eyes were dark, his eyelids squinting to keep the sun out.

"You are *not* my superior officer," Tolle said to Seligman in a firm, clear voice. "I am a *Korvettenkapitän* in the *Ausland SD.* I was put on board to watch the two of you and have determined that both of you are traitors to the Reich and *unser Fuhrër.* I therefore relieve you of your command, *Kapitän.* Wagner, climb up to the bridge and take the helm. Head due west and let me know when land is in sight."

Wagner gave a brisk Nazi salute and said, "Aye, *Herr Kapitän,*" and climbed the ladder to the bridge. On his way up, Tolle shouted to him, "When you get up there, throw that body over the side."

"Aye, *Herr Kapitän,*" he repeated.

Neumann said, "You son of a bitch. You tried to set me up as a traitor. Well, I didn't sink the boat, and I'm not a traitor."

Seligman heard the sound of the American's body bouncing once on the side deck, then splashing in the water. In the next moment, it bobbed behind them and was quickly left behind.

"Ah, but you did sink it," Tolle said to Newmann. "At least, that is what I told *BdU* and *SD.*" He waved the gun at Seligman and Neumann and said, "One of you grab this body and throw him overboard before somebody trips on him." Neither Seligman nor Neumann moved.

"Why did you tell them that?" asked Neumann.

"What are you two talking about?" asked Seligman, looking from one to the other. He didn't know which one to focus his attention upon, but he had a healthy respect for the revolver in Tolle's hand, and Tolle's calm and experienced handling of it, so the captain directed his words at him. "We had a chorine gas release. We had to surface, and a plane sank us." As he finished, he felt a slight adjustment in the tracking of the boat as Wagner brought it around to due west. Seligman's experience told him they were at about half-throttle.

Looking at Tolle, Neumann said, "One of my watch crew told me right before we spotted the plane that you flushed the toilet when we were too deep, and that's what caused the gas leak."

"Is that true?" Seligman asked Tolle.

"Maybe," he replied. "But it doesn't matter. I sent a message to *BdU* and *SD* as we were sinking. I told them Neumann set off the scuttling charges and sank the boat, with much loss of life. That is what they will believe. I also reported that you, *Kapitän,* knew he was going to do it but did nothing to stop him."

"Where did you come up with this?" asked Seligman, his arms spread wide.

Tolle said, "I knew what Neumann wanted to do when I saw him walking through the boat like he was looking for something." Looking at Neumann, Tolle continued. "It was then that I remembered. You volunteered to help Siegfried place the scuttling charges when we were leaving port. You weren't trying to be helpful. You did that so you'd know where they were."

"That's a lie," shouted Neumann.

"Maybe," said Tolle, "but it's a lie the *SD* will believe because I told them so."

"You told them that to cover your own incompetence when you flushed the toilet." Neumann stared at Tolle, then laughed. "You Nazis can't even take a shit without causing problems."

Tolle raised the gun and pointed it at Neumann, but Seligman put his hands up as if to shield his first officer and said, "Wait a minute, Tolle." Turning to Neumann he said, "Shut up, Neumann. Let's think about this. Nobody's in a good situation here."

Tolle lowered the pistol slightly and Seligman said to him, "I'm taking you at your word that you are *SD* and you outrank me." He thought to himself, *I'm also taking into account you've already killed three people and have a gun.* "Let's see if there is some way we can make this situation work for all of us. What do you want to do?"

Tolle said, "I have a plan."

Seligman heard Neumann snicker, so he turned to the first officer and barked, "Shut up." Turning to Tolle, he said, "Let's hear it."

Tolle said, "I'm willing to let you live if you're willing to act like German Naval officers. Will you help me get ashore?"

"And then what?" asked Neumann. Seligman held his hand up in the direction of Neumann, but immediately put it down when he realized the question was valid and non-confrontational.

"I plan to find out exactly where we are, then use this ship's radio to contact *BdU* and determine if there are any targets in the area, things that would help the fatherland if they were destroyed. Then we'll steal some explosives and blow them up."

Seligman half-smiled at what he considered Tolle's naïveté and let out a low whistle. "That's an ambitious plan," he said. "Where do you intend to find these explosives?"

Before Tolle could answer Neumann said, "Let's rush

him, Willie. He can't get us both." Neumann began to slowly move away from Seligman.

Turning to Neumann, Seligman asked, "Were you going to sink us?" He continued to hold his arms away from his body, in deference to the man with the gun.

Neumann said, "Willie, you are afraid of being judged a bad man, but you lack the courage to be a good one. You should have taken a stand against the Nazis a long time ago."

"So you would kill yourself and the rest of our crew because you hate the Nazis?" Seligman replied. "Is *that* how you die for Germany? I'm not so sure Tolle's plan isn't better. At least if we go down, we go down fighting."

"Fighting the *wrong* people, Willie. *The wrong people!*"

Tolle laughed. "I didn't think I could count on you two," he said. And he fired.

Tolle's shot struck Seligman's right shoulder three inches above his nipple. It spun him around and he dropped to the deck. Tolle turned the gun toward Neumann, but the first officer reacted quickly, grabbing Tolle's hand and shoving it into the air just as Tolle pulled the trigger. A split second later the boat surged forward and Tolle, his legs against the back of the boat and his feet slipping in blood, flipped backwards into the ocean. When he surfaced he started firing in the direction of the boat, futilely emptying the last three chambers as he struggled to remain afloat.

Neumann bent over Seligman and turned him over. The front of the captain's shirt was soaked in blood, but he was conscious.

"I'll get you to shore," Neumann told him.

"You're a traitor, Oskar," said Seligman sadly as he gasped for air. "The only thing I want from you is that you get word to my family so they know what happened to me."

"You're talking out of your head," Neumann replied. "Tolle's a liar, I'm not a traitor, and you're not going to die."

When Neumann stood up, he noticed something entwined in his hand. It was Tolle's identification tags. When they were scuffling, Neumann's hand must have grabbed them from around Tolle's neck. He dropped them in his pocket and climbed the ladder to the bridge, timing his steps to allow the ship to bounce across the waves. When he got topside he saw why the boat had surged forward. Tolle's wild shot into the air had caught Wagner in the back of his head. He had fallen forward across the boat's throttles, shoving them into the full ahead position.

Neumann pulled Wagner's body off the throttles and cut them entirely back. He dumped Wagner unceremoniously over the side. He got some perverse pleasure in disposing of the Nazi, even if he wasn't the real spy. He spun the boat around 180 degrees and headed back out to sea, scanning the ocean's surface for Tolle.

It took Newmann about five minutes of trolling, but he spotted Tolle's head bobbing in the ocean. The spy had discarded the gun and was using both his hands to stay afloat. Neumann puttered slowly toward him. When he got about twenty meters from Tolle he gunned both engines and went straight toward him.

Neumann heard "Nein, nein," then a thump against the bow and the sound of the propellers hitting something. Looking behind the boat, he saw a patch in the ocean turning red.

Satisfied that Tolle was not going to be rescued, Neumann

turned the boat westward. Checking the compass quickly, he made a mild adjustment in steering to bring it to due west. He slowed the throttle and returned to the lower deck. After pulling Seligman into the cabin, Neumann searched several drawers for a first aid kit. Not finding one, he took off his shirt, put it over the wound, and placed the captain's hand on top of it.

"Push," he exhorted Seligman. "You must hold on."

Although Seligman seemed to put some downward pressure on the towel, he mumbled something that sounded like, "Go away." His eyes were closed, but fluttered every now and then.

Neumann climbed back up to the bridge and opened the throttle to full ahead. Based on the sun's position in the sky, he estimated it was mid-afternoon. For the next two hours the fishing boat chased the sun west until Neumann finally saw land.

He cut the throttle to a very low speed and went down to the cabin to check on Seligman. He had lost a lot of blood, his shoulder appeared to be broken, and he was unconscious. The towel was lying on the deck next to him, and there was blood everywhere.

"Hang on," Neumann told him. "I'm going to get you to a doctor." But Seligman didn't respond.

He noticed something sticking out of Seligman's blood-soaked pocket. Reaching for it gently, Neumann pulled it out and saw that it was a picture. It was covered with blood and cracking in spots but he could see that it was the picture of Seligman's wife and son that the captain had shown him on Christmas Day. He wiped it gently and stuck it in his own shirt pocket.

Neumann climbed to the bridge again and looked for a good place to land. He saw a few houses down near the ocean, so he steered a few degrees north, until he found a secluded area. Pointing the boat toward it, he increased speed, keeping a watch for rocks.

The boat reached shore in a calm surf just as the sun dropped below the horizon. Neumann ran the boat up onto the beach. After cutting the engines, he climbed down the ladder and went into the cabin.

Seligman was dead.

CHAPTER FIFTY

14 January, 1942
    Somewhere on the Georgia coast

Neumann slept under a tree, wrapped in a blanket he had found in the ship's cabin. At first light he climbed in the boat to retrieve Seligman's body. He was as gentle as possible, but he had to get it over the side. He was glad he had folded Seligman's arms across his chest and laid him out straight, because he was stiff.

He pulled the captain's body about fifty meters inland. Then, using a pot from the ship's galley, Neumann tore at the ground until he fashioned a grave approximately three-fourths of a meter deep. It took him two hours and he was afraid that any minute someone would come along, but no one did.

After laying the captain's body in the grave, Neumann stood at attention, put his right hand over his heart and quietly sang the German soldier's tribute to a fallen comrade, 'Ich hatt'einen kameraden'–'I once had a comrade.' As

Neumann settled Seligman in the grave, Neumann lost his grip and dropped Seligman's body the last one-fourth meter, causing Seligman's right hand to bounce on top of his own. Neumann remembered this, and choked up, when he came to a verse in the tribute that said, *"His hand reached up to hold mine...I can't give you my hand, you must stay in eternal life."*

When he finished burying Seligman, Neumann saluted his captain's grave and placed the picture of Seligman's family under a rock on top of it. He paced away from the ocean until he came to the nearest tree, a loblolly pine a distance of six paces away. With his knife, Neumann scored it with an 'x' about three feet off the ground.

He saluted one last time, then turned and began to walk away from the ocean. He had gone about twenty meters when he stopped, thought for a moment, then returned to the grave and retrieved the picture. When he put it in his pocket, his fingers touched Tolle's identification tag again. Neumann walked to the water's edge, wrapped his own tags around a rock, and flung them as far out into the water as he could. Putting Tolle's around his neck, he walked away.

Neumann spoke little English, so he rehearsed what he would do and say when he found someone, or someone found him.

He had plenty of time to practice. It took him several hours before he came to a road on which there was a cluster of houses. He didn't see anyone around the buildings, but he waited on the side of the road, and fifteen minutes later he heard a car approach. Facing it, he dropped to his knees, put his hands in the air, and said, "German sailor. I surrender." The car slowed to a stop about 10 meters from him and he repeated his mantra as the driver rolled down his window.

"What are you doing?" The driver asked, unable to hear him at first. "That's a good way to get yourself run over."

When at last he understood Neumann, he shouted, "*What?*" Neumann repeated the phrase, and the American pointed toward the first house and said, "Walk."

Neumann stood, but kept his hands over his head. He walked toward the house with the car traveling close behind him. When he got to it, he turned around to face the car.

His "captor" pointed to the ground until Neumann knelt, then said, "Stay put." Neumann didn't understand exactly what he said, but nevertheless replied, "*Ja, Ja.* Stay put," continuing to hold his hands over his head.

The American, who Neumann guessed to be about sixty, mounted the steps between glances back at his 'prisoner,' and knocked on the door. When it was opened Neumann heard an excited conversation between the driver and someone inside, with much pointing toward him.

In a minute, the driver came down and told him, "They are calling the police." Neumann didn't understand the first few words, but he did the last.

"*Ja, Ja, Polizei,*" he replied.

A woman with a cigarette dangling out of the corner of her mouth and a stare that could have cut diamonds came out of the house carrying a rifle with which she seemed to be quite familiar. They both walked behind him, and he was afraid they were going to shoot him, so he said, "Bitte! Bitte!" Please! Please! The man walked back in front of him and said, "You can put your hands down." Neumann didn't understand, so the American held his hands over his head and said, "Hands up." Dropping them, he said, "Hands down." Then he held his hands in the air again, swept them down, and said, "Hands down."

"Ja," said Neumann. With a smile, he lowered his hands, and said, "Hands down." Patting his chest he said, "Erich

Tolle." He pointed toward his 'captor', and said, *"Dein Name?"*

The American put his hand on his chest and said, "Daniel Musgrave."

"Daniel," Neumann repeated, then put his hand to his chest again and said, "Erich Tolle."

"Tell that Nazi bastard to shut up or I'm gonna shoot his ass," said the woman behind him.

The police took Neumann to a small town, where they locked him in a cell. There were two other cells, but he was the only prisoner. Three hours later the same two police officers led another man to the cell. He introduced himself in German as Gerald Updegraff and said he was an FBI agent. "What is your name?" Updegraff snarled. The way he paced back and forth, his frown, even the fact that he left his hat on, all said he was not prepared to believe anything Neumann told him.

"Erich Tolle. Radioman."

"Serial number?"

Neumann rattled it off without hesitation, having memorized it on his walk to the road. Updegraff, however, was having trouble understanding the German numbers. He kept repeating them, switching from German to English, and back.

"Where are your dog tags?" Updegraff abruptly asked.

Neumann took them off his neck and handed them to the American, who was looking him up and down. Neumann's eyes followed the American's gaze down his body. He was wearing a t-shirt, now in tatters, and British army fatigue pants, the outfit that had so enraged Wagner last July.

Raising his eyes to look into Neumann's he asked, "Why

are you wearing British army uniform pants?" He copied the serial number off the tags and handed them back to Neumann.

"When we captured the naval base at Lorient we found many British uniforms in storage there. They are much more comfortable than ours, so we were allowed to wear them on the U-boat."

Updegraff grunted. "We assume enemy soldiers that are wearing our uniforms are spies, and we shoot them. What do you say to that?"

It was all Neumann could do to smile; Inside he quaked at the threat. He knew the German army did the same thing, but had forgotten he was wearing the pants. He shoved his hands into his pockets so Updegraph wouldn't see them trembling, and said, "Why would I wear a British uniform in America if I were a German spy? If you talk to the man who first found me he will tell you that I immediately identified myself as a German sailor and told him I was from a U-boat. A spy who surrenders is not much of a threat, is he?"

"A spy who surrenders is a dead man, if I have anything to say about it." Updegraff stared at him for a minute, then sniffed the air and curled his upper lip. "You stink," he said. "When was the last time you bathed?" He shook his head, as if he were trying to get the odor out of his nose.

"When we left Lorient." Neumann was so used to the stench of fifty men closed up in a U-boat that he didn't notice it anymore.

"When was that?" Updegraff moved back to escape the odor.

Neumann thought for a moment, then said, "December 23."

"So you were out to sea on Christmas?"

"*Ja*. But we had a tree."

"Really? How heartwarming." Updegraff looked at his

notes and asked, "Why was your boat off the coast of the United States?"

"I wish I could help you," Neumann said. "But I was just a radioman. I was not privy to our orders."

"But as a radioman you must have seen the messages sent to your boat."

"Always coded. I would write them down exactly as they were sent to us, then give them to our *kapitän* for decoding."

Updegraff turned around, looking for something. He found a chair over in the corner and pulled it out to where he had been pacing. Sitting down, he folded his arms across his chest and asked, "So what happened to your U-boat?"

Neumann sat on the cot in the cell and recounted what had occurred, including the toilet being flushed at an unsafe depth, although in the retelling it was Frick who had flushed it, not Tolle. He was as accurate as he could be with times and locations, then described the plane that had sunk them. "You can check it out," he told his interrogator. "I bet that pilot has been bragging to everyone about sinking our boat."

"Don't worry, I will check it ." Updegraff already knew there were rumors of a U-boat sunk by a plane several days earlier, but every plane that went out on patrol claimed to have destroyed something. Even though the pilot said he dropped the sailors a raft, Updegraff couldn't believe that anyone could make it to land from as far out as the pilot said they had been when he sank them.

"How'd you get to shore?"

Neumann went through the entire episode, but said Wagner, not Tolle, killed the fishermen. He also didn't mention burying Seligman.

"You say there were four of you? And three Americans? Where are the bodies?"

"Wagner threw everyone overboard when he shot them. Before he could re-load to shoot me, I overpowered him and threw his scrawny ass overboard. Then I ran over him with the ship."

"So Wagner killed the three Americans, Captain Seligman, and First Officer Neumann?"

"Yes, sir."

"And threw their bodies overboard?"

Neumann nodded.

"Why?"

Neumann paused, afraid too quick an answer would sound rehearsed.

"Wagner was a Nazi. The rest of us...we wanted... hoped...to surrender. He said something about getting ashore and blowing things up. Oh, and he also said he thought Neumann and Seligman were traitors."

"He wanted to kill you because you wanted to surrender?"

"I think so, although you are asking me to read the mind of a very troubled young man."

"And no one else made it to shore?"

"No, sir," said Neumann. "We were too far out."

Updegraff nodded slightly. For the first time, Neumann thought the FBI agent believed him. "And the ship is still on the beach?" the American asked.

Neumann nodded. "In the exact condition I described to you, covered in blood where Wagner shot the men."

Updegraff abruptly stood up, and said, "You better hope I can find the pilot of that plane. Otherwise, you're probably going to be shot as a spy. Goodbye, Ensign Tolle. I hope for your sake, you have told me the truth."

"Oh, I have, *Herr* Updegraff," Neumann said, standing up. He extended his hand through the bars, but Updegraff ignored it. He stared at Neumann for a moment, then turned and left.

CHAPTER FIFTY-ONE

Late afternoon of 3 August, 1972
    Atlanta, Ga. Home of Erich Tolle

"So you are not Erich Tolle?" asked Ernst.

"I am known as Erich Tolle, but I am *not* the Erich Tolle that murdered your father. At the time your father was killed my name was Oskar Neumann, and I was the first officer on U-112, commanded by your father, Wilhelm Seligman."

"Were you *planning* on sinking it and killing all the men you served with?" Ernst looked at Tolle, studying his face for some emotion, shame, pride, anything, that would help Ernst understand how a man could do that to his comrades, but at first Tolle's face was impassive.

"I thought about it, even plotted how to do it. You see, I was very strongly against the Nazis and the war. It was all Hitler's doing."

"It couldn't have been all Hitler," said Greta. "The whole country went along."

"*Ja*, but there was some opposition. There were many

failed attempts to kill him. Hitler was a mad man, but he was a genius at manipulation."

"So you *would have* sunk it and killed my father?" asked Ernst.

Tolle sat for a moment, a blank look on his face, and Ernst began to wonder if he would answer. Then Tolle said, "I asked myself that question every night for twenty years. I would go to bed and try to sleep, but always the question came up. *Would I have killed my crewmates?*"

The two men stared at each other. Neither blinked; neither spoke. Greta asked, "But you don't ask yourself anymore?"

"No, because ten years ago, I realized the answer."

"What is it?" asked Greta in a whisper, leaning forward.

"Yes, *Herr* Neumann, or *Herr* Tolle, or *whatever* it is I am supposed to call you. What *is* the answer?" Ernst asked, his fists clenched.

Neumann flinched at Ernst's anger, and he hesitated.

Ernst stood up and said, "My father was on that boat, and the rest of the crew were my countrymen; a different generation, but my countrymen just the same. And so I ask you again. Would you have sunk U-112 and killed my father?"

Tolle leaned forward and rubbed the palms of his hands together. Ernst noticed a tear trickling down his cheek, and more pooled in his eyes.

"They were my countrymen, too," he said, so quietly Ernst almost didn't hear him. "As to what to call me, the whole world calls me Erich. I hope *you* will call me Oskar. Now, to answer your question.

"Except for Tolle, the men on the boat were no more my enemy than the Americans on the ship that rescued us, or the Americans, and British, and every other nationality, on the ships we were sent to sink. Wagner was a Nazi sympathizer and I didn't *like* him, but he was young and misguided; not a reason to kill him. I killed the only man who was my enemy. He was the only one I *could have killed*. But fate punishes me by cursing me with his name for the rest of my life." The tears left his eyes and streaked his face.

"You didn't have to change your name," said Ernst. "Why did you? And to his, of all people?"

Tolle nodded. "While I was digging..." Tolle hesitated and Ernst flinched, realizing what Tolle was going to say. "While I was digging...your father's...grave, I thought about what would happen if I ran into any Nazis in a POW camp. By this time we had been at war with England for two and a half years. There were Germans in POW camps there, and we knew that the Nazi prisoners were allowed to control them. We heard of prisoners being killed because they were sympathetic to the Allies. Tolle had bragged that he radioed the *BdU* and told them that I sabotaged *eins eins zwei*. *BdU* would have gotten word to the Nazis in the all the POW camps to be watching for Oskar Neumann. I would have suffered a 'visit from the Holy Ghost.' That is what we prisoners called the murder of an Allied sympathizer.

"Erich Tolle would not be popular with *all* the prisoners, but the Nazis would protect him. Also, Tolle said he was in the *Ausland SD*, the Nazi foreign intelligence service, and the Nazis frequently gave *SD* members a new identity; chances are his name was *not* Erich Tolle. If it was not, there would never be family looking for a person of that name. I could make up my whole life story and not have to worry about someone finding out it was a lie. If I was going to survive, I had a better chance of surviving as Erich Tolle than as Oskar Neumann."

"And my father?" asked Ernst, his nostrils flaring. "Have you ever returned to his grave?"

Tolle nodded and said, "Many times. I respected your father. One of my greatest regrets is that he died thinking I was a traitor. We disagreed on attacking American shipping, but he was a good man, determined and forthright. I can see him in you.

"When I surrendered, I was taken to Savannah, where I was held in the city jail for several months. Eventually, the United States opened the POW camp at Fort Benning and I was sent there. Every day they sent me to work on a farm nearby, where I met a young woman who lived a short distance away. She would visit me as I worked; fraternization was forbidden but I was there for more than three years. I became friends with the man I worked for, and he allowed her visits. When the war was over I was sent back to Germany.

"I returned to the United States in 1947 and married the woman. You met Barbara earlier. But first, I went to Savannah and from there found my way to where I had made landfall. The 'x' on the tree was faded, but still visible. It is in a protected area."

Ernst and Greta looked at each other. Ernst cocked his head questioningly, but she just shrugged, so he asked Tolle, "What is a protected area?"

"A wildlife sanctuary. No construction is allowed there because of the wildlife that lives in the area. I've gone back every year on the anniversary of his death and placed flowers on his grave." Ernst nodded. "No one knows he is buried there except for me." Tolle paused, then added, "And now, the two of you."

Greta smiled, happy to be included, but Ernst shook his fist and asked, "Why didn't you try to find me? You said my father asked you to."

"Yes, and I tried," said Tolle, holding his hands outstretched. "But I was searching *Dresden* for a boy named Ernst *Seligman*, and his mother, Marie *Seligman*. I didn't know you changed your name to *Möller* and moved to Berlin until today. Dresden was destroyed, so many people dead. I assumed you and your mother had both been killed there." His hands bounced each time he said, "Dresden" and "Seligman."

"Actually, she was killed in Hamburg," Ernst acknowledged, his anger waning as he understood the challenges that had confronted Tolle. He sat there quietly, thinking about everything he had heard. *It all makes sense,* he thought. *Please offer to take me to my father's grave.*

"Would you like to see where your father is buried?" asked Tolle.

CHAPTER FIFTY-TWO

4 August, 1972
   Somewhere on the Georgia coast

The next day, both Tolle and Ernst encouraged Barbara to come along, but she begged off.

"It'll be hot and y'all will be talkin' German," she said to Tolle, "and, you'll feel like you have to translate for me, an' that'll slow down y'all's talkin'. I'm gonna stay here. I know y'all will have a good time."

It was as hot as Barbara had feared, but the car was air conditioned. The drive was part interstate and part two-lane highway, and would take more than six hours. As they rode, Tolle and Ernst in the front seat, Greta in back, Tolle talked about President Eisenhower getting the idea for a system of highways from his wartime experience in Germany, where he saw how beneficial the *autobahn* was.

"Still, he was a military man," said Tolle, "so he insisted that at least one mile of every five be straight and flat so that military planes could land on them, if necessary." Tolle shook his head and said, "We always think about war first."

After a while, they fell into a comfortable quiet. Ernst and Greta recognized the melodies of the songs on the radio even if they didn't always understand the English lyrics. No one had spoken for a while when Ernst, sitting in the front seat with Tolle, turned to him and said, "You told me yesterday no one knew you buried my father there on the beach. Why didn't you tell anyone?"

Tolle grasped the radio knob and turned down the volume. He tilted his head toward Ernst and said, "I thought the Americans would want to move his body. I wanted to let him rest in peace, especially after I found out the grave was in a protected area. It seemed right for a U-boat *kapitän* to be buried within sight and sound of the sea. But if you want to move him I'll tell the authorities what I did."

"Let me see where he is," said Ernst. "If it's a nice place it might be best to leave him there." He started to ask another question, then stopped. Tolle glanced over at him and saw his hesitation.

"You want to know about your father, don't you?" he asked, and Ernst smiled. "You must have been very young when you lost him."

"I was four," said Ernst.

"So young," said Tolle, shaking his head. He cleared his throat. "Your father cared about his men. We lost a man overboard right after Christmas, about three weeks before we were sunk. We searched, but it was only the new crew members who thought we would find him. The experienced men, myself included, knew the seas were too rough, and it was at night, but your father searched as long as we could. I saw it in your father's face, how much he hated to give up. He felt more than just a *kapitän's* responsibility. I could see the worry in his face and knew that with him it was personal. It was like he was searching for his own kin." Tolle shot a glance at Ernst and smiled.

"He cared about the enemy, as well. If we had time and there were no enemy warships nearby, we would surface after we sank a ship and check on the survivors. If they hadn't saved some food he would give them some of ours. He would have the navigator give them their location so they would be able to plot a course to follow. He knew it was our job to sink the ships but he was glad if the crew escaped safely."

Sitting in the back seat, Greta leaned forward to hear better as Tolle told them about the Christmas tree they had on board, and how Seligman allowed the men to come to the command deck to smell it.

"That was 1941, our last Christmas on U-112. Your father made a big deal out of seeing that all the men had letters from home. He knew I had no home, so he came by my bunk with a letter from your mother. He let me read it, even though it was pretty mushy." He paused, then said, "Apparently your parents had, shall we say, a very affectionate visit before we sailed that year."

Ernst thought for a minute, then said, "That was the last time I saw him. My mother told me he had to leave early because we declared war against the United States."

"That would have been it," said Tolle.

"Man, I'd love to see that letter," said Ernst.

"I'm sure you would," said Tolle. "It must have been lost with the boat."

They stopped talking for a moment as the news came on the radio, and they heard that a man named Arthur Bremer was sentenced to 63 years in prison for shooting Alabama governor George Wallace in 1968 while he campaigned for the presidency.

When Tolle returned to his narrative, he focused on

Ernst. "He was always talking about you," Tolle said. "He called you his little man, and would say you were the smartest child he had ever seen. I'd tease him. 'Just how many kids does a U-boat *kapitän* come into contact with,' I'd ask, and he'd say, 'Doesn't matter. Mine's the smartest, and the kindest.'" Ernst raised his eyebrows, smiled, and looked back at Greta.

"The thing I admired about him most, however, was his devotion to your mother. Whenever we were in port, everyone on the crew, married or single, whored around..." Tolle stopped suddenly, remembering Greta. He glanced in the back seat but she just nodded at him as if to say, "Carry on."

Emboldened by her acknowledgement, he continued, "But not your father. He became furious one time when a commanding officer misunderstood him and thought he wanted to see a girlfriend instead of you and your mother. Your father would have hit the man, but he knew he would end up in the stockade, so he held off. Nevertheless, he complained all afternoon about what the other *käpitan* had said."

Here was the father who Aunt Marta wanted me to know, and to emulate, thought Ernst. But *what would my father say about the way I behave towards women?* He wondered. That thought was too unpleasant to contemplate, so he changed the subject. "Why do you think the German archives have no record of U-112?" he asked Tolle.

Tolle shrugged and shook his head. "I guess the other Erich Tolle's message to BdU had an effect."

"What kind of effect?" asked Greta.

"I always wondered how submarine command would handle the idea that a saboteur sank one of their boats. The Nazis didn't like to acknowledge that anyone dissented from their point of view. My guess is that they altered the records."

"That's exactly what Professor Bredow thought," said Greta, smacking her hand on Ernst's shoulder.

"You mentioned Professor Bredow yesterday," said Tolle. "Who is he?"

After Ernst explained who Bredow was and how he had come across him, Tolle nodded his head slowly. "He sounds interesting," he said. "I'd like to meet him."

"Oh, he'd love to meet you," said Greta. "You could help him fill up his U-112 binder with crew member names, patrols, ships sunk, all that stuff that German Archives doesn't have. Did I tell you I used to work in Archives?"

"No," Tolle replied.

"I was there for two years. Gunther Hunt, our archivist, always said the Nazis kept meticulous records. He was constipated, you know."

"No, I didn't," said Tolle, sounding as if that was the most interesting thing he had heard all day. Ernst shook his head and put his hand over his face as Tolle continued. "*Herr* Hunt may be right about the meticulous records, but they were also masters at lying to cover their tracks. I guess they decided to hide U-112 so they would never have to admit what happened. When I was at Fort Benning, there were other prisoners, confirmed Nazis, who asked me if I was sure Oskar Neumann was dead. Someone had gotten word to them. I know they intended to kill him...me...if they ever found him. I guess the Nazis changed their records as a way of killing U-112, also."

Tolle had slowed down as they drove through a small town, and seemed to be looking for something.

"There it is," he said, and turned the car into a parking lot in front of a building with a sign that said, 'Florist'. "Come on," he said to Ernst and Greta. "You two pick them out, and I'll pay for them."

Greta followed along as Ernst chose a bouquet of white

carnations, daisies, and tiny red rosebuds. Tolle didn't notice until they got back to the car that Greta had lagged behind and bought a single red rose with her own money. Holding the door for her to get in, he said to her, "How very nice of you." In return, Greta dazzled him with her dimples.

Twenty minutes later, on a narrow, two-lane road, Tolle slowed, then pulled off to the side. "I think we're here," he said, parking the car.

After locking the car, they walked eastwardly, Ernst carrying his bouquet, and Greta the one rose. She was wearing walking shoes today, instead of her usual high heels. Normally Ernst loved watching her walk in heels; they made her butt roll like thunder. Today, though, they were walking in loose ground, so he was glad she had been practical with her choice.

"Is this the path you followed when you got here?" asked Greta, practically skipping through the loose earth and sand mixture.

"Somewhat," said Tolle, "but the road we came in on wasn't here back then, so it was a lot longer walk." Greta looked at him as he spoke, walking with a carefree gait. He said, "Watch where you step. There are alligators around."

"Are you serious?" cried Greta, looking at the ground and grabbing Ernst's free hand.

"Yes, and they attack people holding hands," teased Tolle. Greta grinned and pointed an admonishing finger at him, but she started watching where she was walking.

"There really *are* alligators around," Tolle said. "Just don't walk right up on top of one, or walk too close to standing water."

It wasn't ten minutes before Greta shouted, "I see the ocean!"

"Indeed you do," said Tolle. "Not too much farther now."

They came into a small clearing and Tolle said, "Give me

a minute. I want to get my bearings." It was quiet except for waves crashing on the beach on the other side of some palm trees. The sun beat down on them. Tolle, sweat stains in the armpits of his shirt, put his hands on his hips and turned in a slow circle, looking around. He stopped, a slow smile breaking over his lips. Walking slowly in a southerly direction, Ernst and Greta following in single file, he approached a loblolly pine. Placing his hand waist-high on the trunk, Tolle turned to Ernst and Greta and said, "Look." He rubbed the tree as if he were applying suntan lotion, and Ernst could see where the bark had healed over a cut. "This is it," Tolle said.

Tolle put his back against the tree and paced six steps toward the ocean. When he stopped, he waved his arm to the couple and they followed his steps, stopping in a patch of sand with a few sprouts of scrub grass poking through in places. Tolle removed his hat, a baseball cap with the Atlanta Braves logo on the front, and placed it over his heart. "Your father rests here," he said solemnly, eyes cast downward.

They stood silently as the summer wind played through the upper branches of the trees, then Tolle began to sing in a rich, strong voice. Ernst recognized the song as *'Ich hatt' einen kameraden'*.

When Tolle finished, Ernst laid the flowers on his father's makeshift grave, then Greta squatted down and placed the single rose next to them. She whispered, *"dankeschön,"* then stood up.

Ernst reached into his pocket and pulled out a box. He opened it, and Tolle recognized a bosun's pipe inside. Greta and Tolle watched curiously as Ernst raised the pipe to his mouth and moistened his dry lips with his tongue.

His eyes glistening with tears and sweat rolling down his face, he blew one continuous high note, which he ended abruptly after a count of eight. Tolle remembered it—"The

Still," the bosun's order to come to attention in the presence of a commanding officer. He snapped his back ramrod straight and gave his best military salute over the grave. After the traditional count of five, Ernst blew "Carry On," a warbling whistle similar to a canary. Tolle snapped his hand down to his side.

Tolle turned to Ernst and held out his hand. Ernst took hold of it with his own right hand, at the same time wiping his face with his left, fearful that his tears would make Greta think less of him. Shaking the other man's hand, he said, "Thank you for bringing me to my father, Oskar. You are an honorable man."

Oskar enveloped Ernst in an embrace and said, "Your father died condemning me. Hearing his son say that is like forgiveness from him. Thank you." When Ernst saw that Oskar was crying, also, he was no longer ashamed of his tears. He tucked his head against Oskar's chest.

Oskar let go of Ernst with his left arm and held it out toward Greta in a welcoming gesture. She immediately slipped into his embrace and the three of them stood there, intertwined, an occasional sob escaping from first one, then the other, until all three were unashamedly crying.

Regaining his composure, Oskar said, "I have waited thirty years to share this with someone. I'm so pleased it was you." He broke the embrace, then said, "I have one more thing for you."

"What is it?" asked Greta, wiping her face with the palms of her hands and bouncing as best she could in the sand.

Oskar reached into his shirt pocket. "Your father had this in his pocket when he died. I almost lost it when I was searched by the FBI. The agent wanted to throw it away, but I told him it was my brother and his family and they had been killed in a bombing raid. He let me keep it. Now that I've met you, I feel like what I told him was true."

Oskar handed Ernst a picture. It was cracked and had traces of a brown substance on it, but the subjects were clearly identifiable. Ernst held it reverently for a moment, marveling at how young they were; noticeably younger than he was at present. He handed it to Greta, and said, "This is me with my ..." Another sob broke through his reserved demeanor, and he couldn't continue. Standing behind him now, Oskar placed his hand on Ernst's shoulder as Greta examined the picture.

"Your mother was very beautiful," she said, then looked up at Ernst. "And you look just like your father." She reached with her right hand to caress his cheek and wipe his tears. "So handsome, so strong."

CHAPTER FIFTY-THREE

17 January, 1942
Reich Chancellery, Berlin

Admirals Raeder and Dönitz went up the steps to the Reich Chancellery, walked through a medium-sized reception room, then between double doors almost seventeen feet high. Passing through a round room with a domed ceiling, they saw the intimidating gallery, 480 feet in length and, by design, twice as long as the Hall of Mirrors in Versailles, where Germany had been forced to admit guilt for World War I. Every time he passed through it, Raeder was glad he was German.

"I don't like delivering unpleasant news to him," said Raeder. "He's not going to be happy when he hears this. How could you let this happen?"

Dönitz said, "I didn't 'let this happen'. I warned Seligman to keep an eye on Neumann. It is Seligman's fault."

Raeder waved his hand dismissively. Dönitz trailed him

by a half-step. *If he's smart, he'll stay behind me,* thought Raeder.

By the time they arrived at *der Führer's* massive office, they had walked almost a quarter mile. They were immediately ushered into his private chambers, only to find Hitler already in full rage.

"*That treasonous dog,*" were the first words out of his mouth as he rose from his chair behind his desk. "How did you let this traitor on board one of my U-boats? I should have you both shot."

"*Mein Führer,*" said Raeder in his most soothing voice as they both snapped to attention, "We cannot be sure that what is being reported actually happened. We are trying to find out if there are any survivors. If there are, we will hear who survived from our prisoners already there when the crew is interned. Then we will know if the report from that radioman is accurate and whether the U-boat was deliberately sunk."

"*That radioman,* as you call him," said Hitler, slamming his fist down on the desk, "was an agent of the *SD.* His name was Erich Tolle, and he had been placed on U-112 by my order, to observe the officers. They were not party faithful. I wanted him to watch them for evidence of treason and if he discovered any, I planned on making an example of them. And you *idiots* sent them to America. Something has to be done. No one can know this." Hitler waved his arm, as if swatting at a fly, and began pacing in front of them.

Neither Raeder nor Dönitz seemed surprised that the government was investigating their officers without notifying them. Instead, they seemed intent on avoiding implication in any wrongdoing.

"I warned the *Kapitän* before he left," said Dönitz. "I told him I had my doubts about Neumann. I told him I wanted a full report when they returned so that if Neumann needed to be replaced, we could do so."

Hitler stopped in front of the U-Boat Commanding Officer and glared at him. Dönitz swallowed.

"We must ensure that the traitorous dogs on that boat receive no recognition. I have ordered all record of them serving in the *Kriegsmarine* be eliminated." Spittle from Hitler's mouth sprayed Dönitz's face as he continued. "Their personnel records are to be changed to show every one of them as a conscripted private in the army. They will be listed as executed for war crimes in Russia. Any record of the officers' attendance at Flensburg-Murwik Naval Academy will be removed. All records of U-112's service will be destroyed. History will show that it was ordered and laid down but cancelled as outdated."

Dönitz's mind was racing. Would they be able to carry this off? Change all the records of a boat and its fifty-two-man crew?

Raeder interrupted his thoughts by asking Hitler, "How will you say it was outdated?"

Hitler said, "We will say that technology passed it by. We had planned for it to be similar to the last one built before it, but we came up with new equipment, so it was cancelled."

He began pacing, again, and said, "The British have already begun shipping our POWs to the United States. We must get word to any of them in America. If any men from U-112 come into their camp, especially Oskar Neumann, they are to be killed as quickly and quietly as possible. All except Erich Tolle. If he is alive, he is to be protected."

Hitler looked at the men, then said, "Go on, get to work on this. I never want to hear the names of these traitors again. They didn't exist. The boat didn't exist. *Every record will be changed.* I never want *anyone* to find *anything* about *U-eins eins zwei* or its crew."

CHAPTER FIFTY-FOUR

5 January, 1972
   In-flight from United States to Germany

Ernst and Greta both fell asleep as soon as their overnight flight back to Germany took off, but four hours in, Ernst awoke to Greta shaking him. "I need to stretch my legs," she said, edging to the front of her window seat.

"Go ahead," he told her, not opening his eyes.

"I will if you'll let me by."

Still half asleep, he didn't move until her fist drilled into his side and he felt her fingers grab flesh and twist. Jerking up in his seat, he said, "OK, honey, OK."

She leaned toward him and whispered in his ear, "You are so sweet. Want to join the mile-high club?"

He looked at her, eyes wide. She batted her eyelashes and flashed her dimples.

"Do you think we can?" he asked, as he stood up, suddenly wide awake.

"No," she said, passing him. "I just needed you to wake up." She patted his chest and kissed him on the cheek.

When she returned Ernst was flipping through a magazine. "I want to ask you something," she said as she squeezed by him and settled back into her seat.

"About the mile-high club?" he asked.

"No, silly. That's not going to happen. Everything we've learned about your father has gotten me thinking about some things you've said about your family."

Ernst nodded, setting the magazine aside.

"You told me once that your earliest memory of Aunt Marta was of her being happy-go-lucky, but that was early in the war. By the time it ended, her personality had changed to the serious woman she is today. Do you think it was because of losing your parents?"

Ernst took her hand. "It wasn't just them," he said. "She lost everyone that was close to her, except me."

Greta looked away and muttered, "And you're not always a day at the beach."

Ernst rolled his eyes. Then he told her, "She lost a baby, too."

"Really?" Greta leaned toward him. "Was that the baby, Greta, that she mentioned when you came to the Archives?"

Ernst nodded.

"When was that?"

Ernst thought for a minute, then said, "I think it was shortly after the war. I can't remember exactly, but we were hungry all the time, and that didn't happen until the Siemens plant closed near the end of the war. Aunt Marta wouldn't talk about it for the longest time. Finally, that day at the Archives she mentioned it to you, so after we left, I asked her about it. I thought the father might have been American but she said the baby was *Russenkinder.*"

"So she was raped by the Russians?" she asked.

Ernst nodded.

"I suspected so," said Greta. "Sometimes she can be so dark, just like my mother. I thought when we first met that she hated me, but that wasn't it. I made her think of that baby."

"I don't know about tha…"

"I do! Ernst, don't you see? It makes perfect sense."

Ernst mulled it over. "It's possible," he finally agreed. "Since you brought up her moods, I want to tell you something. I've decided when we get home that I'm going to see if I can draw her out about a few things."

Greta leaned forward. "Like what?"

"For years, I've had this recurring memory that soldiers came to our flat. I've asked Aunt Marta about it several times, but every time I did she changed the subject, until that day we came to the Archives. I asked her then about the soldiers and she said they were American, but then she said the baby was *Russenkinder*."

"Weren't the Russians there first, before the Americans?"

"That's the problem. I never really remembered, or if I did, the memory was jumbled. But since she told me her baby had a Russian father, I've been remembering little bits and pieces. When we get back, I'm going to ask her about something I think happened, but can't be sure about."

Greta raised her eyebrows, but Ernst looked away, picked up the magazine, and started flipping through it.

"Nooo," she said, pulling it out of his hand. "You can't say something like that, then not finish it."

He looked around the cabin. It was night and most of the people were asleep. Near the front of the plane a baby was crying. Ernst leaned toward Greta and whispered in her ear, "I think Aunt Marta killed a soldier."

Greta gasped and pulled back so she could look at his

face. "With her bare hands?" she whispered. "Because I can see her doing that. "

Ernst shook his head and sighed. He leaned so close that he could smell the shampoo Greta had used that morning, and said, "No, smarty. I think she shot him with his own rifle."

They moved their heads so Greta could whisper in his ear. "Do you think he was baby Greta's father?"

"Who knows?" Ernst said. "Before I ask that, I want to find out if my memory is correct."

"I should be there when you talk to her," said Greta, nodding her head.

"I don't think so," said Ernst. "That might intimidate her."

"Are we talking about the same Aunt Marta? Because the one I know is *not* going to be intimidated by me."

"Why do you want to be there?" asked Ernst, ignoring her comment.

Now it was Greta who looked around the cabin. Everyone close to them was asleep. She spoke quietly. "Are you aware Aunt Marta came to see me?"

Ernst raised his eyebrows and shook his head.

Greta said, "It was right before you got the airline tickets to go to America." She told Ernst about her meeting with Marta at her flat.

"What does that prove?" asked Ernst. The baby had finally stopped crying, and he imagined it latched safely onto its mother's breast. In his mind, the mother looked like Greta.

"It was two days after that when Aunt Marta told you to take me with you to the United States, instead of her. She told me to call her Aunt Marta, too, even though when she came to see me she told me to call her *Fraulein* Möller. I think I connected with her and if I'm there she will be more comfortable discussing it than if it is just the two of you. After all, you're going to ask your aunt, who's practically your mother, about being raped. She may not want to talk to you about it."

Ernst shook his head and frowned. "I don't know," he said. "She and I have always had a special relationship."

He looked at Greta, who raised her eyebrows questioningly and asked, "Is her avoiding your questions all these years the part you consider 'special?'"

Ernst pressed his lips together. He knew she was right; it would be awkward, but he still wasn't sure how his aunt would feel about Greta being present.

"Let me think about it," he said.

"That means no." Greta sat back in her seat and folded her arms across her chest.

"That means let me think about it."

CHAPTER FIFTY-FIVE

6 January, 1972
Berlin

Aunt Marta met them at the airport the next morning. After the subway ride home, Ernst and Greta took a nap, then they spent the afternoon talking about everyone they had met, especially Oskar.

"He wants to come to our wedding, Aunt Marta," said Greta. "You'll get to meet him. Won't that be great?"

"That will be great," agreed Marta. "I can't believe it, Ernst," she said, as her nephew returned from the bathroom. "It's like you found the needle in a haystack."

"Yes, I did," he replied, standing next to Greta. "And there's something else I found."

Marta cocked her head to the side and asked, "What?"

"I found the father you wanted me to know. Oskar told me what a good man he was, just like you said. I want to be more like him."

Greta looked up at him from her chair and smiled as

Marta walked toward him, arms outstretched, and began crying.

"Please don't do that," Ernst said, but he put his arms around her waist and quietly said, "You were right."

"Of course I was," she said, kissing him on the cheek. "Now let's fix supper."

The three of them worked on supper together, catching up on what had happened in Berlin since they had been gone, but every time Ernst or Greta brought up home, Marta somehow got the conversation back to their trip. She wanted to know every detail, even what they had eaten at each meal. Ernst wondered if she knew what he wanted to ask and was controlling the conversation to keep him from doing so.

When supper was over and the three of them were clearing the table, Marta told them, "You must be sure to write Sergeant Johnson and tell him how everything turned out. He sounds very nice."

"He and Sergeant Thomas were both so nice, and so happy for us when they found out we were getting married," said Greta. "Perhaps we should invite *them* to the wedding, too," she said, bouncing on the balls of her feet.

"Perhaps we should send them some pictures, instead," said Ernst, as they finished carrying the dishes into the kitchen. Marta turned on the water in the sink, but Ernst said, "If you will leave those, Greta and I will wash them later. Let's go in the living room. I want to show you something that Oskar gave me."

"Sounds mysterious," Marta said, setting some dishes down on the counter instead of in the sink. They went into the living room, where Ernst took a chair opposite his Aunt and pulled the picture out of his shirt pocket.

"Have you ever seen this?" he asked, handing it to her.

Despite the picture being cracked and faded, with blood stains turned brown with age, she recognized it instantly.

"*Gott im Himmel*," she cried. "I used to have a bigger copy in my room, but I lost it during the bombing." She held the picture in front of her and studied it. "I wonder if we can get this copied so I could have a print." She was rocking a little as she sat looking at it. "There's my dear, sweet Marie, with Willie, and you, just a baby." Looking up at Ernst, she said, "This proves Oskar was with your father on the U-boat, and that it was built. We must take it to the Archives and shove it in front of *Herr* Hunt's nose." Marta put her hand to her cheek and wiped away a tear. "What is this brown stuff on it?" She scratched at the picture. "It's coming off."

"Please don't," said Ernst quickly. "It was…it is…Papa's blood. The picture was in his pocket when Tolle shot him."

"Oh, my," said Marta. "How awful. I don't even want to think about it." She rubbed her fingers on her dress.

"I learned a lot about Papa on this trip, Aunt Marta, but I remembered some things, too."

Marta stared at the picture and said, "I remember that blouse your mother was wearing. I gave it to her for her birthday, then wanted to borrow it. She wouldn't let me have it, though. She said she wanted to wear it for your family picture."

"Aunt Marta," said Ernst, "I'd like to ask you about something."

Ernst heard an ambulance go by outside, its siren blaring. The sound had almost faded before Marta spoke again.

"I think I know what you want to ask about," she said. She continued to study the picture, as if memorizing the faces in it. "You want to ask about the Russian soldiers, don't you?"

Ernst saw a few tears on her cheeks. "Is that all right?" he asked. "I think you were…I know you were raped. We talked about that when we went to the Archives. But I think something else happened, too."

"Yes," she said, her voice fragile. "Some…something else

did happen. I was wondering if..if this trip would bring the memory back to you," she said, brushing another tear from her cheek.

Greta moved next to Marta and touched her arm gently. When Marta looked at her, Greta smiled her silent support.

"You want to know about one particular soldier," Marta said. She rubbed her forehead.

"Yes," Ernst replied. "Can we talk about it?"

Marta stopped rubbing her head. "Yes. It's time," she said, but returned to staring at the picture. "Ask your question, and I will answer it."

Very softly, he asked, "Did you kill a Russian soldier?"

"*Nein*," she said, looking up from the picture. Their stares riveted each other's and a small smile played around her lips. "*You* did."

CHAPTER FIFTY-SIX

6 July, 1945
Berlin

"Marta! Come quick!" Marta heard the voice shouting her name over and over, each time a little louder, like the sound of a train as it approaches the station. Finally it was right outside her door, and an excited hand pounded, demanding that she open it.

When she did, she stood face to face with *Frau* Kleist, who flitted about like a bird released from its cage. "The Americans," *Frau* Kleist panted as she shouted. "They're here! We're finally in the American district. We can go out again!" *Frau* Kleist's face was radiant. "Come see," she said, grabbing Marta's hand and pulling her toward the steps.

"Wait," Marta replied. "Let me comb my hair."

"It doesn't matter what you look like. Let's go." She pulled Marta's hand again, and this time the younger woman followed her.

"It's amazing," Marta said, as they walked through the

street. Even though there was still rubble everywhere amid damaged buildings in need of removal, the absence of the Russians made everything seem cleaner, almost new. They passed a building where the *trümmerfrau*, or rubble women, had formed a line and were hard at work handing debris from one to the other all the way out to street, where it was loaded into a cart. When it was full, the women swarmed around to push and pull, with an occasional curse, until they had moved it a block down the street. There, they threw the debris on a fire that multiple groups of *trümmerfrau* working in the area used to dispose of their debris. For this work, they received extra food rations.

"We can work like that now," said Frau Kleist. She laughed, not at the prospect of doing manual labor all day, but because she was excited about being able to get out. Since they'd been raped and began hiding at night, they stayed indoors during the day, too. They didn't want any of the Ivans who attacked them to spot them out walking and know they were still in the neighborhood.

The women were walking in the middle of the street when an impatient beep from behind sent them scurrying onto the sidewalk. An American jeep with two soldiers sped up and drove by. Both women looked at them fearfully, knowing what the Russians had done to the female population. The Americans, however, looked straight ahead.

"I don't want to be attacked, but I wouldn't mind being acknowledged," Marta fumed as they drove away.

"What are you saying?" asked *Frau* Kleist indignantly. "They don't belong here any more than the Ivans. Being ignored is wonderful. Think of it. We don't have to stay in the attic anymore. We're actually out in the sun. This is so nice!" *Frau* Kleist was smiling and nodding at everyone she saw, except the Americans.

The previous day the Russians had been everywhere,

prowling around after dusk, still looking for women. Marta and the *Frau*, along with *Herr* Kleist and Ernst, had spent the night in the attic, just like they had every night since the Russians raped the women, but this morning the Ivans were gone.

There were other changes besides the Russians leaving. Marta could feel these changes and knew what was happening inside her, but after all the death and destruction, she could not bring herself to do what so many others had done. She could not destroy a new life, even one conceived in hate.

The two women walked on for a short distance, then the *Frau* said, "I need to get back home. I don't have the strength I used to have."

"No wonder," said Marta, as they turned around. "We don't get enough to eat. No one has any strength."

The sun would set in thirty minutes, so Marta began to gather her things for the night, then remembered they didn't need to hide in the attic. Ernst, though, had gotten used to sleeping there and wanted to continue.

"I think I'd like to start sleeping in a real bed, again," Marta told him. "My back is hurting from sleeping on blankets up there on the floor."

"Why did we start sleeping there?" asked Ernst. "Was it because of the Ivans?"

"Goodness, no, child. Why do you ask that?" She laughed nervously.

"*Herr* Kleist told me that he and I had to protect our women from the soldiers," Ernst replied.

"Oh, he was just being silly." Marta couldn't look her nephew in the eye, though, because she was afraid her face would give away the lie. "We just thought it might be fun for a little while, kind of like camping in the woods. But now I want to sleep in a bed."

They had just finished supper, such as it was. Two days earlier, Ernst had found two potatoes growing in a small patch of land behind an abandoned building that was being torn down. Marta made soup with them, and this was the third meal in a row they had eaten it. Every time they ate it she added a little more water, making it last a little longer but taste a little thinner. She gathered up the bowls, the only two they had, and put them in the sink.

"Will you wash these bowls, please, Ernst?" she said. "I want to run down to *Frau* Kleist's to take her the rest of this soup. *Herr* Kleist is going to give us some bread in exchange for it."

"OK, Aunt Marta," he said.

She headed out of the flat with the remaining watery soup, looking forward to having some bread. Where the baker had gotten the baking goods she didn't know and wouldn't ask. When she got to the stairs she heard the front door open, so she stopped and looked over the bannister to see who it was. Four floors below she recognized the Ivan with the limp, and gasped. Turning quickly, she looked around and finally set the soup on the floor in a hallway corner, then ran back to the flat.

"Quick," she shouted to Ernst. "Gather up everything from the table and put it away. Throw out the water." She shoved utensils into the drawer without cleaning them, pushed the chairs to spots she had marked on the floor so they would appear unmoved, then said, as calmly as she could, "I think we'll go to the attic after all." Shooing Ernst ahead of her, they headed toward the bedroom closet.

"Why?" he asked.

"I've changed my mind. I want to sleep there one more night."

She placed the ladder under the attic opening and sent Ernst scurrying up toward it. As she did, she heard the door to the flat opening, and cursed that she had not gotten a new lock on it. *Herr* Kleist had told her not to replace it.

"It will tip off the Ivans that someone still lives here if the lock is changed," he said.

Ernst pushed the hatch cover aside and disappeared into the attic. She was steps behind him, and her head had just poked through the opening when she felt the hand around her ankle.

"So this is where you've been hiding," said the Ivan. He was one of the three with whom she agreed to cooperate if they didn't make Ernst watch them rape her. "Come down here, I don't have much time."

He tugged on her calf and ran his hand up under her skirt. She caught Ernst's eye and mouthed, "Stay up here," then started down the ladder, his hand sliding up her leg. She stopped and tried to swat it away, but he grabbed her foot and pulled it down to the next step with one hand, and pushed his other hand up until he found what he was seeking.

"There it is," he said, as he shoved two dry fingers inside her. She grimaced at the pain. "You're not wearing under-wear," he laughed. "Were you expecting me?" She stopped, so he pulled on her leg and said, "Come on, I haven't got all day."

She worried about what Ernst would see if she didn't cooperate, so she continued down, impaled on his fingers. As she reached the bottom step he kept his one hand between her legs and grabbed her breast with the other, then lifted her off the last step and put her feet on the floor. "Where's that boy that used to be around here?" he asked, looking up. "Is he up there?"

He let go of her and moved toward the ladder, but she said, "He's running the streets with friends. I can't keep him home."

"Getting into trouble, no doubt. While he's gone, we'll have some fun." He pushed her roughly from the closet, sending her bouncing onto the bed. Pushing the closet door closed, he swung his rifle off his shoulder and laid it on the dresser.

He grabbed her arm and pulled her up onto her feet, but when he grabbed her dress she said, "Please, don't rip it. I'll... I'll take it off." She turned her back to him and pulled her dress over her head; it was the only clothing she was wearing because of the heat.

He had pulled his belt off his pants and when she leaned forward to lie down on the bed he raised it over his head, bringing it down hard on her buttocks. It surprised her and she screamed, then clamped her own hand over her mouth. She rolled across the bed and dropped to the floor, cowering between the bed and the wall. *Please stay in the attic,* she thought, over and over. The Ivan never took his eyes off her as he removed his clothes.

When he was naked, he picked up the belt and walked around the bed, his erection pointing menacingly toward her and the belt dangling menacingly at his side.

"*Nein,*" she cried, as he grabbed her hair and dragged her back to the other side of the bed.

He pointed at the bed and said, "On your knees, like a bitch dog." She hesitated and shook her head imperceptibly, so he shoved her onto the bed on her stomach. Pushing down between her shoulders with one hand, he brought the belt down on her. Marta tried to cover her backside with her hands, but when she put them behind her the Ivan grabbed both. He laid the belt down for a moment to gather her hands together in a vice-like grip. Then, pushing them against her back, he picked up the belt with his other hand and brought it down on her so fast she couldn't count all the blows. She screamed as the belt rained down on her, all the while thinking, *please don't let Ernst see this.* Then the Ivan dropped the belt and pulled her into a kneeling position on the side of the bed.

He stood behind her and grabbed her hips, then pulled her back onto him as he forcefully entered her. She threw her head back and cried out in pain, so he pushed forward on her shoulders, forcing her head down onto the bed, then alternately pushed and pulled her hips to force her to move in rhythm with him. "This will be the last time I can have you," he said. "My unit has already moved out and I have to catch up with them before the Americans find me."

She closed her eyes and grimaced, her hands grabbing the blanket and balling it into her fists. "*Bitte, nein,*" she said. Please, no; but he would not be denied.

Suddenly, she felt him turn slightly to the side. He yelled, "You little shit, I'll kill you!" followed closely by a gun shot, so much louder indoors than those she had heard during fighting outside. Instantly, something warm splattered across her back, and she felt the Ivan pull out and drop away from her. She heard something being dropped, followed by two thuds, one loud, one less so. Looking over her shoulder, she saw Ernst and the soldier lying on the floor on their backs. Ernst's upper body was in the closet, his feet in the bedroom. The Ivan was next to the bed, and the rifle lay on the floor between them. Blood and bits of flesh were splattered on the bed and the wall, and blood was beginning to run across the floor.

"Ernst!" she screamed. "Ernst! Oh, God, no! Ernst!"

Rushing to his side, she knelt over him and put her hand

on his chest. His eyes were closed and she cradled his head on her knees. She kissed him on the forehead, saying, "Oh, Ernst, oh, Ernst." She couldn't yet comprehend what had happened, but she could find no marks on her nephew. The Ivan was on his back, a gaping wound in his chest, his blank eyes staring at the ceiling. Blood continued to spread around his body.

She felt Ernst stir, and she began to breathe again. She rocked him and said, "It's all right, it's all right," praying that it was.

Ernst groaned like an old man and reached his hand to the back of his head, rubbing it. He opened his eyes and said, "What happened?"

Ernst had just climbed into the attic and turned to watch his aunt come into their "campground" when he heard a man say something in Russian. Ernst didn't understand it, but his aunt stopped climbing up and her eyes got really big, like he knew they used to when the planes came over and dropped the bombs.

She shushed him, then climbed down the ladder. That's when he heard the man saying more in Russian. His aunt answered him in Russian. *Why didn't she speak German?*

He heard the closet door close. Seconds later, he heard his aunt scream. She sounded hurt. When the planes had dropped bombs, it helped him feel braver when she held him really tight and rocked back and forth, saying, "It's all right, it's all right." He wondered if she needed him to hold her and say, "It's all right," so he crept down the ladder to find her. When he got to the bottom he stood in the closet and listened.

The door was closed so he couldn't see anyone, but he

heard voices coming from the bedroom. He heard a loud slap and his aunt screaming so he opened the door about an inch and peered through the opening. The man had his back to the door and was naked. Ernst couldn't see his aunt, but he heard her crying. She must be really scared because she didn't cry very often.

The man walked around the bed and then Ernst saw his aunt on the other side of it. The man grabbed Aunt Marta by her hair and pulled her around to the side of the bed toward the closet, where he beat her with the belt. Ernst jumped every time he hit her.

Then the bad man got behind her and grabbed her. He seemed to be rocking backward and forward. Aunt Marta was kneeling on the bed in front of the man, who kept pulling on her and saying something in Russian.

"*Bitte, nein*," he heard his aunt say. She was crying even harder.

Ernst put his hands over his ears so he couldn't hear her. He looked away. On the dresser just outside the door he saw the soldier's rifle. *I'll capture him*, he thought.

Ernst crept quietly out of the closet and picked up the rifle. It was heavier than he expected. He couldn't hold it against his shoulder like he saw the soldiers do, so he held it at his side and found the trigger. Papa had shown him where it was on his toy guns. He would make the bad man raise his hands, just like he had seen soldiers do when they captured the enemy.

But just before he said, "*Hände hoch*," the bad man heard him and looked over his shoulder, yelling something in Russian. It scared Ernst and he jumped.

He heard the loudest noise he had ever heard and dropped the rifle. He fell backward, hitting his head on the floor. A wall of black with different colors shooting across it, like the time he fell off the porch and hit his head on the sidewalk, enveloped him.

When he awoke, his aunt was holding him. She rocked him and said, "It's all right, it's all right." His head hurt real bad, so he groaned and reached his hand to rub the back of it, where it had hit the floor. He opened his eyes and saw the bad man lying on the floor, naked, with a lot of blood around him. Ernst looked at his aunt and said, "What happened?"

Marta sat on the floor holding Ernst, kissing the top of his head, and rocking back and forth with him until he asked, "Why are you naked?" She smiled and shook her head.

After helping him stand, she got up and reached for her dress. Before she could pull it over her head, Ernst said, "Aunt Marta, you have blood on your back."

Ignoring it, she pulled her dress on, then looked around the room and assessed the situation. She had a dead, naked, Russian soldier lying on the floor. How was she going to explain that? At least he didn't have an erection anymore.

The bullet had exploded through his chest right about where his heart would have been. She was lucky he had pushed her upper body down on the bed or she might have been hit by the round after it came through him.

Someone was pounding on the door, calling, "*Fraulein*, are you all right?" She recognized *Herr* Kleist's voice.

"Ernst, please let *Herr* Kleist in," she said more calmly than she felt.

"I shot the bad man," Ernst said.

"Is that what you think?" Marta asked, hugging him against her. She tossed her head back and forced herself to laugh. "No," she said, "that's not what happened."

"I shot him," said Ernst, but he didn't sound as sure this time.

The pounding started up again, as did the yelling. "*Fraulein*, let me in. Are you OK?"

"Go let *Herr* Kleist in, then I will tell you both what happened."

Ernst looked at the body on the floor, kicked its foot, then turned and walked to the front door.

The Kleists came bustling in, *Frau* Kleist gasping and putting her hands to her mouth when she saw the dead man on the floor. "*Gott im Himmel*," she proclaimed.

"He caught me before I could get in the attic," said Marta. "Ernst made a commotion and I managed to get his rifle. I shot him."

"*I* shot him," said Ernst. The Kleists both looked at the little boy. By now others were knocking on the door, but their knocking was more what Marta would have expected from the postal carrier, not the frantic, I'll-bust-this-door-down pounding that she had heard from the Kleists.

"No one must know," said Marta, looking from the Ivan to the Kleists.

"Of course not," said Herr Kleist. "I'll take care of them," he said, walking toward the front door. After he left, Marta closed the bedroom door so no one could see in, but put her ear against it to listen. *Herr* Kleist told a few of the people from the cellar that they were mistaken; the sound of the shot had clearly come from out in the street.

"My wife and I just had supper with the *Fraulein* and her son," he told them. "We've been here all evening and there has been no gunfire in here. I did hear one shot from outside, though, that sounded really close. Maybe if you go out you can find someone dead. Be sure to come back and tell me if you do," he said, closing the door in their faces.

Marta smiled. Maybe he wasn't as useless as *Frau* Kleist sometimes claimed.

When *Herr* Kleist returned, Marta said, "I need to tell you what happened."

"Only if you want to, dear," said *Frau* Kleist, pulling a chair in from the kitchen. She sat down, crossed her legs, and looked at Marta expectantly.

"I know what happened," said Ernst. "I took his rifle and shot him because he was hurting Aunt Marta. She was naked, just like him."

"Oh, poor Ernst," Marta said. "Does your head hurt?" She hugged him to her, again, and rubbed the back of his head, where she felt a knot rising on the surface. Ernst jumped when she touched it. "He hit you so hard you are confused, aren't you?"

"I am?" he asked.

"Apparently, *mein kleiner mann,*" said Marta sympathetically. "You came into the room and said, 'Let my aunt alone.'" Marta lowered her voice to make it sound much more masculine than Ernst's. "You said, 'If you don't let her alone, I'll hurt you.' That's what you said, just like that." The Kleists both nodded their heads in approval, although *Herr* Kleist looked around the room and frowned.

"I did?" asked Ernst.

"You sure did," his aunt replied. "You are *so* brave. Then he hit you and you fell down. But he was watching you, so I had a chance to grab his rifle and shoot him. You were knocked out, but you helped me get away from him. You are my hero."

Herr Kleist continued to look around the room, as if he was trying to picture what Marta was telling them. When Marta turned to point at the soldier he noticed blood spots on the back of her dress.

He shook his head and said, "I don't…" but *Frau* Kleist hit him on the knee.

Marta said, "Ernst, I want you to go to with *Herr* Kleist to their flat. *Frau* Kleist and I must take care of things. Perhaps you can go to sleep there. I will come to get you in a little while, OK?"

"I can help," said Ernst.

Marta said, "It would be best if you did what I asked, honey. You and *Herr* Kleist go downstairs." Marta looked at *Herr* Kleist and nodded toward the door.

"Come on, son," said *Herr* Kleist, putting one hand on Ernst's shoulder and raising the other to scratch his head. "You can help me bake some bread." He looked back one time, squinted his eyes, and shook his head.

Frau Kleist went into the bathroom and came back with a bucket. She called after her husband, and when he stopped, she held it out to him and said, "Before you do that, can you go to the pump and get us some water? I think we're going to need it."

As soon as Ernst and her husband were gone, *Frau* Kleist told Marta, "I can't believe Ernst killed one of the Ivans. I wish it had been me, but helping you cover it up is almost as exciting. What's our plan?"

Marta's desire to protect Ernst cleared her mind and she hoped she spoke like a general on the eve of battle. "First, we have to get the body out of here. We'll leave him naked so they won't be able to identify him from his uniform; at least, the Americans won't, and the Russians aren't here anymore. He'll just be another war casualty. But we can't let him be found here, and he's too big for us to carry." She paused as an idea formed in her brain. "Remember the work site we passed this morning?"

"I do. They had a cart they were using to haul wood away."

"We have to find where they left the cart and put him in it. Then we'll take him and his uniform back that way. We can dump him at the site and cover him with debris. We'll throw his uniform on the fire; it will still be burning. He'll be another dead body in a country full of them."

"But he's a fresh dead body," said *Frau* Kleist. "No one will believe he's left over from the war if we hide him in the rubble from the building."

"You're right," said Marta, nodding. "Let's dump him in one of the lakes. There are so many women that jumped into them to kill themselves that another body might not be noticed, even if it has a prick. It might be weeks before he's found and by then the fish will have had a chance to work on him. After we dump him, we'll come back here and clean up this blood."

Marta's decisiveness apparently convinced the *Frau*. "Done," she said, rubbing her hands together. "But how do we get him down the stairs without being seen?"

"We don't," said Marta. "We'll get the cart and hide it behind our building, then we'll throw him out a window in the back. No one ever goes out there, and it's dark now."

Frau Kleist smiled. "Marta, there's a devious side of you that I'm just beginning to appreciate." She stared at the body for a moment, then said, "Let's cut off his prick and shove it in his mouth."

Marta shook her head. "Believe me, I want to. But if we do that, all the *men* in the American army will want an investigation. They'll figure a woman did it for revenge, and they'll want to find the woman. If we dump him like he is, he could have been shot by anyone, even a jealous husband.

Without his uniform they won't know if he's Russian, German, American, or one of the refugees passing through. Maybe he was killed for his clothes. Who knows?"

The *Frau* nodded agreement. "Let's get this bastard wrapped up," she said, but before they began she kicked him in the genitals. When Marta looked at her questioningly, she said, "If we're not going to cut it off, we can at least do that."

Marta nodded and kicked him once, then again. She then picked up his uniform and sifted through the pockets until she found a wallet and opened it. It contained a few marks, which she shoved into her dress pocket. Flipping through it, she found three pictures. Her anger grew as she looked at the children staring back at her. Two girls who looked to be about seven and ten, and a boy about five. He could rape her, threaten Ernst, then go home and cuddle his children. The bastard!

Then it hit her. Those children had lost their father at the hand of her nephew, who was about the same age as them. What had Ernst done? She didn't absolve the Ivan of his wrongdoing, but she wept for the children.

"Why are you crying?" asked *Frau* Kleist.

Marta held the picture out to her.

"What? And we haven't lost family? Ernst didn't lose his parents? You didn't lose yours? You cannot be soft like this, Marta." To emphasize her point, she kicked the Ivan's balls again. "Let's get this scum out of here," she said, and they began wrapping the body.

When they threw the body out the window moments later it came unwrapped and they had to wrap it again. But the streets were deserted; the Germans still weren't convinced the Russians were gone, and the Americans hadn't organized patrols yet.

It took them all night, but by the time the sun came up, the blood was gone, the uniform was burned, and the body was floating in a lake two kilometers away, along with what must have been two new suicides that night. As they returned the cart to the worksite Marta thanked the *Frau* for risking her life to help her.

"Why would I not?" asked her neighbor. "You're my best friend."

"Then I guess it's true what they say," said Marta.

"What's that?"

Marta smiled and said, "Friends help you move. Best friends help you move bodies."

Frau Kleist laughed out loud, then quickly clamped her hand over her mouth. They both looked around and when they didn't see anyone, they threw their arms around each other's shoulders and alternately laughed and cried as they walked home.

CHAPTER FIFTY-SEVEN

6 August, 1972
   Marta & Ernst's flat

Marta looked at Ernst. "Are you angry that I lied to you about who killed the Ivan?"

"No, *Mutter*," he said. Greta continued to hold Marta's hand, but looked at Ernst in surprise. She's never heard me call Marta *Mutter*, he realized. "But why did you?" he asked Marta.

"I was afraid. I had heard of a woman who killed a Russian soldier that raped her. The rumor was that she disappeared and was never heard from again. If that had happened to you..." She put her face in her hands and cried.

After a moment, Marta raised her head and said, "I didn't know how the Americans would react if they found out that a seven-year-old had killed a Russian soldier. What would they do? At that time they still considered the Russians to be their allies. I didn't want anyone to know what happened and if they did, I wanted them to think it was me. After all, I promised your mother I'd take care of you, then I let you kill someone."

"I did it because he attacked you," said Ernst. "That should have counted for something."

"Things were different then," Marta said. "Who knows what would have been done?"

Ernst moved next to his aunt, on the side opposite Greta, and Marta put her hand on his cheek, rubbing it. He felt tears welling in his eyes, and tried to hold them back, but couldn't. His aunt slipped her arm around him and pulled him against her chest, letting him quietly cry with his face against her breast.

"And you've kept this in all these years," said Greta, shaking her head. "That must have been very hard to do…" She hesitated, then added, "*Mutter.*"

Ernst felt Greta join in their embrace, as Marta said, "It's all right. It's all right. I have to admit, though, sometimes I wonder who rocked the children of the dead Ivan."

Ernst had no response to that.

When all of them stopped crying, Marta said to Greta, "When you told me about your mother, I knew it was time to tell Ernst the truth. At the end of the war, so many women in Berlin were raped, everybody talked about it, but of course, not to children."

"Really?" asked Ernst.

Marta nodded. "And it wasn't just working class women. The Russians, and some Americans, seemed to enjoy humiliating German women who had been upper class. If they found a house with servants the woman of the house was sure to be raped, and most likely the female servants, too. It was so commonplace, women talked about it to people that before the war they wouldn't have even nodded to on the street. But eventually, I became ashamed." Marta kissed Greta on the head and told her, "Your mother has a wonderful daughter despite the horror she suffered, and you and she were brave enough to talk about it. You gave me the courage to remember."

Greta smiled at her.

"I want us to look to the future, not the past," Marta said. She looked at Ernst. "We have been the two of us for long enough. It is time we added Greta, and then some little ones."

"Perhaps a boy named Willie," said Greta, "and a girl named Marta."

"Thank you, dear," said Marta, "but I would prefer Marie."

AUTHOR'S NOTE

While *Subterfuge* is a work of fiction and the main characters are fictional, there are people depicted who were real. The following characters are a part of history, some for the good and some for the bad. It is up to the reader to decide which. If a military rank is given, it is what the individual would have had at that time in the story. Some were promoted after the time at which they appeared in the story.

If a character is not mentioned here, he or she is fictional.

Germans
Colonel Heinz Jost
Kapitän zur See Hans-Rudolf Rösing
Korvettenkapitän Heinz Fischer
Vizeadmiral Karl Dönitz
Fregattenkapitän Eberhard Godt
Kapitän zur See Meckel
Adolf Hitler
Grand Admiral Erich Raeder
Korvettenkapitän Reinhard Hardegen
Kapitänleutnant Richard Zapp

Kapitän zur See Ernst Kals
Lieutenant Hans Fuhrmann
Kapitänleutnant Ulrich Folkers
Korvettenkapitän Heinrich Bleichrodt
Herbert Baum
Mayor Willy Brandt
Chancellor Konrad Adenauer
Horst Bredow
Admiral Hans-Georg von Friedeburg
Archbishop Frings

Americans
Colonel Gail Halverson (Uncle Wiggly Wings)
President John F. Kennedy

British
Air Chief Marshall Arthur "Bomber" Harris
Prime Minister Winston Churchill

The meetings depicted in Chapters 20 and 21 did occur, and the actions of the real participants are recreated as accurately as possible from historical records. The thoughts of the real individuals are strictly my perception of what they may have been thinking at the time. The participation of a fictional character in the second meeting is for dramatic purposes only.

All other descriptions are fictional, although the activities and actions of the crew on U-112 are based closely on true events that occurred on other U-boats.

I owe a great debt of gratitude to members of two writers' groups, Second Draft of Louisville and the Louisville Writers' Meetup. Their many suggestions helped enormously. I especially want to thank Rob Davin for accompanying me to Chicago for a tour of U-505, a type IXC boat, the same as U-112. He also corrected one scene in the book that was described inaccurately. I appreciate the guidance, suggestions, and editing of Hydra Publishing, which helped bring this story to you.

ABOUT THE AUTHOR

This is Erv Klein's first book, and shows his interest in history in general, and World War II in particular. He is retired from running a service company for which he wrote many newsletters, which piqued his curiosity as to whether he could write fiction. He is currently working on a family saga set in rural Kentucky, and also spends time as a lobbyist, continuing education instructor, and attorney. Erv lives in Louisville, Kentucky, with his wife, Linda, their two dogs, Snoopy and Bailey, and Castro the friendly cat.

Made in the USA
Lexington, KY
08 May 2019